I'd never thought of Bitty's ex-husband as a particularly handsome man, but in death, he was downright homely.

I'm not sure how long I stood there staring at him with Bitty's vampire cape in my hand, but the voices from the living room finally seeped into my stupefied brain and I hung the crocheted cape on the doorknob and went into the kitchen.

I found a silver tray, an already prepared pitcher of tea and a bowl of lemon wedges in the refrigerator, and somehow put together glasses, ice, napkins and long-handled silver teaspoons to take into the living room.

Seated precariously and obviously uncomfortably on the 1850's horsehair-stuffed couch, the two police officers appeared grateful for a diversion when I set the tray down on the antique Turkish hassock serving as a coffee table. Bitty had produced a linen handkerchief from somewhere in her black ensemble, and dabbed daintily at what I was certain were crocodile tears at the corners of her eyes.

"Bitty," I said while the officers reached for the tea and lemon wedges, "would you mind stepping into the kitchen with me for just a moment?"

Something in my voice must have alerted her, for she gave me a startled glance and promptly excused herself. Neither officer protested.

Before Bitty could launch into a tale of mistreatment by local officials, I said bluntly, "I found Philip."

With her mouth still open, Bitty looked at me. Then she said, "Well, I suppose that's good news. For him, anyway. Where is the philandering Philip? Mexico? Paris? Rome? A Motel Six in Tupelo?"

"In your coat closet."

This book is dedicated to the real Divas—names are being withheld to protect the guilty, but you know who you are, ladies! I will see you at our next meeting.

And to the beautiful town of Holly Springs, Mississippi, where antebellum homes graciously preside and history is celebrated alongside modern progress.

Dixie Divas

Virginia Brown

Smyrna, Georgia

Bell Bridge Books
PO BOX 67
Smyrna, GA 30081

ISBN: 978-0-9821756-5-1

Bell Bridge Books is an Imprint of BelleBooks, Inc.

We at BelleBooks enjoy hearing from readers. You can contact us at the address above or at BelleBooks@BelleBooks.com

Visit our websites – www.BelleBooks.com
and www.BellBridgeBooks.com.

10 9 8 7 6 5 4 3 2 1

Cover design: Debra Dixon

Cover photo:
Legs graphic: ©Madartists | Dreamstime.com
Cocktails graphic: ©Stephen Coburn | Dreamstime.com

Interior design: Linda Kichline

F Bro

CHAPTER 1

If not for long-dead Civil War Generals Ulysses S. Grant, Nathan Bedford Forrest, and a pot of chicken and dumplings, Bitty Hollandale would never have been charged with murder. Of course, if the mule hadn't eaten the chicken and dumplings, that would have helped a lot, too.

My name is Eureka Truevine, but my family and friends all call me Trinket. Except for my ex-husband, who's been known to call me a few other names. That's one of the reasons I left him and came home to take care of my parents who are in their second adolescence, having missed out on their first one for reasons of survival.

We live at Cherryhill in Mississippi, three miles outside of Holly Springs and forty-five minutes down 78 Highway southeast from Memphis, Tennessee. My father—Edward Wellford Truevine—inherited the house from my grandparents around fifty years ago. It wasn't in great shape when he got it, but over the years he's put money, time, and his own craftsmanship into it, and now it's on the Holly Springs Historic Register.

Every April, Holly Springs has an annual pilgrimage tour of restored antebellum homes, with pretty girls and women in hoop skirts and high button shoes. Men and boys in Confederate uniforms stand sentry with old family Sharpshooters and cavalry swords, neither of which could do much harm to a marshmallow. It's a big event that draws people from all over the country and gives purpose to the lives of more than a few elderly matrons and historical buffs.

This year, Bitty Hollandale cooked up a big pot of chicken and dumplings to take to Mr. Sanders, who lives in an old house off Highway 7 that the local historical society has been trying to get on the historic register for decades. Sherman Sanders is known for his fondness of chicken and dumplings, and Bitty meant to convince him to put his house on the tour. It'd been built in 1832 and kept in remarkably good shape. Most of the original furniture is in most of the original places, with most of the original wallpaper and carpets still in their original places. The only modern renovations have been electricity and what's discreetly referred to as a water closet. It's enough to make any Southerner drool with envy and avarice.

"Go with me, Trinket," Bitty said to me that day in February. "It'd be such a feather in my cap to get the Sanders house on our tour."

I looked over at my parents. My father was dressed in plaid golfing pants and a red striped shirt, and my mother wore a red cable knit sweater and a plaid skirt. Under the kitchen table at their feet lay their little brown dog, appropriately named Little Brown Dog and called Brownie. He wore a red plaid sweater. They all like to coordinate.

"I don't know," I said doubtfully to Bitty. "I'm not sure what our plans are for the day."

What I really meant was I wasn't at all sure leaving my parents alone would be wise. Since I've come home, I've noticed they have a tendency to pretend they're sixteen again. While their libidos may be, their bodies are still mid-seventies. The doctor assures me it's fine, but I worry about them. Daddy's had an angioplasty, and Mama has occasional lapses of memory. But otherwise, they're probably in better shape than Bitty and me.

Bitty, like me, is fifty-one, a little on the plump side, and divorced. But she's lived in Holly Springs all her life, while I haven't come back to live since I married and followed my husband to random jobs around the country. Bitty and I have been close since we were six years old and she rode over on her pony to invite me to a swimming party. As I then had a love for anything to do with horses, she fast became my best friend. Besides that, she's my first cousin. I've got other cousins in the area, but over the years we've lost touch and haven't gotten around to getting reacquainted.

Bitty knows everyone. I've only been back a couple of months and am still struggling to reacquaint myself with old friends. Some people I remember from my childhood, but many have been forgotten over the years. Besides, the shock of finding my parents so different from how I remembered them in my childhood still hasn't faded enough to encourage more shocks of the same kind.

"They'll be just fine," Bitty assured me. She knew what made me hesitate. "Uncle Eddie and Aunt Anna can do without you for an hour."

"Maybe you're right." I studied Mama and Daddy. They played gin rummy with a pack of cards that looked as if they'd survived the Blitzkrieg. "Will you two be okay if I run an errand with Bitty?" I asked in a loud enough voice to catch their attention.

"Gin!" my mother shouted triumphantly, or what passes for a shout with her. She's petite, with flawless ivory skin that's never seen a blemish or freckle, bright blue eyes, and stylishly short silver hair that used to be blond. Next to my father, who's over six-four in his stockinged feet, she looks like a child's doll. My father has brown eyes and the kind of skin that looks like he works in the sun. He wears a neatly trimmed mustache, his once dark brown hair is still thick, but has been white since a family tragedy in the late sixties. He reminds me of an older Rhett Butler. Since I'm using *Gone With the Wind* references, my mother reminds me of Melanie Wilkes, with just enough Scarlett O'Hara thrown in to keep her interesting. And unpredictable.

I, on the other hand, am more like Scarlett's sister Suellen, with just enough of Mammy's pragmatic optimism to keep me from being a complete cynic and whiner. I inherited my father's height, my grandmother's tendency toward weight gain, and auburn hair and green eyes no one can explain. I like to think I'm a throwback to my mother's Scotch-Irish ancestry.

"We'll be fine if your mother will stop cheating at cards," my father said.

Mama just smiled. "I'm not cheating, Eddie. I'm just good enough to win."

Daddy shook his head. "You've got to be cheating. No one beats me at gin."

"Except me."

"So," I said again, a little louder, "you'll both be fine for a little while, right?"

My mother looked at me with surprise. "Of course, sugar," she said. "We're always fine."

Bitty and I went out to her car. Bitty's real name is Elisabeth, but it got shortened to Bitty when she was born and the name stuck. Anyone who calls her Elisabeth is a stranger or works for the government. Bitty is one of those females who attract men like state taxpayers' money lures politicians. On her, a little extra weight settles in the form of voluptuous curves. About five-two in her Prada pumps, she has blond hair, china blue eyes, a complexion like a California girl, and a laugh that'd make even Scrooge smile. If she wasn't my best friend, I'd probably be jealous.

"I wish you'd drive a bigger car," I complained once I'd wedged myself into her flashy red sports car that smelled of chicken and dumplings. "I always feel like a giant in this thing."

Bitty shifted the car into gear and we lurched forward. "You are a giant."

"I am not. I'm statuesque. Five-nine is not that tall for a woman. Though I admit I could lose twenty pounds and not miss it."

Gears ground and I winced as we pulled out of the driveway onto the road that leads to Highway 311. One of the things Bitty got in her last—and fourth—divorce was a lot of money that she's found new and interesting ways to spend. I got ulcers from my one and only divorce. Those aren't bankable. My only child, however, a married daughter, makes up for everything.

It was one of those February days that promise good weather isn't so far away. Yellow daffodils and tufts of crocus bloomed in yards and outlined empty spaces where houses had once been. Some fields had already been plowed in preparation for spring planting. A few puffy clouds skimmed across a bright blue sky, and sunlight through the Miata's windshield heated the car. I rolled down my window and inhaled essence of Mississippi. It was cool, familiar, and very nice.

"So what are you going to do with yourself, Trinket?"

I looked over at Bitty. "What do you mean?"

"You've been home almost three months now. A doctor just bought Easthaven. Want me to introduce you?"

"Good Lord, no. I don't want another man in my life."

"He's a podiatrist. Think of how useful that could be. And Easthaven is one of the nicest houses in Holly Springs."

"My feet are fine. And Cherryhill suits me right now." Bitty ground another gear and I checked my seatbelt. Undaunted by my lack of interest, she went right on talking.

"Think of the future. Once your parents are gone, God forbid, you'll be all alone in that big ole rambling house. Is that what you want?"

"Dear Lord, yes. Not that I want my parents gone, but living alone doesn't bother me. I'm used to it. Perry traveled a lot."

"Whatever possessed you to marry a man named Percival, anyway? It sounds like a name out of Chaucer's medieval romances."

"His mother read a lot. Besides, with a name like Eureka Truevine, that's not a stone I felt I should throw."

Bitty nodded. "That's true enough. Percival and Eureka Berryman. Good thing his last name isn't Berry. Then he'd be Perry Berry."

We laughed. It's funny what appeals to middle-aged women past their prime but not their youthfulness. There's a sense of freedom in being beyond some expectations.

When we pulled up into the rutted driveway of The Cedars where Sherman Sanders lives in voluntary isolation and bachelorhood, he was sitting on his colonnaded front porch, serenely rocking with a shotgun across his lap. He stood up, a small man with wizened features, bowed legs, and a nose that juts out like a ship's prow. He wore faded blue overalls, muddy boots that had long ago lost any kind of shape, a flannel shirt that had seen better days, and a straw hat that looked like something big had taken a bite out of one side. A bone-thin black and tan hound lay beside the rocking chair, and when Sanders nudged it with his boot, the old dog struggled to its feet and bayed in the opposite direction. Sherman Sanders casually brought up the shotgun. It pointed straight at Bitty's car. He obviously had better eyesight than his hound.

"Don't mind the shotgun," Bitty said when I made a squeaking sound. "He doesn't shoot women. Usually."

"Dear Lord," I got out in that squeaky tone. "Who does he usually shoot?"

Bitty opened her car door and stuck her head out. She waved her hand and called, "Yoo hoo, Mr. Sanders, it's Bitty Hollandale. You remember me?"

Sanders aimed a stream of brown spit at the dirt in front of the house and nodded. "Yep. I 'member you. You're that pesky female that's been worryin' the hell out of me 'bout my house."

One thing about Bitty, she never lets minor obstacles deter her from her goal.

She smiled real big. "That's right. I brought you something."

Sanders shifted the wad of tobacco in his mouth to his other cheek. "Don't need nuthin'. Might as well go on back home. I ain't in'trested in my house bein' on no stupid damn tour with a bunch of strangers walkin' through it and gawkin' at everything."

I didn't much blame him, but I didn't say that to Bitty.

"Oh, you'll like this," she said, and started to put both feet out of the car to reach in the back for the pot of chicken and dumplings. Unfortunately, she'd forgotten to take the car out of gear or set the brake. The Miata bucked forward. Off-guard, Bitty pitched out of the car like a sack of cornmeal and sprawled face-first onto red dirt. Luckily, she was wearing a pantsuit and not a skirt, but her rear end stuck up in the air like a generous red wool flag. The car coughed, died, and made an annoying buzzing sound.

Sherman Sanders cackled so loud his hound started to bark again, turning its head in all different directions just in case the mysterious noise was dangerous. While Mr. Sanders slapped his thigh and cackled, I set the brake, took the keys out of the ignition to stop the buzzing, then got out and went over to see if Bitty was hurt.

"Are you okay?" I asked anxiously, but could tell she was just more mad than anything else. She sat up and brushed dirt and gravel from her face, palms, and the front of her pants.

"Damn car. I keep forgetting it's got a clutch. Look at my pants. I just got them out of the cleaners, too. Give me a hand up, will you?"

I did and she turned back to Mr. Sanders. "As I was saying, you'll like this, Mr. Sanders. It's your favorite."

Bitty has always been quite resilient.

"Oh my, where *are* my manners?" she said then, and gave me a push forward. "Mr. Sanders, this is my cousin, Trinket Truevine from over at Cherryhill."

I managed a polite smile and "How do you do" while keeping an eye on the shotgun, but a still chortling Sanders looked like what I often call, "ain't right," meaning not right in the head.

Bitty pulled out the big aluminum pot where she'd secured it behind the driver's seat, and marched relentlessly up to the porch. When she set it down on the white-painted hickory planks, the hound immediately found it irresistible. Its nose seemed to be the only one of the five senses still working efficiently.

"Sit, Tuck," Mr. Sanders said, again with another nudge, and the dog reluctantly squatted on its back haunches with nose in the air and sniffing furiously. Sanders leaned forward. "What you got in that pot?"

Bitty smiled. "Chicken and dumplings. Homemade, of course."

I could see Sanders wavering. The shotgun lowered, the bowed legs quivered, and I swear that his nose twitched just like his hound's.

"Huh. Reckon you intend to bribe me with those, do you."

"I sure do." Bitty's smile got bigger. She lifted the lid and a thin curl of steam wafted up. "Fresh, too. Just made early this morning. They have to sit a little bit to let the dumplings soak up all that broth, of course."

"Young hen?"

"Two. And White Lily flour cut with shortening and rolled out to a quarter inch."

While they discussed the intricacies of dumplings, I looked around. The white painted house has a chimney at each end; old brick covered with ivy at one end, bare wisteria limbs on the other chimney. Windows go all the way to porch level on the front, with green shutters that can be closed in stormy or cold weather. Elongated *S* hooks have the patina of age on them, but still look in good working order. A lantern hangs from the center of the porch, and electrical wire covered with conduit pipes painted white run along the porch's edge to make a sharp right angle beside the double front door, and then run parallel above the footings of the house and around the corner. One of the front doors was open, the screen shut. The closed door has one of those old-fashioned bells that have to be twisted to make a noise. It's a bright, polished brass. Everything about the house promises loving attention, while the front yard looks like goats live in it. No grass. Just red dirt, ruts, and gigantic cedar trees with furrowed gray trunks splintery with age.

"Reckon you can come in if you want," I heard Sanders say, and I looked over at Bitty. I thought she might faint. Her face had the dazed expression of someone in a spiritual trance.

Her voice shook a little when she said faintly, "Why, Mr. Sanders, we'd love to come in. Wouldn't we, Trinket?"

I looked at the shotgun. I wasn't so sure.

"Uh . . ."

"Come on, Tuck," Sanders said, and opened the screen door for us. "He don't bite, but I ain't of a mind to leave him out here with that pot."

The hound didn't worry me. When it'd drooled over the chicken and dumplings, I'd seen that it had no front teeth. Mr. Sanders, however, seemed to have all of his teeth but not all of his marbles. Maybe it was the odd glint in his eyes, or the way he kept cackling like an old hen.

Reluctantly, I followed Bitty and Sanders into the house. It has that smell old houses have of meals long eaten, people long past, memories long gone. It isn't a bad smell. It's actually very comforting. Furniture gleamed dully, smelling like lemony beeswax. Bitty paused in the entrance hall and took in a deep breath. She was obviously having a religious experience.

As if afraid to wake the saints of old houses, she whispered, "Beautiful. Just beautiful!"

I have to admit she's right. Oval-framed photographs of family members in garments a hundred and forty years old hang on walls. The walnut mantel over the fireplace holds more old photos in small frames, a chunky bronze statue of a soldier on a horse, and a pair of crystal candlesticks. A low fire burned behind solid brass andirons. The front room is filled with antiques, and just a glimpse into the dining room across the foyer promised more treasures in the heavy furniture and wide sideboards against two walls.

Since I don't know that much about antiques or old houses, I followed along as Mr. Sanders gave us the royal tour. Bitty kept clasping her hands in front of her face as if praying, and murmured in rapture while we looked at huge old beds with wooden canopies and mosquito netting, cedar wardrobes that go all the way to the ceiling and still hold clothes from the 1800s, and gilded mirrors with a mottled tinge betraying their age. Carpets laid over bare heart pine floors look as if they hadn't been walked on in years.

By the time the tour was over, Bitty had almost convinced Sanders to allow his house to be put on the historic register and added to the tour. He still had reservations and muttered about turning his home into a circus, but had definitely wavered. Bitty really is good. She should sell real estate or run for Congress.

When we got down to the foyer again with Tuck tagging along at our heels, Bitty picked up a bronze statue from a small parquet table. "This is General Grant, isn't it?" she asked.

For the historically uninformed, General Grant was a Civil War general who burned and slashed his way across Mississippi in 1862, but spared most of Holly Springs. Legend says it was because the ladies were so pretty and treated him to nightly piano concerts, but historical fact has a different version.

Ulysses Sherman Sanders was named in honor of Generals Grant and Sherman, since his family had taken possession of The Cedars right after the war when taxes were high and Confederate income non-existent. As Yankees, they were not enthusiastically welcomed into the community. A few generations have gone by since then and hostilities have ceased for the most part, even if not been completely forgotten by some.

Sanders bristled at any hint of censure in Bitty's question. "That's right; it's a statue of General Grant. Got a problem with that?"

"Heavens no. General Grant was an absolute gentleman while he and his troops stayed in Holly Springs, though I can't say the same for all his soldiers. With some exceptions, of course," she added hastily, apparently remembering that Sherman Sanders' ancestor had been one of those Union soldiers. "This statue's very heavy. Is it weighted?"

Sanders nodded. "I reckon so. Probably because it'd be top heavy otherwise, what with the general liftin' his sword like that."

Bitty smiled and set it down carefully. "I'll be back in a day or two to discuss what needs to be done before the tour. Even though The Cedars hasn't yet been put on the historic register, we can fill out the paperwork and submit it. I don't think there'll be any problem at all. You've done such a wonderful job taking care of this house. I honestly don't think there's another house in Marshall County that's been kept up nearly this well. Most need extensive renovations."

Sanders puffed up his chest. He still held his shotgun, but just by the barrel now. I hoped that was a good sign.

Tuck suddenly barked and rushed toward the open screen door, making me jump. We all looked outside. Something big and brown had its head stuck in the pot of chicken and dumplings. Before Bitty or I could move, Sanders started to cussing, and banged out the screen door and took a shot at the aluminum pot. Rock salt pellets pinged against metal, and the mule made a strangled sound and took off down the rutted drive wearing the pot up to its eyeballs and shedding chicken and dumplings behind it. Tuck immediately took advantage of this unexpected windfall, and the pot-blinded mule ran into a tree. The impact knocked it backwards so that it sat on its haunches blinking dumplings from its eyes while the liberated pot rolled across the yard. Tuck greedily and happily worked the path the pot had taken, slurping loudly. The mule got up and shook itself free of dumplings, obviously unharmed. And unfazed.

Bitty and I just stood there transfixed by the entire thing. Mr. Sanders heaved a disgusted sigh.

"Blamed mule," he said. "I swear it's part goat. Ate half my hat last week."

Roused from temporary astonishment, Bitty said brightly, "Well, I'll just have to cook you up another big batch of chicken and dumplings. Don't worry about the pot. I have another one at home."

We were halfway back to Cherryhill before we started laughing. Bitty had to pull over to the side of the road so we wouldn't wreck. Finally I wiped tears from my eyes and tried to keep from snorting through my nose. I have a tendency to do that when I'm hysterical with laughter.

"Is putting this house on the tour worth another pot of chicken and dumplings?" I asked as soon as I was snort-free.

Bitty nodded. "As many as it takes. I'll just have to buy more ingredients and take them over to Sharita's house."

"You fraud. Someone else cooked them for you?"

"Good Lord, Trinket, you know I can't cook. If I'd cooked them we'd have been shot, stuffed, and mounted over that magnificent walnut mantel. Did you see it? All those gorgeous hunting scenes carved into the wood . . . I thought I'd pass out from pure pleasure."

Bitty and I have different values in many ways. While I appreciate antiques and old houses and generations of custom, it's more in an abstract kind of way. Bitty has obviously made it her reason for living. There are different ways of handling divorce and that empty feeling you get even if the relationship degenerated into nastiness and you're happy to see the last of him. My divorce was pretty straightforward.

Bitty's last divorce made waves throughout the entire state.

Bitty let me off in front of my house. "I'm going shopping for new shoes," she said, and tooled on down our circular drive with a happy wave of her hand. I smiled and shook my head. Now there's a woman who knows how to cope.

Mama and Daddy had gone from playing gin to planning a cruise. Pamphlets were spread over the kitchen table. Something familiar smelling simmered on the stove, and afternoon light made cozy patterns on the walls and floor. Brownie slept in a patch of sunshine. He's a beagle-dachshund mix with long legs, a short body, a dachshund head and coloring, and a beagle's loud bay. He can be heard three counties over when he scents a squirrel. He's also neurotic.

"Where are you going?" I asked my parents when I'd hung my sweater on a coat hook beside the back door and stood looking over Daddy's shoulder at the array of pamphlets.

"I was thinking we'd enjoy rafting down the Colorado River. But your mother wants to take the Delta Queen down to New Orleans. They have a cruise in March this year. It's usually June before the cruises start, but it's been chartered just for us retired postal employees."

Mama looked up. "I thought it'd be nice to travel down the river like those old gamblers used to do. Do you remember *Maverick*? Not the movie. The old TV show. James Garner always did well. I have a feeling I might be just as lucky."

"Huh," Daddy said. "You just think you're a card shark now because you beat me at gin."

"Three times," Mama said with a big smile.

I thought it best not to interfere. "What's for supper?" I asked instead.

"Chicken and dumplings."

My parents just looked at me as if I'd lost my mind when I started laughing, and I heard Mama say to Daddy in a low tone, "Hormones. Must be *The Change*."

CHAPTER 2

Even though Bitty asked me if I wanted to go along when she took Mr. Sanders another pot of chicken and dumplings, I decided to go in to Holly Springs instead. I had a few errands to run, and besides, I'd been thinking about getting a part-time job.

When I'd quit work I'd taken my 401k and all the money from my savings and invested it in a few CDs and some annuities, but I really don't have any idea where it's best to put it. After all, it's not that much money, but it's all I have for my old age. While some days I feel my old age is already here, I figure it'll be a few years yet before I can spend money without worrying about having to live under a concrete overpass and eat cat food in my "golden" years.

I dressed carefully. I wore tan flats that matched my A-line skirt and jacket and wouldn't intimidate any man under five-nine. Some men equate height with masculinity, and resent females the least bit taller. It can be a disadvantage when seeking employment. I dabbed on a minimum of make-up, just enough to look professional without resembling a circus clown. Age can be tricky with a woman's face, and I didn't want to look foolish. The only jewelry I wore was a watch and a pair of emerald stud earrings my daughter had given me for my birthday a few years before.

Mama and Daddy were cuddled up in front of a fire in the living room and watching an old movie with Clark Gable and Claudette Colbert when I stuck my head in the door to tell them goodbye. Brownie lay on the couch between them, his head resting on Mama's lap.

"Good luck, sugar," Mama said, "I know you'll find work. You've always been quite competent."

Competent is supposed to be a compliment, but somehow, it sounds rather flat to me. An "average" kind of thing. But I knew Mama didn't mean it that way, so I said back, "I'll see you in a little while," and went out the back door and crossed the gravel path to the garage.

Yesterday's beautiful weather had turned into February again. A raw wind blew, and rain bloated heavy gray clouds churning over Cherryhill. I paused for a moment to look at the house. After seeing how well-kept Sanders maintains The Cedars, I have a new appreciation for the years of work Daddy has put into their house and grounds. The two stories rise serenely atop a small hill overlooking rolling meadows around it, painted a white that's only slightly peeling in places. It isn't as big as many of the houses in the county, and doesn't look at all like Tara from *Gone With the Wind*, or even Montrose, a red brick antebellum house with four white columns that's the pride of the annual pilgrimage and seat of the Holly Springs Garden Club.

What it does look like is a comfortable home. The large front porch leads to a generous door outfitted with an old-fashioned doorbell, the kind that has to be twisted to make it ring. Just inside, the staircase goes up to a landing, and then turns right. It has a curved oak banister with a graceful loop at the bottom step, polished to a high gleam by four generations of Truevine kids sliding down it, and oak steps the years have burnished to a soft golden color no paint or varnish can ever match. To the left of the small entrance hall is the dining room, to the right, the living room that used to be the parlor. All the ceilings are twelve feet high. Fireplaces are in each room, some of them just for looks now, some of them still working. Behind the living room, the sitting room has been turned into my parents' bedroom so they don't have to go up and down the stairs. A generous bathroom has been added under the stairs, and a large kitchen has been updated. A laundry room is next to a back door that leads out onto a nice cedar deck that my father and his brother built years ago. In spring, half a dozen cherry trees blossom in what used to be a fruit orchard, looking like a wide swathe of pink cotton candy in the back and side yards.

Upstairs, there are three bedrooms and a nice-sized bathroom that started out as part of the sleeping porch. The west end of the glassed-in sleeping porch runs along the back of the master bedroom to the end of the house. It used to be my parents' bedroom. Now it's my room. I like to go sit out on the sleeping porch early in the morning and at dusk. When it's very cold I light a fire in the bedroom, but just for ambience. Two central heating and air conditioning units added twenty-odd years ago work just fine for the entire house.

One of the other bedrooms belonged to my older brother and my younger brother. They both died in Vietnam. Now their room is empty, kept just as it was the day my brothers left. The other room belonged to me and my twin sister, Emerald. She lives in Oregon with her husband and umpteen children. We've never been that close despite sharing a womb and a room.

There's not much left of our land now since Daddy sold most of it and leases other tracts to farmers with cow herds, but enough so that we still feel isolated and protected. Just down the road, there are new houses with swing sets in the back yards and subdivision streets named things like Whispering Willow Wind and Cherry Blossom Surprise. Our street is still called Truevine Road, named for my great-great-grandfather who started a church right after the Civil War and Grant's march left behind a lot of blackened fields, burned-out homes, and despairing souls. The Eureka Truevine church is gone now, burned down a few decades before when electrical wiring installed some time in the early thirties ignited a fire, but its name lives on in me.

I started my car and pulled out of the garage that had once been a cattle barn, and set out for Holly Springs. It isn't far at all, and in fifteen minutes I pulled my car up in front of the café across from the court house on the square. The old clock in the cupola on top of the court house has been fixed. The hands move slowly but steadily, clicking the minutes with big black hands.

Budgie Mason, who manages the café and serves plain food at good prices, waved at me and I waved back. I knew her from my childhood. Her parents had lived down Truevine Road, and her father had raised cotton and lots of kids. He'd done well with both. Budgie looks a lot like she did as a kid—slender and energetic, with a crop of curly black hair she usually kept tied in a ponytail atop her head. The hair might now have some gray streaks, but it's still tied in a ponytail on top of her head.

It started to rain and I hurried across the street to the court house and stepped inside. In the center of the foyer sits a gigantic glassed-in clock, the machinations whirring. To one side is a staircase that leads up to offices and courtrooms, to the other side are more high-ceilinged rooms that house county government offices.

I went straight over to the county clerk's office and asked for an employment application before I lost my nerve. After all, once I'd been an executive secretary in a large chain of hotels. This was hardly a step up the career ladder. Still, an honest job is an honest job.

Apparently, despite the glowing reports on TV and in the newspapers about the profusion of available jobs, it didn't apply to Holly Springs government offices. Not that week, anyway.

I decided the only thing to assuage my disappointment might be a generous helping of hot peach cobbler topped with vanilla ice cream, so I crossed the street in the rain to Budgie's café. It now belongs to a man from Ohio who decided to invest in Mississippi real estate, but at least he has the good sense to keep Budgie on as the manager. After Budgie's husband took off and her parents went into a nursing home, she had to sell the café to pay for expenses. It's still called Budgie's café, despite the sign out front that says *French Market Café* in fancy lettering

It's a neat little place, with round tables and chairs made out of curved iron, and walls painted in bright colors. A few framed posters of ladies in big hats sitting at French cafés hang on the walls. A long Formica counter holds a cash register, a chubby ceramic chef wearing a Gallic mustache and holding a small sign announcing the specials of the day, and a slender vase filled with plastic flowers. Next to the flowers is a pretty crystal jar with dollar bills inside to encourage tips. Tables sport brightly colored plastic cloths, votive candles, and brass napkin and condiment racks. Menus run more to hot biscuits and milk gravy, grits, cornbread, and chicken fried steak than they do to croissants, but do offer beignets and hot chicory coffee like Café Du Monde in New Orleans. France comes to Holly Springs.

Since the breakfast rush was over and the lunch rush hadn't started, and I was the only one in the café, Budgie met me at a corner table by the window with a cup of coffee and a small pitcher of cream. "How are Uncle Eddie and Aunt Anna doing?" she asked.

Everyone familiar with my parents calls them that, whether they're related or not. When I was a kid, other kids knew they could count on my parents for help or advice on almost anything. Except me. Somehow, I'd never tapped into that. My mother still refers to me as her "most active child." That's a tactful synonym for hellion.

"They're doing fine," I said. "When I left they were cuddled up on the couch watching an old thirties movie of Gable and Colbert chasing each other."

"That's so sweet."

"By the time I get back, they'll have probably planned a camel trip along the Nile." I put a few packets of artificial sweetener in my coffee and followed it with a generous splash of cream. "If they get to the stage of buying plane tickets, I might have to lock them in the basement."

Budgie laughed, and I took a sip of my coffee. She had no way of knowing I wasn't kidding about it. There should be some kind of instruction book on babysitting parents who are elderly, mobile, and have a checking account and credit cards.

"You're lucky," Budgie said. "My parents are in a nursing home and don't even know each other, much less me. The only bright spot is that I finally divorced that rotten husband of mine—Oh. Maybe I shouldn't have mentioned that."

It doesn't matter how well related you are to anyone in Holly Springs, or how long you've been gone; everyone you grew up with knows almost everything there is to know about you. Some people might consider that a disadvantage, but it does save a lot of lengthy explanations.

"If you're talking about my divorce, it doesn't bother me," I said. "We're still cordial. I'm just glad he's far away and out of my life. Today I'm celebrating being turned down for a job in every government department in the court house. Do you have any peach cobbler?"

"With lots of ice cream on top." Budgie knows what makes unemployment, divorce, and a rainy day better.

"Why don't you talk to Carolann Barnett?" she said when she brought back my cobbler with a huge mound of ice cream melting on flaky crust. "She's looking for someone to help out in her book store and lingerie shop."

My spoon hovered over cinnamon and nutmeg spiced cobbler. "Book shop and *lingerie?* Let me guess. She sells copies of *The Kama Sutra* and French panties."

"Not quite, but close."

"Where is it," I asked just to be polite; though I had no intention of working in a book store that doubles as a Frederick's of Hollywood.

Budgie gave me directions and I finished my cobbler. I paid my bill and left a tip in the jar by the cash register. Before I got to the door, Bitty barged in with a look on her face like she'd just seen the Loch Ness monster. Her hair dripped rainwater, and mascara smudged her cheeks. As if that wasn't startling enough, she was nearly speechless. I knew at once that all was not well.

"Trinket," she got out between gasps for air, "something terrible has happened!"

Since I'd already guessed that, I said, "Here, sit down and I'll buy you a cup of coffee."

She grabbed my arm in an iron grip. "No. I can't. You've got to come. I don't know what to do, and when I saw your car out front it was like an answer to a prayer. Help me. You've just *got* to!"

I began to get a little alarmed. Even with Bitty's flair for the dramatic, genuine fear filled her blue eyes and left her skin an uncomplimentary shade of gray. Her smart navy blazer with gold buttons on the cuffs was drenched. She wore navy slacks, sensible low-heeled pumps, and a white silk shirt; a jaunty red triangle of scarf stuck up out of the blazer's breast pocket. Gold gleamed at her ears and around her throat. She looked like a half-drowned Macy's mannequin.

"Over here," she said, and pulled me back to the table in the corner. She clasped and unclasped her hands a few times. The huge diamond ring on her right hand shot splinters of light across the café. She took a deep breath and lowered her voice to a whisper. "You're not going to believe this. I went out to The Cedars to take the chicken and dumplings like I promised Sherman Sanders and that's when I found him . . . he's dead as dirt, and I don't know what to do!"

I whispered back, "Sanders is dead?"

"No, not Sanders. *Philip!* What am I going to do?"

"The Philip who's your ex-husband? The one who just got reelected senator?"

She nodded. "That's the one. The police will never believe I didn't kill him."

Good Lord. "Why on earth was he out at The Cedars? And what did Sanders have to say about him being dead?"

"Sanders wasn't there. Just Philip. Laid out in the foyer with his head bashed in. That heavy bronze statue I admired the other day is right next to him. It has blood all over the top of it. Trinket—" She took another deep breath. "It's bound to have my fingerprints on it. I should have thought of that then, but I was in a hurry to get away. It didn't occur to me about my fingerprints until I was halfway here."

This didn't look at all good. And Bitty may be rattled, but she still knew that.

"Did you call the police?" I asked her, and she gave me a horrified look.

"No! They'll think I did it. You have to know our divorce was pretty nasty, with both of us saying all kinds of stuff, and Philip so mad because I got so much money in the settlement . . . you know what they'll think, Trinket."

I did. I also thought she should call the police anyway. I just couldn't figure out a way to convince her of that without our conversation ending in more dramatics.

"Did Philip know Sanders well?" I asked to occupy her while I mulled over ways to tell the police without upsetting Bitty or incriminating her. "It's quite probable they had an argument of some kind and it ended badly."

Bitty plopped down in one of the chairs. Her hands shook, but she had some color back in her face. "Philip has been trying to talk Sanders out of putting his house on the historic register for some ungodly reason. Probably just to spite me." Her eyes narrowed, and with all the mascara smudges, she reminded me of a wet raccoon. "That *bastard*! He probably knew I was going back to see Sanders and went out there and killed himself just so it'd look like I did it."

Ah. Now she was doing better.

"He was that kind of man," I said. Agreement on character or lack of it is primary in any discussion about an ex-husband. I'd learned that years ago. "But this time, I don't think he'd go so far as to bash himself in the head just to spite you."

Bitty stood up. "Well. I'm not going to let him get away with it. I'm fixing to call over at the Brunettis' office."

The Brunettis are local attorneys with a well-deserved reputation for always earning their money. They aren't cheap, but they aren't known for losing, either.

"Excellent idea," I said. "A Brunetti will know what to do."

"But first," Bitty said, "you and I are going out there to wipe my fingerprints off that wretched statue before someone else finds Philip."

I recoiled. "We can't do that!"

"Of course we can. Sanders isn't there, so we need to hurry before he gets back from wherever he went. It won't take but a minute to go in and wipe off my prints. Come on."

"Bitty no," I protested, and followed behind as she made for the café door. "I'm not going with you out to Sanders'." I crossed my arms over my chest and stared at her. "Has it occurred to you that Sanders may well have been the one who killed Philip? Or that he isn't really dead? Besides, it's raining buckets and I have no desire whatsoever to see Philip Hollandale alive, much less dead."

"Philip's nicer when he's dead." Bitty said it almost wistfully.

"Call the police, Bitty."

"I wonder if he thought about me before he died."

Probably. Not kindly, either.

"The police station is just a few streets over," I said. "I'll go with you."

Bitty sighed. "You're not just family, you're a good friend, Trinket. All these years, and we're still close as when we were kids. Come on. We'll take my car."

"To the police station, right?"

Bitty dashed out into the rain with her purse over her head and keys in her hand. The red Miata beeped and lights flashed, indicating she'd started the engine. I sighed. The phrase "in for a dime, in for a dollar" went through my head, but I followed her anyway. What are friends for if they won't go to the police station with you to report their ex-husband's murder?

I should have known Bitty didn't intend to go to the police.

Instead of going around the court square to Market Street, she took Old 178 down past the Fred's Dollar Store to hit Highway 7 through town. I knew better, but I had to ask.

"Bitty, has the police station already moved?"

"Good heavens, Trinket, you don't really think I go there on social calls, I hope. Last time I was there, that cute Sergeant Nestor flirted with me and I got a little giddy and bought up all the rest of the tickets to the policemen's benefit concert at the Kudzu Festival."

The Miata skidded on the wet pavement when she sped up to outrun a yellow light at the intersection of West Chulahoma Avenue. I made sure my seat belt was firmly fastened. Holly Springs' cemetery is just a block or two over, and I wasn't ready to join family members who'd already homesteaded their last six feet of local real estate. Bitty got the car out of the spin without hitting a curb or ending up in a yard, and headed west on Highway 7 again.

"So how do you feel about professional calls?" I asked when my fingernails were finally detached from the leather dashboard. "Murder tends to fall under that category instead of social."

"Really, Trinket, you're beginning to make me wish I'd gotten one of the Divas to help me instead of you."

The Divas she mentioned are a group of women over thirty and under a hundred. They're nothing like the *Sweet Potato Queens* or *Red Hat Ladies*, since none of them are trying to make a statement or glorify Southern ideals. In fact, rumor has it that membership doesn't require being born in the South, just a sense of humor and high tolerance for chocolate. I don't know how many of them there are since I haven't yet been invited to a meeting, but they call themselves the Dixie Divas and often meet at the old Delta Inn that sits across from the railroad depot and next door to Phillips, a nineteenth century saloon-slash-whorehouse-slash-grocery store. The saloon and grocery store part are fact, the whorehouse legend.

"I take it the Divas are familiar with murder then," I said, and Bitty didn't disagree.

"I trust you most," she said instead. "You're my oldest friend, and I don't mean by age."

"Of course not. We're the same age."

"You have two and a half months on me, Trinket."

I rolled my eyes. "So now I have one foot in the grave? And it won't do you any good to keep going down this road. I'm not taking part in any desecration of a crime scene. I like being able to see the sky instead of just iron bars and cinder block walls."

Bitty sped up a little. We went a mile or so past 78 Highway and turned right onto some road that has no sign post. A blue and white rusted out trailer is parked on a hill overlooking an expanse of pasture, cows, and a few emus. The last gave me a start. Brown, feathery, with long legs like ostriches, the birds stretched up their leathery necks and goggled at us as we went past.

"I don't remember those emus from yesterday," I said, and Bitty nodded.

"Frank Dunlap bought them as an investment. Then he found out it wasn't that good of an investment but he couldn't catch them all. They run wild out there in the trees somewhere, and he just lets them go. They bite."

Reason enough to leave them alone.

The road narrows to a Y flanked by pine trees on one side, hibernating ropes of kudzu on the other. Bitty took the kudzu side to the left. Windshield wipers slapped against glass and metal, and broken asphalt occasionally clacked against the underside of the Miata. Elvis played on the radio, but Bitty had it turned way down. Elvis was singing *Kentucky Rain*, which I thought pretty appropriate for the weather.

Bitty turned into Sanders' rutted drive and stopped just past the cattle gap. It looked silent and deserted. No lights gleamed; no smoke came out of the chimneys. No hound sat on the porch, and no dumpling-festooned mule peered through the rain.

I took a deep breath. My heart thumped, my pulse raced, and my throat went suddenly dry as the Sahara Desert.

"I'm not going in there," I said again.

"Fine." Bitty chewed on her bottom lip and looked resolute.

When the Miata edged forward, I realized I'd been holding my breath and expecting Bitty to back out of the driveway and head back to town. I expelled a long gush of air and futility.

"I can't believe you're doing this."

Bitty's knuckles were white on the steering wheel. "Neither can I."

We rolled to a stop and sat staring at the house. Rain glistened on wood planks, dripped from the corrugated metal roof, and hissed against the car. The front door was open, the screen door shut, the empty porch ominous.

"Can you drive a stick shift?" Bitty asked me. "I may need a quick getaway."

"I can drive anything but a tank," I lied.

Bitty turned off the car, opened the driver's side door, and I got out and went around. We both looked at the house again, and then I looked at Bitty. She had an expression like a determined rat terrier on her face. Whether it was a good idea or not, this was important to her. I sighed.

"Come on," I said. "I'll go with you."

Holding hands like two frightened schoolgirls, we eased up the first step. Planks creaked beneath our feet. Our combined weight elicited another groan when we got to the second step, then the porch. The overhead lantern swayed in the wind, and the chains that tether it so it won't hit against the roof or house clanked loudly.

"Why do I keep thinking of that haunted house at the Halloween carnival when we were eight?" Bitty muttered.

"If a ghost pops out at us, I'm wetting my pants. Again."

"I thought it was a skeleton."

"Whatever."

We were at the screen door now. Bitty faltered, and I just wanted to get in and out of there as quickly as we could, so I grabbed the handle and opened the door. We stepped just inside and let our eyes adjust to the absence of lamplight.

The heart pine floors gleamed dully in the dim light, the small Oriental rug with dragon designs lay in the middle, and the heavy bronze statue sat serenely on the parquet table. No body lay in the floor, no blood puddle, and no sign of murder. I looked at Bitty.

She stared blankly. "He was here. I swear he was . . . I saw him. Philip, laid out like a hog on a butcher's table. Blood everywhere."

I put my hand on her shoulder. "You've been through a lot of stress lately, Bitty."

She looked up at me. "I *saw* him. You believe me, don't you?"

There was such a pleading look on her face I couldn't have said no if I'd wanted to, so I nodded. "Of course, I do. Maybe he was just knocked out, and he woke up and left. There's no other car in the driveway."

Something flickered in her eyes and she frowned. "Whoever killed him must have taken his car."

"Or maybe he's not dead."

Bitty looked doubtfully at the clean floor. "Then who cleaned up the mess? There was a lot of blood. Philip never so much as picked up a dirty sock, much less cleaned up blood."

"Someone did. Probably Mr. Sanders. He does like things tidy." After a moment I asked, "Where was . . . the senator lying?"

"There." Bitty pointed and I took a few steps into the room, half-expecting blood and body to suddenly materialize.

I knelt down, careful to keep my skirt tucked behind my knees and well off the floor, and gingerly touched the heart pine. It was dry. It couldn't have already dried in one hundred percent humidity by itself. After all, even on a sunny day, Mississippi's known for humidity so high your shoes can mildew in the closet.

"Well?" Bitty asked, sounding nervous, and I shook my head.

"It's dry."

"I didn't imagine it. As much as I'd like to see Philip choke and die, I know what I saw."

When I started to stand up, I lost my balance, and put my hand behind me to catch myself. It happened to land on the carpet, and wet wool slicked against my palm. I looked up at Bitty.

"The carpet's wet."

It took me a minute to steel myself, but I sniffed at my fingers and caught the distinct and unmistakable smell of pine cleaner. That didn't eradicate the faint, rusty scent of blood. I stood up.

"Come on, Bitty. We need to get out of here."

"But what about the statue?"

I held out my hand. "Give me the scarf from your pocket."

After a brief hesitation, she whipped it out and I walked over to the bronze statue, my hand shaking so hard I nearly knocked it off the table as I wiped away any and all prints. Then I scrubbed up my muddy footprints, walking backward.

"Wipe the door handles, too," Bitty said as we retraced our steps to the screen door. "Just in case."

"Well, we did visit the other day. It'd seem odd not to leave a few prints behind." Still, I wiped away our prints on the door just in case, and we fled back to Bitty's car in a half-run, half-stumble.

Neither of us spoke until we were well down Highway 7 again. I turned to look at Bitty.

"Something was different in the house. I feel like we missed something."

"What we missed," said Bitty as she slowed down to turn into the Sonic drive-in, "is my ex-husband dead on the floor. I'm relieved and disappointed at the same time. I knew it was too good to be true."

She pulled into a slot and cut the Miata's engine. I smelled fried onion rings. Bitty looked at me. "Sonic has great chili dogs with cheese."

"Order two."

"Footlongs?"

"You bet."

When all else fails, Coney dogs provide temporary comfort as well as dimples on the butt and thighs. Not a bad trade-off.

CHAPTER 3

"What are you doing Saturday?" Bitty asked, and I cradled the cordless phone between my ear and shoulder and kept stirring milk gravy in the iron skillet to keep it from lumping.

"Same thing I did last Saturday, I imagine. Why?"

"The Divas are having a meeting."

"Is this an invitation?"

"Three of the Divas can't come. You can be my guest."

While I thought over that honor, the gravy got thick too fast. I grabbed the cup of milk, poured some in, added salt and pepper, and then said, "Are you sure?"

"I'll pick you up at ten-forty-five. Bring something chocolate."

"What?"

"Believe me, *any*-thing chocolate works just fine. My end is covered. I've bought enough wine to keep California solvent."

No one knows what all goes on at these meetings, but there are rumors of Johnny Depp posters being violated in most interesting ways. Men aren't allowed to attend other than as entertainment.

"All right," I said as if uncertain, when I'd been salivating at the idea of seeing for myself what went on at the Diva meetings, "I'll come to the meeting if you really want me there."

When we hung up, I smiled. Bitty obviously feels a sense of responsibility for scaring me with a false murder. Truthfully, I'm glad she didn't listen to me about going to the police. Not only would we have looked like idiots, but the last I heard, there are penalties for making false reports about dead bodies.

Not to say we both didn't wonder why Philip Hollandale hadn't been making a huge fuss over getting hit in the head and left for dead. He's the kind of man who thrives on things like that. His silence was unnatural. Bitty had even been talking about calling him to see if he'd pick up his cell phone, but couldn't think of a good reason for it if he did answer.

"It's not like I can say, 'Hey, why aren't you dead?' without him being suspicious," she'd remarked thoughtfully.

"I don't know," I'd replied, "that seems to be right in line with a lot of the things you say to each other."

That much is very true. As I've mentioned, their divorce had enough acrimony to fuel the local papers for well over a year.

We came to the conclusion that Philip must be involved in something shady, or as Bitty said, "Larceny is his favorite activity next to having a hot young blond hum *Dixie* on Bobo," and so decided not to let it worry us too much. However, Sanders was still missing and that might be cause for concern if he didn't show up fairly soon. He isn't known for straying far from home.

Mama and Daddy got up early as always Saturday morning, and they went out to feed the legion of stray cats that stay in the old barn and supposedly keep the area free of mice and rats. It seems to me that the only thing getting scarce is twenty pound bags of cat chow, but maybe that's because the mice and rats chew through the bags and eat most of it.

It was one of those early February days that start out so nicely and too often end in storms and flash floods. Best to enjoy the sunshine while possible. I went out to the barn, stepping carefully to avoid cats. They crowded metal feeding pans with only an occasional spat.

"Bitty's coming to pick me up in a little while," I said, and Mama looked up at me with a smile.

"You're going to a Diva meeting?"

A little astonished that she knew about the group, I nodded. "It should be interesting."

Daddy said something that sounded like *"At the very least"* but I wasn't sure.

Mama went back to dipping out scoops of cat chow into metal pans, while Daddy turned on the hose and filled up shallow water bowls. Inside the barn, he's built shelves around the top of the loft and covered them with strips of carpet. Wooden boxes hold soft cotton rags, and small cat-sized ladders climb up walls to reach all kinds of hiding places.

Cats of all sizes, colors, and personalities come running when Daddy yodels, "Heeeeere, catty-catty-catty-catty-catty!"

It's an amazing sight. It's like the horses running at Belmont when the gates open. It's the greyhounds at the dog track bursting out of cages to chase the rabbit. It's a 50% sale at Macy's.

With no children in the house, my parents have become nurturers to the animal kingdom. There are worse things to be. What worries me is who's going to take care of them when my parents grow unable to do it. I have a feeling my name is at the top of the list. While I love dogs and cats, I've always thought of them in manageable numbers. Like one. Thankfully, my parents are also civic minded and work with the local humane society to spay and neuter. If not for that, there wouldn't be a square foot of catless space left in Marshall County.

"I'll be home later," I said when the cat pans were full and I had my parents' complete attention again. "Is there anything I can pick up for you at the store while I'm out?"

Mama patted my arm. "You just go and have fun, sugar. We have all we need here."

That seems to be very true.

Bitty showed up at twenty 'til eleven. She had the top down on the Miata and a scarf over her head, and wore sunglasses. The tangerine scarf was the same shade as her cotton tangerine blouse, cotton tangerine slacks, and tangerine shoes. The belt was a bright yellow with a sunburst buckle. I completely understood the need for sunglasses. I felt drab in my faded blue Lee jeans, long-sleeved green knit shirt, and teal windbreaker.

"Is that some kind of uniform?" I asked as I got into her car, and she laughed.

"Yep. I'm a sunshine girl. What's in the cake pan?"

"Mississippi Mud Cake."

"'Atta girl. Something decadent and rich."

She turned up the radio to a golden oldies station and we blasted down Truevine Road to the rhythm of Jerry Lee Lewis banging out *Great Balls of Fire*.

"You're in an awfully good mood," I said when we turned off Randolph onto Van Buren. "Just get an extra alimony payment?"

"Nope." She smiled so big the face-lift scars by her ears puckered. "I got to gloat at Trina Madewell about getting the Sanders house for the tour. That always makes me cheerful. She's such a spiteful thing."

I turned in my seat to look at her. "You talked to Sanders? What'd he have to say about your ex lying out in his foyer?"

"Well, I haven't actually talked to him since we took that first batch of chicken and dumplings out there. I haven't had the nerve to go back, not after seeing Philip laid out like a Thanksgiving turkey, and, as usual, Sanders hasn't returned my calls."

That worried me. "Maybe that was Sanders you saw lying in the foyer?"

"Good Lord, Trinket, I may be nearly fifty, but my eyesight hasn't gone yet."

"You're fifty-one."

"That's nearly fifty from the other side. It's just as close as forty-nine."

I couldn't argue with her logic. "Don't you think Sanders should have returned your calls by now?"

"Not really. He doesn't use the phone much, if at all. If you want to talk to him, you have to go out there. I don't know why he even has the blamed thing if he won't use it."

"Uh, when are you going back out there?" I wanted to know so I could be busy.

"Next time I catch you off-guard." Bitty knows me too well.

Bitty took the left side of the Y that leads uphill to the Delta Inn just across from the railroad depot, downshifting but not quite coordinating correctly with the clutch. The Miata snarled a protest, she cussed, and then got it right. Whoever gets this car after she trades it in is going to need a new clutch, at the very least.

By the time we parked between the Delta Inn and the former saloon-slash-whorehouse-slash-grocery store, I was sure I heard the car making strange noises under the hood. I hoped Bitty had the local tow truck's number in her tangerine purse.

I got out with my cake and looked at the store. Now it serves locally famous hamburgers, cheeseburgers, and homemade fried pies. It's a two-story with a porch on the top that conjures up images of shady ladies waving to prospective customers as they stepped off the train. An addition to the right side houses the current owners. History seeps from walls, wood, and even the railroad tracks only ten yards away.

The old railroad depot is even more impressive. While it's been there since before the Civil War, it's been burned, rebuilt, and added on to so that the original structure has changed a great deal. It's a beautiful old red building, Victorian in style, emanating history, style, grace, and echoes of a life gone by. What a coup it'd be to get it on the Historic Register as well.

As for the Delta Inn, it's one of the loveliest structures in Holly Springs. It was built in 1852, has three stories, white painted old red brick, and four white columns holding up a porch and balcony all the way across the front. Upstairs rooms have doors onto the balconies, and I could just visualize ladies in hoop skirts sipping morning tea and afternoon mint juleps outside their rooms while waiting for the next train. There's a rambling garden at one side, with rose bushes, flower beds and huge holly trees, and several big dogs that look and sound ferocious but are really dangerous only to butterflies and ham hocks. The iron scrollwork gate is kept locked except for visitors.

Bitty took a cardboard box from what can be referred to as a back seat if you're inclined to be generous, and I heard the clink of bottles and recognized her contribution. California wine country has another month of good revenue.

"Need any help?" I asked, but should have known better. Bitty's always been able to carry her wine well. We walked up the cobblestone path to the front porch. Sweet-faced pansies in big concrete pots flanked the double doors.

The hotel is in a state of renovation. Rayna Blue lives in the lobby, as she has for years. It's been a long time since I've seen Rayna, but I recognized her at once when she came to the hotel door to hush the dogs and let us in. She still looks a lot like she did as a young woman in her teens even though she's fifty-one. Slender, with dark hair and big gold eyes, she's about five-five and wears her clothes with an artistic flair. As an artist, she's usually got a few paint smudges somewhere on her face or hands. Today she was paint-free and dressed in a loose black skirt and belted tunic top, with sandals on her feet. Big silver earrings tangled in her brown shoulder-length hair.

"Trinket!" she said, and gave me a hug. "What's it been, seven or eight years?"

I hugged her back and handed her the covered cake pan.

"Something like that. It was the summer your cousin Possum Perkins robbed the Merchant and Farmers' bank at their drive-in window."

Rayna grinned. "Since he deposits his money in a tin can, he's not that familiar with how banks work. It didn't occur to him to un-tape the big *For Sale* sign from the back window of his truck. The cameras got an excellent view of his phone numbers written in black magic marker. Of course, he also forgot that his ex-wife works there as a teller."

"I remember that," Bitty said with a laugh. "Possum was so surprised when the police showed up at his house later."

Rayna shook her head. "Possum drinks to excess. Bless his heart. Look who's already here. You remember Cady Lee Forsythe and Deelight Tillman?"

Since I remembered Cady Lee but not Deelight, I covered up my lapse with a smile and nod in their direction. "It's been a while, hasn't it?"

Cady Lee put her hands on her hips. "Trinket Truevine. I haven't seen you since we were drunk on champagne in the back of Stewart Carmichael's hay wagon."

"Good Lord. I'd forgotten about that. Stewart was drunker than we were, because he ran the mules and wagon into a kudzu ditch and couldn't get us out. His daddy had to come with the tractor to get that wagon back on the road, so we rode the mules home. What ever happened to Stewart?"

Cady Lee grinned. "I married him. We had three kids and an amiable divorce. We still play poker together every now and then, but only when my husband can make it. I married Brett Kincade the second time around. He was a few grades ahead of us. Do you remember him?"

I shook my head. "Maybe if I saw him again."

Cady Lee had always been the school beauty, even back in elementary school. Back then she had soft brown hair and big brown eyes. Now she has ash-blond hair and big turquoise eyes. One of the perks of new technology. Stewart Carmichael's family owns several farms, a meat-packing plant, and an oil refinery. They may have bought a senator or two as well. Last I heard, newly reelected Philip Hollandale owes a major portion of his campaign contributions to Carmichael influence. The Kincades own a chain of department stores. Cady Lee has obviously done well, in marriage and in divorce.

She wore diamond earrings as big as a butter bean on each ear, had a marquis-cut emerald ring on her right hand, a wedding set that had to be at least fifteen carats on her left hand, and her nails were perfectly manicured. Cady Lee has a tan in the wintertime and it looks natural, so she probably spends a lot of time down on the coast. Biloxi is only about five hours away by car, but my bet is she spends her money across the Gulf on the Florida peninsula.

Rayna set my cake pan on the oak counter of the check-in desk at the end of the gigantic lobby that makes up her living quarters. Pink marble forms three walls. The oak-paneled rear wall behind the desk has double doors that lead to her sleeping area. A lovely, curved staircase sweeps up the wall on the lobby's east side, with a baggage room tucked beneath it. At the west end of the check-in desk is a single door that leads back to the former kitchen. Another door in the west wall leads to a former dining room, with the garden facing the street at the front of it.

You'd think that a hotel lobby as a living room would be cold and stark, but it's not. It has a homey feel to it, greatly helped by gigantic houseplants in waist-high pots that sit beneath a three-story domed skylight, several plush couches and chairs, and antique cabinets that house a television, VCR, DVD, and stereo. Rayna's easel and paint supplies are set up in front of the east windows near a huge pool table. Cats wander in and out of the baggage room at will, where I saw several litter boxes discreetly waiting. A few cats perched in the front windows, and a tabby slept in a pot of elephant ears so big that two of the leaves would make a size ten ladies dress.

Multi-colored aluminum streamers hung in glittery strips above a long table pulled to one side of the lobby. A row of feathered and glittered half-masks with peacock feathers lined one end, and strings of plastic beads swirled through brightly colored plates, and hung around the neck of a papier-mâché head in the table's center. The grinning head wore a mask and a crown.

Bitty took the case of wine to the kitchen behind the lobby and put most of it in the big side-by-side refrigerator. Then she set two bottles of white zinfandel on the check-in desk, and pulled the cork on the first one.

"Here we go, ladies," she said, and poured us each a glass.

It was a little early for me to drink wine but this was a celebration. Of something, I wasn't quite sure yet, but the decorations gave me a hint. We all five lifted our glasses in a toast.

"To the Divas!"

By the time the others arrived, I was nearly drunk on chocolate fumes, but prudently kept the zinfandel refills at a minimum. There were ten women, ranging from thirty-year old Marcy Porter to sixty-ish Gaynelle Bishop, with a few others I didn't recognize at all. A cardinal rule is that no men are allowed to attend Diva meetings, unless they're delivering something or are part of the entertainment. Even then, they must take a privacy oath not to reveal what they see or hear. So far, there have been no violators of that rule, for threats of reprisal are so grim and dire most men pale at just the mention. I also learned other interesting but more flexible rules.

Membership in the Dixie Divas stays at an even dozen. No more, no less. Those who drop out, die or move are replaced by a majority of votes. Visitors are allowed to attend by permission of the hosting Diva since space and food may be a concern. Not all the meetings are held at the Inn. Whoever volunteers to play hostess is responsible for allotting members food to bring, but provides ice, dishes and cutlery, and decides the theme.

This month it was Mardi Gras. Appropriate since Fat Tuesday was next week. We put on the masks and Mardi Gras beads, and ate our way through chicken salad, six different kinds of crackers and bread, and a couple of casseroles. Rayna had a huge crock-pot of red beans and rice simmering, and shrimp bisque that was as good as anything available in New Orleans. Desserts ranged from my Mississippi Mud Cake to a huge platter of iced brownies, and filled an entire end of the check-in desk.

I was introduced to several people I didn't know, and reacquainted with a few I'd known and forgotten. Deelight Tillman was one of the latter. Petite, with gray eyes and a shaggy mop of light brown hair, I just couldn't place her. Over my second helping of red beans, rice, and chunks of andouille sausage, we went over the times and places in our past where we must have known each other. We weren't having any success until we started naming siblings and their friends.

Then it came to me. "I know," I said. "My older brother Jack dated your older sister Deevine."

Deelight threw up her hands. "That's it! Of course. I remember we all used to tease her by saying if she married Jack her name would be—"

"Deevine Truevine," we chorused, both emphasizing the first syllables, and then laughed.

"With our surname of Grace," Deelight said, "poor Deevine got a lot of teasing. It never seemed to bother her, though. I don't know what my parents were thinking, naming her Deevine Faithann Grace, and naming me Deelight Joyann Grace."

Lifting my brow, I said, "You're talking to Eureka Truevine, remember? Our parents must have been tippling too much of the church communion wine."

"You've gone back to your maiden name?" Deelight said in more of a question than a comment, and I nodded.

"It seemed to be the thing to do since I knew I'd be coming back home. Besides, Michelle is married, so having the same name as her is no longer important." I paused. Maybe I'd done it just to eradicate all traces of Perry, which is foolish, since we do share a child together. I'd just been so blamed mad, at him, myself, and mostly my lack of foresight.

"Well," Deelight said, "Rayna kept her maiden name when she married Rob. Of course, if she hadn't, she'd be Rayna Rainey."

"So now she's Rayna Blue Rainey," I said, and we both laughed.

"Any grandchildren?" Deelight asked me after a few moments.

"Not yet. Michelle's in graduate school and her husband's an engineer. They live in Atlanta."

Deelight being several years younger than I, she still has kids at home. We talked about all the things parents discuss, our hopes and dreams versus the realities, and how none of it really matters as long as our children are happy, well-adjusted people with good futures. Money never seems to be a big factor in our hopes for them, just their self-reliance and independence.

"Trinket, come over here and listen to this," Bitty said, appearing at my elbow and taking me by the wrist. "Gaynelle Bishop has a perfect idea."

"About what?" I asked as I allowed myself to be escorted close to the nineteenth century pool table where three of the Divas were chalking cues and spotting the eight ball. At least, I think that's what they were doing. I'm not up on all my pool playing rules and terms.

"Why, about Philip and Sanders, that's what."

I stopped dead in my tracks. My eyes must have bugged out like goose eggs. "You *told* her?"

By this time, Bitty's Mardi Gras mask lay horizontal on top of her head, while the rest of us had removed ours. She looked at me in surprise, and peacock feathers bobbled in front of her left ear. "Of course. I can tell the Divas anything. What happens at the Inn, stays at the Inn."

While I wasn't as sure of that as she seemed to be, I consoled myself with the thought that since the senator wasn't dead after all, it didn't really matter.

Gaynelle Bishop, an older woman newly retired from teaching school for forty years, has the face of someone whom nothing can surprise. Acquired, I'm certain, from decades of dealing with children who lie, cheat, and mess their pants. Gaynelle looked at me as if I was one of the latter when I smiled and said hello.

"Don't I know you?" she asked sharply. "Who's your family?"

I clenched my cheeks to keep my Hanes clean. "Ed and Anna Truevine."

Her face cleared and she smiled. "Of course. You've been gone a long time. Your sister comes back home quite a bit, though."

It took a little effort to keep the smile on my face at her implied criticism. Emerald comes back only when she can't stand another moment of listening to the incessant whine of her kids and demands of her husband. She stays a week or two, drags Mama to Memphis shopping, sleeps until noon, and gets room service from Daddy. My usual consolation is that my sister and I didn't come from the same egg, even if we were born six minutes apart. I came out first, eager to see the world and make myself known. Emerald had to be dragged out and woken up, and yawned all the way through the first year of her life. I, on the other hand, rarely slept, and could be usually found in any spot where I wasn't supposed to go. Family history says my mother didn't sleep more than ten minutes at a time for the first five years of our lives, at which point we went to kindergarten and she finally got a three-hour nap.

"That's what I hear," I said to Gaynelle, "but Emerald and I always seem to miss each other somehow."

She laughed at that. "So you do." Gaynelle isn't stupid. She may be somewhere around sixty or sixty-five but she's got the energy of a thirty-year old, the body of a fifty-year old—one in much better shape than I am—and the sharp mind of a scholar. She also has the sharp tongue of a lame-horse politician. Gaynelle dyes her hair light brown, wears contacts, and has a penchant for silk. This is a radical change from her days as a teacher when she had graying hair, cats-eye glasses, and sensible cotton dresses. Viva lá retirement.

"So tell Trinket your idea," Bitty urged, and Gaynelle nodded.

"It's very simple. We should go out there and talk to Sanders. If he doesn't know about the senator being struck on the head, he'll need to in case of a possible lawsuit. If he does, then we threaten him with disclosure to the police unless he goes to them with his explanation. Or his confession."

Simple? It sounded suicidal.

"Uh, you do know that Sanders carries a shotgun, right?"

"Yes, of course I do. But since he can't possibly maim or kill all of us, I doubt he'll even attempt to try such a thing."

"Safety in numbers," Bitty piped up.

I looked at her. "Except for the tallest target. I'd just as soon not be included in this little group, if you don't mind."

Bitty blew out her breath in a huffing sound. "Can you think of a better idea?"

"Yes. Do nothing. If Philip Hollandale wants to file charges, let him. If he doesn't, we need to keep our noses out of it."

Gaynelle shook her head. "That would certainly be true if we knew the senator to still be alive. What if he's not? Then Bitty has a duty to report it to the authorities."

She had me there.

"It's something to consider," I finally said, and we all agreed on that.

"Until she does," Gaynelle said, "it's really best not to mention this to anyone else. Not a single soul, shall we agree?"

I agreed with that, too.

Thankfully, any further discussion of possible murder and missing bodies ended when the entertainment arrived. Since it was a Mardi

Gras celebration, Rayna had hit upon the perfect idea for our festivities: A transvestite stripper. It embodies all that makes New Orleans unique.

Hoots, whistles, and a few tipsy proposals were shouted at the six foot version of Britney Spears. He—she?—undulated into the lobby, wearing leather, a halter top, some kind of fringe, and knee-high boots. A blond wig shimmied around his face as he mimicked what I assume to be Britney's moves, and one of her songs played on a boom box he strategically placed on a table by the front door. Just in case we became too rowdy an audience, I'm sure. Quick getaways must be frequently required in his profession.

At first I wasn't sure where to look. I mean, the tiny little shorts he wore made it obvious he had more external equipment than Britney, but after Bitty poured me another glass of wine and told me to get the stick out of my rear, I grew more enthusiastic in my appreciation. I may be through with men, but that certainly doesn't mean I can't admire—and remember—the tanned, taut packaging they come in when they're twentyish. I've always been partial to a man's belly for some unknown reason, and this Britney had toned abs and a six-pack that would make a nun sigh with pleasure. Maybe Joan Collins has the right idea but the wrong carry-through. Toy boys should be enjoyed but not married. Not that I have any intention of doing either.

None of that, however, kept me from catching his halter-top when he took it off and slung it into the air. It must have been that fourth glass of wine, but I found myself whipping it around in the air over my head and shouting things like "Yee-haw!" and "Take it all off!"

Shortly after that, Marcy Porter caught the skirt of leather strips he threw out into the room, hollered that she was going to "ride you like a stallion!" then launched herself at him. Britney's eyes got big, he sucked in a breath that made his belly meet his spine, and before he could escape, went down in a tangle of excited, half-inebriated Divas. Gaynelle Bishop must have perfected a few karate moves, because she beat Marcy to him. I believe I heard Britney say what sounded like *"Agghh!"* but since it seemed like he was doing just fine, I assumed he was only expressing his appreciation.

Of course, I'm not allowed to say any more than that. After all, what happens at the Inn stays at the Inn.

I will say that I've rarely spent a more entertaining afternoon.

CHAPTER 4

I've recently realized that childhood memories and adulthood expectations are often at complete odds with reality. Especially when said adult lives far away and visits home are always, of necessity, brief.

My early childhood memories are of idyllic, Norman Rockwell years occasionally marred by one or more of my siblings' misdeeds, of which I was always the innocent and much maligned victim.

My adult expectations before returning to Cherryhill to care for my parents were visions of a loving daughter gently easing feeble, grateful seniors into the twilight of their lives with my serene smile and a saint-like patience.

Neither of those is anywhere close to the truth.

If pressed, I can recall a few, and only a few, times when I might—and I stress the word *might*—have given insult or caused injury to one of my siblings. Emerald has always been known to exaggerate, and my brothers preferred getting even to tattling. My mother remembers it quite differently, but her memory isn't what it used to be. There are still a great many events that my parents are better off not knowing and I'd rather not discuss. But I digress.

The feeble, grateful seniors of my imagination are in actuality hormone-driven, energetic people who have no intention whatsoever of fading into twilight anything. Instead, they're quite obviously determined to blast headlong into eternity riding jet skis or climbing Pike's Peak. If I'd ever possessed a claim to patience or sainthood, my chances are definitely blown now.

"You're going to *what?*" I asked in disbelief when informed of my parents' plans.

I could hear my own voice rise several octaves that caused my mother to look up at me in mild surprise and disapproval.

"Dear, it's impolite and unladylike to shriek," my mother pointed out in the soft tone that I recalled from my childhood. She's never had to lift her voice. All that's required for instant and lasting self-flagellation is that cutting edge of disappointment and disapproval.

More calmly, I said, "Sorry. I'm just . . . surprised that you and Daddy have decided to sail on a clipper to Brazil. It's operated by wind. Not reliable engines. *Wind.* It will take months. Or years. What if you have a medical emergency?"

"There's a medic aboard ship," Daddy said enthusiastically. "And radios. A helicopter or the Coast Guard can find us if there's an emergency."

"The American Coast Guard doesn't cruise off Brazil. Besides, you have obligations here that you've acquired."

Daddy looked stunned. "What obligations?"

"Well, that cat colony in the barn for one. Your neurotic dog for another."

"But isn't that why you came back," Mama asked, "to help us enjoy our last few years?"

I stood there for a moment with my mouth open but nothing came out. I'd never admit I'd entertained visions of them as invalids sitting cozily in chairs before the fire while I brought them cups of tea and turned the radio to a classical music station. I tend to get wrapped up in my own imaginary scenarios that no one appreciates but me. This seemed to be one of them. And really, did I *want* my parents to be feeble and needy? Of course not.

But neither did I want them stuck on some ship in the Atlantic with a crew of possible white slavers or drug smugglers. I approached from a different angle.

"Of course I want you to enjoy your lives," I said. "You've earned it. I'd just rather you start off more slowly, work your way up to Boston clippers. You might have a tendency toward seasickness, for instance. Or the ship's captain could be mentally deranged."

"Oh, I doubt anything terribly awful will happen," my mother said. "It has a Triple A rating."

Their expectations obviously leaned toward high adventure with no risks. My imagination ran toward burials at sea.

We compromised.

Reservations were made on the Delta Queen for a cruise down the Mississippi to New Orleans in March. They'd be gone seven days. That gave Daddy three weeks to get the majority of work done on the house before the April pilgrimage and me three weeks to rest up from taking care of a herd of cats and a neurotic dog. I don't know who dreaded it more, me or Brownie. He gave me an occasional untrusting look that said quite plainly I'm not qualified. I agreed.

With this major crisis narrowly averted, I drove my beige Taurus over to Bitty's house for mimosas and sympathy. It was a pretty day, lots of sunshine and wind-driven clouds.

Bitty lives in an 1845 house on Walthal Street a block from the Delta Inn. It's named Six Chimneys, has six bedrooms, a front porch that goes all the way across the front and around the sides, is painted a soft pink with white trim, has a black iron picket fence, a white gazebo in the side yard, and a carriage house converted to a garage on the north side. It's beautiful.

It's not the house Bitty truly wants.

Since she's been six years old, Bitty has wanted a particular house on West Chulahoma Avenue. The Walter Place is built of stone, has twin turrets like a castle, estate size grounds, and was a temporary home for General Grant and his family when they stayed in Holly Springs in 1862. It's probably the main reason Bitty married her third husband, Franklin Kirby III. His elderly aunt owned the house, and Franklin was her favorite nephew. If not for their falling out when Franklin married Bitty and his devoutly Catholic Aunt Mary disapproved of his marrying a divorced woman, maybe she'd have at least gotten to live in it a while. And wouldn't you know it? Not long after Bitty's divorce from Franklin, Aunt Mary died, the house went up for sale, and Bitty lost the winning bid. She was fit to be tied. Sometimes things just don't work out.

As it is, Bitty makes do with Six Chimneys. Not a shabby bargain, in my opinion. It's a lovely old house with a nice history that always sounds impressive on the pilgrimages. Cherryhill on the other hand, is basically a farmhouse built in 1898, and is only included on the pilgrimage because the original foundations of 1859 are beneath the "new" structure, the first house having been burned at the hands of Grant's soldiers. While there was nothing left but the basement and footings, Cherryhill has the distinction of having suffered at the hands of the enemy. If there's one thing Southerners appreciate, it's past suffering. Especially if Yankees are the cause. That alone lends the structure, person, or battlefield, a revered sheen of heroism. Messy details tend to be glossed over, and past honors glorified far beyond anything possible.

I'd seen the same sort of reasoning when visiting London several years before. Though the Norman duke, William the Conqueror, defeated Saxon King Harold in 1066, books upon books are available at Westminster Abbey about Harold. When I inquired about the availability of a book written about William, the clerk gave me a rather startled look and said coldly, as if I should already understand, "William was a *Norman*." And being from the South, I completely understood. Holly Springs doesn't have a single monument to General Grant, either.

Bitty and I sat out on the front porch of Six Chimneys and sipped mimosas from crystal goblets. Sunshine didn't quite reach our wicker chairs with fat blue cushions that we pulled back into the shade of the porch.

"We have Strawberry Plains again this year," Bitty said as if it didn't matter at all, but I knew from the way she said it that it was a major coup.

"That's wonderful. The renovations are completed?"

Bitty nodded. "A few years ago. Now it's a nature walk as well as on the historic register. Every year there's a big deal about the hummingbirds. Thousands of them appear for a few weeks in the fall before migrating south. It belongs to the Audubon Society now."

Strawberry Plains is very close to Truevine Road, a lovely old house Yankee soldiers burned after putting the women and children of Rebel soldiers out into the cold. The family watched their home burn, and after the Union army left on their march south to Vicksburg, the women set to work rebuilding, living in the roofless ruins with their children because there was nowhere else to go. Marshall County has dozens of stories like that one, as does the entire South, and no doubt a fair share of homes up North as well. Civilian suffering isn't restricted to any one area, I've noticed.

What I really wanted to discuss with Bitty hovered on the tip of my tongue. It had nothing to do with my parents, old houses, old wars, or the pilgrimage.

Finally I said, "Budgie mentioned that Philip voted against funds to renovate the Inn as a historical building. Did you know about that?"

"Philip's always been a horse's patoot. He's been a thorn in our sides since Rayna first applied to the Historical Register." She waggled her glass at me. "Mark my words, the minute we get the Inn approved for state funds, he'll find a way to screw it up or delay it."

"Have you heard anything about him since Friday?"

"Not a word. Thank God."

"Nothing from Sanders either?"

Bitty looked at me. "You think something's happened to Philip?"

"Well, if you saw him with his head split open, you'd think there'd have been something in the papers or on TV by now about an assault or accident. It's been three days."

"Maybe he's lying unconscious somewhere. Maybe he tried to drive to the hospital and passed out. He could be in a kudzu gully." Bitty began to look alarmed.

I wasn't sure if it was because she cared about Philip or her alimony checks. It's not that Bitty is insensitive or greedy, but there *is* the whole scorned woman thing that she takes quite seriously. Philip's extracurricular activities were quite humiliating for her.

"We should have reported it," I said. "I know better. Even if he wasn't there anymore, we should have immediately informed the police and let them investigate."

"Anonymously, of course." Bitty took another sip of champagne and orange juice. "No sense in being silly about it. I'm just glad no one knows I was out there. Except Gaynelle and you, of course. Do you think Sanders has something to do with it? He must," she answered her own question, "for I'm sure no one else would have cleaned up the floor but him. I'm just trying to figure out why Philip would even visit him if he didn't mean to screw up The Cedars getting registered, but we've heard nothing. There has to be some good reason he went out there, since he's not known for his good works or philanthropy. I can't see Philip taking a pot of chicken and dump—oh . . . my . . . *God!*"

Bitty sat straight up in the white wicker rocking chair with its fat blue cushions, her eyes so big and round they looked like Blue Willow dinner plates. I nearly spilled my mimosa.

"What on earth's the matter with you, Bitty?"

"My chicken and dumplings. I left them."

"Didn't the mule eat—oh my. You don't mean you left a second batch of chicken and dumplings out there, do you?"

Silent and white-faced, Bitty nodded. I tried to think back to what we'd found out there when we'd gone, but for the life of me, I couldn't recall any pot on the porch or in the foyer.

"You didn't leave them in the car?" I asked, more hopefully than rationally and of course she shook her head. "Okay. Just try to remember everything you did from the time you got there until you left. And remember—Philip is alive, just mad as blazes and plotting revenge."

Bitty sucked in a deep breath and set the crystal flute down on the wicker table by her chair. Then she folded her hands and sat with her feet together on the porch floor, her spine stiff, and her chin only slightly quivering. She spoke with the elucidation but hesitation of a student in the finals of a spelling bee.

"I got out of the car . . . I remembered to take it out of gear this time . . . I pulled out the pot from the back . . . I used pot holders because it was still too hot since Sharita had just finished them when I got to her house. I remember thinking that by the time Sanders got around to eating them, the dumplings would have soaked up the broth just about right . . . since I had to hold the pot with both hands, I couldn't knock on the door, and he didn't hear me call him, so I set it down on the porch right by the door. Then I opened the screen door and stepped inside . . . at first I thought maybe Sanders had fallen. When I realized it was Philip, I was so surprised, then a little angry, because . . . you know, he always seems to muck up things I'm trying to do, just for spite. The statue was lying there next to him, like someone had just dropped it and left it there. I picked it up because it seemed like sacrilege for such a fine antique to be on the floor. And in case I might need it. That's when I saw the blood on the floor and the big gash in Philip's head."

She closed her eyes as if seeing it all again. When she opened them, she gave me a tragic look.

"I dropped the statue back on the floor and turned and ran out of there like a scalded dog. I never even thought about the pot of chicken and dumplings again until just now."

"You're doing better than me. I never thought about them at all. I should have noticed that your car didn't smell like boiled chicken and biscuit dough."

We sat there in silence for a moment. There didn't seem to be too much to say that'd make either of us feel any better, but now I understood Bitty's insistence on wiping off the statue.

Finally I ventured, "Well, at least Philip isn't dead. Think how bad it'd be if he was."

Bitty pursed her lips. "The pot holders have our initials on them. Wedding gift. If he took that pot with him, he's probably got the potholders, too, and is going to try to get me charged with assault or attempted murder. Then he gets out of paying alimony. I am *so* screwed."

"Surely not. Sanders can verify that you were to bring him the food, and obviously he let Philip into the house. I still think they quarreled for some reason, and if Sanders didn't bash him in the head, someone else did. Maybe Philip had someone with him. Maybe it was the mule."

"Oh, don't kid about it, Trinket," Bitty wailed, flopping back in the wicker chair. "I'm *doomed!*"

I think I've mentioned that Bitty is prone to dramatics. I've always thought she'd have been a mega-star if she'd ever gone to Hollywood. Not that she's done badly for herself staying in Mississippi. Bitty and I grew up in the era between June Cleaver and Janis Joplin. It was an exciting but confusing time. We never knew whether to wash our bras or burn them, but at least we had choices, while our mothers and grandmothers options were more limited.

"You're not doomed," I said. "Philip would have to have proof you assaulted him. All he has are pot holders and a pot of chicken and dumplings."

She brightened immediately. "That's true. And I could always charge him with theft."

"Of a pot of chicken and dumplings? I can see the headlines now: 'Senator Hollandale of Holly Springs, Mississippi has been charged with the theft of two embroidered pot holders and a pot of chicken and dumplings valued at eight dollars and thirty-four cents. While the senator protests his innocence, his former wife, the luscious Bitty Hollandale, asserts that although the senator ate the evidence, the empty pot is certain proof of his guilt. This is Trinket Truevine of Channel Eight in Holly Springs reporting to you Live from the Marshall County Jail.'"

Bitty's mouth twitched, then she laughed. "It is ludicrous, isn't it?"

"Drink your mimosa, Bitty. Sanders has probably eaten every bite of chicken and licked the last dumpling from the pot. When you take the necessary papers out to him, he'll be so sated with boiled bird, broth, and biscuit, he'll sign anywhere you tell him."

Lifting her champagne flute, Bitty said, "To the power of chicken and dumplings!"

"And to happy endings," I added.

I've always been a sucker for happy endings. There are far too few in life as it is, and even if the ones on television, in the movies, and best-selling novels are mostly fiction, just the hint of a Happily Ever After is enough to make me sigh with bliss.

That emotion is nearly always followed by the certainty that Prince Charming grew a beer belly and belches his comments at the dinner table, and the only one who listens to Cinderella's dinner conversation anyway is one of the mice. Fairy Godmother has moved to Vegas, won big at craps, but forgot to turn the pumpkin back into a coach before she left so Cinderella can leave Charming and his shrewish mother behind.

If only there could be as many Happily Ever Afters in real life as there is in fiction, life's trials and tribulations would be much easier to bear. It's the promise of catching that brass ring on the merry-go-round, winning that blue ribbon, becoming champion of the spelling bee, getting that great job, that keeps most of us slogging on toward our own personal goals.

Sometimes, however, someone moves the goalpost. And it's *never* closer.

I want world peace and fiduciary responsibility. I want the lions to lie down with the lambs. I want an end to hunger, poverty, disease, and our methodical extermination of species, human beings included. I want religious and racial tolerance, if not acceptance. I want honest politicians without their own agenda and with only the best interests of their constituents at heart. I want the huge hole in the ozone to close. I want clean air, pure rivers and streams, an unmolested rain forest and an end to clear-cutting old forests. I want oil corporations to invent environmentally safe energy, cars to run on vegetable oil, and TV reality shows to disappear.

For myself, I want to live quietly after I win the lottery.

Bitty just wants the Walter Place.

Neither of us is likely to achieve our goals, but neither of us is likely to give up hoping for miracles, either. My life outlook, however, is the pragmatic optimism I mentioned earlier. It's a nice dream to have, but it just ain't gonna happen.

Bitty's outlook is more "Full speed ahead and Damn the torpedoes!"

I realize my goals are always likely to be unfulfilled. Bitty is certain that just one more swipe at the brass ring will be the one that succeeds.

Truth be told, I'd much rather be like Bitty. Her failures are just small obstacles on the way to success. My failures tend to be life-altering disasters. Maybe Bitty will rub off on me a little. That'd be nice.

Meanwhile, we needed to find out if Philip Hollandale was enjoying good health and a sound skull, and whether Ulysses Sherman Sanders had returned to home and hearth with his deaf and blind coon hound and gluttonous mule. My optimism hoped all was well. My pragmatism expected trouble.

CHAPTER 5

"You go up and knock."

"No, *you* go up and knock."

Bitty and I had been having this back-and-forth since we'd pulled up in front of Sherman Sanders' house. The single wood door was still open and the other one closed. The screen door banged softly against the frame when the wind blew just right, which meant it wasn't locked from the inside. There was no sign of Sanders, his hound, or the mule. There was, however, a rather skinny chicken pecking desultorily in the gravel around the side of the house.

The sunshine of the day before had been swallowed by rolling gray clouds that promised rain, but the temperature was still warm. I shivered anyway.

Then I took a deep breath. "We'll go up together."

"We probably look like we're in a three-legged sack race," Bitty said with a giggle when we clumsily climbed up the second step to the porch. That was because I clung to her arm as tightly as a baby possum to its mother's tail.

I untangled my arm from hers and checked to see if I was still wearing my own shoes. It'd somehow seemed safer to present a bigger target, which made no sense at all.

"We're adults," I said aloud, more to convince myself than Bitty. "We're just here to see if Mr. Sanders enjoyed his chicken and dumplings, and is ready to look over the paperwork for the historical register."

"Right." Bitty straightened her charcoal gray pinstripe jacket, smoothed her matching pinstripe slacks, and adjusted the neckline of her low-cut ecru silk blouse. Apparently she was leaving nothing to chance.

While I hesitated, Bitty took two purposeful strides forward, rapped sharply on the wood of the screen door, and waited expectantly. The only sign of indecision was the way her right foot tapped against the hickory plank floor.

"Yoo-hoo, Mr. Sanders," she called through the wire mesh, "it's Bitty Hollandale." After a brief wait, she turned to look at me. "I don't hear a single sound. It's like it's deserted."

"Maybe he's out back. Feeding chickens. Or the mule."

We walked around back, me in my sturdy Nikes and Bitty in her pretty Manolo Blahniks. It was obvious I'd chosen more wisely when she wobbled in a rut and nearly toppled into a lanky bush. Good thing I was there to grab her. While Bitty took the median between ruts that looked to be pick-up truck width, I crossed a small patch of dirt and grass to an L-shaped back porch that ran alongside what had to be the kitchen. In the past, kitchens were separate from the main residence for the purpose of fire safety. Not that it always helped.

This kitchen had been connected to the house by a breezeway. It was just as well-kept as the front of the house, even though the surrounding yard looked like a hog-wallow. Well behind the house were remnants of chicken coops and out-buildings that had seen much better days. An air of desertion hung over them.

"Nothing here but a couple of chickens," Bitty said with obvious disappointment, and I turned to see her peer into a weathered shed with the door hanging by one hinge. "Oh, fresh eggs! There are several—do you have something we can put them in, Trinket?"

"Forget the eggs, Bitty. I'm beginning to think something happened to Mr. Sanders. An accident, maybe. Didn't he have a vehicle of some kind? A truck or car?"

"I should know? Still, he had to have something. How else would he get into town to buy supplies?"

There was no sign of a truck or car, not even a rusted one. I began to get the inescapable feeling that Sanders had been hijacked. No dog. No mule. No Sanders. As much as he took care of the house, he wouldn't go off and leave it unlocked. While the area isn't known for vandals or crime, most people at least shut their doors in chilly weather.

"What's that smell?" Bitty stuck her face up into the air and wrinkled her nose.

"Chicken poop?"

"No. Worse than that. Like . . . a cow lot. Or roadkill."

We just looked at each other for a moment. I could tell she was thinking the same thing I was thinking, but neither of us wanted to be the first to say it out loud.

Finally I said, "Where do you think it's coming from?"

Bitty looked at the badly leaning shed next to the one housing chickens and fresh eggs. I drummed up my courage, forced my feet to move through the weed stalks and dirt, and went as close to the shed as I dared. I've always had a rather weak stomach. Someone can just talk about bodily fluids or what the contestants on *Survival* or *Fear Factor* had to eat to stay in the game—I really think most of television's reality shows are created by sixth grade boys—and I begin to get queasy. My stomach rolls, my face feels hot, and it takes all my effort not to hack up a giant size hairball. Motherhood was a shock to my system. Only perseverance and love got me through it without barfing on my beloved child. But it's been a long time since I had to deal with that sort of thing, and my once-acclimated stomach has reverted to its former intolerance.

So I held my breath, stuck my head quickly into the shed, and hoped I'd find rotting fruit or cow patties, and let my eyes adjust to the dim light seeping through cracks in the weathered gray wall-boards. A dark, familiar shape lay on the floor of the shed, half-covered by a ratty old blanket, placed there on cushioning straw as if laid by loving hands. I stared a moment.

Eyes watering, I pulled my head out of the shed and walked back to Bitty. She had a look on her face of hopeful expectation, and I slowly shook my head.

Bitty put a hand to her chest and sucked in a deep breath, then coughed before asking, "Is it Sanders or . . . or Philip?"

"No. It's Tuck."

Bitty blinked. "Tuck?"

"The hound. Sanders' coon hound. Remember? Loud? Blind?"

"Of course, I remember, Trinket. I just can't figure out why you're crying about it."

"I'm not crying. The smell made my eyes water. Though come to think of it, I'd cry over Tuck before I would Philip."

"Wouldn't we all." Bitty looked toward the house. "So what do you think this means? Maybe Sanders got so upset when his dog died that he went off someplace?"

"I don't think the dog just died."

"Well, I'd say not. From the smell it has to have been a few days."

"No," I said, "I mean that the dog looks like . . . like he's been hurt. There's blood." I didn't go into details. Just thinking about it was enough to make my stomach roll a little bit.

"Then maybe Sanders went off to confront whoever killed his dog. I can't see him killing it," Bitty said, and I agreed with the last.

"No, I don't think he would have done that. But I do think we need to find out how Tuck died. Then maybe we can figure out why Sanders went off, or if he's gone at all. We still don't know that he's left. I'd hate to call the police if there's no need."

We both looked at the house.

"It's open," Bitty said, and I nodded.

"Yep."

It took a few minutes to dredge up our courage, for after all, we might be dealing with a crazed dog-killer at best, a murderer at worst, but we finally went back to the house. Bitty's heels clacked on the heart pine floors. My sports shoes made squeaky sounds. An air of abandonment hung in the rooms as we went from one to the other, checking under beds, in armoires, the water closet with its old-fashioned clawfoot tub and antiquated plumbing, and the closed-in space under the stairs. No locks kept us out of any of the rooms, even the attic that was a historical buff's wildest dream come true. Bitty kept making little sounds like a hamster as we looked through metal racks of old clothes covered with plastic. A hoop made of horsehair and folded on itself would billow out any of the skirts on the old dresses. Bitty flapped her hands in distress.

"Not plastic! Oh, clothes will ruin if they're kept in plastic . . . . "

"If they haven't ruined in fifty or so years, there's time to suggest other methods of storing them."

I tried to keep her focused, but she kept getting sidetracked by cracking leather saddles and saddlebags, a doctor's black bag with instruments dulled by time, and a horsehide and brass chest containing an assortment of letters tied in ribbon, old invoices, and some documents that could be almost anything. At one point, I thought Bitty might just pass on out with emotion. I'd rarely seen her that overwhelmed, not even at her first wedding. This rivaled the birth of her twin sons, now professional students and party-goers at Ole Miss. Twins run in our family. That's why I stopped at one child. I didn't want to risk twin boys with my husband's genes and my tendency toward ignoring the obvious. If I'd been more alert, I'd have seen that Perry's multiple jobs were not a sign of a career on an upward trend, but the lack of long-term employability. All I'd seen at the time were washboard abs and a tight butt. Not excellent marriage qualifications.

Our thorough, if often distracted, investigation turned up neatly made beds, evidence of a morning shave—men never notice all those tiny bristles they leave in the sink—and a used bath towel that seemed out of place in the otherwise tidy bathroom. Plain cotton, it lay atop the bath mat by the tub as if hastily dropped and never retrieved.

Outside, the wind began rattling the windowpanes and threatening rain. I hurried Bitty ahead of me, and we passed through the breezeway to the kitchen out back. There, on a stove that would have been at home in the pages of *Little Women*, sat Bitty's pot of chicken and dumplings. Two pot holders lay near it, embroidered with fancy initials. Bitty stuffed them into her purse.

Fruit flies hovered in a thick swarm, and we didn't need to check to know Sanders had never had a chance to eat his chicken and dumplings.

"Well," Bitty said after a long minute of silence, "*someone* had to bring the pot inside."

I looked at her and opened my mouth, but she beat me to the punch.

"*No,*" Bitty said forcefully. "Calling the police will only complicate things."

"Bitty. This isn't a complication. This is a missing man and possibly murder. We have no other choice."

"Don't be ridiculous. Of course we have other choices. Sanders may be having an affair with a truck stop waitress. Think how mad he'll be if the police track him down at a Motel Six and his name is in all the papers. He can't be dead. He owns The Cedars, and it's not yet signed up to the historical registry. If he doesn't have any heirs, it'll go up for sale at some sky-high price the Holly Springs Historical Society can never afford, and they'll tear down the house and put up a Mini-Mart."

"Out here on a strip of asphalt road frequented only by stray dogs, tractors, and slightly hysterical women? Come on, Bitty. The only thing they'd put up here is a Beware of Mule sign."

Bitty stuck out her chin, looking very much like the mule I'd just mentioned. "This land backs up to Highway 7. They could build a Wal-Mart on it."

I rolled my eyes. "They just opened a new Wal-Mart right off 78 Highway. I hardly think they'd build another one a mile or two down the road. We have to involve the police. If you don't want to, I completely understand. I'll leave your name out of it, but I think we should at the very least report Sanders missing."

"Fine." She looked at me crossly, and then sighed. "I hate it when you're right."

"Don't worry," I comforted her as we left the kitchen and went back to her car, "I'm not right very often."

"I know," Bitty said.

*

Sergeant Maxwell looked at us with an expression that gave nothing away except an air of resignation. A hefty man, with skin the color of polished mahogany, he has black eyes and a broad, strong nose, high cheekbones, and full lips that he kept pressed together a little bit too long before he shook his head and said, "Repeat that, please."

"You see," Bitty began again, "I've been talking to Mr. Sanders about putting his house on our historical registry and permitting it to be on the annual pilgrimage. We've come to a tentative agreement, but when I went out to take him another pot of chicken and dumplings— I did mention those already, didn't I?—he wasn't there. He's still not there. His dog is dead in the chicken coop and the pot of chicken and dumplings are on the kitchen stove. Uneaten."

I nudged Bitty. This version as well as the last one had left out any mention of the senator lying on the floor or a pool of blood.

She elbowed me back quite sharply in the ribs, and smiled at the sergeant. "So I thought perhaps something dreadful has happened to him and it should be checked out by the authorities. Just in case he's met with an accident on the road."

Maxwell cleared his throat and leaned forward, elbows on his desk, tapping a pencil atop a yellow pad of paper. "Mrs. Hollandale, there could be a dozen explanations for his absence. He could be visiting relatives or on vacation. What I find curious is that you broke into his home."

Bitty gave me an *I told you so* look and shook her head. "There was no breaking into anything, Sergeant. The door was left open. Only the screen door is shut, and it's not locked. Out of concern, we investigated to see if he'd hurt himself. Sanders isn't the kind of person to go off and leave his house open, but we didn't notice any sign of burglary. It's just odd."

"We'll check it out," the sergeant said after heaving another long sigh.

"Thank you," Bitty said and stood up. "When you contact him, please tell Mr. Sanders that I'll make another appointment to meet with him at his earliest convenience."

Once we were outside on the pavement, I looked at Bitty. "You didn't tell everything."

"Of course not, Trinket." She hit the little button on her remote and the Miata started and the lights flashed. "There's no point in alarming the police unnecessarily. You've obviously forgotten, but the Holly Springs police are quite sharp. They have a habit of finding out the truth even when it's very inconvenient. You just remember that I told you so when this good citizen stuff blows up in our faces, all right?"

"Okay," I said, and crossed my fingers. When Bitty's the cynic instead of me, it's never a good sign.

Rain changed from a light mist to a heavy downpour before we even got to Market Street, and Bitty parked right in front of Budgie's café without asking me if I wanted to stop. My mouth was already watering for homemade cobbler anyway. We may have our differences at times, but in so many ways Bitty and I are very much alike.

Parking spaces slant diagonal to the sidewalk. On one side of Budgie's is a real estate office; on the other side is an attorney's office. There's an empty storefront by the attorney's office, and an antique store at the end. The café is on the bottom floor of the three-story building built in 1854. It has old-fashioned ornate facings and false front, and the outside brick walls have been painted a nice bright white. Black wrought iron railings and small flower boxes that drape red petunias and cascades of verbena in the summer give it a New Orleans flair.

Budgie's had a nice lunchtime crowd, but we found a table in the rear that had just been vacated. Dirty dishes, wadded up napkins, and a red plastic basket still full of cornsticks cluttered the table. Such a waste of excellent cornbread.

Since the rain had chased away the warmer temperatures, we wavered between chili and cornsticks, or hot potato soup and cornsticks. Followed, of course, by the cobbler of the day with as much vanilla ice cream on top as could fit into the bowl.

I ended up choosing the potato, cheese, and bacon soup, and Bitty had the chili. The red plastic basket of bread and cornsticks are complimentary with every meal. We both had sweet tea instead of coffee with our meal. Coffee comes with dessert.

"After such a wretched day," Bitty said, licking melted butter and cornstick crumbs off her fingers just like she was at home, "we deserve two helpings of cherry cobbler."

"Well, it wasn't as bad as it could have been," I reflected. "And I'm not sure I'll be able to finish one bowl of cobbler, much less two. I ate too many cornsticks."

"Budgie makes them just right. Not sweet, light on the top, golden brown on the bottom. I could eat a barrel of cornsticks if I didn't have to worry about staying a size ten."

I looked at her. "The last time you were size ten was in sixth grade."

"You're thinking of your shoe size, dear," Bitty said without a blink, and we both smiled.

Things were getting back to normal if we were trading casual barbs. I didn't want to think about Sanders, or the senator, or even poor Tuck anymore. We'd done our duty.

"What are you going to do about Uncle Eddie and Aunt Anna?" Bitty asked when we'd put away our cobbler and were sipping coffee. "Are they really going to take the Delta Queen downriver?"

I nodded. "All the way to New Orleans. At least they'll be confined on a boat. And they'll only have one night and half a day in New

Orleans before they fly back home. Maybe that's not enough time to be a problem."

Bitty had taken her compact and lipstick out of her purse and started applying a top coat to her lips, stretching her mouth into that odd-looking "O" women always make. Since I hadn't put on any lipstick in the first place, I felt no compunction to follow suit. Unlike Bitty, who's had a face-lift, injected Botox and collagen and whatever else costs a lot of money and doesn't last, I'd decided to face old age *au naturel*. It has nothing to do with lack of money. Okay, maybe a little, but I've never been one to fuss with my hair or make-up a lot, and figure there's only so much plastic surgery that can be done before a woman begins to look freakish. Bitty's probably a decade or two away from qualifying for the circus. I'm sure I'll be the first one to tell her when it's time to put away her checkbook and let the wrinkles win.

"I think it's good for them," Bitty said, using her forefinger to touch up the corners of her mouth. "This is the first time they've really been free to go anywhere. And of course, they never had the money when they were young, or even after Uncle Eddie got back from the war. It's got to spice up their sex life to travel a bit."

"Please," I said with a shudder, "I'd rather not have that vision in my mind while they're gone. I'd rather think of Mama playing five-card-draw with a cigar hanging out one corner of her mouth than visualize them playing leapfrog in a single bunk."

Bitty laughed. "You can be such a prude. How do you think you got here?"

"I have it on good authority that I was found under a cabbage leaf."

"Then it's amazing that you have even one child."

"And apathy about gardening," I mused. "Perry never could figure out that some kinds of plowing take time and attention. When I realized all he cared about was his own harvest, I took up reading instead. Much less frustration, and always a happy ending."

Bitty snapped her mirrored compact closed and stuck it back in her purse. "Honey, you just need a master gardener instead of a field hand in bed, and you'll forget all about reading."

I doubted it, but since Gaynelle Bishop was bearing down on us like a ship at full sail, I saved my argument for another time.

"Bitty Hollandale," Gaynelle said abruptly, "I think it's just awful what's happened. I know that even though there was all that trouble and nastiness, it's got to be hard for you. Do let me know the first time you get any news, you hear?"

"Excuse me?" Bitty said with a puzzled look on her face. "What's happened?"

Gaynelle put a hand to her chest. "You mean you don't *know?* It's all over town—I thought for sure you'd have heard by now."

"Know what?" She inhaled sharply and half-rose to her feet. "My boys? Has something happened to Clayton and Brandon?"

My stomach thumped, and the undigested cobbler shifted uncomfortably.

"Good heavens no," Gaynelle said and put out her hand as if warding off even the thought of it. "It's your ex-husband. The last one. You know, Senator Hollandale."

Since Bitty sat down hard and just stared at her, it was up to me to ask the obvious.

"What about him?"

"He's missing. Kidnapped or car jacked, I suspect. The police found his car in the river over by a Tunica casino, and no one's heard from him for three days. It's on all the local and national news stations. CNN even reported it."

To Bitty's credit, she never turned a hair. "Philip always has loved publicity," she said. "I imagine he's off somewhere with the flavor of the month, and will turn up with an explanation that won't fool anyone but the idiots who voted for him."

Gaynelle lifted a brow. "I voted for him."

"And I married him." Bitty's smile took any sting out of the implication that Gaynelle was an idiot, or at least, alone in her idiocy.

"Did they say anything about Philip being inside the car?" I asked.

"The car was empty, but they have divers in the river right now to see if perhaps he might be . . . he must have been hurt badly, after all. *You* know. It's so awful, isn't it?"

We all agreed that it was, and Bitty stood up and said she should probably go home since her ex-mother-in-law might be trying to call. I knew that was a whopper of a lie. Bitty's ex-mother-in-law had once accused her of marrying Philip only for his money. As that accusation was only partially true, Bitty had taken offense and called the senior Mrs. Hollandale a dragon of a mother who'd spoiled her son rotten and turned him into a pervert. Things degenerated from there, and their already cool relationship never recovered. Rumor has it that when Bitty's divorce from Philip was final, Mrs. Hollandale celebrated with a ten thousand dollar garden party.

Rain had slacked off when we went outside. The Miata lit up at the punch of the remote and we got into the car and sat in brief silence. Then Bitty looked over at me.

"I always knew that he'd do something like this to me."

"Don't take it personally," I said. "I'm sure he didn't plan to get murdered just for spite."

"Heavens, Trinket, don't be naïve. Philip's not dead. He just wants me to think he is. It's part of some plot to get out of paying alimony. It wouldn't surprise me if his mother thought up this scheme. She's a lot smarter than Philip, even if she is a vicious crone who's turned out a son with an Oedipus complex and a narcissistic daughter that has all the finesse of a black widow spider."

"Try not to be so tactful. Say what you really mean."

Bitty grinned. "If I did, your ears would burn to a crisp. Come home with me. I may need someone to hold me back while I watch CNN."

It always amazes me just how quickly Bitty recovers from disasters.

CHAPTER 6

"Did you hear about Philip Hollandale?" Mama asked me within seconds of my return home. She cornered me in the kitchen right next to the laundry room, eyes bright with curiosity.

"It's been mentioned."

I'd come in the back way, hoping for a respite before having to even think about him again after the last hour and twenty-three minutes spent listening to Bitty fuss and fume that it didn't matter what he did, he wasn't going to get out of paying her every penny he owed her for the years of suffering he'd caused. While six years may not sound like a lifetime to some people, I can tell you from my own personal experience that three minutes in the company of someone whose very name causes an agonizing migraine should earn some kind of compensation, whether personal, monetary, or legal.

"Do you think he's dead?" Mama whispered with an avid interest she'd never have displayed when I was a child. Gossip was frowned upon then.

My mother is one of those people who's come to enjoy many activities in life she'd once eschewed as improper. It's as if reaching a certain age entitles one to so many degrees of vice. Forty earns the right to talk about current music trends as "noise" while speaking admiringly of the musical artists in your era that have *real* talent. Fifty earns the right to go without make-up and not be considered slovenly. Sixty qualifies for pretending you can't hear annoying relatives, and seventy obviously earns a second adolescence, with sexual adventures in unexpected places. I hope I never reach eighty. I don't even want to think about what vice is acceptable then.

"It's possible he's dead," I said, and Mama nodded wisely.

"Philip Hollandale never was a very nice man. Of course, Bitty knew that when she went off and married him. Bless her heart, she just never thinks beyond next week."

For the unfamiliar, the phrase "bless her heart" is used often in the

South to soften criticism. I'm sure it's used elsewhere, too, though perhaps not with the same intent.

"Bitty thinks he's just gone off with one of his women again," I said. I hung my sweater on the rack and ran a hand through my hair to dislodge some of the rain that made it lie close to my scalp like a red and gray squirrel. More than once, I've caught Brownie staring at my head as if his enemy, The Squirrel, masquerades as my hair. That dog is absolutely fixated on squirrels.

Mama followed me into the living room where Daddy sat watching CNN on the main screen, with an old movie flickering on the small picture-in-picture. I've never quite figured out how people can be facile enough to watch two television shows at the same time. It's all I can do to stay focused on one, and even then, I find myself forgetting the plotline before it's halfway finished.

"Do you think so, Eddie?" Mama asked, and Daddy looked up from the TV.

"Think what?"

"That Philip Hollandale has run off with a woman again and isn't really dead."

Daddy shrugged. "I wouldn't put much past that shyster. He's liable to do almost anything."

"Makes you wonder how he ever got elected, doesn't it," Mama said, and Daddy laughed.

"Like most politicians get elected, sweet pea," he said. "They make promises to the big corporations in exchange for contribution money. The contribution money then buys them votes. Getting reelected depends on how well the politician keeps his promises, not how well he's done in the job."

"Oh Eddie, you sound so cynical," Mama said, and went to sit down on the couch by him. "I'd rather think it's the individual voters who elect a man to the job."

"So would I, sweet pea," Daddy said. "So would I."

Brownie jumped up on the couch next to Mama and snuggled close, then looked up at me. When I saw his nose twitch and eyes focus on my hair, I decided retreat was in order and went upstairs to wash my hair and soak in the tub.

Later, after supper had been eaten, the dishes loaded in the dishwasher, and my parents left in front of the TV to reminisce with a Bob Hope movie about the madcap antics of World War II, I went back upstairs to sit out on the sleeping porch off the master bedroom and listen to the rain hit the windows. Days were getting longer, and a hint of gray light still lingered so that I could see the pale dots of cherry tree buds in the yard below.

As a little girl, I'd come here to sit with my mother in a comfortable chair for her to brush my hair and tell me stories or sing songs. There were a lot of cherry trees back then. A lot of people. This old farmhouse that had been home to my father as a boy, and his father before him, was always noisy with life. After Jack and Luke were killed within days of each other in the Tet offensive, the house seemed to draw in on itself, like the people inside. It's odd how inanimate surroundings can take on the mood of its residents. Familiar rooms and furniture grow darker, somber, and no bright sunlight reaches the interior. Light filters in all muted and hazy, as if reluctant to dare shine at all. Visitors speak softly, afraid a loud word may shatter walls. Or break hearts.

Then, as futility and sorrow recede, maybe just a fraction at a time, the air gets a little bit lighter. Shadows shrink, and when someone laughs for the first time, the darkness slowly fades into memory. Only the faces of loved ones remain, fixed forever in our minds and hearts.

As great as my own grief was when my brothers died, I cannot imagine how my parents felt. Just the thought of losing my daughter, my only child, always prompts me to pick up the phone. Even if I only get her answering machine, I hear her voice and a connection is made, a reassurance that she's still there, that she's all right. Then I feel foolish for being a sentimental, needy mother with so much time on my hands that I interrupt my child's life. And I think back to all the times my mother called me when my baby was fussy, or Perry and I were about to go out, or more likely arguing, and how I cut her short far too often and sometimes became annoyed that she seemed to call too much. Now I'm my mother.

Bitty's right. My parents deserve every single moment of their lives to spend just as they want to, not as I expect them to live. It's almost like having teenagers again, watching them make plans for the future without a thought as to possible dangers. I just hope I can survive it.

But I draw the line at white water rafting with them down the Colorado River. I just know I'd humiliate myself by falling out of the raft while they shot the rapids with no problem.

*

I woke up the next morning feeling as if there was something I'd missed, that nagging feeling you get when you just know something important is supposed to be remembered, but for the life of you, you can't think what it is. While sure it probably had something to do with Philip Hollandale, nothing came to mind even when I'd finished my first cup of coffee.

Mama and Daddy were out cooing to the cats and opening more twenty pound bags of cat chow. I saw them out the kitchen window, Mama already dressed in snazzy new tennis shoes and a pair of jeans, and Daddy wearing new Levi's and a flannel shirt that he'd no doubt purchased at Sears. It doesn't matter how many new department stores open up, my father is unwaveringly loyal to Sears, Roebuck, and Company. It doesn't matter that Roebuck took off years ago for an undisclosed location, and that only Sears is sticking it out these days, minus the catalogue that I always pored over every Christmas if I could wrest it away from Emerald or my brothers. No tool or article of clothing worth having is sold anywhere else but Sears, according to Daddy.

When the gigantic Sears up in Memphis closed down thirty or so years ago, my father was devastated. Even I felt a twinge, remembering how I'd anticipated our annual Christmas visit to the twelve story department store on Cleveland with all the excitement and enthusiasm usually reserved for Santa's slide down the chimney. Going to Sears was almost as good. Until that trip, the Christmas season hadn't officially started for the Truevine family.

Back then, we took our 1951 dark blue Oldsmobile, three in the front, three in the back, up what's now Old 78 Highway. That car was built like a tank. Either Emerald or I always had to sit between my brothers so they wouldn't fight, but that only meant we risked getting punched or pinched instead. Getting chosen to sit up front was not only a privilege, but a relief. Mama took a supply of food along in case there was car trouble or traffic, and by the time we got to the parking lot we kids were so wound up that only the walk through the cold air to the store kept us from just spinning off like tops.

I remember the rush I always felt when the front door to Sears opened and that gush of warm air washed over me, smelling like popcorn, hot peanuts, leather gloves, and new denim Levi's. None of the stores have that special fragrance anymore. If it could be bottled, any store using it would have to post traffic guards at all the entrances. It's that potent.

Those are the kind of memories Bitty and I share, because she and her parents and brother always followed behind us in their car. Daddy's brother, Bitty's father, died a few years back, and Aunt Sarah not long after. Steven, Bitty's brother, lives down in Jackson where he's the CEO of a company that makes rubber grommets for machinery of some kind.

So there's lots more to my connection with Bitty than just friendship or kinship. Coming back to Holly Springs is like reclaiming my childhood.

The phone rang just as I poured my second cup of coffee, and I knew it was Bitty.

"Are you ready for this?" she said before I got out all of my cheerful *Good morning*. "No body was found in the river. So instead of assuming he's alive and off in Mexico, or somewhere in Europe with an eighteen year old girl whose bra size is bigger than her IQ, the reporters are suggesting that Philip has been murdered!"

Reasonable, I thought. "Bitty, have you forgotten seeing him laid out in Sherman Sanders' foyer with a bloody head wound?"

"Honestly, Trinket, you don't really think he's dead, do you?"

I wasn't sure, but I didn't want to rule anything out, either.

"It's possible," I said cautiously.

"Yes, and it's possible that Hugh Hefner can be monogamous, too, but I wouldn't want to bet any money on it. I'm telling you, this is just one of Philip's schemes. If he wants something, he'll go to almost any lengths to get it, and I wouldn't put it past him to have run off with all the money in the state treasury and leave me behind to go hungry."

Since Bitty had gotten substantial amounts in three other divorce settlements, I didn't think there was any danger of her starving to death in the next month, but it didn't seem like the time to point that out.

"I'm not sure state senators have free access to treasury funds," I said, "and even if they do, not even Philip is cunning enough to figure out how to pull that off without getting caught. Or dumb enough to try it. He'll turn up soon." *One way or the other*, I didn't add.

"Well, they just need to focus on finding out where that weasel went instead of dragging the river and looking under rocks. I should call the police and tell them his favorite rendezvous spots where he hides out with his Slut of the Month."

"No," I said as firmly as I could. "Just stay home and off the phone. Read. Watch an old movie. Try not to think about it. You're working yourself into a frenzy."

"Maybe I'll go visit Rayna. She's always calming. Want to go with me?"

"Sure." What else did I have to do anyway? No one had called me in for a job interview, and my parents were feeding the furry flocks with fishes and loaves while their neurotic dog ran madly around the yard barking at birds sitting in oak and cherry trees. It drives him crazy to have the yard invaded by birds or squirrels, but he ignores several dozen feral cats like they don't even exist. Go figure.

When I got to Bitty's house, she met me at the door before I could knock. Bitty always wears her hair in the latest styles, something suitable for a fifty-one year old woman going on thirty. It's usually loose, soft, and frames her face very attractively. It startled me to see it pulled straight back into a knot on the nape of her neck. She wore a black jersey and matching pants, and no jewelry. Even her flat shoes and opaque socks were black.

"Good God," I said, "who are you supposed to be? The grieving widow?"

She narrowed her eyes. "He's *not* dead, just absconded with state funds and a bimbo."

"Ah. I keep forgetting that. So what's with the death clothes?"

"Black is slimming. I've put on a few pounds. Stress makes me eat. Last night I ate an entire box of chocolate cupcakes. Then I threw up, but since my stomach was empty, I had a bag of potato chips to settle it. Do I look fat in this?"

"No. You look like you belong in a heavy metal band. All you need is a ring in your nose and one in your eyebrow. Use gold. It's shinier."

"I suppose you think you're funny." Bitty went to the coat closet right off the wide front entrance hall and took out a black crocheted cape. "They're in style," she said when she saw me staring at her. "It's a poncho. Don't you like it?"

"It's lovely, Elvira. But doesn't it get too warm in your coffin?"

"One more death joke," Bitty muttered, "and I swear I'll make reservations in Vegas for Uncle Eddie and Aunt Anna. My treat."

If there's one thing I've learned, it's when to shut up.

Rayna was in the middle of painting a landscape when we arrived at the hotel. I mean that literally. It was something new she was trying. A gigantic canvas propped up by an easel under the skylight had swathes of vivid red, blue, and yellow paint. Rayna squirted green paint out of a tube onto her palm and swept her hand across the canvas, then dragged her fingers up in a twist that produced definite blades of grass. She used her thumb or fingertip to dot seed pods here and there, and a couple of entwined fingers formed tree trunks. Daubs of paint covered her from her scarf-protected head to her toes, like she'd actually rolled around on the canvas at one point.

"What do you think?" she asked, standing back and looking at it critically. "A finance company in Memphis wants something bright, new, and huge. Innovative."

"Use real seed pods in a few places," Bitty said. "They dry nicely. That'll give it a three-D effect."

Rayna pointed in the direction of a bunch of twigs, bark, and grass lying on a small table. One of her cats happily chewed on a chickweed stem. "I thought of that, too. It's not exactly an entirely new art form, but I think it will be striking enough to catch the eye when hung behind the receptionist desk, don't you?"

We all agreed that it would be. Rayna has an excellent eye for color and form. She's very artistic. In first grade she drew people with actual arms, legs, fingers and toes, dressed in pants with belts and hats with feathers, while the rest of us were still trying to master stick figures.

When Rayna divested herself of her paint-drenched mechanic's overalls and scarf, we all went outside in her garden to sit in the sunshine and drink sweet tea. After paraphrasing Dolly Parton's line from *Steel Magnolias*, "Have a glass of sweet tea, it's the house wine of the South," Rayna got right down to the subject on all our minds.

"Do you think Philip is dead?"

"I think he's laughing his butt off in Acapulco while some sweet young thing is waxing his ding-a-ling is what I think," Bitty said tartly, hardly a surprising comment to Rayna or myself. We both just nodded.

"If he is," Rayna said after a moment, "the police will find him. It's amazing the things they can do now. And you have to admit, Bitty, Philip never was that good at hiding his covert activities. Remember the time he told you there was an emergency meeting of Congress and he had to go to Washington?"

Bitty rolled her eyes. "And he shacked up in the Holiday Inn right next to 78 Highway with Naomi Spencer and left his car out front for God and everybody to see. Dumb as a box of rocks, both of them."

"If Robby did that, I'd use *hot* wax on his ding-a-ling," Rayna observed, and we all got a good laugh out of that. Everyone in Marshall County knows Robert Rainey would rather cut off his afore-mentioned part than mess with anyone else than Rayna. I've never seen a man more in love with his wife, except maybe Daddy with Mama. Not to say Rayna and Rob are sickly sweet about it, though. They're both independent people with independent interests, lives, and friends. They just know how to balance their relationship and keep the excitement alive.

It was one of those spectacular late February days that Mississippi produces just to remind residents why we choose to live here, with warm sunshine, soft breezes, and a false sense of spring. Weather here has an often wickedly turn of humor. People start shaking mothballs and cedar out of their summer clothes, get out the lawnmower and make sure it's ready for Bermuda grass, and begin sprucing up gardens. Then winter slams back with a vengeance, bringing ice and hail, weather reports of coming snow that usually don't quite materialize, and bone-chilling wind that cuts to the bone. The day before could be a pleasant seventy-two degrees. The next, an icy twenty-two.

"March first is tomorrow," Bitty reflected, "so we've only got six weeks to get the houses listed and ready for the pilgrimage. Cady Lee printed up the brochures this year. She found a place that's doing it for twenty percent less than we paid last year. Of course, we can always add The Cedars at the last minute with a quick print of a flyer once I get Sanders to sign the papers."

"Do you think there'll be enough time for that?" Rayna asked. "I mean, with the details that have to be confirmed, inspection, insurance verified and all that."

"I've got everything done but his signature on the bottom line," Bitty said. "I just have to get that and we can expedite it. I mean, the house needs hardly anything done at all. We have the history of it all written out, highlighted historical data, and a few personal details I was able to find in the museum archives. Sanders can add whatever he likes, and we'll print that out, too. I imagine he'll want to focus on his ancestors' involvement, but that's okay."

"There's always been rumors about his great-great-grandfather being a carpetbagger," Rayna said. "But of course, that's our history, too. Good and bad, we can't rewrite it and no one should even try."

It was a matter of complete agreement that revisionist history is a disservice to current generations as well as past.

"Philip spearheaded a campaign to have state funding ended for historical research," Bitty said darkly. "Not just to spite me, though I'm sure that was the biggest perk, but to get votes from people who don't like certain parts of history. I think he even tried to rewrite a few pages of it."

"You're talking about General Forrest's third cousins or whatever asking Philip to have portions of the Mississippi school history books rewritten, aren't you," I said.

"Actually, those people weren't even related to him. They just had the same last name and thought they'd get some easy money if they filed a lawsuit for slander. Idiots."

"Well, like it or not, Nathan Bedford Forrest not only owned slaves, but he traded in them at times, just like he did mules," Rayna said. "It's awful, I know, but back then, even General Grant owned slaves. Why, when Grant occupied Holly Springs, his New York wife brought her own personal slave with her, and made no bones about her not being freed. After the war ended, General Grant had to be forced by law to free his slaves. Forrest just gets a lot of bad publicity because of the Ku Klux Klan."

Bitty shook her head. "That was an act of idiocy in retrospect, though I'm sure at the time Forrest had some kind of reasoning for it. I mean, something needed to be done about all the criminals running around the South after Union troops moved out and the carpetbaggers came in. It's historical fact that Forrest removed himself from the Klan when they began committing random acts of murder and violence. Of course, most history books don't mention that fact."

"Why, Bitty," I said in surprise, "I had no idea you even cared about actual history."

"Well," she said, "I've been doing a lot of research since working with the historical society. And of course, Forrest only lived fifteen miles away from here in Ashland, so there's a lot about him in the museum."

"New Salem," Rayna said. "Forrest lived in New Salem. Ashland was built a couple of miles over after the Yankees came through and burned down New Salem. Governor Matthews named the new town after his Kentucky plantation. It was called New Salem when Forrest lived near there."

"But his home place was where Ashland city limits are now, I think," Bitty said.

I felt very uninformed. Maybe I'd heard all this growing up, but none of it had stuck. One thing about a certain element of small town citizens is their addiction to local history, their pride in their forbears' part in it, and a determination to educate as many as possible. Every town, north and south, east and west, has these citizens, and if not for them, far too many personal histories and historical data would be lost. Thus the purpose of National Historical Societies.

For some reason, all the discussion about Nathan Bedford Forrest tickled the back of my brain with a reminder that there was something I should remember. I hate it when that happens. It makes me feel as if senility has hit and soon I'll be gibbering in upstairs windows and trying to fly. Anyway, my brain kept making some kind of connection between Forrest and the senator, but I didn't know why. Of course, thinking about Philip Hollandale made me think about him lying in a pool of blood in Sherman Sanders' foyer, and that was unpleasant.

"Hellooo? Trinket? Have you been beamed up?" Bitty was asking, and I gave the lame excuse:

"I was just thinking."

"Hah, I thought I smelled something burning. What's got you thinking so hard your eyes are all squinty?"

I didn't want to go into the details about Philip laid out in Sanders' foyer, so I said, "My lunch. I didn't take time to eat breakfast."

"Let's walk over to Phillips' store and get a burger," Rayna said, and we all thought that was an excellent idea.

Phillips, the former saloon-slash-whorehouse-slash-grocery store now serves hamburgers, cheeseburgers, fried bologna sandwiches, homemade fried fruit pies, and a variety of sandwiches and fried vegetables. Of course, the prerequisite choice of sweet tea or unsweetened is offered, as well as bottled drinks in a big cooler against one wall.

The interior is a historical buff's delight. Big metal signs from the thirties to the sixties hang on the walls, old farming implements decorate odd corners and wall spots, and old-fashion wood shelving holds racks of chips and an assortment of mass-produced desserts. Ceilings are at least fifteen feet high, and bead-board walls and a low ceiling enclose an added bathroom right off the rectangular dining area. A gigantic wasp nest hangs from the dining room ceiling by a cord, but without current residents. Tables are plain and round except for a trestle table set by the front window. Right over the trestle table hangs a corkboard with clippings from local papers and the *Memphis Commercial Appeal* attesting to the fine quality of the cheeseburgers offered at Phillips. Chairs are eclectic. A long bench that looks like it came from the railroad depot sits in front of the counter, providing comfortable seating for those waiting on take-out orders.

I ordered the cheeseburger and a fried pie, Bitty—no doubt watching her weight—had a fried bologna sandwich and fried vegetable sticks, and Rayna ordered a grilled cheese with bacon sandwich. Of course, we all had sweet tea, though I did eye an Orange Crush in the cooler.

While we were eating our lunch, two of the Divas came in to pick up their take-out order. I only recognized one of them, but as I've said, there are so many new or forgotten faces now in Holly Springs that it's not that unusual for me.

After a spate of greetings that involved a couple of hugs, Bitty looked at me and said, "I swear, I don't know where my manners have gone. Trinket Truevine, this sweet young thing on the left is Melody Doyle. Melody grew up here, but went off to college in Georgia, found a job and a boyfriend over there, and just came back about— what, six months ago, wasn't it?"

"Seven," said the sweet young thing with a smile, "though I come and go since I work up in Memphis a lot. It's very nice to meet you, Miz Truevine."

She properly waited until I put out my hand, and then gave me a nice, firm shake that was still soft enough to be ladylike. Obviously, someone's taught her well. It's a bit complicated at times, but there are rules about this sort of thing that I try to remember and usually forget, so I'm always impressed when someone a couple of decades younger is paying attention.

Melody is quite pretty in an understated way, with flashing dark eyes, shiny hair, a slender figure shown to advantage in snug jeans and form-fitting sweater, and a face with a little bit too much make-up to hide a few spots on her skin. She also has a little bit of an overbite, in an attractive Gene Tierney resemblance. If you don't know who Gene Tierney is, you're under fifty and don't watch very many old movies. Trust me; Tierney was a great beauty in her day. I put Melody's age at mid-thirties, but only because of her eyes. There's something quite mature about her eyes. Maybe it's the few corner lines that suggest she's a regular smoker.

When Bitty started to introduce me to the other young lady, we both said at almost the same time, "We met Saturday."

Cynthia Nelson is a newcomer to the Holly Springs area, having just moved into Snow Lake, a community and corporation between Holly Springs and Ashland. It's about ten miles east of Holly Springs, five miles west from Ashland, situated on a two hundred acre fresh spring lake that sports dozens of homes on the lakefront and backs up to the Holly Springs National Forest. It's mainly retirement homes, weekend homes, and hunting and fishing cabins that used to be seasonal. But in the past few years, families wanting a slower pace of life for their children and themselves but within commuting distance of Memphis or even closer locales have been moving in to the corporation. Cindy is one of the latter. Her husband, I'm told, works for a major satellite dish company, and Cindy stays home with their two children and a menagerie of animals. Their house is right on the lake with a dock, a pontoon boat, a fishing boat, and a heavily wooded lot; they get free satellite, and Cindy drives her school-age children all the way to Marshall Academy in Holly Springs, because it has a better school system. Having seen the Ashland schools, I must, alas, agree with her. An air of shabbiness and neglect hangs over the high school despite the best efforts of dedicated teachers and the local school board.

Cindy is cute, bubbly, but not silly. Before the entertainment began at Saturday's meeting, we'd enjoyed a discussion about William Faulkner, writing, and the occasionally tedious but always rewarding value of keeping a journal. While I don't bother to date my entries or write everyday, Cindy prefers a daily account of events that may run from a single sentence to pages of impressions, emotions, or just venting. We share that last trait.

"It's so nice to see you again," I said to her, and I could tell she felt the same. Cindy has light brown hair, gray eyes, a no-nonsense way about her, wears a minimum of make-up and casual clothes that are nice but not flashy. In some way, she reminds me of my daughter Michelle who's younger than Cindy's thirty, but as my mother would say, "has an old soul." Both young women seem to know what they want from life and aren't afraid to work for it.

Melody and Cindy have been volunteering at the historical society copying old documents and getting data entered into computers.

"I can't stay long," Cindy said when we invited them to sit down with us for lunch, "since I have to pick my kids up at two-fifty-five, and before that I have to pick up Pudgy from the vet."

"Is Pudgy a dog or a cat?" Rayna wanted to know.

Cindy laughed. "Neither. He's a hamster that foolishly decided to bite our cat. Until then, the cat had been accepting if not terribly excited to have Pudgy in the family. Fortunately, I think both of them just wanted to get away from the other. Dr. Coltrane said there's no real damage."

"Dr. Coltrane?" Bitty frowned. "I thought I knew the names of every vet at Willow Bend Animal Clinic. Is he new?"

Nodding, Cindy said, "Sometimes he's in the clinic, other times he's out tending to cows, horses, or whatever."

Melody leaned forward, her voice lowered and her eyebrows waggling a little. "I've heard he's absolutely *gor*-geous! I'm thinking of adopting a dog or cat just so I can meet him."

"How old is he?" Bitty asked immediately.

"Um, I'd say in his late forties, maybe," Cindy replied, "but only because of the dates on his framed diplomas hanging on the wall. He looks much younger."

Bitty's smile was absolutely feline. Have I mentioned she's very resilient?

"Well," said Rayna, "the new foot doctor who just opened up an office over by the bank and health clinic is quite attractive, too. Of course, he's only in his late thirties or early forties, I think. There's a candidate for you, Melody. Doctors always make a good living, even when they're podiatrists."

Melody blushed a little. "Truthfully, I'm not sure I'm ready to date quite yet. You know. My last break-up was pretty bad."

"Heavens, sugar," Bitty said, "don't let any grass grow under your feet. You won't get over the last one until you've tried out the next one. I should know. I've had four of the worst divorces in the history of Mississippi, and I can truthfully say that men are like buses. If you miss one, another one will come along in ten minutes."

"Not that it's always going in the right direction, as your four divorces prove," I observed, earning a grimace from Bitty.

"Don't listen to Trinket," she said with a roll of her eyes. "She's sworn off men."

Melody looked over at me. "Does that mean . . . well, I do know a lady over in Potts Camp who prefers other women. She's had a recent break-up. I could introduce you, if you like."

Bitty choked on her sweet tea, and Rayna got really interested in the crusts of her grilled cheese with bacon sandwich.

"Thank you," I said, "but I'm not quite ready for any kind of relationship yet."

"I certainly understand *that*," Melody said with a wise nod of her head. "I guess it doesn't really matter if it's a man or a woman, when you're in love you do crazy things. Then when it's over . . . why, life just seems empty for a while. Unless you do find someone new, I guess."

Apparently to change the direction of the conversation, Cindy said, "When I took Pudgy to the vet this morning, the strangest thing happened. I had to wait in one of the rooms just off the waiting room, and if the door's open you can hear everything. A police officer came in with a dead dog wrapped up in a blanket and plastic. Said he wanted to know what'd killed it. Well, it smelled just awful, and three people in the waiting room had to take their pets and run outside to get away. I was gagging, too, I can tell you."

"How horrible," Rayna said, and looked worried. "Did you find out what happened to it? I do hope there's not some kind of jackass out to poison dogs with anti-freeze again. People like that should be locked up and dosed with salts, then given no access to a toilet."

"Forget the lock. Glue their butt cheeks together and let them explode," said Bitty.

"At the least," Melody agreed. She looked over at Cindy. "What did happen to the poor thing? Was it the policeman's dog?"

"Dr. Coltrane came in before I heard what happened, but that kind of examination would take time anyway, I imagine." Cindy shook her head. "And you never can tell what some people are feeling, so I don't know if it was the policeman's dog or not. He sounded straightforward about it, even when the receptionist got a little testy and told him he should have come around to the other door like he'd been told. I think she knew him, because she called him Jimmy Joe."

"Ah. Jimmy Joe Wellford," Bitty said. "My second cousin. Or is he my third? Sometimes I forget that kind of thing. Do you remember, Trinket?"

"Third cousin, I believe, even though I have a hard time keeping all that straight myself." Actually, I was still trying to envision the explosion of a villain dosed with salts and butt cheeks glued together. "Don't you think it more likely that the glue would come undone before someone really exploded?" I asked no one in particular, and Bitty looked thoughtful.

"Not if it was that gorilla glue, or super glue they show on TV that can hold chairs to the ceiling."

"I no longer believe all those commercials," Rayna disagreed. "I can't tell you the stuff I've bought because it looks so good on TV, and then it sits in a drawer until I either throw it away or donate it to the church bazaar to see if they can make use of it. Robby always tells me I have a too-trusting nature. I guess most women do."

"Not Trinket," Bitty said. "I bet she's never owned a bottle of gorilla glue in her life."

Since I hadn't, but saw no need in giving fuel to Bitty's teasing, I vowed that I had three tubes packed away somewhere in one of my moving boxes. It's not that I'm untrusting, it's just that sometimes I like to look at both sides of an issue, and prefer to see proof before I commit myself either way. Most of the time, I strive for optimism, but I'm never really surprised when and if something doesn't work out. Disappointed, perhaps, but rarely surprised.

"Well," Rayna said, and stood up with her sandwich remnants wrapped in the paper, "I think I'll go on back home. I've got work to do. And I want to check on the stray cats that hide in that old compress building. Just in case there's some crazy animal hater running loose again."

About that time a freight train came by, rattling the windows and shaking the floor even though it was moving pretty slowly. Most trains use the tracks a hundred yards down the hill, but engines always sit outside the depot, and a small crew mans the old cinder block building just a few yards away. Illinois-Central Gulf Railroad owns the tracks, but a local schoolteacher owns the depot that's been in her family for years.

We all waved our farewells, and then separated in front of the hotel to go our own ways.

Once we were in my car, Bitty said, "I have the most perfect idea."

I shuddered. I've had vast experience with some of her ideas, and when said in that particular tone, it doesn't bode well. Too few of Bitty's ideas have satisfying endings for me.

"I'm scared to ask," I finally said. "Can you keep it to yourself?"

"I could, but it's too good not to share. Did you hear what Cindy said about Jimmy Joe bringing in a dead dog to find out what killed it? I think it might have been Sanders' dog. Why else would the police care?"

Sometimes Bitty really surprises me. "You may be right," I said.

She nodded. "Well, I know better than to go around and just ask him questions, because Jimmy Joe is naturally contrary anyway, and close-mouthed as a dead man if it has to do with police business."

"Lovely analogy," I observed, but Bitty hardly slowed down.

"So, if I take in my dog to see this new vet, he won't know me and may just tell me all about what killed that dog. That way, I get to see if it's Sanders' dog, and at the same time, I get to meet this gorgeous new vet who's just my age."

"Ah. You were paying attention. Cindy said he's in his late forties. And you don't have a dog."

"Well, good heavens, Trinket, there's probably only a year or two's difference between us, and besides, everyone says I look much younger than my age."

"You do," I said truthfully, "but you still don't own a dog."

She waved that small detail away with a flick of her wrist. "I'll just borrow Aunt Anna's dog. He's fairly small, though not at all the kind of dog I'd choose. He'll do in a pinch."

I had a vision of her dragging the neurotic Brownie into the vet's, then a vision of her crossing the rural highway to the county hospital's emergency room to get stitches in her hand.

"Brownie isn't very sociable," I said. "And even if you could somehow get him into the vet's without an escort or getting half your arm chewed off, Mama would never let you take him off without her. She adores that dog."

Bitty mulled that over for a moment or two, and I thought maybe she'd rethink ways to get information and meet the new vet, but I should have known better.

"I have it," she said as we turned off Van Buren, "I'll borrow a dog from Luann Carey. She has several, and probably won't even miss one."

"Uh, you are going to ask her first, I hope?"

"Honestly, Trinket, sometimes you act like I'm an idiot."

"Sorry. I just know you get carried away when you've got a mission. And obviously, your current mission is to snag you a new husband. I'm just not sure why, since you're still having problems with your last husband."

"I'm *not* looking for a new husband. Are vets rich?"

"Some are. Bitty, is that what you base a good marriage partner on? His bank account?"

"I might as well. Look what basing a marriage on love did for me. And for you, for that matter."

"You've got me there. And which one of your husbands were you in love with? Just out of curiosity."

Bitty laughed. "The one with the most money, of course."

"Oh, that narrows it down. Except Frank—your first husband, father of the twins, in case you don't remember. He started out with a lot of money. Was it him?"

"Frank was definitely the best-looking one. We made beautiful babies, didn't we?"

"You certainly did. Clayton and Brandon have turned into good-looking young men, too. Or were the last time I saw them. How are they doing?"

"Driving all the girls at Ole Miss crazy. They've each changed their major a few times. I think it's a ploy to keep from graduating so they can keep drawing money from their trust funds. Good thing Frank set those up before he got involved in all that mail fraud business."

"Is he still in prison?"

"He's got eight more years left, I think. Those Federal guys really do take some things to the extreme."

Frank Caldwell, Bitty's first husband, had done a lot more than mail fraud, but good lawyers and a sympathetic judge that used to go fishing with the senior Caldwell kept him from getting life. Bitty's third husband had been a Frank, too, but she called him Franklin so as not to get them confused. I've always thought her choices were repetitive, and not very wise.

Since the mystery of which husband Bitty might have truly loved held a limited appeal for me, I changed the subject.

"Speaking of prison—I wonder if Philip's disappearance has anything to do with Sanders disappearing."

I pulled up in front of Bitty's house and parked at the curb. Her lawn service keeps the beds mulched and tidy, and before long the pansies planted in the front beds and in twin concrete pots on each side of the walkway to the porch will be replaced with summer flowers.

"Oh, I doubt it," Bitty said. "Philip will turn up in some bimbo's bed, and Sanders doesn't look like the type for threesomes."

I went inside with Bitty to use her phone to call my parents and see if there was anything they'd like me to bring home from the store.

I had to pass by the Piggly Wiggly anyway, and it's much less trouble for me than for them. There's a nice phone in Bitty's front hall, one of those fancy white French retro copies that has punch buttons instead of a dial. She keeps it on a small table that has a pretty mosaic tile garden pattern.

"You should get a cell phone," Bitty said. "Then you could call them from anywhere."

"And they could call me."

"I see your point."

She started toward the coat closet to put away her poncho, and the doorbell rang. Since I was already on the phone dialing home, Bitty went around me to get to the door.

About the time Mama answered, I heard Bitty's voice rise indignantly and turned to see several policemen at the door.

"Trinket," Mama asked, "what's going on there? What's all that noise?"

"Mama, I'll have to call you back—everything's fine, I'm sure. I think Bitty's alarm went off and the police are here to check things out."

Of course, I knew that wasn't it at all. The way Bitty barred the door with one hand on her hip and shaking her finger at the tallest officer standing his ground couldn't mean anything good.

Sometimes I hate it when I'm right.

"Mrs. Hollandale," the officer repeated politely, a nice young man with a stoic face and patient tone, "it's just routine. We're not here to arrest you, but we would like to ask you some questions."

"Do you know Lieutenant Jimmy Joe Wellford? He's my cousin," Bitty said, still waving a finger. "I've a good mind to call him right now!"

"Yes, ma'am. Lieutenant Wellford said you might want to do that."

"Well then!"

"He also said to tell you he's not accepting your calls and to cooperate."

Bitty looked outraged. I decided I might be able to help, fool that I am.

"Officer, Mrs. Hollandale has been very upset by the disappearance of her ex-husband. I think if you'll just give her a moment to calm down, she'll be most glad to answer any questions you have for her."

I ignored the look of betrayal Bitty shot at me, and took her by the arm to drag her a few feet deeper into the hall and away from the officers.

"Bitty," I said in a low tone, "by not cooperating you look guilty of something. Invite them in, we'll give them some sweet tea, and you'll politely, calmly, and *truthfully* answer every question they ask. Okay?"

"You've gone over to the dark side."

"I prefer to think of it as the sensible side. Now I'll go fix the tea and bring a tray, and you take the officers into the living room."

One thing about Bitty, she can be very flexible when she chooses.

Turning with a brave smile, she went back to the doorway and said, "I do apologize for my rudeness. It's been such a terrible time for me lately, with all the uncertainty and everything. Of course you may come in and ask me some questions. My cousin will bring us some sweet tea while we talk. Do either of you take lemon?"

Both officers stepped inside. I've noticed that as I get older, professional people tend to get younger. I'm not sure why that is. These two young men looked as if they should be juniors in high school. The one obviously in charge had caramel-colored skin and refined features, and the other officer, pale white, thin, and jumpy, kept looking around the room like he'd never been inside a house before. He reminded me of Barney Fife.

"Trinket, would you mind hanging up my poncho for me?" Bitty asked, giving me a sweet smile while her eyes shot daggers in my direction.

"Why, of course I would, dearest cousin," I replied as I held out my hand for it, leaving it up to Bitty to decide if I meant I minded or not.

Bitty and the two officers went into the living room with its tall windows that let in lots of sunlight through the sheer curtains, and antique couches and chairs probably uncomfortable for any man over five-two, while I crossed to the coat closet to hang up Elvira's cape. The door was already slightly ajar, and I seized the brass knob and pulled it wider to reach inside for a hanger.

And I stared Philip Hollandale right in the face.

CHAPTER 7

Shock rendered me momentarily speechless and immobile. I knew it was the senator, for I'd met him at Bitty's wedding to him, and one or two times after that, though only for very brief moments. I've never thought of him as a particularly handsome man, but in death, he's downright homely.

I shut the door and stood there, poncho in my hand, heart racing and mind darting to and fro like a scared rabbit. What should I do? There's a dead man in the closet. The dead man is Bitty's ex-husband. Their divorce was loud and nasty. He's known to have been missing for the past few days. Not only that, but Bitty swears she saw him lying in Sherman Sanders' foyer. And Sanders is now missing, too. Bitty is the only obvious common denominator.

But a dead man is in her closet, and that's not something that can be ignored for long.

I'm not sure how long I stood there with all that going round and round in my mind and Bitty's vampire cape in my hand, but the voices from the living room finally seeped into my stupefied brain and I hung the crocheted cape on the doorknob and went into the kitchen.

The police would have to be notified, of course. Dead bodies are their purview. I've very little experience with dead bodies, nor is it one of my ambitions to cultivate that interest. And, sadly, it occurred to me that Bitty might have some knowledge about her ex-husband being in her coat closet that she hadn't yet shared with me. If so, I couldn't imagine her reasoning, but then, there are times when Bitty and I have very different viewpoints on things.

It'd only be fair to ask her before I came to any conclusions on my own.

I went into the kitchen, found a silver tray, an already prepared pitcher of tea and a bowl of lemon wedges in the refrigerator, and somehow put together glasses, ice, napkins and long-handled silver teaspoons to take into the living room.

Seated precariously and obviously uncomfortably on the 1850's horsehair-stuffed couch, the two officers appeared grateful for a diversion when I set the tray down on the antique Turkish hassock serving as a coffee table. Bitty had produced a linen handkerchief from somewhere in her black ensemble, and dabbed daintily at what I was certain were crocodile tears at the corners of her eyes.

"Bitty," I said while the officers reached for the tea and lemon wedges, "would you mind stepping into the kitchen with me for just a moment? I can't find another clean glass."

Something in my voice must have alerted her, for she gave me a startled glance and promptly excused herself. Neither officer protested.

Before Bitty could launch into a tale of mistreatment by local officials, I said bluntly, "I found Philip."

With her mouth still open, Bitty looked at me. Then she said, "Well, I suppose that's good news. For him, anyway. Where is the philandering Philip? Mexico? Paris? Rome? A Motel Six in Tupelo?"

"In your coat closet."

For a moment she just stared at me, then her brows snapped down over her eyes and she turned toward the kitchen door. "That *no-good, dirty pervert—*"

"He's dead, Bitty," I said, cleverly deducing she hadn't stuffed him in between her taupe Evan Picone raincoat and Elvira's black cape, after all.

Silence. It didn't seem to register with her. I completely understood.

After a moment I said gently, "We have to decide how to tell the police."

Bitty grabbed my arm in what can only be described as a Vulcan death grip that's certain to be in the Secret Service Training Manual for presidential bodyguards.

"Oh no we don't!"

"Bitty—"

"You listen to me, Eureka May Truevine, you are *not* going to tell the police anything! Do you hear me? Philip's already dead. It's not like rushing around yelling our heads off is going to accomplish anything more than getting me arrested. You see that, don't you? We had a knock-down-drag-out divorce and have been mortal enemies, and if the police find him in my coat closet they're going to automatically think the worst."

"It seems likely."

"How dead is he?"

"Very. But I'm not an expert on these things. Shall I go ask him?" I was a little perturbed that Bitty didn't seem to realize how much worse it would look if the police discovered Philip in her closet for themselves.

"No. Let me think a minute," she said.

My jibe apparently went over Bitty's head, evidence that she was much more focused on her own solutions than the inevitable outcome.

"Bitty, there's only one thing we can do. You have to know that. If you didn't put him in the closet, someone did, and the sooner the police can start looking for the killer, the better off you'll be. After all, he wasn't killed in your coat closet; he was moved here from Sanders' foyer."

We'd been talking in low tones. One of the officers called from the living room to ask if Mrs. Hollandale needed assistance. Bitty's resilience took her to the living room door where she looked in on them and said she'd be right back after cutting them each a piece of angel food cake.

"I'm just famished, and this is such an exhausting conversation, I think we all need a bit of nourishment." Returning to the kitchen, she hissed, "See if there's any angel food cake left in the cupboard. I think I have some raspberry sauce to go over it."

"What are you going to do?" I asked as I went to the cupboard she indicated with a wave of her hand.

"I'm calling the Divas. We need some help getting Philip out of here."

That stopped me in my tracks. "You're not serious."

"Dead serious," Bitty said. "Listen, he was killed somewhere else anyway. I didn't put him in the closet, and it's not like it's the crime scene. Let someone else find his body. Naomi Spencer, maybe. She liked riding him. We'll put him in her car. Or her bed. Anywhere but in my house."

Actually, it had a bizarre kind of logic. I mean, I was certain Bitty hadn't killed him—or almost certain—and if the police found him in her house they'd immediately arrest her. Like she said, it wasn't as if

Philip had been killed in her coat closet. I could vouch for her that he hadn't been in there when she'd taken out her poncho before we went over to the hotel. And we hadn't been separated the entire time until we got back, so really, Bitty couldn't have had anything at all to do with Philip's sudden and mysterious appearance in her closet.

Which brought up the immediate question—*who did?*

That question, however, would have to wait until later. Right now, Bitty was calling in the Divas and I was cutting angel food cake and drizzling raspberry sauce over it to feed the two young and hungry police officers sitting in the living room. Priorities, I told myself, priorities.

After what seemed like an eternity but was really only another thirty minutes or so, the two young officers left with a promise to inform Mrs. Hollandale immediately when the senator turned up.

Bitty stood at the door smiling tearfully and dabbing her eyes with an artful sniffle or two just for good measure, and thanked them from the bottom of her heart for their kindness and the magnificent job they were doing.

"Philip and I may have had our differences," she said, "but the love we once felt for each other never completely faded away. It's just so hard for politicians to balance their dedication to keeping our country safe with their private lives. But I've always understood that Philip's first duty is to his country, of course, even if it cost us our marriage. Why, both of you gentlemen must surely understand that, since you place your lives on the line every day for all of us."

The youngest officer, the pale young man with a buzz-cut, earnest eyes and rapt expression, nodded. "Times are hard for a lot of us now, what with terrorists on the loose."

I wondered what part of Holly Springs terrorists would target first, the defunct toy factory or the aluminum siding plant. Apparently, so did the senior officer, a young man with a stoic face and sharp eyes. He gave his partner a quelling glance, thanked us both politely, and accompanied his companion down the sidewalk to the patrol car at the curb.

Bitty shut the door and leaned against it. "What do you think?" she asked.

"I thought you were about to break into a chorus of *God Bless*

America."

"Not that. Do you think they suspect anything?"

"The young one doesn't even suspect gravity is a law. He's got to be Barney Fife's son."

"Farrell. His name is Rodney Farrell and he graduated from Marshall Academy three years ago. His daddy works at the brick factory."

"Uh hunh. Watch your step around the other one. He's more like Andy Griffith."

"Marcus Stone. He graduated at the top of his class from Holly Springs High School, then took two years of college at Mississippi State. His mother used to work three jobs just to put food on the table, and his grandmother draws disability. Heart, I think."

I stared at her. "It amazes me that you know so many details about other people's lives, but could never remember your third husband's middle name."

Bitty pushed away from the door. "Rayna is calling as many Divas as she can get, and they'll be here within a half hour." She looked toward the closet. "While we wait, I'll take a look at Philip."

She strode purposefully toward the closed closet door, hesitated, took a deep breath, and pulled it open. I wasn't sure what she'd do, so I hovered close just in case she had hysterics or assaulted the senator with an umbrella.

But Bitty tilted her head to one side and studied him curiously, almost dispassionately.

Clad in dark pants, an expensive Italian shirt, and no coat, Philip Hollandale was propped up by wool coats, windbreakers, and raincoats. His eyes were open and sightless, his lips curled back in what looked to be a slight snarl, and his hands clenched in loose fists. A bath towel had been wrapped around his head like a turban. A dark, reddish brown stain discolored its right side.

"Good thing I keep my furs in cold storage," Bitty finally said. "I think some blood came off on my new windbreaker."

She sounded oddly detached. I wasn't certain if that was a good sign or not. In fact, the line between good and bad was getting awfully fuzzy. It felt like what we used to call Backwards Day when we were kids. Left was right, up was down, good was bad—you get the picture.

That feeling didn't go away when trusted Divas descended *en masse* on the scene. Gaynelle Bishop, who had voted for the senator, supervised the stuffing of him into black plastic Leaf and Garden bags. Rayna Blue grabbed Bitty's stained windbreaker from the closet and stuck it into a garbage bag. She looked up when Cindy Nelson asked what on earth she was doing to a brand new Land's End windbreaker.

"It has to go. I watch CSI. Not even bleach will get this blood completely out."

There had been a brief, if not detailed, explanation when the Divas arrived concerning the urgent necessity of removing Philip Hollandale from Bitty's closet, along with firm assurances that Bitty nor me had any hand in putting him there or shortening his lifespan. That was all it took to enlist the Divas' aid. I wondered if they took some kind of loyalty oath when becoming a member that might involve sacrificial rituals, but since most are avid animal lovers, I suspect the only kind of sacrifice entails bottles of wine to the California Grape Gods.

Cindy—whom I'd last seen riding behind Marcy Porter on the sweaty back of a Britney Spears-like stripper doggedly crawling toward the hotel doors wearing only thong underwear and one leather boot—and Georgie Marshall, to whom I'd not yet been officially introduced, helped stuff the senator into black plastic. Both are younger women in their early thirties. Sandra Dobson, solid, sensible, with short brown hair and a pretty face, and with whom I'd only briefly spoken at the Diva meeting, estimated the senator's time of death—TOD, she called it—at being approximately three to four days, judging by the body's condition.

"He's obviously been kept in cold storage," Sandra said, and since she's a nurse, we were all inclined to take her word for it. "He's still pretty stiff, though rigor doesn't seem to be the cause. I'm not an ME, but it looks to me like he's been frozen. See here on his head where the blood is beginning to thaw?"

Bitty peered at Philip. "He does have some little ice crystals on his eye brows and in his hair. I didn't even notice. Of course, alive he wasn't much warmer than this unless some hottie happened along to thaw out his wiener. I don't know why he was always so proud of that thing. I've seen much better lying on a barbecue grill."

We all got quiet, and of course, you know where we all had to immediately look, even if it was covered up with black plastic. Some of us were no doubt imagining Polish sausage and bratwurst compared to Philip when Gaynelle said, "Pull the end of the bag over his head. I can't stand him looking at me with those frozen fish eyes."

Voter loyalty is often fickle. Diva loyalty is apparently steadfast.

"Where are we taking him?" I asked, obviously having subconsciously committed myself to an active participation in this lunacy.

That question stopped everyone for a moment, and we all looked hopefully at each other. No one spoke for about ten seconds, and then Bitty's grandfather clock chimed the hour. Some of the Divas jumped at the unexpected sound, and so did I.

"It's three o'clock," Cindy Nelson said in a quavering voice, "and I have to pick up my kids. Is there anything else I can do?"

"No," Gaynelle said, "we can manage. Just do be discreet, dear, and don't mention this to anyone quite yet."

Cindy promised, and then fled with what I can only describe as a mixture of terror, relief, and a determination to get as far away as possible. The rest of us looked at each other silently.

"It's still daylight," Rayna said at last, "but if we can put him somewhere until later tonight, I have a key to the old ice house and feed supply. It's not like he isn't already frozen. We can keep him there until we figure out what to do."

"Isn't there a dog food packing plant close by?" Bitty asked, and we all recoiled.

"No!" some of us said simultaneously.

"Jeez, I was just kidding," Bitty muttered, but I had the feeling that wasn't quite true.

"He's wrapped up pretty well," Sandra said, "so we could put him in your cellar, Bitty."

Bitty staggered sideways as if physically struck. "I'd rather be stripped naked and left on the church steps on Sunday morning," she said vehemently. She sounded pretty positive about it.

Peering at Bitty with a slight frown, Gaynelle asked, "You're saying you *don't* wish him to be put in your cellar, am I correct?"

Her question made me ponder Bitty's past activities, but I just said, "I think what Bitty means is that the police have already been here once, and if they come back with a search warrant it won't look very good for Philip to be in her cellar next to bottles of twenty year old wine."

"Well," Georgie suggested almost timidly, "he's already dead, so why don't we just hide him in the cemetery?"

Gaynelle patted her arm. "That is indeed the logical place, dear, but I'm afraid they'd be certain to notice a new grave, even if we were able to dig one without being seen. We'd be rather conspicuous, I fear."

Georgie, rather shy and bookish, with long red hair in a French braid down her back, blue eyes, and horn-rimmed glasses, shook her head. "I know that, Aunt Gaynelle, but you know how so many of those above-ground vaults are cracked and broken. They took off some of the broken lids to repair the vaults. They use a kind of resin that dries fairly quickly, but once it bonds, it lasts longer than the original stone." She paused and pushed at the glasses sliding down her nose, then bit her bottom lip before adding, "I was out there yesterday and I happen to know where there's an empty vault with the lid mostly off. The gates close at five this time of year, but the workers are already back at the maintenance sheds by four-thirty."

"It's an excellent idea," Gaynelle said, and looked at Rayna. "What do you think?"

Rayna looked around at us. "Divas?"

We all looked at each other. Unanimous agreement was signaled by raised right fists and thumbs pointing toward the ceiling. I wasn't certain if I'd just been unofficially inducted into the Dixie Divas or not, but I was definitely included in the graveyard shift.

*

There was some difficulty loading the senator into a vehicle for his journey. I pulled my Taurus up into the driveway behind Bitty's sports car and close to the back door. When I opened my trunk, I looked doubtfully from the car to the plastic and duct-taped figure lying on the back porch. The senator had been nearly six feet tall, and probably weighed a hefty two-fifty.

"I don't think he'll fit," I said.

Bitty put her hands on her hips. "We can cut off his legs. I have an electric kitchen knife I only use at Thanksgiving and Christmas."

"Someone get Bitty a Jack and Coke," Rayna called, and gave her a gentle nudge toward the house. "We'll get it all worked out, hon. You just go on inside and have a drink."

"Come along, dear," Gaynelle said, her usually brusque manner softened to a tone useful with a five year old. "We'll have us a toddy while we wait. Won't that be nice?"

Rayna, Sandra, Georgie and I studied the situation with the combined skills of women completely out of their league. I'm glad to say that none of us had ever before encountered the necessity of carting off and hiding a dead ex-husband.

Sandra finally suggested, "Let's wrap him up in one of Bitty's old rugs and stick him in my SUV."

"Bitty doesn't have an *old* anything," Rayna replied. "She donates to charities a lot. It's a great tax write-off and she gets to flaunt the way she's spending her alimony so Philip can seethe. I guess now she'll have to find another entertainment."

"God forbid," I said. "She'll have to get a new ex-husband to make miserable, and I'm not sure any of us want to go through that again."

"Just be glad you weren't here during the worst of it," Sandra said with a shake of her head. "I thought they were actually going to end up in a gunfight in court square after one of the hearings."

Thank God for small favors.

Now that we had a plan, we had to make it work. Sandra seems to be very organized. In her mid-forties, about five-four, sturdy, and practical, she works only part-time now, filling in at hospitals or doctors' offices when and where as needed. As a matter of practice, she keeps a well-stocked kit similar to that of an EMT in her car. Handily enough, if a spot of blood gets noticed in her car, it's less likely to arouse suspicion.

So Sandra's SUV was backed up the driveway, the senator rolled into a rug that Bitty grudgingly let us haul down from an upstairs guest bedroom, then carried out by six sweating pallbearers, including Gaynelle Bishop who refused to shirk her Diva duty. Even Bitty grabbed a hunk of fringe and wool rug, though a bit unsteadily since she had a whiskey glass in one hand. We all heaved at the same time, and Philip thunked into the back of the SUV like a sack of Irish potatoes. We looked at the results of our efforts. A good two feet of him still stuck out.

"I'll put the back seats down," Sandra said, "but we'll have to take two cars now."

Georgie and I got in the front seat and pulled, while Sandra and Rayna pushed from the rear until we managed to get the respected member of Congress wedged into the cargo area.

"I think I've got a hernia," Georgie gasped when we finished, and she collapsed in the driver's seat with a hand pressed against her side.

"And just think," I reminded her cheerfully, "we get to carry him from the car to the vault next."

Georgie gave me a pained look. I smiled. Maybe I'm not as old as I thought.

With the back seats laid flat and Philip dragged forward, only wool tassels hung slightly over the edge. When we slammed shut the cargo door, we breathed a collective sigh of relief. Bitty refrained. She sucked down the rest of her whiskey and glared at the SUV.

"That rug costs more than Philip's hair-weave and his last underage tart's new boob job combined," she said, and as Gaynelle escorted her back into the house to freshen up her glass, Bitty added, "I just hate it when bad things happen to good carpets, don't you?"

Rayna elected to ride with Sandra just in case of trouble. None of us knew exactly what kind of trouble might arise, but then, when we'd awoken this morning, I daresay none of us had expected to soon be hiding a frozen corpse, either.

Georgie, our designated time-keeper, pointed to her sports watch and said, "Three minutes until lift-off."

That gave us added incentive, and Gaynelle hustled Bitty from the house and out to the curb, while the rest of us tried to appear as normal as possible, just friends donating a carpet to the local charity or Goodwill box. We had ten minutes until law offices, banks, and government employees got off work and into their vehicles to crowd the streets. Since everyone practically knows everyone else, should the police ever ask, someone was bound to remember that Sandra and Rayna had been hauling a carpet around, followed by Gaynelle, Bitty, Georgie and me.

When Sandra pulled out, the rest of us piled into Gaynelle's twenty year old light blue Cadillac and followed the SUV at the seemly pace of a funeral procession. At the intersection of North Maury, Sandra went straight and we turned right, just in case. A few streets up we turned onto South Market Street by the court square, tooled at a reasonable speed past old homes and office buildings, then passed Chulahoma Street and under the wrought-iron sign at the main entrance of the cemetery.

Hill Crest Cemetery, also known as "the Little Arlington of the South" because of the notable generals buried here, is enclosed by fencing and wrought-iron gates. It's not the only cemetery in Holly Springs, but it's the biggest. There's another cemetery on East Boundary Road just off Old 78 Highway, but it's new and doesn't have the ancient, gnarled holly trees, oaks, and marble monuments dating back to the early nineteenth century like this one. Truevines are buried here in several plots, being a rather fertile family in the past. There's even a Truevine here who joined the Union army. His grave has a small marker with a carved Confederate flag crossed by a Union flag as testament to the love borne a son despite parental disagreement.

Five wrought-iron gates mark the entrances; three are left open during the day. Sandra chose the one farthest from the maintenance sheds and office. The narrow road dips sharply and loops around, branching off through twenty-five acres. At the far end of the cemetery lies a small trough that makes a path between neatly mowed grass and tall pines. In front of that is the newer section. It's rather bare-looking. Near the old gates, tall monuments mark old family plots and the passage of two hundred years.

Sandra's SUV slowed down, and she seemed to be looking in her rearview mirror for directions.

"When we get to the right vault, tell me and I'll stop so you can get out," Gaynelle said to Georgie in the back seat, looking at her in the rearview mirror. "I thought to bring some flowers."

Bitty, sitting up front with Gaynelle and the bottle of Jack Daniel's, stared at Gaynelle as if she'd just said she'd voted for a Democrat in the last election. Gaynelle's known to be an ardent Republican. "You'll put flowers on that pervert's grave? I think you've lost your mind, Gaynelle Bishop."

To Gaynelle's credit, she didn't fly off the handle, but then, after years of teaching pupils liable to do everything from throwing spitwads to setting the chemistry lab on fire, I imagine she has a great deal of self-control. She just reached over to pat Bitty on the arm.

"Bitty dear, the flowers aren't for the senator. They're just in case anyone should notice us and wonder what we're doing. It's a ruse. Once we've gotten him into the vault, you can burn them if you like."

"I think I'll do just that."

"Suit yourself, dear. It's a lovely dried arrangement I took from your dining room table."

Bitty's answer to that was another splash of whiskey into her empty glass. Apparently, Coke and ice took up too much room.

Fortunately, Georgie spied the vault just ahead. It was getting close to five, and soon the cemetery gates would close for the night. It occurred to me that no one had suggested just how we were going to get back in to get him moved before morning.

Before Georgie got out of the car I asked, "If we're supposed to come back for him after dark, how will we get in?"

"It won't be that hard," she said, and held up a cell phone. "Before we left Bitty's I called the cemetery office and told them I had a little more work to do for the historical society, and it might take me until dark. I come here a lot. The caretaker gave me a key last week, and I haven't given it back yet. It fits the lock on this gate. I like to sit out here sometimes at night. It's quiet."

"I think you need more friends your age, dear," Gaynelle said, but I began to realize that Georgie is probably used to being underestimated. She just smiled and closed the car door.

It must have been a strange procession, should anyone happen to have seen it, six women advancing on a broken vault with a bulky rug and an expensive arrangement of dried flowers. It was going pretty well until Bitty tripped over a carved statue of a boy and his dog. She held on to the edge of the rug to keep from falling, and put us all off-balance. We struggled valiantly, but the rug came open, the senator fell out, and Bitty sat down hard on the grass right in front of the stone statue. As the senator rolled downhill toward her, she put out a foot to stop his progress.

"Don't even *think* about it," she said to the plastic-wrapped corpse, then knocked back a slug of Jack Daniel's.

"How did she do that," Sandra wondered, "without spilling a drop of whiskey?"

"Bitty is a woman of many talents," said Rayna as she covered the senator discreetly with the dark burgundy carpet.

We got him tucked into it again, ignoring Bitty's suggestion that we "Just stick his head back up his ass and roll him like a truck tire the rest of the way to the vault."

"You stay right there, dear," Gaynelle said to Bitty, "and hold the flowers."

Bitty, I'm happy to say, agreed.

As Georgie had said, a broken vault had half the top off to one side, the other half still in place but askew. It was a plain vault, about three feet high and eight feet long, with one of those thick stone slabs supposed to be set in place on top. The cover had broken in half, right across the carved names that are almost illegible, worn away by time and weather. I could barely make out the date of 1835. No coffin resided inside, and with a great deal of huffing, puffing, a few words suitable only for pool halls and maybe jail cells, we managed to slide Philip Hollandale into the burial vault.

"This is . . . a lot of trouble . . . if we're just coming . . . back in a few hours," Rayna got out between gasps for air. "I say . . . we leave him here."

It sounded like an excellent idea to me. At least the police would be notified and could begin looking for whoever murdered him.

Bitty reached us, limping slightly with the flower arrangement under one arm and empty glass in her hand. She peered into the vault. "I say we mount him naked on a pole in court square. Philip loved to be naked and mounted."

Sandra looked at her. "Now that we've got him far away from your house, just exactly how did Senator Hollandale get that fatal head wound?"

"I know how," Bitty said, "I just don't know who did it."

Gaynelle gave the others a swift summary of the events at Sherman Sanders' house, and ended by saying, "Now Sanders is missing, so it's quite probable he killed the senator and fled."

"So you see," said Bitty rather plaintively, "unless I tell the police that I saw Philip in the foyer and didn't report it, they won't suspect Sanders at all. Though they do know he's missing."

"What about the dog the police found?" Rayna asked. "Do you think it's Sanders' dog, and if it is, do you think it has any connection to all this?"

"We can ask Faye Harper," Gaynelle said. "She works part time in the animal clinic. She may very well know something."

A cold breeze rustled the holly branches of a tree, and whistled through the bare limbs of an oak nearby. I shivered. Things were getting too complicated, as if hiding a dead body wasn't complication enough.

I wasn't quite sure how to bring up the subject, so I just dove in. "Listen, I think we all should keep this to ourselves for now. The less people involved, the better it will be. If the other Divas don't know anything, the police can't accuse them of obstruction."

"Trinket's right," Rayna said firmly. "Let's just keep this among ourselves for now. So, do we come back for him tonight, or leave him here?"

"We can leave *him* here," Bitty said, "but we're not leaving my rug. I paid nearly ten thousand dollars for that rug, and Philip Hollandale threw such a fit when I bought it, then had the nerve to demand it in the divorce settlement, that I'm damned if I'll let him get it now."

"Bitty," I began, but she gave me one of those mulish looks that had always promised a fit when she was in elementary school, and the tenacious resistance of a wolverine ever since she'd hit junior high school. I sighed and looked at the others. "Maybe you should take a vote," I said.

The final decision, I think, made us all a little uncomfortable, but it seemed like there was nothing else we could do.

CHAPTER 8

"Yes, Mama, everything is just fine," I lied to my mother without the least bit of guilt. Why should both of us be terrified? "I'm staying the night with Bitty. Yes, she's a bit upset with all those Breaking News interruptions on TV, as well as everyone in Marshall County calling to tell her how sorry they are to hear about the senator missing, and they hope she's doing all right."

Mama's still sharp as a tack, and she knows very well that the real reason people keep calling Bitty is to see if she knows anything reporters aren't telling. But here I was on the phone telling my mother a whopper of a lie so I could go back out at midnight and steal a corpse from a vault in the cemetery. I hadn't told her this big a fib since I'd told her that Perry was doing just fine in his job and we were still deliriously happy. That'd been last year. The truth does have a way of coming out eventually.

"Well sugar," Mama said, "Bitty's a lot stronger than anyone thinks. But I'm glad you're staying with her tonight, anyway. Maybe Eddie and I can chase each other around the kitchen table while we're here alone."

Lately I've wondered if the doctor over at Williams Clinic has given Daddy a prescription for Viagra, but not only have I not had the nerve to ask, I don't want to know the answer.

"Don't fall and break anything," I just said, and Mama laughed.

"No chance of that. I have no intention of running very fast. It's much more fun when I get caught."

When I hung up, I looked over at Bitty. "I'm not at all sure those people are my parents. I think someone abducted my real parents and replaced them with sixteen year olds in wrinkled birthday suits."

Bitty, stretched out on the couch in what she referred to as her parlor but what was really more of a den, smiled and took another sip of hot coffee that I'd forced on her as soon as we got back to her house. "They're just frisky. I hope I'm still like that when I get their age."

"I don't think I've been like that at any age."

"Like I told you, your problem is just that you've never had an orgasm." Bitty laughed when I made the usual uncomfortable sound I make whenever she says something like that. "I'm telling you, Trinket, once your eyes roll back in your head and you shout 'Hallelujah Jesus, I'm comin' home!' you'll know exactly what you've been missing out on for thirty years or so."

"That's sacrilegious," I mumbled as I looked at a picture on the wall of a young woman in a flowing dress and big hat with trailing ribbons being pushed on a swing by a handsome young gentleman dressed in nineteenth century clothes.

"What's sacrilegious is that you've been cheated all these years. It's against nature. Besides, I haven't noticed you showing up at church on Sunday mornings lately."

I looked at her. "I'm afraid the walls will cave in. Especially if I sit by you."

"You've got God confused with Darth Vader. Keep in mind that God created us just like we are, and all we have to do is follow a few rules and everything will be just fine. It's very simple. No cheating, stealing, or killing, and we can go to heaven and visit with Elvis."

"There are seven other rules you've left out," I said. "What about lying?"

Bitty gave me a pitying look. "Bearing false witness means you shouldn't tell lies that'll get other people in trouble. I only stretch the truth when absolutely necessary to save myself or to spare someone else pain. That's not at all the same thing."

Discussing theology with Bitty is something like finding a talking frog. While you're amazed the frog can talk, you just know there's a trick to it somewhere.

"What time are the Divas coming back over?" I asked, though I knew very well that we'd set the time at eleven-thirty, well before the sinister hour of midnight, and late enough to ensure that most of Holly Springs would be sound asleep in their beds.

Bitty yawned despite the massive amounts of caffeine I'd been pouring into her. "Really, Trinket, you need to pay attention to things. We're to meet at eleven-thirty at the Inn. Georgie and Gaynelle are going to meet us, and Sandra promised to come, too. No one's liable to notice, especially if we go in the back way."

With that fervent hope in mind, we did what I can only describe as skulking outside the back garage door of Rayna's section of the hotel. I've often thought it would be wonderful to live in that big old building, with its former suites rented out to nineteenth century passengers, the lovely marble lobby, and what was once a dining room that served over a hundred people. Rayna has plans with a few developers to renovate and turn the room into a gift shop and a small, quaint restaurant. It'd be an excellent stop on the railroad if ever we could get a historical train to run down the tracks from Memphis or up from New Orleans to bring tourists. Especially during the April pilgrimage.

Anyway, there we were in the dead of night, clustered outside the rear of the Inn and waiting on Rayna to come out and meet us. Rob's car was gone, so chances were good that he'd had to go out on a call. That happens a lot since he owns a bail bonding business as well as an insurance investigation company.

"Good Lord," Rayna said when she saw Bitty, "who are you supposed to be?"

"Well, we all agreed that dark clothing is best," Bitty defended her *haute couture*. She'd poured herself into a tight black jumpsuit that I swear looked like a leather body stocking, wore a black leather jacket, mid-calf suede boots with high heels, and had a black purse on one shoulder.

"I couldn't talk her out of it," I said. "She thinks she's one of the *Charlie's Angels.*"

"She looks more like one of the Hell's Angels," Sandra observed, and we all nodded in a silent agreement except for Bitty, who chastised our sadly lacking fashion expertise.

Since I still had on the clothes I'd worn earlier, the comfortable blue Lee jeans and yellow shirt and jacket, I'd borrowed Bitty's black crocheted poncho to cover up my bright colors. It still smelled faintly of *Beautiful*, that perfume by Liz Taylor.

"All right, Divas, let's go," Rayna said, and we set out in grim determination to retrieve what we all hoped was a still-frozen senator from the cemetery.

As promised, Georgie did indeed have a key to the gate lock, and with car lights off and the only illumination a ragged half-moon to guide us, we made our way very slowly down the narrow, sloping road to the vault that held Philip Hollandale. My heart was thumping so hard I worried it'd fracture a rib, and my dry mouth prevented speech. Apparently, the others were having similar reactions, as no one spoke until we reached the stone vault.

Then we just stood and looked at it for a few moments. Wind sighed through holly limbs and oak branches, and in the distance a dog howled. It was very Sherlock Holmes. If a sudden fog had sprang up and curled around our feet, none of us would have been surprised.

Finally Rayna, our undeclared leader, said softly, "Let's do it."

We positioned ourselves around the opening, and reached inside to grab the carpet and haul the senator out by his feet. To my surprise, he was much deeper than I remembered, because I felt only empty air. I wasn't the only one. Bitty reached so far inside I thought she might just fall all the way in, so I grabbed her by her purse strap. It was the only thing loose enough to grip. Her jumpsuit looked painted on.

After a few moments, Gaynelle said the obvious: "The senator is no longer here."

We all looked at each other, dumbfounded.

"Where the hell is my carpet?" Bitty demanded, but I could tell from the slight quiver in her voice that the expensive rug had lost some measure of importance to her.

"No doubt," Gaynelle said, "still with the senator. Oh dear. This could be a problem."

That was an understatement. It couldn't have escaped anyone's notice that all our fingerprints were likely to be on the plastic Leaf and Garden bags, and Bitty's rug could certainly be traced back to her. But what puzzled and bothered me most, was the question of just who had found the senator in the cemetery, and who had put him in Bitty's coat closet in the first place. It was quite likely to be the same person or persons who had killed him in Sanders' foyer.

Even in the dim light afforded by the moon, when I looked at Gaynelle, I saw from her expression that she'd come to the same conclusion.

"Perhaps we'd best leave and discuss this matter elsewhere,"

Gaynelle said, and most of us instantly agreed.

"Shouldn't we just look around a little bit first," Georgie asked, "to see if maybe dogs or something dragged him out?"

"It'd have to be really *big* dogs," Sandra said uneasily.

"Not to mention dogs with a key to the gate since the fence keeps them out," I observed.

"No, sections of the fence are down," Georgie said with a shake of her head. "But I don't really think dogs could drag him away."

"Maybe he thawed," Rayna said. "Or even melted. No. That's ridiculous. I must be a little bit hysterical. The rug would still be here."

"My lovely rug is *gone*," Bitty said. I decided that focusing on the non-essential details kept her from descending into hysteria, and gave her a comforting pat on the shoulder.

"Bitty dear," Gaynelle asked, "do you still have that bottle of Jack Daniel's with you?"

Wordlessly, Bitty reached into her purse and took out a bottle. "I brought it along just in case," she said, and we passed it around, then went and got back into our cars.

*

Back at the Inn, the general consensus was that we were all in a great deal of trouble. If the police had been notified of a body being found in an empty vault, their investigations would certainly lead to us.

"If pranksters saw us," Sandra suggested hopefully, "maybe they just hid the body somewhere else and it'll turn up in a day or two."

"What kind of pranksters," Rayna asked, "Transylvanian teenagers? Who steal bodies?"

"Apparently," Gaynelle said darkly, "*we* do."

Bitty brushed that aside. "Oh for heaven's sake, Gaynelle, we didn't steal him. We just moved him. Knowing Philip, the devil probably threw him back up here and he just landed in the wrong place."

"What are we going to *do*?" Sandra asked plaintively, and silence fell for a moment.

Finally Georgie said, "I'll go out there and look around for him tomorrow. I go out there so much anyway, no one will ever suspect

I'm trying to find the senator or a clue as to who took him. Everyone will just think I'm still doing my historical work."

"An excellent and practical solution," Gaynelle approved. "I'm glad to see my brother's intellect is thriving in you, my dear."

Georgie looked very pleased.

"And if we don't find him? What then?" I asked, hating to prick their bubble of hope but forced to ask the unavoidable question.

A discussion ensued in which several ideas were passed back and forth, everything from reporting it to the police, to staking out the cemetery like resident ghouls and waiting to see if the killers or pranksters returned to the scene of the crime. The former idea of reporting it to the police did not, I regret to say, gather much support. Even Gaynelle thought it a risky idea.

"There was so much rancor between the senator and Bitty, that they may very well jump to the immediate supposition that she killed him. Especially since he's still wrapped in the carpet that made the judge in their divorce threaten to cut it in two and give each a half. Solomon's solution is still remarkably effective in so many instances."

"I don't know about Solomon," Bitty remarked moodily, "but Philip was more than happy to cut it in two rather than give it to me."

"That's the idea, Bitty," I said. "The judge then knew who really wanted the carpet most, the person willing to destroy it, or the person willing to give it up to preserve it. See? Solomon's choice."

Bitty just looked at me. "Well, that's just the dumbest thing I've ever heard. Solomon Schreiber would never cut up an expensive carpet, and neither would I."

There are times Bitty can be quite obtuse, but since we were all under a great deal of stress, I thought it best not to continue with explanations.

"So then," Rayna said, "why don't we go home and sleep on it tonight, and when we get up in the morning, we'll see what's happened. If the police announce they've found Philip Hollandale's body, we should all go in immediately and tell them exactly what happened before they get to the truth themselves. If no one says anything, we can assume pranksters—or the murderer—found him and did something with him. Either way, I think we're going to have to tell the police what's happened. We can't just keep moving the senator around like a chess piece, especially once he starts to really thaw out."

Rayna said it so much better than I had, and after the shock of the evening's events, Bitty seemed to listen. She nodded thoughtfully.

"I'm sure you're right. Chess never was my game. Philip was always much better at it, but then, aren't politicians supposed to be good at strategy as well as lying and stealing?"

"Most of them are multi-taskers," I agreed.

We all parted with a flexible game plan of waiting for the morning, then making a much more informed decision.

Once back at Bitty's house, she turned off the alarm system she rarely used, and had me check the upstairs while she checked the downstairs. I wasn't quite sure what I was looking for other than burglars or a body, but finding neither, I went back downstairs to find Bitty sitting at the kitchen table.

"Are you all right?" I asked, and she nodded.

"Just waiting on you to go with me to the cellar. If Philip is down there, I don't want to go alone."

That thought hadn't occurred to me, and frankly, I couldn't drum up any enthusiasm for going into the cellar. They always smell musty no matter how many windows or air circulators or dehumidifiers they may have, and make me think of being buried alive. Rather macabre, I know, but when I was a child a Vincent Price horror movie about being buried alive had made a lasting impression. To this day, I don't care to sleep in a completely dark room. Perry had preferred pitch black surroundings at night—unless he felt like doing the horizontal tango, at which time he wanted every light in the room so bright we could have been in an operating room. Two more reasons we're entirely unsuited for one another. What sane woman wants all her flaws lit up like an appendectomy patient on the surgery table?

Anyway, Bitty and I did our osmosis thing again, where we tried to meld into one another to present a bigger target as we crept down the cellar steps. When Bitty turned on the overhead light switch, I blinked.

"You've done some redecoration."

"I know. It's the family room."

"For what family, The Sopranos?"

"Oh for heaven's sake, Trinket, the boys chose the decorations. I just paid for it."

That explained it. A massive pool table commands the middle of the room, but there's a giant TV, an electronic dart board, some poker tables, a refrigerator, and a wet bar strategically placed against dark paneling. A black leather couch and matching chairs are in the middle. All that's missing are layers of cigar smoke and a few men dressed in black suits, white ties, and shoulder holsters.

"What's that door over there?" I asked while we still stood on the stairs and peered around the 'family room.'

"The wine cellar. It's temperature controlled. Not very big, though. I keep it locked."

"And that door?"

"To the back yard."

We stared at it for a moment, both knowing it should be checked but neither of us in a great hurry to do it. After a moment, I gathered my courage—which I can do with a thimble—and said firmly, "We'll check it together."

Thankfully, there was no sign of intruders or forced entry. We congratulated ourselves on being so composed and Bitty's foresight in installing iron bars over the cellar windows, and then we went back upstairs.

I took a shower in the guest room bath that had one of those stalls with water jets spraying from five different directions, washed my hair with a shampoo that smelled like an exotic fruit, and slathered on conditioner. If I don't use conditioner, my hair feels like straw. It's very coarse.

Afterward, wrapped in three different towels big enough to use as sheets, I examined my face in the mirror for signs of depravity. People who hide corpses should have bulging eyes, rat-like teeth, and a nose like a weasel. So far, my depredations hadn't made it to my face. I just looked very tired and fifty-one years old. Not an attractive combination, although I suppose with a little rest and a life free of crime, I might be presentable enough. My auburn hair has darkened with the years and has a few streaks of gray I do my best to pretend aren't there, and while my green eyes aren't the vivid hue of a Hollywood starlet's, they're fairly bright. My brows are thin and arch naturally, and my lashes and brows are light brown. My nose is short and straight, my round chin has a dimple I've always hated, and my complexion is fair with a few freckles I've done my best to eradicate all my life. Freckles, like cockroaches, are indestructible, it seems.

Bitty had laid a shapeless caftan on the bed for my nightwear. Once I'd towel-dried my shoulder-length hair, brushed my teeth with a toothbrush Bitty thoughtfully provided, and rubbed some kind of face cream into my skin that probably cost more than I'd made in a week, I got into the caftan and then the bed. It was antique, of course, with a half-canopy and mosquito netting that was pulled back at the sides in a graceful swoop. A quilt I was certain had been crafted in another century smelled clean and fresh, and pale light came through tall windows covered by sheers and damask drapes.

I fell asleep almost immediately, a surprise since I've always thought criminals must lie awake at night plotting more crimes or worrying about imminent apprehension.

When I awoke the next morning, rain pattered on the windows and dripped from eaves, and the smell of coffee drifted up the stairs. I lay there for a few minutes. In the past, Bitty got up at the crack of noon, but lately she's been an early riser. Joining the Historical Society has been very good for her, on one hand; on the other hand, it's led to murder, although indirectly. Which led me to mull over the improbability of Hollandale visiting Sanders by coincidence.

While Bitty frequently suspected the senator's motives, it was quite likely she was very correct this time. Philip Hollandale was not the kind of man to visit constituents unless there was an advantage to be had. Sherman Sanders doesn't seem like a large donor, though stranger things have been known to happen.

So what reason would take Hollandale out to Sanders for a visit other than some scheme to delay or prevent The Cedars being put on the historical register? Perhaps the first thing that should be investigated were connections between the senator and Sanders, then possible deals in which he was involved that might affect Bitty. It sounded far-fetched in one way to think Philip Hollandale would go to such lengths for petty vengeance, but it's been my experience that in the case of lost love and divorce, petty is the norm and vengeance figures in somewhere. Money, of course, is the biggest and most frequent factor.

My clothes from the day before were gone, so I found a pair of white socks in a chest of drawers to cover my feet, and went downstairs, caftan billowing around me. Bitty was nowhere to be seen, but a pleasant young woman with light brown skin, black hair styled in attractive curls around her face, and a big smile stood in the kitchen.

"You must be Trinket," she said, and poured coffee into a big mug and put it in front of me along with a blueberry muffin dripping in butter. I just looked at it with my heart beating fast.

"Are those freshly baked muffins?" I asked hopefully.

"Took them out of the oven only ten minutes ago. Kept them warm in a biscuit keeper."

"You must be Sharita," I deduced, remembering the chicken and dumplings.

She laughed. "Was it the muffins that gave me away?"

I'd already bitten into the muffin and had closed my eyes with utter ecstasy. After a moment of pure bliss, I opened my eyes and nodded. "And the chicken and dumplings."

Sharita laughed again, her milk chocolate dark eyes lit with amusement as she went on with her tasks. Flour, sugar, eggs and milk were being used in a most business-like way atop the Corian counter.

"I heard about old man Sanders' mule eating those dumplings," she said. "I'd like to have seen that."

"It was definitely a once-in-a-lifetime sight," I said. "So do you come in every day? Bitty never mentioned she has someone help her in the kitchen, though Lord knows she'd either starve to death or have to eat out all the time if she didn't."

"I come in once a week and prepare all her meals," Sharita said as she worked a flour sifter, one of those aluminum ones with the pull handle. "Sometimes Bitty has parties or special events, but most of the time it's just a weekly menu that I put up in the freezer for her."

"You ought to sell these muffins," I said as I finished the last bite. "They're the best I've ever tasted."

Sharita grinned. "I do. I own a catering company and small diner, and we also make up gift baskets of baked goods, jams, jellies, and apple butter we'll deliver for a small extra fee. Of course, I charge a little more if I go to clients' homes to cook, but those who want me to do that can certainly afford it."

"Like Bitty," I said, and Sharita nodded. Thinking of my parents and how much they'd like a basket of muffins and jellies, I asked, "Do you have a business card?"

After getting to a stopping place with the sifter, Sharita reached in her smock pocket and took out a business card. Though obviously printed on a home computer, it was as business-like and attractive as Sharita. It read *Sharita Stone Professional Catering* and had the address of her diner, business number, and a cell phone number, all in a burgundy color against cream stock.

"Don't be trying to steal her," Bitty said, coming in the back door with a newspaper under one arm and a big coffee mug in her hand. "I've got Sharita this time every week. Put your name on the waiting list."

"Unfortunately, you don't have to worry about that. Though I am going by her diner to pick up a gift basket for Mama and Daddy to take on the Delta Queen with them."

Bitty poured herself another cup of coffee. "I'd forgotten they were going on that trip. So much has happened—" She stopped abruptly with a glance at Sharita, and then beckoned me to go with her back to the screened porch just off the kitchen. "It's nice out there this time of morning, Trinket. Come get some fresh air. You look like you need it."

"Is that a passive-aggressive way of telling me I look like hell?"

"When did you learn all those kinds of terms? You've been paying too much attention to the wrong things. I think you need to meet a man, get some new interests in your life."

By this time we were out on the screened porch and far enough away from Sharita that she couldn't overhear us, and Bitty motioned for me to sit down in a wicker chair with fat pink cushions that looked remarkably similar to the ones on the front porch.

"Apparently," I said in a low tone, "getting new interests in my life involve grave-robbing and desecration of a corpse."

"Don't go overboard. You have such a tendency to do that. It's just that Sharita's brother is that nice young police officer who came to question us yesterday, and I'd just as soon not get either of them involved right now."

Before I could point out that the officer would inevitably be involved quite soon, she thrust the morning paper at me. The local headline

read: *"Senator Missing, Foul Play Suspected"* and right below that
an article detailing a search of The Cedars for the missing Sherman
Sanders.

"No mention of Philip's body being found," I said.

"So I noticed. Of course, it was midnight last night before we
even knew he was missing. Along with my carpet."

"What is it with you and that rug?"

"It broke up my marriage. Not like you may think." Bitty sipped
at her coffee and tucked her feet under her in the chair. She wore a
thick cotton robe that still managed to look stylish on her, and matching
blue house slippers with a band of fur and glitter marching across the
instep. "I wanted the carpet, Philip refused to buy it, so I used my
own money. Philip was furious. So he bought his legal assistant a
boob job then tried them out just to be sure they worked. Of course,
he made sure I knew all about it. He's lucky I didn't shoot his ass with
my forty-five. Instead, I filed for divorce on grounds of infidelity. He
nearly went through the roof. Worried more about how it'd look to
his constituents than how I felt about everything. Not that it was his
first time to stray. Usually, he bought me something expensive to make
up for it. That time, I had to pay for it myself. So, I have the carpet to
remind me not to be an idiot again."

It actually made sense to me.

However, what I said was, "You have a *gun*?"

Bitty sighed. "Yes, Trinket. A forty-five. I keep it locked up in a
gun safe. I've always hoped that by the time I remembered where I
put the key and got it unlocked and had the damn thing loaded, Philip
would either have had time to get away or I'd be out of the mood to
shoot him. Now that someone else has saved me that necessity, I may
just get it out and keep it handy for other annoyances."

Since her tone of voice already sounded a bit hostile, I decided to
forego any further discussion of the wisdom of her owning a lethal
weapon, and went right on to the next topic.

"At any rate, we need to call Rayna and all present a united front,
whatever else we do."

"You're still set on telling everything to the police, aren't you."

"Bitty, I just don't see that we can do anything else. I'm so afraid
they'll view it badly if they learn you saw him out at Sanders' and

didn't report it. Once his body is found, you know it's going to be such a mess. And of course, we'll all have to be truthful when questioned. It's bound to come out."

"I suppose so. It'd be so helpful if Sherman Sanders would show up. I really need him to sign those papers so we can get his house on our tour. And of course, apply for the historical register."

There was a short silence during which I pondered Bitty's remarkable ability to focus on non-essential issues while her ex-husband's frozen corpse hop-scotched around town, then she gave a decided nod of her head.

"Yes," she said, "that's what we'll do."

"Go to the police?"

"Later. First, we'll go out to The Cedars and go through Sanders' desk to see if he signed the paperwork I sent him last year. He could have, you know. I think he just likes all the attention he gets by making me come back all the time. Not to mention bribes. Last month, I took him out a nice gift basket of muffins and jellies Sharita made up, and before that, it was a tin of pralines. It wasn't until Budgie reminded me that he always orders chicken and dumplings when he eats at the café that I hit on the idea of getting Sharita to make those for him."

I stood up. "If you go out to The Cedars, it won't be with me along. I'm going home."

Bitty looked up at me in faint surprise. "You'd let me go alone?"

"I prefer you don't go at all. However, if you have some kind of suicidal proclivity, I can't stop you. Just tell me where you put my clothes, and I'll leave you to your insanity."

A crafty look came over Bitty's face, and I swear she looked like one of those cartoon villains. All she needed was a long curling mustache she could tug and say, "I've got you now!"

Instead she said, "I sent them out to be cleaned. You can wear something of mine, if you like."

"You're seven inches shorter than I am. Even this caftan hits me at the knees. Where did you send my clothes, Elisabeth Ann Truevine?"

"Don't worry. They have a two hour special. Of course, if I call and tell them not to hurry, delivery will be delayed until this evening."

"You're a horrible little person."

Bitty smiled. I sat back down. The rain had finally stopped, but eaves still dripped.

"You do know that the police are investigating Sanders' disappearance, too, don't you?" I asked without much hope it'd faze her.

"If you'd read the article, you'd know that they already searched his home but found no evidence of foul play, and because of his advanced age, have asked people to be on the watch for him in case he's had a stroke or forgotten where he lives."

"They found *nothing?* How convenient for you."

"Isn't it?" She stood up. "It won't take long, Trinket. Especially with both of us looking through his paperwork."

A sense of fatality settled over me. I began to understand how prisoners on Death Row at Parchman must feel as the time of their execution draws closer. Actually, it brings with it a sense of peace, knowing that doom also brings an end to uncertainty. At least, that's my interpretation of how it must feel. If asked, the prisoners may well provide contradictions.

"All right," I said, "but you have to pay for my lawyer."

"That goes without saying. I keep the Brunettis on a continual retainer."

When the doorbell signaled the arrival of my clean clothes, I went immediately to the front door in case Bitty wanted to negotiate other terms. To my not-so-great surprise, Officer Marcus Stone and several other officers I didn't know greeted me.

"Is Mrs. Hollandale here?" Officer Stone inquired.

I think I said something like Yes, but because my heart beat so fast and my knees shook so hard, and I found it hard to hear anything over the buzzing in my head, I'm not sure of that.

At any rate, Officer Stone and the other gentlemen presented a signed search warrant and asked us to please step outside to the porch while they performed their duties. Bitty, who had been upstairs troweling on her make-up, came down just in time to hear the last.

"On what grounds, may I ask?" she demanded somewhat haughtily, not an endearing tone to take with policemen sent to search your house, in my opinion.

"We received a tip this morning that Senator Hollandale may be imprisoned here," the officer said more politely than he probably felt.

"Step outside, please, Mrs. Hollandale."

Bitty puffed up like a toad, said something like "Search away, the sonuvabitch isn't here," then stomped out to the front porch. The sun had come out at last, thankfully warming the air.

Clad in my short black caftan with bright pink flowers, and a pair of white socks and no underwear, I huddled in a wicker chair and hoped no one came along to see me. The caftan was cotton and fairly thick, but with the light behind me, I'm sure I showed everything there was to see. It's not a nice feeling.

Leaning around the door frame, Bitty called inside, "If one thing gets broken, Marcus Stone, I'm telling your mama!" then sat down in a chair and crossed her arms over her chest. "If this just doesn't beat all," she fumed. "Why on earth would I want to be around Philip Hollandale longer than three minutes? I couldn't stand the man when I was married to him, I sure don't want to be around him now. Dead *or* alive."

As an officer stood guard at the door and didn't wear a hearing aid, I motioned to Bitty to be quiet. She looked at me, her lips pressed into a taut line.

"You're making wrinkles," I said, and instantly her muscles relaxed and her face settled back into a fairly normal expression.

"Thanks. I wouldn't want all Doctor Pearson's nice work to be ruined. He gave me Botox injections around my mouth, and it got rid of every one of those horrid wrinkles. You should try it, Trinket. It gets rid of squint lines between your eyebrows, too."

Since most of my squint lines had formed in the past week, I doubted Dr. Pearson would be of any benefit to me unless I kept him on retainer.

It wasn't long before a crowd began to gather out front, gawking at the police cars and all the officers standing on the porch and looking around in the yard. Bitty, ever the consummate hostess, called inside to Sharita to bring out a pitcher of iced tea and some of those cookies she'd baked that morning. After a brief discussion with the officer at the door, during which Bitty said she'd tell his auntie how rude he was being, Sharita was allowed to bring out a tray with sweet tea and shortbread cookies.

Soon, quite an ensemble sat in wicker chairs on the front porch.

Mrs. Tyree, an elderly black lady who has lived in the house next
door for the past thirty years, sat in a wicker rocking chair sipping
sweet tea and eating a shortbread cookie. Allison Kent, who lives
across the street and is about our age but married into Holly Springs
life, pulled up a chair and talked about her grandchild who attends
Marshall Academy. Richard Simmons—not the adorably prissy person
who bounces around so energetically on TV—came to sit on the porch
with us, too. Mr. Simmons used to work for the tax assessor's office
and knows just about everything there is to know about people in
Holly Springs.

My attire, or lack of it, was briefly explained, and we chatted
amiably about the weather and the upcoming pilgrimage. Naturally,
that led to talk of the history of the area. One of the pilgrimage highlights
was the fairly recent Ida B. Wells Museum dedicated to the young
black woman who had helped pioneer civil rights. The old white house
sits right where Highway 4 ends by Rust College, the first Negro
college in North Mississippi

Tiny little Mrs. Tyree was proud of the fact that she was one of the
hostesses and tour guides for the museum. "I have it all just about
memorized," she said: "At the age of sixteen, Ida B. Wells nursed her
parents and siblings through a yellow fever outbreak. Her parents
died, so she then took care of her five surviving siblings by working in
the country as a teacher. But it was a day on the train in May of 1884
that set Ida Wells on the path to her writing career and work as a
crusader for justice and democracy.

"Ms. Wells was the Rosa Parks of the nineteenth century," Mrs.
Tyree continued, rocking back and forth, "and the first Negro female
to make history by refusing to give up the seat she'd paid for and be
moved to the back."

"I didn't realize all of that," Bitty said when Mrs. Tyree's spiel
ended. "What sorrows she had to endure."

"And what triumphs those sorrows led her to," Mrs. Tyree
observed with a wise nod.

"Maybe that's what you're going through, Bitty," Allison Kent
said. "A time of sorrow that will lead to personal triumph."

The truthful but vague explanation that the police were searching
for any clues to the senator's disappearance had been given and

accepted by those present. Since he certainly wasn't in the house any longer, and the only thing worrisome was a possibility of evidence indicating he had recently spent time in her coat closet as a frozen corpse, Bitty had channeled her anger into gracious hospitality. I, on the other hand, always expect the worst. That way, when it happens, I can deal with it much more easily. It's when the worst fails to happen that I find myself surprised and a bit off-balance.

"You know, Allison," Bitty said thoughtfully, "you may be right. All this turmoil will pass and I'll just rise above it, like a phoenix rising from the ashes of disaster."

As I've said, Bitty tends to be melodramatic, especially when she's center-stage. She'd spread her arms out wide, in the manner of a rising phoenix, I suppose, when Officer Stone came out of the house onto the porch.

"Mrs. Hollandale, please stand up," he said, and I knew at once from the tone of his voice that something dreadful was about to happen. I reached blindly for Bitty, but still caught up in her vision of rising from ashes, she stood up to face him.

"Elisabeth Hollandale, you have the right to remain silent," Stone said as he caught her wrist and tucked her out-stretched arm behind her. "Anything you say can and will be held against you in a court of law. You have the right to an attorney. If you cannot afford an attorney, one will be provided for you."

It was that last sentence that sunk in for Bitty, and she drew herself up straight and looked him right in the eye. "I can afford whatever has to be paid, Marcus Stone, so don't you dare put handcuffs on me without telling me what in the blazes you think you're doing."

Stone, a rather formidable young man, seemed a bit taken aback. Then he gathered himself and said politely if nervously, "I'm arresting you, Mrs. Hollandale."

"Well for the love of all that's holy, I can see that! Why?"

"For the murder of Philip Hollandale."

Bitty paused for only half a second, and then said firmly, "It's my understanding that murder usually requires a dead body."

"Yes, ma'am. And we have one."

I half-rose from my chair, but to Bitty's credit, she didn't blink an eye. "And how does that affect me?"

"Senator Hollandale's body was just found in your wine cellar."

CHAPTER 9

I'd like to report that I then woke up in my own bed in the upstairs master bedroom that used to belong to my parents, but unfortunately, the nightmare only grew worse. In front of God and every neighbor a quarter-mile in all directions, the police then arrested *me*. Even Sharita was taken in for questioning, though as the sister of Marcus Stone and not having spent the night, she wasn't required to wear handcuffs or ride in a police car.

So there I was, wearing a flowing caftan and white sports socks, my hands cuffed behind me and my hair sticking out like a wire brush, sitting in the rather cool confines of the Holly Springs police department at the apex of Market and Spring Streets, waiting to be questioned. I shivered so badly that a woman working there brought me a thin blanket and tucked it all around me.

"Is that more comfortable?" she asked with a smile. She wore a blue shirt and dark pants that looked very much like a police uniform. Or that of a crossing guard. She probably had on underwear, too. I didn't, and the lack made me very uncomfortable.

I nodded. "Thank you."

She patted me on the shoulder. "They'll be through with you soon."

That's what I was afraid of. Never having ridden in a police car before, nor been escorted to jail by men in uniform, however polite they may be, visions of hard time danced in front of my eyes. Instead of Camp Cupcake, I'd be sentenced to life in Parchman. I'd participated in the cover-up of a crime. I'd violated the sanctity of a corpse by hiding it in a cemetery, though a good lawyer could probably come up with a winning argument on that point. *Lord.* It'd cost me the rest of my savings to pay for a good lawyer. I'd either have to end up on the streets or living off my parents, neither of which I found appealing. Nor could I ask or expect Bitty to provide me with legal representation, since I had been a willing accomplice.

Just about the time I'd worked myself up into a state of

unexpurgated guilt, the door to the room where I sat in my caftan and sock-clad feet opened. A rather hearty man of near six feet in height entered. He wore a tan cowboy hat, muddy boots, a plaid flannel shirt, and Levi's. His belt buckle was big, round, and bright. He took off his hat, swiped a hand through his brown hair, and affably greeted the lady who'd brought me a blanket.

"Afternoon, Miss Claudia."

"Afternoon to you, Jackson Lee," she replied. "You been out in the fields today?"

"One of my prized heifers got cut up by barb wire. That new vet came out, stitched her right up. Seems like he's going to work out pretty good around here."

He glanced at me then back at the woman he'd called Miss Claudia. "Reckon we got us a little problem here."

"Seems like," Miss Claudia agreed, and I wasn't at all certain I liked some farmer making remarks about me when he knew nothing of the situation. I sat up a little straighter and lifted my chin to indicate that I was above rude speculation, an effect no doubt diluted by the fact I wore only a caftan, socks, and a blanket with MARSHALL COUNTY JAIL printed on it.

Then I looked away and wondered where they'd taken Bitty. I hadn't seen her since she'd gone one way and I the other, riding in separate police cars the three blocks to the police station. I hadn't been given my one phone call yet, and dreaded calling my parents. They may seem to be in their second childhood, but the shock of having their daughter arrested for desecration of a corpse might be enough to cause a heart attack or stroke. Or both.

The farmer came to stand right in front of me. He smelled like mud and cow manure. I tried to breathe through my mouth.

"Miz Truevine?" he asked, and I looked up at him, rather startled he knew me.

"Yes?"

"I'm Jackson Lee Brunetti." When I just stared at him blankly he smiled and added, "Your attorney."

"Oh. But I didn't call—"

"Miz Bitty called. She might be here a little bit longer, but as soon as you answer a few questions, I'll give you a ride back to her house.

I'd have been here sooner, but I got stuck way out in the back pasture and it took me a while to get to my truck. Sorry about that."

I tried to remember if I knew this man, but whether from stress or senility, nothing came to me. I knew of the Brunetti family, of course. Most of them are lawyers. I just didn't remember this particular Brunetti.

Since there didn't seem to be anything else to say, and I'm not one to ignore a life preserver flung my way, I nodded and said, "Thank you."

Within what seemed like hours but was probably only fifteen minutes, I'd had my police interview, answered the few questions allowed by my attorney, and was in the muddy red truck cab next to Jackson Lee Brunetti. I decided the cow manure smell wasn't that bad at all.

"Mr. Brunetti," I began, and he stopped me.

"Jackson Lee. Nobody ever calls me Mr. Brunetti unless they're strangers or want some money."

"I'm a stranger."

"No, you're not. I'm a few years behind you, but I remember your brothers. They were my heroes back in school. When Jack and Luke got killed, they became even bigger heroes."

A lump formed in my throat and tears stung my eyes. It must have been my weakened stamina. Just the mention of my brothers right now crumbled my reserves.

Finally I got the lump worked down and could talk, so said, "All right. Jackson Lee. I'll be responsible for your bill. I wasn't coerced into anything, but acted of my own free will and sound—if temporarily non-working—mind. Besides, I'm more worried about Bitty than I am myself right now."

He smiled as he hit the blinker to turn onto Walthal Street. "That's what she said about you."

For some reason, that made me tear up again. I sniffled, and Jackson Lee reached over to open a compartment and pull out a box of tissues. I used three of them.

It wasn't until he'd pulled up in front of Bitty's house where the police still worked and had yellow crime scene tape strung all around that I remembered him from grade school. I turned to look at him.

"You were in the sixth grade play that ended up in a brawl. You had the part of Stonewall Jackson, and Dougie McAllen played General Bernard Bee, only you had rock salt loaded in what was supposed to be an empty shotgun."

Jackson Lee grinned. "That was the second time General Bee got whupped by Stonewall Jackson."

I started laughing. "And Dougie got mad because he hadn't wanted to play a Yankee, even a general, and the Civil War was re-fought in the elementary auditorium. Even a few parents got in on it."

"My daddy didn't. When I got home, he took me out to the barn and gave me a real good reminder that the Civil War had ended." He chuckled and I laughed with him. No wonder Bitty gave the Brunettis all her business. Any lawyer this charming would probably have a jury eating out of his hand.

I was still smiling when I opened the truck door to get out. Jackson Lee appeared on the curb before I could manage the descent with my caftan and blanket all wadded up around me and impeding my progress, and scolded me for not waiting.

"A lady always waits to have her door opened, Miz Truevine."

"Jackson Lee, I'll remember I'm a lady if you'll remember to call me Trinket."

"Done."

Jackson Lee smoothed my way into the house, getting me past policemen, ensuring that I wouldn't be retained for any reason, and assuring that I wouldn't interfere with their investigation but only wanted to retrieve my clothes. The cleaners had delivered my cleaned clothes, and since the plastic bag was gone, I assumed they'd already been checked for evidence. There was a brief moment of tension when an officer insisted on keeping them, but Jackson Lee quoted some point of law that the search warrant didn't extend to items not at the house when the warrant was first served, or items not belonging to Mrs. Hollandale.

I got dressed the quickest I think I've ever done. My purse had been dumped on the bed and contents catalogued, apparently, but Jackson Lee got those released as well. By the time I got out the door, he'd also had my car released and handed me the keys.

"Go on home, Trinket, but expect a search warrant to be served on you for your clothes and maybe your car. Call me when it is. You and Bitty come in to my office tomorrow afternoon, okay?"

"Won't Bitty still be in jail?"

He lifted an eyebrow. "I didn't spend eight years in law school to let my best client sit in jail a minute longer than she needs to. By the time I get back over to the jail, she'll be waiting on me to bring her back home. It'll probably be best if you're gone. It's going to be hard enough to keep Bitty from tearing these officers a new one without worrying about one of them getting you off in a corner to answer their questions."

I could see the sense in that. Once Bitty saw the mess in her house, she'd go ballistic. It'd be all Jackson Lee could do to keep her from finding the key to her gun safe. I didn't envy him the task.

When I got in my Taurus, I pulled out onto the street by Jackson Lee's truck and rolled down my window. He leaned over with an arm propped on the car roof and I said, "You know Bitty hides an extra key to the gun safe."

He looked at me with a smile. "I know how to handle Bitty."

I smiled back at him. I had every confidence he did.

*

"Oh my," Mama said faintly when I'd related the entire story of Philip Hollandale and Sherman Sanders, from when we'd first gone out there with a pot of chicken and dumplings to when Jackson Lee came to spring me from prison. "All you had on was a caftan and socks? I'd have just *died* being in public with no underwear."

The Truevine women have firm priorities, because truth be told, that was the part that bothered me the most, too.

"I know," I said. "It was awful."

Daddy, who has never appreciated some of the subtleties of the female psyche, looked at us as if we'd just said we were voting Republican. The Truevines have always been Democrats and Methodists, if I haven't mentioned that before. Right or wrong, we hold to our traditions.

"You mean to tell me," he said slowly, "that you carted the dead body of a United States senator around town in a rug?"

"We didn't know what else to put him in," I apologized. "A thick carpet seemed less likely to leak if he started to thaw out."

"Dear me," Mama breathed, eyes getting huge. "That's not a vision I want to linger in my mind for very long."

I nodded. "He never was a particularly handsome man alive. Death has done nothing to improve on that."

Daddy made a deep sound in the back of his throat, put both hands palms down on the kitchen table, and got up. Without saying another word, he took his thick sweater off the coat hook by the back door and went outside. Mama and I just looked at each other.

"Your father never has much stamina when it comes to this sort of thing," she said, and I nodded again. Women in our family tend to be the ones to handle funeral details, and of course, the cooking and baking when close friends or loved ones die. The amount of food on the table of the bereaved indicates just how well-liked they are in the community. Baptists and Methodists vie for the honor of receiving the most casseroles and cakes at a single funeral. It's been an unacknowledged contest going on for decades. There's a certain protocol for this kind of thing that women instinctively know and men are unaware exists. Recently, a lady from the South has published a book on how to give a proper funeral. Since the large influx of residents from other parts of the country, it's way overdue, in my opinion.

At any rate, Mama and I discussed the ramifications of the senator's unexpected demise, and drank tall glasses of sweet tea with lemon wedges and fresh mint from her small greenhouse. It summons the taste of summer, the lemon and mint a reminder of idle evenings in lawn chairs with cricket serenades and lightning bug starlight.

"I'm sure Bitty didn't do it," Mama said. "She'd never be so crass as to mess up someone else's house like that."

"I agree. If Bitty was going to kill Philip, she'd either do it at his house or outside where the mess could be easily cleaned. Unless, of course, he made her so mad she just couldn't stand one more minute of putting up with his foolishness."

We looked at each other over the rims of our glasses, sipping tea while both our minds had to be focused on the obvious question: Who *had* killed Philip Hollandale? While his list of enemies had to be endless, as he'd never bothered about stepping on the toes of people he'd considered useless to him, which of them had taken it so far as to go out to The Cedars and bash him in the head with a heavy bronze statue?

The only name that came immediately to my mind was Sherman Sanders. Bitty would certainly tell the entire truth to Jackson Lee, who would then decide how much of it she should convey to the police and at what stages of the investigative process. It's a shame it has to be that way, that people can't just say what really happened without fear of it being used against them, but since there are so many people prone to stretching the truth or outright lying, it's necessary to let a good lawyer take charge of such situations. Really good lawyers do the lying for their clients, but outstanding lawyers tell the truth and get them off anyway. Or just enough of the truth to sell the rest to a jury. There are subtleties in the legal system I freely admit I don't understand at all.

"How well do you know Sherman Sanders?" I asked Mama.

"Not very well. He's more your father's age, and since they both grew up here, they'd know each other, I'm sure."

Mama was born in Hardeman County, Tennessee, not that far away out Highway 72, then Highway 45. She's a Crews, related to a branch of Crews in Marshall County, which is how she met Daddy a long time ago. They courted right before World War II, married right after, and for a while, times were pretty tough. Farming no longer made more than a bare living unless backed by a big corporation. Daddy has a natural distrust of conglomerates, a view he'd inherited from his own father. So he went to work at an insurance company in Holly Springs, Mama took care of the house and my brothers, then about the time Emerald and I came along, Daddy went to work for the post office. After my brothers died, Daddy sold off some of our land he'd always thought they might want one day. Later, he sold most of it when he realized neither Emerald nor myself would be back to build houses and rear our children. Since a developer bought a large chunk of it several years back, he and Mama are pretty well off for the first time in their lives.

Anyway, Mama added, "I've had a few discussions with Sherman Sanders. In fact, not so long ago I ran into him at Carlisle's." Carlisle's is the local Big Star grocery store. "He said he might be coming into a lot of money soon, he just hasn't decided yet. I thought that a rather odd thing to say, since you either come into money or you earn money. Unless, of course, you just go out and steal money, but then, I doubt very seriously Sherman Sanders would be bragging about that, would he."

She hadn't said the last as a question, more of an observation. I agreed. "No, I don't think he'd do that. So did he say how he expects to come into this money?"

"Not a word. We were at the meat counter, and he was getting a ham shank sliced and I was trying to decide if I wanted the center cut pork chops or a pork roast. Then I saw butterfly pork chops on sale so I bought those. Remember? We had them Wednesday last."

"I remember. They were excellent. At least an inch thick."

Mama smiled. She's always been a good cook, and hasn't lost her touch. "Anyway, I wouldn't put most anything past Sherman Sanders. Sometimes he's today, and then sometimes, he's yesterday."

I knew what she meant. There are people, especially older people, who stray back and forth between the yesterdays and todays at the flip of a hat. Or turn of a thought.

"Do you think him capable of murder?" I asked, and Mama didn't look surprised or even shocked at the suggestion.

"I suppose, under the right circumstances," she said after a moment of thought, "anyone is *capable* of murder. Most people have something inside them that stops short of violence, but if fear or the urge to protect a loved one is extreme, then yes, I think Sanders is capable of murder."

It occurred to me later when I thought about what she'd said, that Sanders didn't seem to love anything but that old hound and The Cedars. If either was threatened, he'd certainly react to protect them. Obviously, Tuck, the hound, had been killed. But Philip Hollandale, as vile as he could be, had never seemed physically vicious. Immoral, snaky in politics, yes, but would he go to an extreme that would anger a constituent and definitely risk unfavorable publicity, at the very least? And if he had killed Sanders' dog, why? None of this made any sense.

Bitty called before bedtime, sounding very calm and composed.

"Are you all right, Trinket?"

"Yes, I'm doing fine. How are you? Did you just get out of

custody?"

"Heavens no. Jackson Lee got me out right after he got you out. We sat here talking while the police conducted their search. Since Philip wasn't killed here and this isn't a crime scene, they just have the wine cellar closed off now. Jackson Lee managed to get me out a few bottles before they padlocked the door, though."

"Jackson Lee certainly is efficient."

Bitty laughed. "Oh yes. I don't know what I'd do without him. He may not look like the sharpest tack in the box, but he's what Daddy used to call a good ole country lawyer. If he wasn't so young, I'd think of Ben Matlock."

"I think we both have watched entirely too much TV in our lives. We relate everything to a television show we've seen. So were you charged with anything?"

"No. I was just held for questioning. I imagine they've gone back out to Sherman Sanders' house to look for traces of blood and my fingerprints." She sounded unconcerned.

"You don't seem very bothered by that," I said.

"Well, I didn't kill him, so I seriously doubt I'll be charged, much less convicted for it. I trust Jackson Lee. He says the fact Philip was found frozen in my wine cellar is circumstantial at best."

"Are you sure he said that?"

"Pretty sure. Why? You're not saying—"

"Good Lord, no, Bitty, don't even think anything like that. It's just that you assured me the Holly Springs police are very efficient, and even though I was with you all day when he was put into your coat closet, and I saw how upset you were after you found him in Sanders' foyer, I admit, if you weren't my first cousin and best friend, I'd have to lean toward you being guilty."

"Oh, so would I. But the law requires more than just thinking it. It requires proof. And of course, I didn't kill him so they won't find any proof at all."

It did sound likely. Possible. Hopeful.

"Was Jackson Lee your divorce attorney?" I asked, and when Bitty answered in the affirmative, I felt much better. "Well, he certainly did well for you then. And he's charming enough to sweet-talk the bark off a tree, so if it comes down to it, I'm sure he can prove your innocence to a jury."

"He can be charming, can't he? If he just didn't smell like cows all the time."

The inference didn't escape me. "I take it he's not married?"

"Widowed. Widowered? You know, Meg Ryan had a good point in that movie. Why are women widowed, and men not widowered if we call them a widower? Anyway, his wife died a few years back. Maybe as long as six, I don't quite remember. Oh, she was a fiery little thing! I think he met her up north somewhere, I never could keep that straight, but I liked her right off. Of course, they lived up in Memphis then and I didn't see much of them, but she always came down with Jackson Lee to visit family. Tiny, with dark hair and eyes, and a regular little spitfire. Knew how to make Jackson Lee toe the line, as well as their boys. I sure do miss Carmella."

Bitty sounded rather sad, so I asked, "Mama and Daddy are supposed to leave day after tomorrow on their cruise down the river. Want to go up to Memphis with me to see them off?"

"I'd love it. A change of scenery would be just the thing. We can eat in one of those little places that look over the river. Watch the barges go past. Or we could go to The Peabody and sit in the lobby, see who walks past. One time that I was there, I saw an Arab sheik and Tom Cruise. They weren't together, of course. Tom Cruise was still with Nicole Kidman then."

"These days, his better choice would be the Arab sheik," I said dryly, but my reference to the high price of oil went right over Bitty's head.

"I've always wondered if he didn't swing both ways. You know. Being so pretty and all."

I decided to ignore that.

"Since it's obviously been a while since you've sat in The Peabody lobby," I said, "it might be nice to go watch the ducks in the fountain. But it'll have to be after Mama and Daddy get on the Delta Queen, because they need to check in early."

We made our plans, and I hung up and went to the living room to visit with my parents. It was a pleasant evening, with only a few remarks about the subject at the back of all our minds, until the evening news came on at ten. We have cable that shows Memphis and local channels.

About ten minutes into the broadcast detailing verbal skirmishes between the Memphis mayor and the city council, the Memphis mayor and the media, and the Memphis mayor and the city and county citizens, an anchorman said, "And in Holly Springs, Mississippi today, the body of Senator Philip Hollandale was discovered in the cellar of his ex-wife's home. Police are still investigating, and while Elisabeth Hollandale is being questioned, she has not yet been charged in connection to his death."

Mama said indignantly, "He makes it sound like Bitty is going to be tried for murder!"

Since that does seem likely, Daddy patted Mama on the hand and said, "Jackson Lee has it under control, honey. Things will be just fine."

The tone of Daddy's voice, however, indicated the opposite, and neither Mama nor I were much comforted by his assurance.

I caught the last part of the anchorman's usual information about Philip's age and party affiliation—at which Mama sniffed and observed that no *Democrat* would be found dead in his ex-wife's cellar, completely ignoring national and local scandals involving illustrious members of the Democratic party—then the serious-faced anchorman went on to say, "And in what may be related news, Sherman Sanders, a Holly Springs resident being sought for questioning in the senator's death, has been missing for five days. Mr. Sanders is five feet-six inches tall, seventy-six years old, and may be suffering from a stroke or senile dementia. It is thought that the recent death of his only companion, an elderly hound dog that was found dead of natural causes at his home, may have precipitated Mr. Sanders' current condition. If anyone has seen or does see a man answering to the description now shown on your television screens, please call the Holly Springs police at the number listed . . . ."

My ears heard what he said after the *hound dog dead of natural causes* part, but my mind had ceased absorption. Do natural causes include caved in ribs and blood? If so, Parchman prison is no doubt crowded with innocent men convicted of murder.

Ten seconds later the phone rang. I stood up. "It's Bitty," I said without bothering to look at the Caller ID, and Mama and Daddy nodded. I went into the kitchen to take the call.

"I thought you said that dog was all bloody?" Bitty asked before I even got out the usual polite telephone greeting.

"Yes, that's what I said because that's what it was." I squeezed my eyes shut and tried not to see poor old Tuck's body.

"How can natural causes be bloody?"

"An interesting question. I suggest we ask someone who can answer it."

After a brief silence, Bitty said, "Since your parents are leaving day after tomorrow, why don't I just keep their little dog for a few hours when we come home?"

"*No.*" The possibilities for trouble if Bitty and a neurotic dog like Brownie get together are too much like the possibilities created by splitting the atom.

"Fine then. Luann Carey lives over on Higdon Street. She's always got extra dogs."

I rubbed at the recent crease permanently formed between my eyebrows and sighed. "I'm sure Jackson Lee will know about Sanders' dog. Why not just ask him?"

"At five hundred dollars an hour, I'd just as soon keep our professional conversations at a minimum."

"Good Lord, Bitty! Is that what it cost for Jackson Lee to pick me up at the jail and—"

"Don't get your panties in a twist, Trinket. He did that for free. He does a lot of what he calls *pro bono*. I think it means legal aid for poor people. Anyway, he'll be in New Albany most of tomorrow."

I let her insinuation of me as one of the poor slide, since alas, it's very close to being true. "Is there really a big hurry to find out if Tuck died of natural causes or not?" I asked.

"I suppose not. But if he did, then why did Sherman Sanders kill Philip?"

"You're assuming Philip killed the dog, then Sanders killed Philip and ran away?"

"That's the only thing that makes sense."

I thought about that for a moment. There are times Bitty sounds very logical. Normally, those times incite caution. Now, however, I had to agree with her. It really was the only thing that made sense.

What I said was, "My head hurts, Bitty. I'm going to bed."

"We have an appointment with Jackson Lee tomorrow afternoon at four."

"We can ask him then about the dog."

"And my rug. Get some sleep, Trinket. You really do sound tired."

Bitty sounded wired, and I suspected she'd been sampling some of the wine Jackson Lee saved from the locked cellar. "You too," I said anyway. "I'll talk to you tomorrow."

I went back into the living room. Daddy looked up at me. "They made a mistake." When I looked at him blankly, he said, "On the news. Sherman Sanders isn't seventy-six. He's eighty-one, five years older than me. We were drafted together, and he was in my squad in Okinawa right after the war. Stayed after I left, though. He'd met some Japanese girl named Nobi or Sato or something like that. Wanted to marry her, but because he wasn't discharged yet and some of the states over here didn't allow Japanese across their borders then, he couldn't bring her back with him. I remember he talked about desertion, but in the end, he didn't do it. Wonder what ever happened to that girl? He never did talk about her after he came home, just sat out there in that big empty house and got older every day."

"I wonder why he never got married," Mama mused.

Daddy shrugged. "Probably never did find another girl he fancied like he did Nobi. Or Sato. I never can remember which it is. Pretty little thing, though. I met her once when she came out to our base in Tachikawa. I could see why Sherman wanted to marry her."

After I got into bed and turned out my lights, I lay there with moonlight making oblong patches on my rug atop heart pine floors and thought about Sherman Sanders leaving behind a woman he loved. I guess most people have some tragedy in their lives, whether they talk about it or not.

CHAPTER 10

At twenty minutes to four the next day, I showed up at Bitty's front door. I hadn't heard from her all day, which I thought unusual, and had left a message on her home answering machine as well as her cell phone, but she hadn't called back. If I hadn't gone by Sharita Stone's shop to buy a basket of muffins and jellies to give Mama and Daddy, and heard that Bitty had been in earlier, I'd have worried that she'd been rearrested, or disappeared into the same black hole that seemed to have swallowed Sherman Sanders.

To my consternation, when I turned the antique doorbell to announce my arrival, I heard the ferocious barking of a dog. It didn't sound like a large dog, but nonetheless, it was a *loud* dog. I knew right then that Bitty had done just what she'd said she was going to do: gone out to Willow Bend Animal Clinic with a dog to get information from the new vet, who most likely wouldn't be familiar with her methods of extracting information. Jackson Lee and Bitty could make a devastating team. Both of them have loads of charm and ulterior motives.

I heard Bitty coming down the hallway into the spacious entrance hall and speak to the dog, but the barking didn't abate. I braced myself, expecting to find an ankle biter at my feet, but when Bitty opened the door, I saw that she held the animal in her arms. It barked. I blinked.

"What is that?"

Bitty smiled. "A Chinese pug."

"What's a pug? Chinese for a cross between a pig and ugly?"

"Don't be insulting, Trinket. This is Lady O-ya Moon Chen Ling. She's very exotic. Not at all like other dogs."

I had to agree with the last. Lady O-ya Moon Chen Ling looks like a cross between a pig and a teddy bear. Cuddly, in a homely kind of way.

"Lady Ling is dribbling snot all over your sleeve," I said instead, seeing that Bitty meant to defend not only her reason for temporarily possessing the dog, but her choice of breed.

Bitty made some kind of cooing noise and left me to come in and shut the door behind me as she went to what looked like a diaper bag sitting on the table by the telephone. Bemused, I closed the door and watched while she wiped the dog's nose with a tissue, then tied a bib around its neck. Dark brown bug eyes stared at me over Bitty's arm, and I swear the animal had a smug smile.

"That wasn't snot," she explained, "Chen Ling drools. She can't help it. She has an awful underbite."

"I can see that." Indeed, anyone within a hundred yards can see it. Chen Ling has the underbite of a Louisiana alligator. When Bitty put her on the floor, I also noticed bowed legs and pigeon toes. The back legs turn out. "Are they supposed to have legs like that?" I asked.

"I can see you know absolutely nothing about dogs, Trinket. Luann Carey assured me that Chen Ling has papers a mile long. Her coloring is called fawn and silver, with chocolate something or other. I can't remember the last."

"Uh hunh. How long is Chen Ling going to be with you?"

"Oh, I just borrowed her for the day. Luann rescued her from someone who intended to have her put to sleep. Can you imagine? Just because she's a little past her prime and has a few medical problems. Besides the dental work, and her jaw being a little out of synch so she drools all the time, and her being born with some kind of congenital thing that makes her toes turn in a little bit too much in the front, why, she's just fine."

Inhaling deeply, I asked, "Have you talked to Clayton and Brandon lately?"

Bitty looked up in surprise. "Just last night. I called Ole Miss to assure them that I'd be quite all right and not to worry if they heard anything on TV that says different. Why?"

"It seems to me that you're getting a little broody."

"Oh Trinket, I'm way past that. I don't want to mother anyone, I just borrowed Chen Ling for the day. Luann said I can take her back anytime."

Bitty smiled at Chen Ling and then kissed her right on top of her furry little head. I stared at both of them. Chen Ling obviously had mastered the situation, but I wasn't at all sure about Bitty.

"Well, put her out in the back yard or wherever you're going to leave her so we can go," I said, and Bitty gave me a startled look.

"I'm not leaving Chen Ling here by herself."

"Good heavens, Bitty, then where does Luann Carey live? We don't have much time if we have to make too many stops on the way to the law offices, and since Jackson Lee has been kind enough to come back from New Albany just to see us, I'd think you'd want to be prompt."

"Luann hasn't answered my calls, and when I tried to leave Chen Ling alone earlier she made such a fuss that I thought it best to take her with me. She does just fine. No car sickness or anything. Stop looking at me like that. I have a little carrier for her, and while we're on the way to the office, I'll tell you all about our visit to Dr. Coltrane."

Since there wasn't enough room in Bitty's Miata for us all to ride in the front and I had no intention of holding Chen Ling, we took my car. I threatened Bitty with all kinds of terrible reprisals if that dog threw up, but both she and the dog didn't seem to be paying any attention.

"About that new vet," Bitty said as I pulled out of her driveway, "the rumors are true. He is absolutely gorgeous. I've thought about it, and decided that he'd be perfect for you, Trinket."

Still a little miffed that she always gets her way, and that Chen Ling kept staring at me as if to say *ha ha* while sitting in that ridiculous looking baby sling Bitty had next to her chest, I said quite coolly, "If I decide I want a man, I'll find one myself, thank you very much."

"No, you won't. I know you. You'll just wither away on the vine out there at Cherryhill, and never have a single orgasm before you die."

"Bitty!"

"You deserve an orgasm, Trinket. I intend to see that you get at least one."

I almost ran up on the curb at the intersection of College and Randolph. "I'm not going to point out the sound of that, and I do *not* want to discuss my sex life," I got out when I managed to get the car straightened up again and headed for Center Street.

"Since you don't have a sex life, there can't be any discussion,"

Bitty said. "We'd have to sit here without saying a word."

"An idea I find remarkably attractive right now." Something in my tone must have gotten through to Bitty, because she changed the subject.

"Anyway, Dr. Coltrane—his first name is Christopher, by the way—said that he did the autopsy on Sanders' dog, and that it'd died of old age. Something about the liver and a cyst or tumor that was malignant. Said Sanders knew about the tumor, so there wouldn't be a reason for him to run over the dog since it didn't have long to live anyway. But maybe that was just to make sure it was really dead."

"Wait. Was the dog run over *after* it died?"

"Post-mortem, he said, which is another way of saying Sanders ran over his dog after it'd already died. I just think that's the strangest thing I ever heard of in my life. Don't you?"

I certainly did.

The Brunetti law office, or one of them, is located on Center Street not far from the court house. It's one of those old buildings painted white with black wrought-iron balconies and stairs, and flower boxes that hold bright red geraniums in the summer time. Law offices are mainly on the ground floor, with conference rooms and storage areas upstairs. Parking spaces slant close to the front door. Jackson Lee's office is painted in dark green and burgundy, his furniture big and masculine. Shelves line one wall all the way to the ceiling, holding law books, and behind his desk is another set of shelves with some glassed-in cabinets in the top middle. We sat in two of the plush chairs arranged in a half-circle in front of his desk.

After we'd discussed with Jackson Lee all the possibilities that might arise from our lunacy, and been given the bad news that participating Divas would have to come forward and answer police questions, I told him what Bitty had learned from the vet.

Jackson Lee sat back in his office chair and linked his hands together behind his head. He had his right ankle balanced on his left knee, but since he was dressed in nice pants and a button-down shirt, there was no danger of muddy boots. His cowboy boots were quite clean.

"Damn strange," he said after a moment. "Of course, that may well have nothing at all to do with Philip Hollandale. Once Sanders is found, a lot of this can be cleared up."

"What if he's never found?" I asked.

In the silence that followed my question, any hope I had that Sanders' disappearance may positively affect Bitty's situation faded. Finally, Jackson Lee leaned forward and smiled.

"Whether we ever see or hear from Sherman Sanders again, Bitty didn't murder Philip Hollandale and won't be convicted. Especially not in Marshall County."

That made sense. Bitty grew up here and remained here. She's deeply entrenched in the community. Even citizens who don't know her personally have heard of her, and while Bitty may be known as a little flaky at times, there's not a malicious bone in her body. Everybody knows that. So what Jackson Lee said made me feel a lot better.

Then Bitty ruined it.

"Well, everyone knows if anyone had a reason to kill him, I did, so I hope they don't hold that against me," she said, not looking up from wiping drool from Chen Ling's snout, or mouth, or whatever it's called. Cradled like a baby in her arms, having been removed from the sling, the dog lay back with half-closed eyes, paws dangling, underbite oozing saliva onto a tiny pink bib with BABY spelled out in embroidered blocks.

I closed my eyes. When I opened them, Bitty had looked up at Jackson Lee, her wide china blue eyes innocent of deception. Jackson Lee sighed. Then he smiled.

"That's not something you need to mention to anyone else, Bitty," he said. "Let me do all the talking right now. If anyone asks you questions or mentions anything about the case, tell them that your attorney won't allow you to discuss even the smallest detail. Think you can do that for me, sugar?"

Bitty smiled back. "Anything you say, Jackson Lee."

If I hadn't already been sitting down, I'd have had to look for a chair. Since she'd reached thirteen years old and found out she has a certain power over most males in her general vicinity, Bitty has never had the least inclination to give ground on anything. In fact, if a man so much as says red, then she'll say green just to tease him. What's always been the biggest mystery to me is that men can't get enough of it. It's my opinion that if Bitty had set her sights on Rhett Butler, she'd have given Scarlett O'Hara a run for her money. That would have been a dust-up I'd pay good money to see.

Jackson Lee walked us out to my car. He towered over Bitty, and I noticed the protective way he hovered around her. Bitty noticed that Chen Ling didn't like the baby sling.

"Here, precious," she said, fussing over the dog, "let me take you out of that ole thing."

When I looked up over her head at Jackson Lee, he was smiling down at Bitty like she'd been talking to him. He had an expression on his face that said she meant a lot more to him than just as a client. Then he glanced up, saw me looking at him, gave a somewhat sheepish grin, and shrugged. I nodded. Sometimes we just can't help who we find irresistible. There's not always a lot of rhyme or reason about it.

"So," Bitty said once we were safely in the car and Jackson Lee had gone back inside, "I think it's going to be so nice to go in to Memphis with you tomorrow. Do you want me to come to your house in the morning, or do y'all want to pick me up?"

"It'd be just as easy to pick you up since we'll be coming this way anyway and it's not so far out of the way. We'll pick you up at six-thirty."

Bitty sucked in a sharp breath. "Six-thirty! I thought they didn't have to check in for the cruise until eight-thirty. Memphis is only forty-five minutes from here."

"Barring rush hour traffic, eighteen-wheelers jack-knifed in the middle of the interstate, and Mama forgetting to pack something so we have to stop at a Walgreen's drug store. Besides, we have to go to downtown Memphis and find a parking place."

"It's probably just as well. An early start means more time in Memphis. Do you know if The Peabody allows any kind of animal other than ducks in the lobby?"

"We're not taking that dog with us, Bitty Hollandale."

"They must have some kind of accommodations for guests' pets."

"They do. Guests leave them at home or in kennels."

"Honestly, Trinket, when did you become anti-animals?"

"Don't be silly. I'm not anti-animals. I used to have dogs, remember? I just didn't wrap them up in baby blankets and bibs and pass them off as ugly infants."

Bitty brightened. "I hadn't even thought of that! You're absolutely brilliant."

Sometimes I feel like if I could just inhale deeply enough, the stupid things I say will be sucked back into my mouth and swallowed. However, since I haven't yet mastered that ability, I contented myself with, "If you insist on taking Chitling, we're giving up The Peabody."

"*Chen* Ling. And I've been to The Peabody before so it doesn't matter if I go again or not. I just want to get out of Holly Springs for a day. I want to go where no one knows me and won't be looking at me with one of those fake smiles and slopping sugar while they're really thinking I had something to do with Philip ending up dead in my cellar."

Technically, we all shared some blame for that, but since Bitty was already under enough stress, so much that she'd started carting around a dog I was nearly sure I'd seen in some movie about space aliens, I just said, "We'll be in Mama's car. It's bigger than mine."

"See you at six-thirty."

After I got home the day didn't much improve. That morning, I'd spent with Mama as she walked me through the schedule of cat-feeding and Brownie care. The evening I devoted to more of the same, but not quite as complicated. A chalkboard on the barn wall details which cat gets which medicine, and thankfully, said cats were in wire cages covered with plastic to prevent the spread of germs, but none of the patients were particularly appreciative of the medical efforts on their behalf. Daddy had welder's gloves draped on a shelf, and a six-inch plastic tube called a pill shooter, with which I could shoot a pill down the victim's—I mean patient's—throat. The trick is apparently getting the patient's mouth open. That morning it'd been easy enough, but that was because the cat had sunk its front teeth into my left thumb so I was able to wedge the pill shooter between the cat's teeth and my thumb, push the plunger, and when the cat choked, I extricated my bleeding digit. Very simple. Mama and Daddy have pill splitters, pill crushers, and pill shooters. Everything handy but a gun.

Don't get me wrong. I'm not anti-cat, either. I always had kittens when I was young, and as an adult, I had a cat that lived to be twenty and a half years old. Since she died, I've steadfastly refused to get another pet. It hurts too badly to lose them.

Anyway, we did another run-through before my parents trusted me with their care, and we went inside where Mama gave me another list of *Things To Do for Brownie*. My head started to whirl and a dull thud spread from behind my eyes to my temples. Brownie eats homemade dog food on top of his special dry dog food. Boiled chicken breasts and long-grain rice only. No salt, no preservatives, and only a little of the broth with *all* the fat strained and discarded.

"I froze a two-week supply," Mama said, and when I staggered at the implication, she smiled. "Just in case of the unexpected. He has digestive problems. And he'll eat around the pills if you don't watch him, so you can either dip it in plain no-fat yogurt for him or in the chicken broth, and if that doesn't work, use the pill shooter. He has his own right here in this basket. Oh, and don't let him eat anything he's not supposed to eat. It could kill him. He ate so many terrible things when he was young, hairbrushes, razor blades—half of your father's dental bridge once—I fear it's done a great deal of damage to his intestines and bowel."

When I glanced down at Brownie, he looked up at me with anxious eyes and drooping ears, one paw held up, the very picture of a pathetic sufferer. He reminded me of one of those old paintings people went crazy over back in the seventies, of big-eyed, soulful dogs, cats, and kids that made you cry just looking at them. But I know better.

This is the same dog I've seen leap four feet into the air to try and snag a bird winging past or a squirrel off a tree limb, and I'm not buying the pathetic pretense.

So I looked at the neat little plastic containers of Brownie's chicken and rice to go on top of his dry dog food—that can only be purchased at a vet's for three times as much as you'd pay for dog food in Wal-Mart—read the list of his medications, and was very glad I hadn't gotten a job yet. This was obviously going to take up all my time.

"And I'm sorry," Mama was saying, "but I just didn't have time to put you up some meals while I'm gone. There's meat and frozen dinners in the freezer, and cans of soup in the cabinet."

"I'll manage. If I get too hungry, maybe Brownie will share."

"Of course, he'll sleep with you at night. He likes to burrow under the covers. I've been told it's the dachshund in him. Apparently, the breed used to go into rabbit and weasel holes after their prey."

"Now, we might have a problem there. I don't want a dog on my sheets."

"Oh, he's clean. Besides, I usually just throw an old bedspread on top of our bed and he gets under that. I left a quilt in your room for him to use. Sometimes he likes to bunch it around him. Let's see, is there anything else I've forgotten to tell you?"

I waited patiently. I knew where keys were, had phone numbers, schedules, pharmacy and doctor numbers—"Which of the vets do you prefer?" I asked.

"Any of them at Willow Bend are wonderful, even that new vet. Quite a charming young man. Brownie took right to him."

I narrowed my eyes. Suspicion is an ugly thing, but it seemed there was some kind of conspiracy going on.

However, Mama didn't say anything else about the new vet, just gave me phone numbers of church ladies in her Sunday School class if I decided I needed prayers. Those would definitely come in handy.

Finally, there was nothing left to write down, remember, or show, and we all sat down to a light dinner of grilled cheese sandwiches and tomato soup. They'd be up at four, probably. I'd sleep until six if I used ear plugs.

A sense of energy bubbled in them, and they laughed about the least little thing, looked at the brochures of the Delta Queen and tried to figure out exactly where their stateroom would be by looking at the outside of the river boat. I sat and watched them for a while.

It's funny, but I felt like I used to feel on Christmas Eve. Not when I was a kid, but when my daughter was four and five, old enough to know about Santa Claus, and young enough to still believe. Her excitement, the sense of wonderment and magic, had always been in her eyes.

That wonder and magic sparkled in my parents' eyes right now.

"I won't be able to sleep a wink tonight," Mama said, and Daddy leaned close and said something in her ear I was glad I couldn't hear, and then they both laughed.

"If you two lovebirds are through with dinner," I said, getting up from the table and taking dishes to put in the dishwasher, "I'll clean up, then go upstairs. It's been a long day for me, and I think I'll read a little before I turn out the light."

I saw immediately my long explanation was completely

unnecessary. They hadn't heard a word. That made me smile. Crazy kids.

As I'd suspected, I woke up at five-fifteen and turned off my alarm clock. None was needed. Even upstairs, I could hear the excitement below. For one thing, Brownie had obviously seen the suitcases. He's not a completely stupid dog. In fact, he's quite the little survivor. From the time he showed up in an ice storm, looking pathetic and shivering, he'd insinuated himself into their lives and hearts quite firmly. And most of the time, I think he's really a sweet, cute creature. Except when he's constantly barking, as he does the minute he sees suitcases. He relates suitcases to people going away. For a dog, I think that's a pretty good connection. I've worked with hotel employees who wouldn't be able to figure that out. Bless their hearts.

"So," I said when I'd dressed and gone downstairs, raising my voice to be heard over the incessant barking, "is anyone ready to take a voyage on the Delta Queen?"

Mama just laughed, and Daddy grinned. They had on coordinating clothes again, Mama in sharply creased navy pants with a navy and yellow sweater over a white turtleneck, and Daddy in navy Dockers with a yellow shirt and navy sweater. Brownie wore a navy and yellow sweater on his indignant little body, barking furiously at the suitcases sitting in the hallway.

I rolled my eyes and reached for a bottle of aspirin Mama keeps over the sink. Three cups of coffee and a cinnamon roll later, I followed them out to the car. Daddy had gone out early to feed the cats so I wouldn't have to, and Mama fed Brownie and held him in her lap and stroked his head and told him she'd be back soon. Brownie whimpered, playing it up for all he was worth.

I felt like doing the same.

It was still early, but behind the morning fog, I saw the pale glimmer of sun that promised a nice day. Daddy opened the trunk of Mama's car to load suitcases, and saw the big basket of muffins and jellies from Sharita's I'd hidden in it. They were both delighted, as I'd known they would be.

Daddy stopped Mama's big 1995 Lincoln at the curb in front of Bitty's house. Just as I got out to go up to her door, it opened and out she came, wearing one of her elegant pantsuits and a matching fringed cape. She also wore a black canvas sling across her body.

"Did Bitty break her arm?" Mama asked, startled.

"Not yet," I replied, giving Bitty a fierce look she totally ignored.

"Aunt Anna, Uncle Eddie," Bitty said, sweeping toward us with a beaming smile, "aren't you both so excited? Going to New Orleans on a river boat—that's just so romantic!"

After the first bubbling minute or two, Bitty got into the car, and Daddy finally addressed the subject I knew he'd been dying to since she'd come waltzing down the sidewalk.

"Did you get a chimpanzee, Bitty?"

"Of course not, Eddie," Mama said, "It's one of those Star Wars dolls. A Wookie or Yodo or something. Isn't it?"

"It's a pug," Bitty said before they could offer another insulting guess. "A very expensive dog."

Mama squinted." It's alive?" She sounded doubtful and vaguely alarmed.

"Girl, someone saw you coming. Get your money back," Daddy advised.

"I didn't pay for Chen Ling. She belongs to someone else. I just borrowed her . . . I mean, I'm taking care of her for a few days."

"Come to think of it," Daddy said, glancing into the rearview mirror when he stopped at the corner, "it does look kind of like a chitling."

Until he said that, I hadn't realized just how much Daddy and I are alike at times.

"*Chen Ling* is her name." Bitty pulled the canvas edges of the sling back, and Mama, who had been looking over the back of the seat, made that sound people make when they see cute babies.

"Oh, just look at her! Why, Bitty, she's absolutely precious. Isn't she, Trinket?"

"Precious," I said. "Just precious." And actually, looking at her again, I have to admit it's the kind of face that really grows on you. There's something about those big eyes and nose like a closed accordion. Of course, the fact that she wore a bib, and Bitty had her in some kind of outfit that I swear looked like a ballerina's tutu, just made her look like a homely baby. On her own, she's quite cute. In an exotic, drooling kind of way.

Bitty beamed at the praise, and I realized she'd found another distraction. I envy her that ability. I really do. My solution to a problem is to lie awake at night worrying it to death. Then I resurrect it in the morning, chew it over, approach it from different angles, and if I'm lucky, find an answer before I expire from sleep deprivation.

Bitty pretends it doesn't exist. With other people, that solution would end in disaster. Not her. Most of the time, something happens to smooth out the difficulty, and she's happily on her way, unaware—or pretending to be—how close she came to utter catastrophe.

So by the time we got to the river bluffs in Memphis that morning, Bitty had talked about the dog, the approaching pilgrimage, how chunky Marilee Thompson was getting since she'd hit *that time of life*, and a buffet luncheon she's planning for April 1st. Daddy and I mostly stayed out of the conversation, he no doubt from abject boredom, and I in a sort of hypnotic trance at the amazing propensities of women in our family to completely ignore the unpleasant. My twin sister Emerald has successfully ignored the unpleasant all her life. Maybe I had been found under a cabbage leaf, after all.

The Delta Queen is one of those huge, gracious river boats that truly summons the flavor of an era gone by if you overlook all the modern conveniences. The closest I'd ever been to a river boat before was the mock-up of one at Mud Island, a nineteenth century reproduction of gamblers in string ties and jaunty bowlers, and elegant ladies in satins and silks. Mud Island is a spit of land just off the Wolf Harbor on the Memphis river bluffs, accessible by a tram. The name is inelegant, but the museum, and the reproduction of the Mississippi River all the way from its mouth near Canada to where it spills out into the Gulf of Mexico, is really nice. Kids love to walk in the flowing water that's ankle deep, and then say they've walked across the Mississippi River.

After verifying their tickets and checking luggage, the line that had formed at the gangplank to the huge paddle-wheeler began to embark. We were allowed to go with Mama and Daddy to look at their cabins since it was a chartered cruise and we're family. I have to say, I've rarely been so impressed with accommodations. Their stateroom had a window with white wooden shutters and stained glass over it, a very comfortable bed draped in what looked like an antique quilt, brass lamps with milk-glass shades, and a spacious bathroom.

I set the basket of muffins and jellies on the beautiful mahogany dresser placed against one wall as Mama went excitedly from one new discovery to the next. A brochure listing daily activities and points of interest where the river boat would be docking lay on a small silver tray next to the bed. Bitty read aloud, "'Relax in the cozy comfort of the Betty Blake lounge—' I wonder who she was? Anyway, it says you can sip tea in the Forward Cabin Lounge then join in rollicking fun—are you going to do that, Aunt Anna? Oh my! All their furnishings are antique." Bitty looked up at me with glittering eyes. "A vintage calliope in the Texas Stateroom."

"We have to stay home," I said, "and this is a chartered cruise."

"They're stopping in St. Francisville. Have you ever been to St. Francisville, Trinket? They have the most gorgeous old plantation homes, dripping in Spanish moss, filled with antiques . . . . "

Fortunately, the river boat gave a short blast of its whistle, and by the time I removed the brochure from Bitty's hand and got her and Chitling to the stateroom door, another blast or two had sounded. There was a flurry of kisses and well-wishes, a reminder to call me when they got to New Orleans, and I hustled Bitty out of their room and down the hallway to the exit.

"Lord, Trinket, stop pushing," Bitty said when we stood out on the old cobblestones made decades before the Civil War. "I'm going to drop Chen Ling."

"Chitling will bounce. Besides, she's in a sling and you've got a death grip on it."

We turned with our backs to the sun to wave at Mama and Daddy, who'd come out to stand at the rail and wave. Daddy had his arm around Mama, and they both looked so sweet and familiar and excited that tears came to my eyes. I sniffled. Bitty handed me a tissue, which was surprising since I'm usually the one prepared for such situations.

"They'll be back in a week," she said, and I nodded.

"I know. They just look so . . . happy."

"That's because they are. Now come on. I have no intention of standing out here on these uneven cobblestones in my heels. It's a wonder people don't break a leg on these things."

Once we were back in Mama's car, and Bitty had the dog out of the sling and seated on her lap where she could look out the window,

I said, "We can't take that dog into The Peabody."

"That's ridiculous. They already have ducks in the lobby. If they allow ducks, they should allow dogs."

"I suggest you take that up with the general manager. Unless the policy has changed since I was employed there, dogs are not allowed."

"Oh. Do you know I'd forgotten you used to work there, Trinket? That was what, back in the eighties?"

"Right after they reopened. Then a year or so later Perry got transferred and we moved to Jackson. And after that, we moved to North Carolina. And after that, we moved to Virginia. And after that, we moved to Arkansas. I think Idaho was next—or was it Oregon? I can't recall."

"Perry was a serial employee when you met him. You shouldn't have been so surprised that he didn't change after you got married."

I looked at her incredulously. "Are you giving me marriage advice?"

Bitty blinked in surprise. "No, not at all. Just making an observation. Oh honey, I didn't mean anything *mean* by saying that. In fact, I've always thought it a shame that you got married with blinders on."

"I'm not sure that explanation is an improvement," I said, but I knew what she meant. It's true. I was so gullible I didn't suspect a thing when I married a man with a great set of abs and the work ethic of a hobo. True to her nature, Bitty married expecting things to work out in the long run. And the odd thing is, they usually did. Maybe not the way she expected, but certainly in her favor.

"So what's with you and Jackson Lee?" I asked as I pulled out onto Riverside Drive and drove along the curving road built atop the lower bluffs. Expensive homes and apartments line the upper bluffs looking over the Mississippi River.

"Cybill Shepherd has a house right here somewhere," Bitty said, "and so does that man who was married to Liza Minnelli—I can't remember his name. Jackson Lee is my attorney, so what are you asking?"

"Cybill Shepherd's house is farther down, and David Gest was married to Liza Minnelli. I just think Jackson Lee is very nice, very smart, and very protective of you."

"He better be at five hundred dollars an hour. But he is a sweet ole thing, isn't he? Stayed with me until the police left, made sure all the doors were locked and I felt better, then I nearly had to push him out the door. Oh Lord—do you think he was on the clock all that time?"

Sometimes I could just shake Bitty. She can be so obtuse, that I have to wonder if it's not something she does on purpose.

"Probably not. I'd be surprised if you ever get a bill from him."

"Don't be silly, Trinket. I always get a nice bill from Brunetti and Brunetti. I think there's another name in there, maybe another Brunetti, but it's fairly new so I don't remember. Oh, this is Beale Street. Turn left."

Reluctantly, I turned left. Then I decided it'd be up to the management at The Peabody to inform Bitty that no animals are allowed in the lobby, and not to stress myself over it at all. Let her find out the hard way.

Of course, the lobby waitress who brought me a mimosa without the champagne and Bitty one with extra, thought Chen Ling was just "the cutest thing *ever*," and there shouldn't be any problem at all as long as that precious darling stayed in the sling and didn't chase the ducks once they came down to the fountain. I wanted to ask if that was current policy, but sipped my orange juice instead. There are times it's just best to let things go.

Even as early as it was, a little after nine-thirty, the lobby had quite a few people sitting in chairs or on couches positioned around marble top tables. At one end of the lobby is the five-star restaurant named Chez Philippe after the patriarch of the Memphis family who owns the hotel and quite a few other properties around town. At the other end, up marble steps, is another restaurant that serves a kind of blended cuisine, very modern and very delicious, with its own chef. Chez Philippe has a chef who's been there for years and is known worldwide for his dishes. Jose was there when I worked at The Peabody back in the mid-to late eighties.

The name Chez Philippe reminded me of Bitty's Philip.

"I don't suppose the results of the autopsy are out yet," I said as Bitty fed Chen Ling a piece of dog biscuit she'd apparently brought in her purse. She shook her head.

"I think they come in today or tomorrow, but I already know what killed him. General Grant. That statue is very heavy."

I frowned. Something still tickled the back of my overloaded brain. It had to do with General Grant, but what? And how could that possibly have anything to do with Philip's murder? Maybe everything that's happened is getting to me and I'm becoming unhinged, I thought. It was certainly a possibility.

"Did you know Sherman Sanders has a lost love?" I asked after a minute of brain strain produced no answer and Bitty began to look like she meant to take Chen Ling out of her sling.

Bitty looked up, mouth slightly open. "He *does?*"

I nodded. "Daddy told me. It's really a rather sad story."

"That may be where he is, then," Bitty said, sitting up a little straighter against the back of the upholstered loveseat we'd chosen. "He's gone to be with her—it is a her, right?"

"From what Daddy told me, I'm pretty sure. But I don't think he's gone to be with her, although I admit that's a possibility."

"Oh Trinket, not everyone gets as soured on love as you are just because things don't work out every time."

A little indignantly, I said, "It's not *that*. She lives in Japan. Or did right after the Second World War, anyway. Sanders was still enlisted in the service, and since some states had laws refusing to allow Japanese across their borders and he didn't know where the military might send him next, he had to leave her behind. At least, that's the way Daddy told it."

"Why, how tragic. There were laws like that? That's simply archaic."

"Yes, but if you put it in the context of the Patriot Act and today's fear of terrorists, it's a bit more understandable, I guess. A leap, but maybe understandable."

We both sat quietly and thought about that for a moment; then Bitty sighed and said, "I hope he comes back soon. Maybe he can explain how Philip ended up on The Cedars' floor with his head bashed in."

"It'd be nice."

At eleven each morning the Peabody ducks are brought down from the roof and Penthouse duck suite that had cost twenty-five thousand dollars back in 1982. They march across red carpet that leads from the elevator to the marble fountain in the center of the lobby. A Duck Master ambles along behind them, carrying a long stick just to guide the mallards along should they decide to stray. Heaps of corn are positioned on ledge corners in the middle of the fountain, and John Philip Sousa's march plays on speakers as tourists crowd around with cameras to take pictures. The ducks seem to take it all in stride, tourists are delighted, and the hotel gift shop sells dozens of duck-related items from shoehorns to mallard telephones. I still miss the original Duck Master, Edward Pembroke, a former circus roustabout and acknowledged attraction in his own right. On any given day, Mr. Pembroke was liable to say almost anything. He'd been quite a hit on *The Tonight Show*. I've always wished I'd spent more time talking with the elderly gentleman, as his life story was more interesting than anything I'd ever heard then or since. A real piece of not only Memphis history, but human history. I hope he somehow knows that he is irreplaceable.

Anyway, right after the ducks marched, so did we. Bitty had insisted on valet parking as the bright morning sunlight might hurt little Chen Ling's eyes, so I let her pay for it. We always go Dutch even though Bitty sometimes grumbles that she can afford it better than I can. She's right, but there's a certain sense of failure and embarrassment that I'm this old and have no more money put back than I do.

That led me to wonder how Sherman Sanders paid for the upkeep on The Cedars, since I know firsthand what it costs to pay for old houses' tendency to need frequent, and often costly, repairs. How had he sustained it? Family money had long since dwindled, if rumor was correct.

"I don't remember if I ever knew Sanders had a job of any kind," I said once we were on the I-55 interstate and heading toward I-240 and the exit of 78 Highway. "Did he?"

"Not that I know about. He did some farming, leased out some pastures, cut hay and let people come buy it, but that doesn't sound like a lot of money, does it."

"Not enough to keep up an old house as well as he has," I mused. "Although if he took care of the small problems before they became big ones, that wouldn't cost as much."

"Maybe that explains why his front yard has always looked like a hog wallow. He used to have goats, but I don't know if he has any now. Just that mule."

"And Tuck," I murmured, thinking how isolated he was from society.

"You're feeling sorry for that old man, aren't you," Bitty said. "He may be a murderer, you know."

"I know."

"Of course, if he murdered Philip he deserves a medal for it. That man was a boil on the backside of humanity."

"I know," I said again. Bitty was wrong about me feeling sorry for Sanders. He'd chosen to live as he did. I had more of a pragmatic view of the entire situation. How did he afford to live on so little money? I wanted to know his secret. It may come in quite handy. Maybe he dabbled in stocks. That's too risky for me. Most people don't have enough reverence for others' money.

"Mrs. Hollandale called me last night," Bitty said then, and I gave her a startled look. A smile of satisfaction curved Bitty's mouth, so I knew that her ex-mother-in-law must have gotten as good as she'd probably given. "I let her go on for a few minutes, you know, since she is his mama, and even if he was a rotten sonuvabitch and a pervert, she loved him. But after a little while, I got tired of listening to her rant about how I'd ruined him financially and tried to ruin his career, and so I told her a few things about her son that I've wanted to say for years."

"You didn't!"

"I did. Before I got to the part about incest and how she might want to talk to her daughter about a few things, she hung up on me. A pity. Maybe when I see her at the funeral I'll suggest she go on TV and talk to Dr Phil. Or Jerry Springer."

"You intend to go to the funeral?" I was both appalled and awed.

"I've already called Tina over at the Dress Barn and she's ordered my outfit. Black silk, with tiny seed pearl buttons, and the cutest little hat with delicate wisps of net and more pearls. I should look quite respectable, a nice balance between grief—which would be too obvious since everyone in Marshall County and probably the entire state of Mississippi has to know how much I wanted that man dead—and formal regret that a United States senator has passed."

"Bitty, you have to stop saying things like that."

"Like what?"

"That you wanted Philip dead. Remember what Jackson Lee told you, to just let him do the talking."

"That really is convenient, don't you think? I can just sigh and look away and say, 'I'm afraid my attorney has asked me not to comment' when people bring it up, and then they can go on thinking whatever it is they wanted to think in the first place anyway, but they won't be sure. I just love that."

"You do know I won't attend his funeral," I said.

"Of course you will, Trinket. It wouldn't look right if you didn't. He was family."

"Since Miss Manners advises against brawls with the bereaved, I'll follow her suggestion. It seems best."

"Miss Manners," Bitty sniffed. "What does she know? She's probably a Yankee anyway."

"Unless etiquette rules have changed a lot since I've been gone from Holly Springs, I don't think I recall brawling as an acceptable part of Southern funerals."

"Then obviously, you haven't been to very many funerals. Good Lord, Trinket, don't you remember my Uncle Fred on Mama's side? We may have only been eleven, but you can't have forgotten *his* funeral. Aunt Lilly took a swing at Karleen Shepherd, who'd been sneaking around with Uncle Fred, then Karleen's brother Sid hit our cousin Jerry and knocked him down into the open grave, and the preacher from the Red Banks Baptist Church fell in on top of him trying to get out of the way. You can't tell me you've forgotten that!"

"Mama took me and Emerald to the car," I said, "but I do remember people with torn clothes and bruises coming to the house afterward to eat. And red dirt smeared everywhere."

"I had a ringside seat, up on Uncle Fred's coffin where Daddy put me so I didn't get hit and get dirt all over my pretty new dress. Anyway, that's a funeral I don't think I'll ever forget. Or all those grieving kinfolks taking swings at each other."

"That kind of grief isn't usually expressed until the reading of the will," I commented, and we both started laughing.

Maybe going to Philip's funeral wasn't such a bad idea after all. While I certainly didn't want to be witness to a brawl like at Uncle Fred's funeral, whoever had killed Philip might just be among the mourners.

CHAPTER 11

Those first hours in the house by myself felt not only odd, but blessedly peaceful. After dropping Bitty off at her house and suggesting she take Chen Ling back to Luann Carey before she got too attached, I returned to Cherryhill and parked Mama's Lincoln in the garage, went inside, took off my nice slacks and sweater, put on a sweat shirt and pair of old jogging pants that I'd used when painting walls, and let the comfortable silence close around me.

Sunlight seeped through tall windows to warm the rooms, just as it had when I was a little girl and played with the dust motes. Now, while I might be thinking about having to dust those motes off furniture, I still enjoy soaking up the light.

Brownie followed me around, looking lost. I tried to get him to go outside, but he stood in the open doorway peering into the yard and refused to move. When I tried to make him, he curled back his upper lip in a snarl. I let it go. For now.

"Experts say," I promised him when he followed me upstairs to my room, "that dogs don't have any concept of time. It doesn't matter if Mama is gone an hour or a month, you won't know the difference. Be glad. It has to be one of Mother Nature's compensations for being unable to make your own peanut butter and jelly sandwiches."

Tilting his head from one side to the other, he looked at me like he understood every word, but I knew that was just my imagination. I'd said some unkind things in the past that he'd no doubt still remember, if that were true.

I retrieved my book off the night stand where I'd left it the night before, and put the pair of emerald earrings I'd worn to Memphis into a little crystal jar with my watch, a habit I'd begun years ago. Brownie went back downstairs with me, and cuddled up next to me on the couch while I read a book and he fell asleep with his head nestled against my hip. The grandfather clock in the hallway ticked softly, marked the half hours with a deep-throated *bong*, and squares of sunlight moved slowly across the warm beige carpet. After the frenzied hours of the past week, the total peace closed around me like a security blanket.

Something woke me, and I opened my eyes, blinking. I sat up slowly, and wiped a thin line of drool off my chin. Sunlight squares had changed to dim rectangles and a fuzzy glow. I hadn't meant to fall asleep. I've never been a person who takes naps. Usually I feel worse when I wake up than I did before I fell asleep. Maybe because of the weird dreams I have in the daytime.

When I stood up, Brownie appeared at my feet from wherever he'd been in the house. He wagged his tail expectantly, and I yawned and went to get a glass of Coke, then I put on the thick rubber yard boots kept on the back deck to perform the afternoon ritual of cat medicating and feeding. Brownie was quite happy to help me by scattering birds pecking around Mama's feeders and keeping sinister squirrels at a distance.

Everyone has their own routine and way of doing things, but I've always thought it more efficient if Mama and Daddy would feed the loose cats before medicating those inside the barn. That way, the cats would be gathered around the pans of food outside, unless there's inclement weather, and the sick cats would be more eager for their food and less likely to resist medication.

Remind me never to apply for a position as an efficiency expert.

Caged cats tend to be cranky when other cats are eating within eyesight or smelling distance and some person is trying to poke pills or squeeze liquid down their throats. Even with the welder's glove, which is bulky and clumsy, it's really hard holding on to a struggling cat and using the plastic pill shooter at the same time. By the time I got to the third cage and last patient, sweat had made my hair wet and my antiperspirant had stopped working. My underarms were uncomfortably damp.

"Come on," I coaxed out loud while inside I was screeching *Take the damn pill!* "Just open a little bit wider and it'll all be over."

The cat, a fat orange and white male with malevolently narrowed gold eyes, hissed so loud and hard that globs of spit sprayed my face. That's when I jammed the pill shooter down his throat, hit the plunger, and injected a small tablet almost all the way out his other end. About that time, Brownie, still on his mission of clearing the area of terrorist squirrels, chased one into the barn. Baying like the hound of the Baskervilles and stretched out in a dead run, the dog passed me long before I saw the squirrel a good ten yards ahead of him. The cat hacked up the pill that shot at me like a missile, used the welder's glove as a launching pad, and flew over my shoulder and up into the air where he landed a good six feet behind me.

I turned just in time to see an orange tail streak up into the hayloft. Hayloft is more of a reminiscent name for it. What's in the hayloft now is just remnants of molded straw. And probably thriving mice colonies. Maybe even rats. I don't like rats. I briefly debated, sighed, and reluctantly pursued the escapee. A broken promise to my mother just isn't something I want to contemplate.

Distracted by this new prey, Brownie had already climbed halfway up the ladder to the loft by the time I got there. I pulled him down and told him to *Sit* without a hope he'd listen, then went up after the cat.

What happened in the loft, shall stay in the loft. Suffice it to say I triumphed, though only because the cat boxed himself into a corner and the welder's gloves held up.

I deposited the cat back into his cage, gave him another pill, then fed him, cleaned three cages and litter boxes, and wobbled toward the open barn door. Several empty tin bowls and no cats waited for me. Brownie had disappeared. I'm sure I saw the squirrel he'd been chasing up in an oak tree eating dry cat food. He seemed to be laughing, but I'm not so sure about that.

"Brownie," I called after I'd washed out and put away tin bowls and refilled water tubs.

No dog. No bark. Light deepened into purple shadows. They settled around the house and barn, and the air turned brisk. I walked around to the front of the house where dogwood trees had buds and daffodils were already opening. Probably a half acre stretched between the house and the street. It sloped gently downward, ending in a drainage ditch Marshall County had put in back when the subdivision down the road was being built. White river rocks lining the ditch gleamed in the dusk.

There was no sign of Brownie, and I had a moment of panic. Stories of dogs traveling great distances to find their owners flashed through my mind. Not that I think Brownie is smart enough to do that, but he is dumb enough to try. I walked up and down the road, peered into thickets of blackberry bushes, wild plum, and river willows growing in the wet land along the drainage ditch, calling him until I was hoarse. Now, this is a dog that can be heard over three counties when he sets up a howl. Just how far away could he have gotten in such a short time?

Weary, discouraged, and more than a little upset, I finally went back to the house. I'd call Bitty and ask if Mama had ever mentioned the dog doing this before, and if so, where Mama had found him. Other than that, I didn't have a clue what to do. There's no Amber Alert for dogs, and the alarm for lost or stolen children has only been in use here a short time anyway.

When I got to the back deck and the dark top step, I tripped over a furry rug that I didn't remember ever being there before. The rug yelped loudly. I hit the wood deck with both palms out flat, fortunately missing the sleepy rug.

"Damn you, Brownie," I said more calmly than I felt, relief that he wasn't lost or on some canine excursion obliterating my anger that he'd been napping while I'd been in blackberry bushes.

We both went into the kitchen. I turned on a light and plopped down in a chair to look at Brownie. He stared expectantly at the refrigerator.

"I suppose you think you deserve your supper after all the trouble you caused?" I said, but since it was a rhetorical question anyway, I got up and prepared his food by the directions Mama had printed out from her computer and left taped to a cabinet door.

While Brownie ate chicken and rice warmed in the microwave, I made myself a peanut butter and jelly sandwich. I poured a glass of milk, got out some chips, and put it all on a plate. Just as I sat down with it, Brownie came up to me, nudged my knee, and threw up on my bare foot. For a moment, I just sat there, thinking more fondly of my ex-husband and my last job. I'd hated working in the personnel department of a motel chain for little more than minimum wage, but it began to look better every minute. Then I remembered my parents' faces while they stood there at the river boat rail, and I sighed, got up, threw away my sandwich, and reached for some paper towels.

I cleaned my foot and jogging pants first, and then knelt to wipe up chicken, rice, and expensive dog food from the kitchen floor. Something hard was in the middle of the soft goo. I debated looking, and then decided it might be best.

A glint of green shone under slimy stuff. I used the edge of a paper towel to clear away goo and saw my emerald earring. For a minute I just stared at it, uncomprehending. Then it hit me, my mother's warning about Brownie's unusual taste for inedible objects. Brownie sat nearby watching me with great interest.

"Aren't there two of these?" I asked him, knowing he would only lie even if he could tell me. I hurried up and wiped the floor clean, dropped my soiled earring into a paper cup, then flew upstairs to check my crystal jar.

It'd been pulled off the night stand, and lay empty. My heart nearly stopped. My emerald earrings my daughter had given me four years before at Christmas. My watch. Gone. No sign of them. I lay flat on my stomach and searched under the bed with a flashlight, and found my watch up against the wall. There was no sign of my other earring.

Brownie had come upstairs with me, and now he eyed the watch I'd put on the bed. Then he coughed, a choking, sputtering sound, followed by a long moan.

"Damn," I muttered, a word I seemed to be using more frequently lately, "I've got to call the vet."

It was near seven and the vet's office closed at six-thirty, but I tried anyway. On the fourth ring, a man answered. Before he finished saying "Willow Bend Animal Clinic" I blurted out, "My dog ate my earrings. What do I need to do?"

He asked the size of the dog, the size of the earrings, then my name. When I said Truevine he immediately said, "Ah, Brownie. You'd better bring him in, I'm afraid. Just to be sure. I'll wait for you."

"I'm on my way."

I hung up the phone, glared at the dog still looking greedily at my jewelry jar, and stuck my bare feet into a pair of untied Keds.

All the way to the vet's clinic on Highway 4, I thought about having to explain to my mother that the very first night she was gone I'd let her dog kill himself. It wasn't something I wanted to ever do. And besides, now Brownie leaned up against me with his ears drooping, his eyes all big and sorrowful, and his muzzle resting on my right arm. Every once in a while he'd let out a soft groan. I'd imagine the sharp post of the solid gold earring piercing his intestine, and then I'd press harder on the accelerator. I got there in less than fifteen minutes, which I thought was pretty good.

A light was on inside the clinic, and I slammed my car into gear, cut it off, cradled the dog in my arms, and nearly ran down the slightly sloping concrete walk to the front door. A young girl met me and immediately led me to an examining room just off the main waiting room.

"The doctor will be right in," she said, and stroked Brownie's ears back. "Poor Brownie, you sweet thing. We'll take good care of you like always."

Brownie groaned pitifully. His eyes half-closed, he gave a feeble thump of his tail against the cold steel table top, and quivered so hard I heard his teeth clack together. I focused on him with something like panic. How could this have happened? What was the matter with me, that I couldn't even care properly for a dog? I should have put my jewelry up higher. It wasn't like I hadn't been warned.

The other door opened, and a man in a white coat open over a pale blue shirt and faded Levi's stepped in briskly. He wore one of those masks doctors wear that cover their lower face.

"What'd you do, boy?" he asked, his voice gentle yet reassuring as he took Brownie's muzzle in one palm while his other hand moved over the abdomen. Brownie licked the heel of his hand, a lethargic stroke that alarmed me.

"Is he dying?" I asked, and couldn't help the emotion that clogged my throat.

"Oh, I doubt it. Not from a little old earring. If it was the Hope Diamond, or dental work again, it'd be a lot worse. We're going to take him back here and run an X-ray just to be sure. It depends on where it is as to whether you'll need to leave him with us." He lifted the dog and put him into the assistant's arms, then pulled the mask down from his face to let it rest around his neck.

When he looked up at me, I knew immediately this had to be Dr. Coltrane. Unless there were two drop-dead gorgeous vets working in the same clinic. The odds of that are astronomical, but not impossible.

And, stupidly, I immediately became aware of my sweatshirt, paint-stained jogging pants, and untied Keds with no socks. Not to mention, my hair probably looked like hell.

"Now, I know you're not the Mrs. Truevine I usually see in here," he said.

"I'm her daughter. They've gone on a short vacation. I was supposed to be taking care of their animals, but obviously, I'm not doing that good a job of it."

He grinned, and I noticed the way it reached his eyes, dark brown eyes with faint laugh-lines at the corners. Dark brown hair streaked with gray at the temples, a little more lightly in the rest of it, feathered over his forehead in a tousled look that was probably usually neatly combed. He had at least a good six inches of height on me, but I'm willing to bet we're pretty close weight-wise. I have big bones. Really.

"Brownie is one of those dogs that have a way of finding things that aren't good for him," he said. "Most dogs just don't usually eat metal."

"It's my opinion he's part goat," I said, and the grin widened.

"I wouldn't doubt it. Since we haven't been introduced, I'm Dr. Coltrane."

We shook hands, then he said he'd go back and help with the X-rays and I should make myself comfortable out in the waiting room if I liked. I wandered out there, flipped through some magazines, then glanced up at a mirror hanging on the wall and nearly had a stroke.

Good Lord! My hair looked like frayed electrical wire sticking straight out, my mascara of earlier smudged under my eyes raccoon-style, and I had a grape jelly smear on one cheek that defied logistical explanation. Cat spit stiffened one side of my hair, and I found the ejected pill stuck above my right ear. Stunned, I could only stare at my reflection. No wonder the vet had been grinning. He'd probably had to go into the back room to collapse in hysterical laughter.

Now, I'm not usually a vain woman. But neither do I want to leave the house looking like the village idiot. When I heard footsteps, I searched frantically around the waiting room for an empty grocery bag to pull over my head. Plastic would be best, especially if I took deep breaths.

Dr. Coltrane carried Brownie in his arms. The dog looked up at him adoringly, floppy ears flat against his head in an attitude of submissive joy.

"Did you have to sedate him?" I asked.

"Oh no. Brownie's a good boy, aren't you, fella."

In what alternate universe, I thought, but mindful of my frightening appearance, decided not to reinforce the impression of village idiot. It wasn't that I wanted to impress an admittedly handsome man; it's just that I didn't want my parents to have to deal with whispers of inherited insanity. Honest.

"So how is he?" I asked. "Did you find the earring?"

"Afraid not. I've given him some Metamucil with an antibiotic, and Tiffany is making up some more for you to take home. If he did swallow it, the earring should pass naturally in a day or two, but if he has any problems bring him back in."

"By 'pass naturally' you mean . . . . "

"In his stools, yes. That shouldn't be a problem. Put him on a leash when it's time for his regular movement. If you notice any blood, call me immediately. Tiffany will give you my card with my home number on it as well, should it happen after hours. I'll carry him out for you."

"Shouldn't I pay the bill first?"

"Don't worry about that. Mrs. Truevine is a regular client and we have all her information if we need it."

Great. My mother has a vet on retainer. My cousin has a lawyer on retainer. And I need a psychologist on retainer. Is it psychologist or psychiatrist? I get those two confused. Not that it matters. I probably need both.

"Thank you," I said with as much dignity as I could muster when discussing dog poop with a handsome stranger. "I appreciate this very much."

"No problem. Brownie's one of our favorites."

And I bet you say that to all the clients.

I used my remote to unlock car doors, opened the passenger side for Dr. Coltrane to set Brownie inside on the front seat, and then bent to move my purse to the floor. When I straightened, Dr. Coltrane leaned closer to me. Startled, I stood there only six inches from him, inhaling an exotic mix of rubbing alcohol and shaving lotion while my heart lurched into double time and my stomach did a weird flip. My lips parted, and what little oxygen was left got stuck in my lungs as he reached out, put his hand behind my head, and leaned in to kiss me. I swayed toward him.

He put a hand on my arm to steady me, and pulled something from the hair at the back of my head. When he held it up I blinked, then recognized a wad of molded straw.

"I hope you're not feeding this to horses or cows," he said, and I shook my head while I tried to find a hole in the asphalt that'd swallow a five-foot-nine-inch fool.

Since there was no available sink hole, I said, "It must have come from the hayloft. Old barn. Used just by cats now." Was that my voice? I sounded like a Munchkin.

I think he said something like "That's good," but about that time Tiffany showed up with the Metamucil in a little plastic bag and I grabbed it and mumbled that I had to get back home, thanked the empty space right beside Dr. Coltrane for his care, then went around to the driver's side and got into my car. I remember nothing about the drive home except that my face felt hot enough to fry eggs all the way down 311. Oh yes. And that I intended to scream vile invectives at Bitty for ever mentioning the vet to me, or anything at all about orgasms I've never had.

After I got inside, locked the door, and gave Brownie a scathing look he never noticed, I stalked directly to the cordless phone and dialed Bitty.

"Oh Trinket," she said when she heard my voice, "I'm so glad you called. I've thought—"

"If you *ever*," I broke in, my voice low and shaking, "mention anything at all to me about not having an orgasm, or not wanting a man, or should be wanting a man, I will take you out in the middle of court square at noon and tell everyone who walks past that you got so drunk at your wedding reception with Franklin Kirby that you peed in your Evan Picone pantyhose."

Dead silence fell. I heard something humming that could have been Bitty's brain trying to figure out if she should push me on that or not, but it was probably just static on the line.

"All right," she finally said. "No orgasm talk. No man talk. Not unless you start it first."

Since I figured donkeys would fly before that day ever came, I said, "Fine."

After a brief moment, she said, "I don't suppose you want to tell me what happened."

"You're right. I don't."

Ever flexible, Bitty said, "As I was saying before being interrupted, I've thought of an excellent plan."

"I don't want to hear it."

"You're just in a pissy mood. You're going to like this. It involves two of our favorite things."

That would be chocolate and champagne. My interest was piqued. "Go on."

"Dr. Johnston—he's the new podiatrist that bought the Easthaven House—is giving an early St. Patrick's Day party and I thought if you and I dressed up really nice—"

"Bitty, I just warned you—"

"Don't get all bent out of shape, Trinket. I'm not matchmaking. If anything, I've got my eye on the doctor. Just think of the wonderful foot massages I'll get. Anyway, I'm sure we'll be invited, and many of the people already on the guest list are former acquaintances or business associates of Philip. If we pay attention, we might hear something that'd relate to Philip and Sanders. What do you think?"

It'd been a long day. I'd gone up and down the spectrum of emotions, hitting all of them pretty strongly. Even so, it sounded like a good idea.

"I'm sure I'll be sorry," I said, "but it does sound like a good idea."

"I just knew you'd think so," Bitty said enthusiastically. "And since I already accepted invitations for both of us, I'm so glad I went ahead and talked to you about it."

"As opposed to showing up at my door and abducting me?"

"Be fair, Trinket. I only did that once, and it was a long time ago."

"I was in my pajamas at a party where everyone else was wearing clothes!"

"If I'd known you hadn't *meant* to dress like that, I'd have said something. It was a Come As You Are party. I thought you knew that."

"And if I'd known that, of course I would have worn my ratty old teddy bear pajamas with the big rip in the rear seam where everyone could—and did—see my panties."

"Honestly, sometimes you have the longest memory for the worst things."

"That's so history won't repeat itself."

Bitty sighed. "Anyway, it'll be a chance to see Easthaven since the doctor bought it, to see if he's done anything new. He's very nice, and cute, in a rough, dangerous sort of way."

"A dangerously rough podiatrist? That has to be a professional drawback."

"Well, it's only a tattoo, and I only saw it once, when he'd rolled up his sleeves to wash his hands before examining my feet."

"Bitty Hollandale, you have no shame. There's not a thing wrong with your feet."

"Well, I know that *now*."

I rolled my eyes. No point in trying to shame Bitty. It was too exhausting and very nearly impossible.

"I'm tired and I'm going to bed, Bitty," I said. "It's been a stressful day."

"Oh honey, I never thought of you still worrying about Aunt Anna and Uncle Eddie. You know they'll be just fine. You should have come home and taken a nap, rested up, got your mind off it by walking the dog or something."

"Yes," I said, thinking of the past two hours, "That's exactly what I should have done."

When we hung up, I looked over at Brownie sitting on the couch beside me, and I set the cordless phone down on the end table. He looked so sweet and harmless lying there. But I knew the truth.

"Come on, you little fraud," I said, "it's bedtime. And I hope you don't wake me up in the middle of the night with a Metamucil meltdown."

You'd think after the day I'd had, sleep would be instant and deep, but I tossed and turned most of the night. It could have been because I wasn't used to sharing my bed with a dog rolled up in a blanket like an enchilada, but that was only part of it. Brownie, I'm happy to say, slept through the night with no digestive emergencies.

Of course, I'd put up all jewelry, small metal objects, hairbrushes, and safety razors just in case he decided to have a midnight snack.

It was the murder and the missing Sanders that kept me awake. Most of the time. Other thoughts kept trying to sneak in, but I did a pretty good job of keeping them at bay. Still, right before I finally fell asleep, I had a brief flashback to the veterinary clinic and Dr. Coltrane. With any luck, I'd never see him again.

*

"You look a little tired, Trinket," Bitty said, "are you getting enough sleep?"

We sat in Budgie's having coffee and blueberry cobbler. Bitty was armed with a pug, so we had to sit over in the smoking section that consisted of a metal screen and two tables. No one ever sat there. They smoked wherever they liked.

"It's not the sleep, though more would help." I pushed around a piece of crust and three blueberries left on my plate. Maybe I should start a diet. I already had to shop in the Tall section for clothes. Did I really want to shop in the Big and Tall section?

Bitty sighed. "I know. It's all this worrying about the pilgrimage. I just wish Sanders had waited until he signed those papers before killing Philip and running off."

I looked up at her. She was feeding Chitling a piece of pastry crust. The dog made sounds similar to those of a pig sniffing out truffles, but finally decided the crust was safe to eat.

"Bitty, do you *ever* think about the possibility of being convicted of murder?"

"Not really. Jackson Lee told me to let him think about that, so I do. Isn't that right, you precious thing?"

The last was directed to the dog, of course.

"When are you taking that dog back to Luann Carey?"

"Soon. I talked to her this morning. She called to check up on Chen Ling, make sure she's been eating right and taking her medicine. Luann's very particular about who she lets take one of her dogs, you know. That girl will stand up to a two hundred pound man and give him what-for if she even thinks for a minute that any dog is being mistreated. I've seen her do it. Riley Simpson did, too. He kicked a skinny stray one day over by Phillips' and Luann nearly took his head off. First time I've ever seen a two hundred pound man cower and run."

"That can't be true. Your second husband used to cower and run all the time."

Bitty made a piffling sound. "That man couldn't run. He got too fat to hardly walk. Only five-seven, and two-hundred-sixty-five pounds. It was like sleeping with Namu. Nemo? You know, the whale. And forget sex, unless I wanted to climb on top, but that was like riding a big old beach ball with a tiny little knob sticking up. Sometimes I had to turn on the light to find it."

"Keep talking like that and I'll lose my cobbler."

"It does conjure up some awful images, doesn't it?" Bitty looked up at me and smiled. "I still wouldn't have divorced him if he hadn't been so mean when he got sloshed. Bourbon seems to do that to some men. Makes their weenies limp, too. Try doing anything with *that*."

I remembered Delbert Anderson quite differently, but of course, I hadn't been married to him or even lived in Holly Springs during that marriage. There had been enough witnesses to attest to the fact that Del tended to get loud and boisterous when drunk, and also tended to lash out at whoever came within range. I understand there were photos of Bitty with black eyes and blue bruises. She got quite a nice settlement out of that divorce not to make a big fuss about it, and Del Anderson took what was left of his inheritance and skulked back to Sunflower County.

Desperate to change the subject, I said, "What are you wearing to the St. Patrick's Day party?"

"Something green, of course, though that really isn't my color. It's more yours. I've got a floaty little dress that's rose-colored, but it does have tiny green jewels that swirl up and over one shoulder, then down the back and on the skirt. That'll do, don't you think?"

I agreed, and when Bitty asked what I was wearing, I had to think. I have lots of pants and sweaters, blouses and jackets that are very nice, but my supply of party clothes is limited to a sheer bronze blouse worn with my black chiffon pants, or worn with my black chiffon skirt.

"Something green, of course," I finally said. "I'll put a ribbon in my hair."

Bitty looked at me. "You don't have anything to wear, do you. Well, that's just not right. Come on. We'll go right over to the Dress Barn and find something for you. Tina is excellent. I don't know why she has that horrid name for her shop, when she has all those beautiful clothes made by Versace and Wang and Chanel in the back room. But then, I think the name was already there when she bought it, so she just left it. People get accustomed to things, you know, and change is always risky."

Despite my protests, we ended up at the Dress Barn, where Tina, obviously a fashion maven, sized me up, measured me, clacked through a row of clothes hanging on a rack inside a closet that'd survive Armageddon, and pulled out a gorgeous dress that took my breath away. Not so much because it was absolutely stunning, but because the price tag was more than I'd made a month in my last job.

"Nonsense," Tina said when I made a choking sound and backed away, "you're very well proportioned. This will be lovely on you."

I looked at her. Well-proportioned must have a new definition in the clothing industry than it does in fashion magazines and doctors' offices. Granted, I have a nice-sized chest, but that's just to balance out my generous hips and thighs so I won't spin hopelessly around on my ample rear like one of those Weebles my daughter played with as a child. You know, a plastic toy person or animal shaped like an egg that never turns over because it's bottom heavy. That's me.

Before I knew quite how to get out a word since my lungs were depleted of air just looking at the price tag, Tina and Bitty had me stripped down to my cotton Hanes and sensible bra and poured into the dress. They stood me in front of a three-way mirror so my humiliation could be tripled, told me to open my eyes and stop being so silly, and then Tina—who's much taller than Bitty and can manage it—pulled my hair up off my neck.

"So you can see the lovely way it drapes over your shoulders," she explained. "Of course, you'll wear a different bra with this. Or none at all."

Already lightheaded from lack of oxygen, I nearly passed out at that last thought, so to shock myself back to consciousness, I looked in the mirror.

Was that *me*? A dark green thin velvet draped over my body down to my knees, where it flared out just a little bit in one of those diagonal hemlines that dip lower on one side than the other. The neckline scooped into a soft vee shape, it had long fitted sleeves, and designs in pale green swirled from one shoulder to waist and down one thigh to the knee. Somehow, it had the effect of being slimming while accenting my bosom and minimizing my thighs and hips. It's amazing the deceptive packaging men can create and women can wear.

Bitty laughed. "She's speechless. We'll take it."

"I love it," I said, "but we won't take it. I'd have to cash in my 401K."

"Your birthday is in a few months. Consider this a gift," Bitty said.

"No," I said. "It's too much. We don't exchange gifts anymore, remember? We stopped doing that years ago."

"Then it's my treat. Consider it payment for all I've put you through lately."

Tina wisely remained silent and didn't offer any comments, though everyone in Holly Springs and Marshall County would know what Bitty meant by that.

"Payment is a free lunch, not a two thousand dollar dress, Bitty."

"Now you listen to me, Trinket, in the first place, I get a hefty discount here, and in the second place, I don't want you showing up at the party looking like Orphan Annie. It's rude. And I have the money and want to do this, and you know one of the cardinal rules of courtesy is that one must know how to politely accept a gift."

"But this is too much, Bitty."

"Good Lord, Trinket, it's not like I'm buying you Montrose or anything. Take the damn dress!"

"Fine. But I'm buying the shoes."

Bitty smiled. See what I mean about her always getting her way?

CHAPTER 12

So there I was, two nights before Mama and Daddy got back from their cruise, decked out in a dress Joan Collins would love, complete with my emerald necklace that matches my emerald earring—the last in the singular, since Brownie either never passed the other earring or it's still well-hidden for later consumption—and my new shoes, strappy, short-heeled sandals in a lovely warm gold that Bitty finally approved after accepting the fact I was not going to pay six hundred dollars for the shoes she wanted me to buy. We'd had to drive all the way to Memphis for them anyway, and I'd had enough of shopping with Bitty by then, as I think she had of me.

The night of the party, I met Bitty at her house, and instead of her sporty little Miata, we got into the larger black Mercedes she usually keeps in the garage for such occasions. It's part of the settlement from her third husband, Franklin Kirby III. If Bitty had a vehicle to signify every divorce, her house would soon look like an Import dealer's car lot.

Truth be told, I was a little nervous about going to this party. It wasn't so much that I was shy or anything about meeting new people and seeing old acquaintances, or even that I felt like a complete fraud in a dress with a price higher than a cat's back, but I've just never really been one for socializing with people who earn more in an hour than I do in a month. It's the opposite of being a snob, I suppose. It's not like I have an inferiority complex or anything, but what on earth can people from two such opposite poles have in common to discuss? The TV season getting shorter every year? Politics and religion are two definite no-nos. Not that I'm not fairly well-versed in such subjects, but it's certain death to the festive mood of a party if guests begin to scream and sling canapés at each other.

Bitty, whose childhood was very different than mine because her mama came from an old money family, and her daddy went into their family business and made scads of money, was at home with these people. Not me. We weren't poor, but neither did we always have new cars and trips to Europe. Or even ponies.

Anyway, my stomach was jittery and I hoped I was more composed than I looked when we pulled up in front of Easthaven, a four-columned white house on the fringe of Holly Springs. A valet came immediately to take Bitty's car, and we got out and I sucked in a deep breath.

"I wish you'd have let me eat something before we got here," I grumbled to Bitty.

"Honestly, Trinket, the days of Scarlett O'Hara are long past. There will be plenty of *h'or d'oeuvres* to nibble on, and besides, you don't want your tummy sticking out in that dress. First impressions are important. You do look spectacular, by the way. Tina is always right."

I felt spectacular, in a quivery, uneasy sort of way.

The interior of Easthaven definitely lived up to the promise of the exterior. Antiques filled every room, expensive carpets cushioned guests' feet and covered glowing heart pine floors in plush designs, crystal chandeliers hung in several rooms, and stained glass transoms over tall double doors lent a lovely glow. Bitty was right. I'd have looked like Orphan Annie in my own clothes. These guests wore understated but expensive elegance like I wear comfortable jogging pants and sweatshirts.

Bitty introduced me to senators, doctors, lawyers, even a Holly Springs mayor or two. Past and present, I presumed. I had just managed to grab a crystal flute of excellent champagne from the silver tray of a passing waiter dressed in black, hoping we'd soon get to the table that held food, when Melody Doyle approached us, arm-in-arm with a smiling man of medium height and rather uneven good looks. He reminded me in one way of Ashley Wilkes—yes, another *Gone With the Wind* reference, this time to the movie—slender, slightly bookish looking, but like Bitty had noticed, with a definite edge. Maybe it was his eyes. Hazel, narrow, and close-set. But his smile was very nice. His pale hair swept to one side, and he wore it a little long.

"Bitty," Melody said, "I know you've met Dr. Johnston, but I thought you two should get better acquainted."

Introductions to me were made, and Jefferson Johnston seemed the proper gentleman as he politely shook hands, welcomed us to his home, asked after our needs, and then turned his smile on Bitty. "I understand you have extensive knowledge of antiques, Mrs. Hollandale."

"Oh please, call me Bitty. Everyone does." Bitty returned his smile with one so dazzling I swear it was like a flashbulb going off. I took a sip of champagne to keep from saying something regrettable.

"Only if you call me Jefferson," Johnston murmured, sounding much too intimate in a square of two too many people. I looked over at Melody, who had a fixed smile on her face. Uh oh.

"Bitty dear," I said, "would you mind helping me find the buffet table? I'm famished."

"Oh, I'll take you right there," Melody said immediately, and linked her arm through mine to turn me away. "It's against that wall over there, out of the way so people have room to mill about. Everything seems to be going nicely, don't you think?"

I looked at her. She sounded rather proprietary, a note I've heard before in countless tones from countless hostesses, usually at Tupperware parties.

"Yes," I said, "it's absolutely lovely. Dr. Johnston's home is magnificent."

"You should see the nineteenth century sunroom off the back. It has one of those peaked roofs so popular back then, all this Victorian scroll work, and big elegant wicker furniture that Queen Victoria herself once owned."

"I see you've taken the fifty-cent tour," I said with a laugh, and Melody smiled.

"Actually, since I started work for Dr. Johnston as his receptionist, I helped him plan this party. I hope everything goes smoothly so he doesn't fire me."

"I'll bet you get a big raise. This is a wonderful party."

That was sincere. There didn't seem to be a false note anywhere, from the complicated flower arrangements sitting on tables, to the immaculate sheen of wood floors and brass work, to the expansive buffet spread out on a table right in front of us. An ice sculpture of intricate design rose from a gigantic bowl filled with ice and shrimp. A closer look at the sculpture, and I saw it was a castle.

"Is that Blarney Castle?" I asked, and Melody looked very pleased.

"Yes it is, you have a good eye for things. Dr. Johnston is part Irish, and of course, I am as well, so this is a favorite holiday. We have soda bread, Irish stew, and of course, tidbits to snack on, all the dishes you could want. There's Beluga caviar in that dish."

I nodded politely, though I had my eye on the stew and soda bread. Something filling. I hadn't been exaggerating when I'd told Bitty I hadn't eaten all day. I'd had a half-slice of toast for breakfast that morning, taken Brownie out on a leash with plastic bag in hand and a futile hope he'd eject my other earring, then fed the cats and released the caged ones after their final dose of medicine—thank God—and gone with Bitty to get my hair cut, nails done, and even a pedicure. By the time I got back, it was time for another round of canine and feline room service; then I'd soaked in the tub with bath salts while soft music played, and had fifteen minutes before I needed to dress. Quite a busy day.

Melody, as assigned hostess, left me at the buffet to tend to other guests. I watched her go across the room, her slender figure clad in a form-fitting emerald green dress that highlighted her dedication to exercise or excellent genes, her dark hair loose and flowing around her shoulders. A very pretty girl.

"Bitty seems to be having a fine time tonight," a familiar voice said, and I smiled up at Jackson Lee.

"Bitty always has a fine time." I noticed that Jackson Lee couldn't take his eyes off her, and felt a little sorry for him.

"She's always the belle of the ball," he said.

"Yes. I'm not sure how she does it, but I think it has something to do with those hypnosis classes she took in college. You know, How to Mesmerize Men and Make Them Mindless Minions."

Jackson Lee grinned. "Whatever she does, it's pretty powerful."

"So I've observed."

"She's wrapping Jefferson Johnston around her little finger right now."

There was something wistful in Jackson Lee's tone, so I said, "That doesn't worry me. He is not only too young for her, but I don't think a foot doctor makes that much money, despite this house. Not in

Holly Springs, anyway. There can't be that many people here with bad feet and good insurance."

A slight frown creased Jackson Lee's brows. "You know, I've worked on some medical cases, so I had to do a little research one time on podiatry. Maybe things have changed, but I'm not so sure Dr. Johnston is that good at it."

"Well, he must be doing something right, because I've heard he stays booked up and it's hard to get an appointment."

Nodding, Jackson Lee said, "Then he probably makes more than enough money."

"Last time I heard, no one got rich from taking Medicaid patients."

Jackson Lee laughed. "You have a sharp sense of humor, Trinket."

"It's a gift," I said modestly. "Most people think I'm just bitchy. I'm glad you're able to recognize the difference."

"Being bitchy has definite advantages, so don't give up hope."

"Are you kidding? I prefer it this way. Keeps the rabble at bay."

Bitty's laugh rose above the conversation and stringed quartet, and Jackson Lee looked her way again. "Think I'll just go on over and join in," he said.

"Take your hip boots," I advised, "it might get pretty deep."

With all distractions temporarily aside, I applied myself to the buffet. Shrimp and cocktail sauce, of course, three different kinds of cheese, soda bread and stew, several olives, a slab of roast beef, slice of ham, generous chunk of roast chicken topped with pulled pork, and tender asparagus tips in cheese sauce. My plate was almost too heavy to hold, so I looked around for a place to sit.

"The sunroom," a deep voice said at my left shoulder, and when I turned, he added, "It's almost empty of people, and has lots of little tables and comfortable couches and chairs."

I didn't know quite what to say. The last time I'd seen this man, I'd had moldy straw in my hair and jelly on my face. And we'd discussed canine bowel movements.

"Dr. Coltrane," I said faintly, then lied, "It's so nice to see you again."

He grinned. "How's Brownie?"

"Alive only by the grace of God and Metamucil," I replied.

"And the other earring?"

"Unseen. He may have hidden it for a midnight snack. I've been watching him, but so far haven't been able to track him to his secret lair."

It was ridiculous the way my mouth went suddenly dry and my heart plummeted to my stomach. The plate of food became superfluous. No doubt, my heart would soon be digested.

"Brownie probably has several hiding places. It's his nature to burrow. Look under beds and in the back of closets," he said. Coltrane continued to smile while I continued to babble.

"My parents will be back soon. My mother may be familiar with his current lair. I think he has the ability to become invisible. He makes me nervous when he just disappears for a while. I'm considering a bell for his collar."

"That might help. Care to join me?"

While I briefly pondered the implications of that invitation, Dr. Coltrane spooned some caviar onto his plate next to crackers and chicken, and picked up the glass of champagne he'd set down on the table. Light from tall candles in Hurricane glass flickered on his face and hair, and picked out the distinguished silvery strands that only make men look handsome and women look old. I remembered suddenly that I had no use for men.

"I'm fifty-one," I blurted, and he smiled kindly.

"My middle name is Hayes. The sunroom is this way. We'll continue sharing statistics where it's quieter."

I found myself being pulled by some magnetic force that sucked away free will. I played rat to his Pied Piper. That's how I found myself alone in a Victorian sunroom with subtle lighting and Dr. Coltrane. Music from the stringed quartet playing in some alcove drifted out to us, a nice background for conversation. The inevitable buzz of conversations, laughter, and occasional loud voice sounded far away.

"Much better," Dr. Coltrane said when we were seated in white wicker chairs with six-inch cushions, and tiny little white wicker tables held our plates. "It got a bit noisy out there for me."

"I hate parties," I said, and internally cringed at the implied insult to Dr. Johnston, who may very well be his best friend. "Not the people who give them, of course. Or the people who go to them." My underarms got damp and my face felt hot.

"I'm only here because I have the night off and am supposed to be representing the staff of the clinic. Or whatever excuse they used to get me here to meet single women."

Brain function ceased. So did the physical ability to move. I wondered how long it'd be before I keeled over onto the floor out of sheer embarrassment. If only I could be like Brownie and become invisible. Then I'd go out to the parlor or living room, or wherever Bitty was flirting her curvaceous little ass off, and pound her to an unrecognizable pulp. Then I'd pull out every last strand of her blond hair and weave it into a poncho I could wear to prison. Like a reverse Martha Stewart with her pretty poncho made by a fellow prisoner at Camp Cupcake.

Dr. Coltrane looked up at me. "Aren't you going to eat?"

"Suddenly, I'm not as hungry as I thought." I tossed down the flute of champagne and harbored other mean thoughts about Bitty while Dr. Coltrane pushed caviar onto a cracker and ate the disgusting stuff.

"I hope I'm not inconveniencing you by bringing you out here with me," he said after a moment. "It's just that when I saw the friendly face of someone capable of discussing more than a TV reality show or be-bop, I grabbed you like a life preserver. Can't women under forty talk about anything else?"

It occurred to me then that Bitty *might* not have sabotaged me, that Dr. Coltrane had been lured here to meet candidates others considered suitable; like sweet young things most men of his age and stature wore as arm candy.

Rather cautiously, I said, "Hip hop." When he looked at me with a puzzled expression, I added, "Not be-bop. That's fifties music. Hip hop is today's preference."

He shook his head and sighed. "Just someone screaming language my daddy would have taken his belt to me for when I was a teenager. Fifty-three."

"Excuse me?"

"I'm fifty-three. You're fifty-one, I'm fifty-three."

"And your middle name is Hayes. My middle name is May."

We both smiled.

Since I realized that I was really just a life preserver and not a romantic candidate, I felt much better about the entire sunroom thing, and we both relaxed and talked about whatever came into our heads. Mostly how much Holly Springs has changed since I came back and he came here to work, having spent a summer here on an internship years before.

"I got tired of big towns and bigger cities," he said, leaning back in the wicker chair that looked much too flimsy for his large frame. "The pace is hectic, and the clients more spoiled than their pets. I've had women bring their cat or dog in to be euthanized just because they've redecorated and the animal no longer goes with their new furniture. The first time that happened to me, I thought the client was kidding. When I realized she was not only serious, but impatient that I didn't understand Fifi went with the French style and she'd changed to Oriental, I'm afraid I said some very unkind things that vets aren't supposed to say."

"Did you euthanize Fifi?"

"Hell no. I gave her to my mother. Of course, I told the client that since I'd spoken out of turn, there was no charge for the euthanization and disposal of her precious poodle. I was young then. I've learned more subtlety now."

"I think that sounded pretty subtle."

"But it's what I should have said first. Then I started charging for it, since we usually had to hold the animal a while before finding it a new home with no danger of it being traded in. So what brings you back to Holly Springs after being away for a while?"

"Divorce. And of course, I had this ridiculous impression my parents needed me to care for them in the twilight of their years. I had no idea they'd turn into hormone-driven teenagers the minute I came back."

He laughed. "They probably just hid it from you when you came for visits. There's a point when the kids leave home and you're alone that you suddenly remember how it felt to be teenagers again."

"You sound like you speak from experience."

Some of the laughter faded from his face and I felt as if I'd intruded. Before I could change the subject he said, "My late wife and I had a very brief span of the second honeymoon syndrome. Then she was diagnosed with melanoma. We hardly had time to accept it before she was gone."

"I'm so sorry. What a terrible time it must have been for you."

After a moment, he said, "There's nothing like the death of someone you love to make you appreciate the time you had together, and even the time you've got left when they're gone. For me, it made me think about my priorities, and I came to the conclusion making more money than I need isn't one of them. Making memories is."

Transfixed by his tone of voice, the way his mouth curved up in a smile when he talked about his late wife, and his personal philosophy, it took a moment for me to realize that we were no longer alone.

"Trinket," Bitty said in a tone of voice indicating it wasn't the first time she'd spoken, "I've been looking for you everywhere!"

I looked up at her. "And now you've found me. Good job."

A vision in her rose dress with delicate green jewels, and her blond hair loosely framing her lovely face, Bitty looked from me to Dr. Coltrane and smiled. "You can't hide forever, either of you. Come brave the masses. People will begin to talk about you, and I prefer being the topic of local conversation."

"Then you should always be happy," Dr. Coltrane said with a grin, having already risen to his feet when Bitty showed up, "because I've heard more about you in the past few weeks than I ever knew about anyone."

"The best part is, most of it's probably true," Bitty said, linking one arm through his and one through mine to lead us back toward the crowd, "unless you've been talking to a few people I shall leave nameless. Naomi Spencer is one of them, a catty little thing with breast implants and a nose fixed so often she could be kin to Michael Jackson. Have you met her, by chance? She's out here talking to a congressman. She's the plastic Barbie with the bleached hair and personality of a cactus. I'll introduce you. Lovely girl."

Part of me wanted to pinch Bitty and part of me wanted to laugh. I'm sure Dr. Coltrane felt much the same way. But who can resist her?

Once Dr. Coltrane stood with a look on his face like a deer caught in headlights while Naomi Spencer chattered about being a cheerleader at Ole Miss, Bitty took me off to a relatively quiet corner.

"So?" she demanded, sounding rather like an indignant garter snake. "How many people other than Kit Coltrane have you asked about a connection between Philip and Sanders?"

"Not a single one," I confessed promptly. "And you?"

Bitty looked taken aback. Indignance disappeared, replaced by self-defense. "Trinket, you know you're much better than I am at that kind of thing. I tend to rattle on, and forget what I'm supposed to ask, while you have a way of asking things without people even realizing it."

"Compliments get you nowhere with me. You should know that by now."

"Only because you're too cynical to ever believe any."

"I prefer to think of it as pragmatic. Compliments are usually offered right before someone sticks their hand in your purse or sells you down the river."

"If you weren't so often right about that sort of thing, I'd continue this argument, but we really should talk to some of Philip's former companions. Not Naomi Spencer. She's got the mental capacity of a goose. Every day she wakes up, it's a whole new world. I think you should talk to Representative Bellew. He knew Philip well, and he's a Democrat. You two should get along famously."

"I never discuss politics at social gatherings," I said, but Bitty had stopped listening.

Before I could blink twice, I was being introduced to a stocky man in his mid to late forties. Russell Bellew has one of those mega-watt smiles that never quite reach their eyes that most politicians cultivate, but you usually don't notice anyway because they're dazzling you with the light of their presence and their brilliant wit. That talent should be considered a viable alternative to fossil fuel sources.

"Why, Miz Truevine," Bellew said while I wished I'd brought sunglasses, "I'm always glad to meet a constituent."

Before Bitty could slither off, I grabbed her arm, smiled at Bellew, and said, "I'm not registered to vote yet, but Bitty is."

Some of the wattage dimmed in his smile, but ever vigilant, he said he'd be glad to send someone around to register me with the Democratic party while I renewed my God-given right to exercise my privilege as an American to make the world a better place.

"Why, I'm sure Trinket would appreciate that," Bitty said while she tried to detach her arm from my grip without anyone noticing, "and I'll be glad to give you her phone number and address if you like. You know, she's been talking about becoming a Jehovah's Witness, and I know that you're a deacon over there at First Baptist Church."

Bellew got a look on his face like Bitty had just said I was a member in good standing at the Church of the Damned. If there's anything a good Southern Baptist likes, it's saving the soul of a misinformed Catholic or any other religion that isn't Baptist but certainly should be.

Belatedly, I recalled there's no way I can ever beat Bitty at this sort of thing. She's been a practicing Southern Belle since birth. Bitty can insult people so tactfully they never know they've just been compared to camel spit unless someone kindly takes them aside and explains it to them. I've seen her do it. And I've also seen her put people in situations that hardened prisoners in Parchman would fear. I'd overstepped my abilities and I knew it. I released her arm immediately.

Bitty smiled at Bellew. "I was just kidding about Trinket becoming a Jehovah's Witness, but I'm sure she'd love talking to you and hearing what all you've been up to down there in Jackson lately. Trinket is very civic minded."

Feeling a blend of awe and envy, I watched her sail off toward her next victim. It's always humbling being in the presence of a master.

My conversation with Russell Bellew resulted in little more than impatience and a strain on my courtesy level. Fortunately, after listening to intricacies of the state senate's stand on the waste disposal bill and how the Republicans were stonewalling at every turn, a man standing nearby joined in our conversation.

"Philip Hollandale wrote that bill," he said. "Only because one of his biggest contributors owns the land where the new landfill is supposed to go."

My attention immediately transferred to this new source. "Hollandale seems to have had so many big contributors," I said. "It's my understanding that he did very little for the ordinary citizens, and everything for corporations that helped elect him. Like most politicians."

"Most people don't understand the immense amount of money it takes to get elected," the Democratic representative protested, "or how much time is taken up campaigning. If it weren't for our big contributors, we'd never get any bills written or passed between elections."

"So Senator Hollandale was looking out for his constituents," I said to the man whose name I didn't know, "by promoting the new landfill?"

"Not really. Looking out for himself, mostly."

Both men seemed to agree on that, nodding sagely, and then Bellew wandered off to talk to a woman whom I thought to be Naomi Spencer or a lookalike.

"I'm Trinket Truevine," I said to the dissenter, and with a smile, I held out my hand.

Returning the smile, he said, "John Carr Daniels. Most of my friends call me Jack."

"Is that a description or a warning?"

"Sometimes both." His smile widened into a grin, and I laughed.

"You know, Senator Hollandale was my ex-brother-in-law, but I have to admit, never one of my favorite people. Not because of any particular party affiliation, but because his policies were far too often self-serving."

Jack Daniels nodded. "I'm an Independent, and I can tell you that even if Hollandale had been a Moderate, I'd never have voted for him. Crooked as a snake's back."

"I'd heard from Bitty that he used to walk a fine line, but then, no one in the family could believe she'd actually gone and married a Republican anyway. Truevines have been Democrats and Methodists since the First Crusade. Are you from Holly Springs?"

"Ashland. I don't usually talk politics at parties. A lot of people don't often agree on much these days."

"I certainly understand that." I paused; then I said, "I heard the senator had taken to visiting Sherman Sanders, and wondered what on earth he'd be doing that for since Sanders isn't likely to be a big donor."

"Probably has something to do with that new Nissan plant going to be built in a couple of years. They've been looking at land around here, and down around Jackson and all points in between, as well as up in Tennessee. We've got the edge because our taxes are lower and we're still close to Memphis. The railroad's close by, truck terminals are all around."

"What could that have to do with Sherman Sanders?"

"He owns land that backs up to Highway 7, a big chunk of it. Mostly pasture and already pretty flat there, costs less to grade it and build. I guess Hollandale thought he could talk Sanders into selling, wave a couple of carrots in front of him, but that old man's got a lot of horse trader in him."

"But wouldn't Sanders make a lot of money if he sold to developers?"

Daniels shrugged. "Sure. But people like Sanders don't care as much about the money as they do their privacy. And besides, he's smart enough to know that Hollandale would cut himself a bigger piece of the pie than Sanders would get, kickbacks, stuff like that. If he wanted to sell, he sure didn't need Philip Hollandale to act as go-between."

"Was an offer ever made to Sanders?"

"Not by Nissan. They haven't made any offers to anyone yet. Still mulling it over."

"So Sanders wouldn't have turned the senator down, because there'd be no solid offer to consider."

"That sounds logical," Daniels said, and I saw from the way he looked at me that he had a good idea where I was going with this line of thought.

I thought about Sherman Sanders and how he'd enjoyed being "courted" by Bitty to sign up with the Historic Register. Maybe he'd been playing that game with Hollandale and it'd gotten out of hand. One word led to another, a fight broke out, and the senator was killed.

But thinking that and proving it were two entirely different things.

"Well," I said casually, "when Sanders comes back home from vacation or wherever he is, he might just surprise all of us and sell off that land, take all the money, and go live in Mexico with a pretty señorita."

Jack Daniels laughed, and we chatted a little longer before being distracted by the hidden string quartet playing *Danny Boy* so Dr. Johnston could show off his baritone. After the applause faded, he invited everyone to join in a second round of the song, and of course, we all did.

While I've always fancied I have a decent voice, though more suited to country-western than Irish ballads, the big surprise was Naomi Spencer's clear, soaring soprano.

"Well, well," Bitty said behind me, "Barbie can sing as well as blow. Implants must increase lung capacity. No wonder Philip paid for them."

"Do I detect a hint of malice, dear cousin?"

"Just a soup can of it."

We both laughed at that, my having mispronounced the French word *soup-çon* in a home economics cooking class we'd shared in high school. It's still our favorite pronunciation of it. As I've said before, it's funny what middle-age women find amusing.

"How's your chat with the foot doctor going?" I asked.

"I do believe he likes me," Bitty said demurely. "He's asked me to dinner next week."

That widened my eyes. "Bitty, he's probably not even forty!"

"Oh Trinket, you know forty is the new thirty, so fifty is the new forty. A few years' difference is nothing these days."

"Uh, ten or twelve years are nothing? What could you possibly have in common?"

Bitty just smiled. I rolled my eyes. "Bitty Hollandale, it's too soon after your last divorce to go hunting down another husband, and I know you—you marry every man you sleep with just so you'll still be a 'good girl.' Technically, anyway."

"Who said I'm going to sleep with him? I enjoy the hunt much more than I do the capture most of the time. Men are much nicer, more gallant and attentive in pursuit than they are in bed. I think it's the thrill of the chase thing. They're born hunters, after all. Once they're well-fed, they tend to get fat and lazy. Or look for new prey."

In a way, her skewed logic has a kernel of truth. Of course, not all men are like that, just like not all women are manipulative. But people too often do tend to get comfortable in marriage, and forget the key elements that brought them together in the first place. That's my observation, anyway, and since I was guilty of that to a certain extent but it wasn't the real sticking point, I'm probably not a good spokesman. Spokeswoman? Spokesperson. Mercy. All this politically correct stuff can be very tiring and annoying.

"Well," I said, "just so you don't take it too far. I think his receptionist is very fond of him."

"Melody?" Bitty looked surprised. "I'm sure you're wrong about that. She's the one who suggested we get better acquainted, said we have a lot of common interests since we both love antiques and old houses."

"Oh. Maybe I'm wrong. It was just my impression, but then, everything's a little hectic. At any rate, I still don't think you're ready for another relationship."

"Trinket, you worry too much. And since I'm not allowed to discuss your relationships, or lack of them, it seems unfair we have to discuss mine when I don't want to."

She had me there.

"Fair enough," I said.

Bitty held up her right hand, little finger bent, and I laughed as we did the pinky promise thing. Really, for women in our fifties, we can be so adamantly juvenile. Maybe my parents are on to something. Maybe I'm the one who needs to change perspective, take life a little less seriously most of the time, learn to enjoy the ludicrous more, worry less about things I can't possibly change, focus on the good things and deal with the bad as they come up. It certainly seems to work for my parents, and certainly Bitty is more youthful than most people our age. In a way that's not dependent upon a plastic surgeon, too.

Of course, Bitty is the consummate Southern belle, and that lasts until death. My sister is more a Southern belle than I am, and that's the main difference that's defined us since birth. I'm a woman who prefers denim to lace, plain speech to coy implications. Bitty and Emerald have perfected the fine art of flirting. I suck at it. Not that I don't occasionally find myself trying it, just to see if I've gotten any better, or out of an insane urge to make a complete fool of myself, but it's nearly always a failure. I'm the poster personality for Don't Try This At Home.

However, I do have my compensations. Most of the time, I'm the cool head in an emergency, I tend to be organized with possessions even when my thought processes muddle up, and I still have the dress I wore to my Senior Prom. I also still have the very first vacuum cleaner I ever bought, a Sears Kenmore, of course, and it's in excellent working condition. Bitty changes vacuum cleaners more often than she does shoes, although she has no idea how to turn one on. That's not a criticism. It's just a fact. She's been fortunate to have people around her who do know how to work vacuum cleaners, and they're hourly so they don't mind at all.

At any rate, we agreed the evening was a success, as I had gotten a clue to what Philip may have been after with Sanders, and Bitty had fresh meat for her relationship grinder.

I mean that last as a somewhat accurate simile. Most men feel like they've been through a meat grinder when Bitty walks away from them. Southern men expect it when they become involved with a "belle." Newcomers or visitors are quite often traumatized. It's been suggested by one dazed man staggering away from a belle, that warning signs similar to Beware of the Alligators should be posted at state lines. Posting Beware of the Belle signs would be a complete waste of time and energy. Men caught in the spell of a proper Southern belle are as helpless to resist as Ulysses was the Sirens, although at least that worthy Greek hero took the precaution of having himself lashed to the ship's mast. True belles have an awesome power, but not all use it wisely. It's a responsibility I'm rather glad I don't possess.

On our way home, Bitty mused aloud, "Girls today don't have any proper notion of how to behave, have you noticed?"

"I assume you're referring to Naomi Spencer."

"She does come to mind, yes. It's not that I have anything against flirting, or even having one of those things you won't let me talk about anymore, because Lord knows, it does make life interesting. It's just that so many young women don't leave any mystery in the male-female thing at all. They just put it out there like slabs of catfish on ice for the men to look over and pick what they want. You know what I mean, Trinket?"

"I'm not sure. We're talking about Naomi's lack of restraint, right?"

"I suppose. Watching that empty-headed little tart bounce around swapping spit with first one man, then the other tonight, I had to wonder just what Philip was thinking."

"Obviously, he was thinking with the head below the belt, Bitty. Men tend to do that far too often."

"Did Perry ever cheat?"

"Not that I'm aware of, though he could have, I guess. I've just never thought about it. By the time I realized that he wasn't the person I'd thought he was, or wanted him to be, I'd ceased caring what he did. Doesn't that sound awful?"

"It sounds sad."

I nodded even though Bitty was watching the road and not me, thinking that it summed up my marriage. Most of it, anyway. While Perry wasn't what I thought he was, I'm quite sure I wasn't what he thought I was, either. We both ended up disappointed.

"You know, Bitty, it wasn't that Perry couldn't keep a job. It was more that he didn't think it was important. Uprooting the family to go halfway across the country chasing another pot of gold that'd turn out to be empty didn't matter to him. He didn't like staying in one place long anyway. I finally got to where I could tell that he was getting restless. It'd be little things, minor things that didn't matter, but they'd pile up into big things. Then one day he'd come home and say he'd been fired, replaced, resigned, or whatever, but there was a great job opening three states away where we'd all be happy as pigs in mud. Of course, it'd never last."

"Perry just has happy feet. But after all, Trinket, you did meet him at a sit-in when he was hitchhiking across the continent."

I smiled. "It was a protest for Native Americans' civil rights. I thought Perry was the most wonderful man I'd ever met when he started talking about how civil rights affect us all, regardless of race or religion, that if one segment of the population faces discrimination, then we're all vulnerable to it. We sang freedom songs all night, slept all day. And rallied for the cause, of course."

Bitty pulled into her driveway, hit the remote, and her garage door slid up. "I thought Uncle Eddie was going to bust a gut when he saw you on the six o'clock news. There you were, right up front holding a poster. Long hair, sandals, hip-hugger pants. Your belly button showing. Did you ever burn your bra?"

"Good heavens, no. I was never that foolish. The reason my breasts don't sag today is because I knew enough to wear proper support."

"Perky boobs is probably what kept you from being a real hippie."

I laughed. "Not to mention the fact I didn't do drugs. A shot of good whiskey, yes, but no drugs. Being a fringe hippie was a brief phase I grew out of quickly, but Perry could never quite leave it behind. Maybe I was just luckier."

"We always seem to miss the shipwreck somehow, don't we?"

"Bitty, sometimes we *are* the shipwreck."

CHAPTER 13

After my interesting night, I slept in the next morning. Brownie, once more rolled up in his blanket with only the tip of his nose sticking out one end, snored softly next to me. I lay there after waking, watching the soft light muted by sheers and curtains slowly crawl across the floor and walls. Peace settled around me. I wanted to nail it to the floor to make it linger.

Thoughts of going to Philip Hollandale's funeral weren't cheering enough to get me out of bed. I dreaded it. But of course, I couldn't let Bitty go alone, and not just because I worried so much about her emotional state. Frankly, I worried that Bitty and Parrish Hollandale, Philip's mother, would make a graveside scene. Unlike Bitty, I'm not as accepting of exciting funerals. I prefer brief, respectful services with a few hymns and no preacher trying to save mourners' souls. Soul-saving is for a Sunday morning or other scheduled event. Reminding widows and loving family members, even obliquely, that the dearly departed may well be shoveling brimstone is the height of insensitivity. Most present have their own opinions about the deceased's current destination anyway, so brief eulogies offered by those who wish to comment on the life and character of the recently passed suffice quite nicely in place of lengthy sermons.

Of course, that's just my opinion, and unfortunately for me, not one shared by all.

Certainly not one shared by the planners of Philip Hollandale's funeral. Perhaps it was the exalted company gathered to pay respects to a man fictionalized as humble, proud, generous, in touch with the common people, and a good Christian—the last of which I feel most of us are unqualified to judge, since the state of one's soul requires knowledge of one's heart, and that may often contradict one's actions. Nonetheless, community members droned on and on about the good works of Senator Hollandale and his eligibility for sainthood, based on such events as his reluctantly signing a bill to increase benefits for the ill and handicapped to receive more medical treatment—a feat that required concessions from his political opponents to a watershed project in south Mississippi to be contracted by one of the senator's corporate donors—and the generous donations he made yearly to various charities, of which Bitty told me the amounts were doubled when he filed his taxes and claimed deductions. Not to say Philip was a terrible person. He loved his mother and was devoted to his sister. According to Bitty, *very* devoted.

"Look at her," Bitty leaned close to me to say, "straight as a stick. No boobs at all. She looks mannish, doesn't she. Do you think Philip liked boys, too?"

Since I had no desire to discuss Philip's sex life, and certainly not at his funeral, I gave Bitty a stern look meant to indicate my feelings. It went unheeded.

"I mean, he always wanted to do it doggie-style. Or I had to sit on top and turn my back. I wonder—"

She stopped only because I pinched her arm. "That woman is looking at us," I said while trying not to move my lips. "She can hear you."

Bitty followed the direction I was looking. "Oh, that's Philip's Aunt Itty. Deaf as a post. She's looking at us because she's trying to remember who I am. We usually got on fairly well together, but Aunt Itty is a bit forgetful."

Perversely, I thought of Philip's aunt and Bitty being introduced to guests at Hollandale functions, and a bubble of laughter percolated right up my throat. I did my best to hold it back. It wasn't the time, and certainly not the place. Nonetheless, a muffled snort escaped. I covered it with my handkerchief and hoped it sounded like a sob.

Bitty gave me puzzled look, and I whispered, "Itty-Bitty."

She whispered back, "Teensy-Weensie," and we both struggled to keep from falling out laughing. Frequently, I'm sad to say, our main source of amusement is a comparison between our lives and the fictional world of television characters. "Teensy and Weensie" was a reference to two very healthy farm girls pursuing Tennessee Ernie Ford on an old *I Love Lucy* show.

Bitty chewed her lip, her nostrils flared with amusement, and we both tried to listen to the preacher promise eternal damnation for the heedless foolish. Even though I most likely fit into that category, I just couldn't control myself. It's a terrible thing to know you're helpless in the face of emotion, even if it's uncontrollable laughter.

My unfortunate predilection for snorting when caught in the throes of hysterical laughter coincided with the preacher's thundering Biblical quote, "'I also will laugh at your calamity—I will mock when your fear cometh . . . '"

Two snorts escaped, the second louder than the first; heads turned, Bitty began to shake, and I held my breath in a vain effort to stifle the laughter I felt pushing up from my chest. I pressed the white handkerchief harder over my nose and mouth. My shoulders shook, tears of hysteria stung my eyes. Bitty grabbed my arm and I did hers. We both squeezed hard. Pain might shock us into soberness again, as well as the fear of unsightly bruises.

It seemed to take forever, but may only have been a few minutes, and we heard the end of the sermon and beginning of a hymn, then everyone rose to their feet to pay final respects to Senator Philip Hollandale. I've seldom been so relieved. As the senator's burial was to be in his family cemetery, all we had to do was slip away and any confrontation would be safely avoided. Just a few yards, a few scant moments away, lay our escape.

Of course, the very subject of our near hysteria appeared right in front of us as we neared the chapel door. An elderly woman with stylishly cut white hair barred our exit. Medium height, ramrod straight, and with a patrician nose, she reminded me of my ninth grade English teacher.

"Aunt Itty," Bitty said calmly, "it's so very good to see you again. Have you ever met my cousin, Trinket Truevine?"

"Truvy?"

"Trinket Truevine," Bitty said more loudly and slowly.

Aunt Itty cupped a hand behind her right ear. "Twinkie? That's rather an odd name, isn't it?"

"Yes, ma'am," I said, though I had to bite my lip. "My real name is Eureka."

"Ore-Ida?" she said. "No wonder you prefer Twinkie. Of course, my parents saddled me with Itta Bena, named after that town over in Leflore County. Terrible what some parents do to their children, isn't it?"

Before I could think of an answer to that, she turned to Bitty and took her hand, covered it with her own pale, blue-veined hand weighted down with enough jewels to shame crown princes of any self-respecting country, and said softly, "We all noticed your emotion, dear. Even after all that happened between you and Philip, I find it so comforting that you still cared for him."

Bitty, ever quick on her feet, put her other hand atop Aunt Itty's and said smoothly, "Of course, I care about what happened to Philip. I just wish I could have been there for him at the end. I had so much I still wanted to say."

"Yes, you certainly should have stayed together. But I'm not quite sure what you mean about his hair."

"Philip died too young," Bitty said more loudly.

"Oh no, I'm sure you won't be hung. They don't do that nowadays, do they? Besides, I don't believe a word of that nonsense about you killing him. Just vicious rumor."

"It certainly is." Bitty patted her hand. "I'm glad Philip's family realizes that. The person responsible for his death will be brought to justice soon, I'm sure."

"Sooner than she thinks," a cool voice behind us said, and with a sinking feeling, I turned to see the elder Mrs. Hollandale staring daggers at Bitty. "Aunt Itty always likes to believe the best of people, but unfortunately, she's sometimes mistaken."

Bitty smiled sweetly. "Yes, I understand she welcomed *you* into the family as well."

Her meaning didn't go past Mrs. Parrish Hollandale. Nor did it get past her daughter, who reminds me of Cher when she played in *Witches of Eastwick*.

"You tawdry tart," Patrice spat, sounding like an angry cat, "I can't believe you had the nerve to show up here today!"

Rarely is Bitty intimidated, and she wasn't then, either. She stuck her chin in the air and said, "No matter what happened in our marriage, Philip deserves my last respects."

Patrice Hollandale towers over Bitty, but not me. When Patrice stepped too close and loomed over Bitty like an avenging angel, I straightened to my full height, put on a polite but uninviting smile, and said, "It was so nice to meet you, Aunt Itty. I've heard such nice things about you. I'm sorry to have met you under these circumstances, but we must leave now."

My comments were directed at Philip's elderly aunt, and quite plainly did not include his mother or sister. I'd met them before, and while I'm not at all sure I believe in the implied incestual relationship that Bitty does, I've never cared for either of those Hollandale women. It's been my experience that people who treat others as inferiors are really only covering up their own lack of class.

At any rate, Aunt Itty, who obviously has class, smiled sweetly and thanked me for being so kind as to attend Philip's memorial service, then looked at Parrish Hollandale with a steely glint in her eyes. "Parrish dear, I believe the funeral director is waiting for us by the limousine."

To her credit, Mrs. Hollandale took Aunt Itty by the arm, ignored Bitty and me with a lofty sniff of her nose in the air as if smelling something foul, and started toward the chapel door.

Bitty stepped to one side to allow them all room to pass, but Patrice Hollandale gave her a rude shove that sent her staggering against a christening font set to one side for what was probably a later service. Water sloshed out of the font and onto Bitty's black Chanel dress.

For one horrible instant, I thought Bitty might actually slug Patrice Hollandale, but she just took a deep breath and said, "Oh you poor thing, I see that the Betty Ford clinic didn't help at all."

Patrice narrowed her eyes. "I've never been to Betty Ford!"

"No? I thought that was part of your plea bargain, but maybe Judge Farris modified the order from your last DUI. Sixth, wasn't it? Of course, since you have a reputation for praying on your knees in a lot of closed chambers, I'm sure both of you benefited."

While Bitty's tone was pleasantly concerned, it held that unmistakable Southern belle cattiness that wouldn't escape the attention of anyone familiar with polite social warfare. Three women within hearing stepped back a pace, but made no pretense that they weren't listening to every word. After all, this is the kind of show that makes the tiresome rules of etiquette bearable.

Sunshine through the open chapel doors streamed inside, highlighting Patrice and Bitty in a rather surreal glow usually found only in Lifetime TV movies for women. If a stringed quartet had begun to play *Leibestrom* by Franz Liszt, I wouldn't have been a bit surprised.

Patrice sucked in a breath of brimstone and sulphur, and let it out in a bellow like an enraged bull. "You bitch!" Then she lunged at Bitty, who is no stranger to such maneuvers and waited until the last second to step aside. Patrice hit the christening font, a lovely and heavy slab of pink and gray marble set on discreet wheels, and then slid down it, knocking herself breathless.

That may be because I'd put my foot out at just the right moment, in case Bitty wasn't quite quick enough. Having big feet can occasionally be an advantage.

"Oh my," Bitty said, peering down at Patrice, "I think she's having a fit of some kind. Due to grief, no doubt. A cool cloth on her face will help."

Patrice made sounds like a strangling frog, very unattractive. Her hands reached up as if to choke Bitty, but lying on the chapel floor, she couldn't reach her, of course. It took a couple of strong men to lift Patrice, since she was still making choking motions toward Bitty and gargling in unknown tongues, but they managed. The three women who'd overheard every word smiled. Nothing like a good funeral to bolster one's spirits.

I'm happy to report that we left without further incident. But unfortunately, I didn't see a single person attending the services who didn't seem quite capable of killing the senator. Except maybe the preacher. And I wasn't entirely sure about him.

*

"You know," Bitty reflected when we sat in front of her fireplace sipping bourbon and branch, "Philip wasn't always hateful. I think he got in with the wrong sort of people and they changed him. He could be very sweet, and we had such a wonderful time the first few months we were married."

I looked at her over the rim of my glass. "Oh Lord. You're not going to turn him into Saint Philip now that he's dead, are you."

"Oh no. I still remember all the awful things he did, too, but seeing Aunt Itty today made me think of the good times as well. Too bad some of her class didn't rub off on Parrish and Patrice, but there you have it. It's something you're born with or you're not. If it could be bottled and sold like perfume, Patrice would still wear *Evening in Paris.*"

"Eeew," I said, and we both laughed at the memory of the cheap cologne we'd once found so exotic. Of course, we were only eight. Then I asked a question that'd been on my mind for a few hours. "Why on earth do you think Philip and his sister had a physical relationship?"

Bitty took a sip of bourbon and said, "Because I caught her with her hand down his pants one night. It was right after he was first elected senator, and we'd all had a lot to drink, but I'd never drink so much I'd put my hand down my brother's pants. I love Steven, but not that way."

"What on earth did they say when you caught them?"

"Something stupid like she was helping him adjust his trousers. I was so shocked, I didn't listen that closely. Anyway, Philip said I'd let my imagination run away with me, that of course he wouldn't ever do anything like that, and I believed him because I wanted to. Ever since then, though, Patrice has hated me." Bitty smiled. "She's just sure I'll tell everybody she and Philip played hide the sausage together."

"Isn't she divorced?"

Bitty nodded. "Three times. Well, technically only twice, because her first husband killed himself before their divorce was final."

Not wanting to linger any longer in the dynamics of the Hollandale family circle, I said I had better go home. "I have to pick up Mama and Daddy at the airport tomorrow."

"It's been a week already? Everything just flies by, doesn't it. Isn't that right, precious?"

Of course, the last was directed at Chen Ling, who'd been left home alone while we went to Philip's funeral, and demonstrated her distress by eating two pillows and an antique doorstop. My amazement didn't stem from the dog's dietary choices, but from Bitty's calm acceptance of them. After all, this is a woman who values antiques so highly they became the major issue in her last divorce.

"When are you taking Chitling back to Luann Carey?" I asked, though I'd begun to feel the probability of that ever happening lessened each day.

"Oh, I don't know," Bitty said vaguely, and broke off a piece of high-priced dog biscuit that Chen Ling sniffed at before turning her face away. "She doesn't thrive in an atmosphere of so many other animals, I think. Lately, I've noticed she hasn't been eating well."

"You don't think it might be because pillow stuffing and wood chips are a bit filling?"

"Chen Ling didn't actually *eat* all that, Trinket, she just expressed her separation anxiety with a nervous reaction. She's high-strung."

I looked at Chen Ling, who stared back at me rather haughtily. Two lower front fangs stick out over the top of her upper lip, if a dog can be said to have lips, and her flat little nostrils flare slightly. She only has one upper tooth, that tucks in somewhere between the lower two. Drool often seeps from the space where her upper and lower jaws don't quite meet. It saturated a bib embroidered with her name and Chinese pagodas.

"And who told you all that nonsense?" I asked Bitty in reference to the separation anxiety that I knew she wouldn't have come up with on her own. "Luann Carey has ulterior motives, I'm sure. It's not everyone who'll take in an old dog with a severe underbite and bow legs."

Bitty's chin came up in much the same manner as when she'd faced Patrice Hollandale. "In the first place, Chen Ling is not old, she's mature, and in the second place, her underbite only adds to her charm, her bow legs are genetic to her superior breed, and last—Luann Carey said nothing about separation anxiety. It was Dr. Coltrane."

Mention of Dr. Coltrane made my stomach do an annoying flip. I stuck my face into my bourbon and branch even though I'd lost interest in its reviving effects.

"Which reminds me," Bitty continued, "you two were thick as fleas on a hound dog at the St. Patrick's Day party. What's going on?"

"What a lovely analogy. Did you learn that phrase down at the Farmer's Co-op?"

"Never mind that. I couldn't believe my eyes when I found you two together all cozy and friendly. You've been holding out on me, Trinket."

"No, I haven't. Well, maybe a little bit. Only because I forgot to mention it, though."

"Right." Bitty rolled her eyes in disbelief. "So, how long has this been going on?"

"Nothing's going on," I said quite firmly. "Mama's dog sucked down my emerald earring, and I had to rush him to the clinic a few nights back. That's all."

I'd already decided I had no intention of telling Bitty about my scruffy clothes and straw in my hair, much less my thinking Dr. Coltrane intended to kiss me. It was just too embarrassing. I have a tendency to dwell on these things and relive them. Bitty turns her embarrassing incidents into victories or entertaining stories. I like her method better, but have never mastered it.

"And?" Bitty lifted a freshly waxed eyebrow.

I stared at her. "And what? That's it. End of story. I've been pawing through dog poop the past few days in the hopes my other earring might show up, but all I've gotten for my efforts is nauseated."

"Well," Bitty said after a moment, "just tell me when you're ready. I have some excellent edible body paint and panties, and lotion that gets really warm when you apply friction. I'll be glad to give them to you, since I'm certainly not using them right now."

As the words *edible, panties*, and *friction* in the same sentence conjured up images certain to haunt me, I went on the offensive. There's no better distraction from an uncomfortable topic of conversation than to give someone an opportunity to talk about themselves.

"So how's it going with the foot doctor? Have you talked to him since last night?"

Of course, Bitty recognized my ploy. It's probably in the Southern Belle's handbook. She smiled. "As a matter of fact, I have. Jefferson and I are going to dinner tonight down in Oxford."

"Well, aren't you just too-too."

"Aren't I?"

"I'll hear all the details tomorrow, I hope. I should be back home with Mama and Daddy by noon. Unless their flight's late."

"Don't they have round-trip cruises on those river boats?"

"Probably, but Mama and Daddy wanted to spend a night in New Orleans anyway, and I imagine a week away from home has exhausted them. They'll come dragging off that plane."

As so often happens, I was wrong. Mama and Daddy came down the long corridor of the airport to where I waited at the security gate, laughing and looking energetic. I have to admit, I felt a twinge of envy. I know; it's terrible to envy your parents such a thing as complete love and trust in one another, that comfortable security that only good marriages have. It isn't that I want to take that away from them or anything, it's just that I wish I could have found that kind of magic. From my observations, it's rare. Maybe like finding an ivory-billed woodpecker, an extinct bird that hasn't been spotted in sixty years. There are rumors it exists, but too often prove to be false.

Anyway, all the way home they chattered and laughed about their trip, told stories about other passengers and some of Daddy's former co-workers, then their sojourn on Bourbon Street. Mama's eyes got big when she talked about the men dressed as women who looked better than most women, even if they were dressed up like floozies.

"Why, one of them looked just like that pretty little blond girl I see on TV all the time. She used to be so sweet, but now she wears all this leather and lets her rear end hang out of her black drawers—didn't she used to be a Mouseketeer? I bet her mother and Mickey Mouse cringe every time that child's on stage."

I thought about the Britney Spears male stripper at the Diva meeting, and found it hard to keep from laughing. Mama might think it a hormone imbalance again.

As expected, Brownie was deliriously happy to see his regular caretakers return. He spun around in circles barking frantically until Mama picked him up and talked softly in his ear. Then he melted into her embrace and stared up at her with adoring eyes, one paw quivering.

Since I'd already ratted him out about the earring and our dash to the clinic, and I could now relinquish all responsibility for his care, I thought him quite endearing.

"Little horror," I said affectionately, but he had eyes only for my parents. A defection I didn't mind at all.

Bitty called late that afternoon to be sure my parents had made it home safely, and said she wanted to come out for a visit and hear all about their cruise. I relayed that information to my parents, who were quite pleased at the prospect of having fresh ears for their stories.

Before I had a chance to ask Bitty about her date with Jefferson, she had one of her melodramatic moments.

"Are you alone?" Bitty asked, her tone lowering, and I rolled my eyes.

"Bitty, I just told Mama and Daddy that you're coming out for a visit. You know I'm not alone."

"For heaven's sake, Trinket, you know what I mean. Go into another part of the house where no one can hear you."

"Is this international espionage? I'm not up to it right now."

"There's been a Sanders sighting."

"Hold on." I took the cordless phone into the formal dining room and pulled closed the pocket doors. "Did you see him?"

"No. Melody Doyle's cousin Serena saw him. You remember Serena? Used to be pretty until after that fourth child. Now she looks like a giant spider sucked all the blood out of her. Just skin and bone. No more life than a dead fly."

"Bitty, sometimes you frighten me."

"Anyway, Melody mentioned it to Cindy Nelson—they go to yard sales together—and Cindy mentioned it to me when she called to talk about us being on the evening news."

"Who's on the evening news, you and Cindy?"

"Of course not, Trinket. The news coverage of Philip's funeral. As a senator, his murder has gotten national attention. Cindy saw the shots of us on the news last night and this morning. We'll be on again tonight, too."

My head got light, and I pulled out a dining room chair and abruptly sat down. I stared at the polished length of pecan table and saw where I'd missed a few places when dusting.

"News? *Us?* As in me and you?"

"Good Lord, Trinket, what's the matter with you? Don't you watch the news? I'd have thought someone would have told you by now. My phone hasn't stopped ringing all day. We look quite good. Nice shots of us."

"Tell me these shots are of us walking sedately into the chapel or out to our cars."

"Now why would they want to show that? The newscaster starts saying how many people showed up, dignitaries and things like that, the camera shows us talking to each other, and then it goes to a shot of Patrice plowing into that marble sink."

"Font," I corrected distractedly, my mind immediately going to my foot stuck out to trip Patrice Hollandale and the possible ramifications of that act.

"Anyway, that's not what I called to talk about, though you may want to watch the news in a little while. Serena Sawyer said she spotted Sherman Sanders walking down Highway 4 just yesterday, and the police are out looking for him everywhere between Holly Springs and Snow Lake. Now maybe we can get him to sign those papers."

"And find out what really happened to Philip," I said.

"That, too. Isn't this nice? I think things are going to work out just fine. Isn't that right, precious?"

Since I knew the last had to be directed toward Chitling, I asked, "How reliable is Serena Sawyer if she's had all the life sucked out of her?"

"Well, just because she staggers around like a zombie doesn't mean her eyesight's gone. She's got four boys, each less than a year apart. That's enough to suck the life out of anyone."

I felt sure that had to be true, and spared a moment of gratitude for my only daughter.

Then I said, "I hope Sanders is able to clear things up, though he may not know anything at all, or want to tell it if he does."

"Well, he'll just have to tell. That's all there is to it."

Since Bitty usually gets her way, I was sure Sanders will end up telling everything. But I cautiously said, "I hope so."

"I'll pick you up at ten, though I may be running a little late if Chen Ling's tummy is upset again."

"Pick me up for what?"

"Have you been listening at all, Trinket? Sanders has been seen. You know as much as he loves The Cedars, he's got to be staying out there, or at least close by keeping an eye on it."

"I'm not going back out there, Bitty."

"It won't take long at all."

"Then the police can go check it out."

"For heaven's sake, Trinket, do you think Sergeant Maxwell cares one fig about getting The Cedars on the historical register? That's all I want, for Sanders to sign that authorization and application, and then if he goes to jail The Cedars won't be bulldozed for some car lot!"

I sighed. Trips to Bitty World can sound logical, but more often than not leave the visitor knee-deep in trouble. I know this. Yet I heard myself say, "All right, but if he's not there—"

"We'll leave immediately," Bitty promised.

When we hung up, I laid my head down on the dining room table and thought about the years I'd spent in the hospitality industry and all the unexpected crises that could and did pop up. There were occasions when occupied rooms were given to guests before the original guests were checked out, so bellmen stumbled into intimate situations none of them appreciated. Before the advent of the key card, keys broke off in locks, were left on restaurant tables, dropped down elevator shafts, and once, became lodged in the private area of a guest's body. Don't ask. Drunk guests had sex in elevators and passed out for the next passengers to find. You wouldn't believe things guests—and a few employees—have been known to do in hotel swimming pools despite the obvious presence of security cameras.

Yet all that I'd encountered in my years paled in comparison to Bitty's latest escapades. I should have realized earlier that she'd had a lot of time to perfect her ability to make insanity seem logical. At least temporarily.

I heard my father call me about the same time the grandfather clock chimed six. Ah. The evening news. My parents may want me to fill in a few details I'd felt best to leave out when telling them about the senator's funeral. I went in to the living room and sat down in a chair close to the TV.

Wouldn't you know it? We rated the lead story. What I'd thought was sunlight had been strobe lights from TV cameras trained inside the chapel doors to highlight departing dignitaries and mourners. Of course, it'd caught the squabble between Bitty and Patrice, though it went by much faster than it'd seemed to then. Bitty came off as cool and calm, Patrice as a berserk harpy, which must certainly delight Bitty. While the cameras didn't detect the presence of my foot in Patrice's path, I knew the exact moment of impact. Patrice's headlong rush turned into an arm-wheeling attempt to stay upright. She looked like a deranged pinwheel, and I freely admit I felt a certain amount of satisfaction in that.

After the funeral clip segued into a story about obesity in the South, Mama said, "I'm glad you tripped her. I never did care much for that girl."

I didn't ask how she knew. Maybe it was my smile that gave me away.

When Bitty got to Cherryhill at five after ten the next morning, I was still sitting at the kitchen table with my third cup of coffee and the remnants of a cheese and bacon omelet. Mama and Daddy were out at the barn reacquainting themselves with the cat crowd, and I was dressed, fed, but definitely not ready to go. I eyed Bitty with what I hoped was a disapproving glare.

"This is insanity," I said. "No good will come of this," I said. "There will be trouble," I said.

Bitty waved away my objections and poured herself a cup of coffee. Chen Ling squatted on the kitchen floor like a grumpy Buddha. She wore a plaid sweater and jaunty cap. Bitty wore a plaid sweater and jaunty cap. I wore Lee jeans and a gray pullover sweatshirt with Ole Miss on the front. If I ever get another dog, it will surely be the worst-dressed canine in Holly Springs.

"Where are Aunt Anna and Uncle Eddie?" Bitty asked.

"You must have parked out front. They're serving buffet at the Chez Cat café. Is that redundant?"

"Probably. But it has a certain rhythm. Are you ready?"

"No. But I can see that no amount of reasoning will persuade you to give up this crazy notion."

"You're quite perceptive. Isn't that right, precious?"

"If that dog ever answers," I said, getting up from the table and putting my plate and cup in the sink to wash off, "she'll probably tell you her name is Chitling, not precious."

"*Chen* Ling. You're only trying to irritate me, but it won't work. This is just something we have to do."

"This is just something you want to do. The police are probably out there as we speak."

"Then why are you so ill-tempered? As long as I can get Sanders to sign these papers, and the police have Philip's murderer, we'll all be happy."

"Except Sanders," I said, then added, "and poor Tuck. Maybe the mule."

"I knew you were an animal lover."

Sometimes Bitty makes my head hurt.

The police were not, of course, at The Cedars. That would be far too easy. Bitty parked her car in front of the house, I immediately handed over Chen Ling, who hadn't liked riding in my lap anymore than I'd liked her riding there since she also seems to have a weak bladder, and we got out. It was a nice day, with a brisk wind, lots of sunshine, and bursts of spring color popping up everywhere. Except in Sanders' yard. Ruts had dried into hard clay. Chickens must have flown the coop since there wasn't even a feather lying around. Fields stretching on each side and behind the house sported a carpet of yellow buttercups and white dogwood.

Oddly, the house seemed to have settled in on itself like a tattered lady, sunlight picking out faded paint and flaws. The front doors were shut and probably locked. All windows closed up tightly. The porch lantern creaked back and forth as far as the tether chains allowed.

A sudden loud bang made Bitty and I both jump and squeal. We grabbed each other, with Chitling squashed in between us. A good thing, or my boobs might have put out Bitty's eyes. I've been wearing a new bra that has underwires and a lift that defies gravity.

"What made that noise?" Bitty squeaked.

"It didn't sound like a gunshot. I think it might have been a door slamming shut."

Bitty didn't let go of my arm, though we had separated when Chitling peed on our shoes. Her voice shook a little. "Then that means he's here. Hiding somewhere."

Detaching herself and clutching a soggy pug to her ample chest, Bitty took a few steps closer to the front porch. "Yoo hoo, Mr. Sanders, it's Bitty Hollandale. Are you here? I've been worried about you. Mr. Sanders? Are you all right?"

The only reply was wind through the cedar trees, a sighing sound. I don't know why, but I suddenly thought of Carl Sandburg and his lovely poetry. Or was it Longfellow? Something about the wind through the trees being a lovely melody.

Bitty took my attention from poetry to the present by turning around and saying, "I think the door's open."

"I'm not going in there."

"You'll let me go in alone?"

"Heavens, no. You have Chitling."

"Trinket, you have a mean streak in you a mile wide. Now come inside with me. What if he's dead?"

"I'm not falling for that again. Fool me once, shame on—"

"Get up here right now!" Bitty stomped her size five foot on the hard bare clay.

I began to understand how she'd managed to keep two wild young boys in line during their younger years, when everyone else in town leaned toward cages and rope to corral Clayton and Brandon. Bitty can look positively fierce. And when she uses that no-nonsense tone, it's easy to see the iron inside her lace glove.

Rather meekly, I followed her up onto the front porch. It didn't help that Bitty was right. The front door was not only unlocked, but slightly ajar. A creepy feeling came over me.

"Bitty, I really don't like this. Let's go. Please."

"We've come this far. I know he's hiding in here. I've got the papers in the car, and once he's signed them, I won't ask you again to come out here with me."

"Can I get that in writing?"

"Well, he'll probably be in jail soon anyway," she said after a moment.

Despite the bright sunshine outside, the interior was dim, musty, with that closed-in smell old houses get if they're not kept aired out and clean. Dust covered tables, floors, picture frames and statues. I couldn't help it. My gaze strayed to the table that had held the heavy bronze statue used to bash in Philip Hollandale's head. It was gone, of course. Taken by the police as evidence when Jackson Lee allowed us to tell them what we'd seen. So far, most of the crime details were being kept quiet, but you know how things have a way of getting out. It would soon be all over Marshall County, if it wasn't already. Too many people knew.

We stood in the foyer and Bitty called for Sanders again. There was no answer, but I'd not expected one. Bitty seemed to think she might be able to coax him to come out, but if he'd indeed killed the senator, that was unlikely. If Sherman Sanders had any intention of surrendering himself to the police, he'd have already done it.

"There has to be dozens of places in here to hide," I said to Bitty when she insisted we go a little deeper into the house. "He could be anywhere. He's not going to come out, Bitty."

"He might. *Yoo hoo, Mr. Sanders* . . . if I leave these papers on the table here, you can just sign them and I'll come back later. It will save your house, you know. No one can take it away from you as long as it's on the historic register, I'll make sure of that. It can be held in trust."

One thing I'll say about Bitty, she's tenacious. And single-minded when she wants to be.

Another noise sounded, muffled this time, and Bitty turned quickly, startled. She must have relaxed her grip on Chen Ling, because the pug hit the floor at a dead run, nails clacking against wood floors and bowed legs scrabbling. Barking like a Rottweiler, the dog headed for the back of the house with Bitty calling after her.

"Chen Ling! Come back, precious! Oh, come back here!" Bitty's size five feet trotted after the dog, whose jaunty cap had come off when she hit the floor and now lay in the dining room. I shook my head and went to pick up the cap. Then I went back into the main parlor with its ornately carved walnut mantelpiece, and stared up at the crystal candlesticks and oval-framed photos. Grim faces stared back, women in stark, high-necked gowns and hair pulled back looking weary and resolute. Men in starched white collars, vests, and long-tailed jackets had whiskers in varying lengths, and looked as grim as the women.

That annoying tickle came back. There just seemed to be something awry, and I had no idea why I felt that way. I'd been in here twice. Neither time for very long, and neither time had I wanted to be here.

Bitty's voice came from the back of the house, and the pug's loud barking sounded like it had gotten farther away. We'd end up being here until dark if I didn't go help her catch that dog. How could a ten pound, bow-legged, pigeon-toed dog wearing a bib and sweater run so fast?

"I'm coming to help, Bitty," I called, and turned away from the mantel.

A burst of light flashed in front of my eyes, I had a brief sensation of falling, and then everything went dark.

CHAPTER 14

One reason I hate funerals is because it's too easy for me to imagine I'm the one closed up in a wooden box, no matter how beautiful the wood and ornate handles. It's not the thought of death that gets me; it's the closed-in space. I think the Native Americans have the best idea, the ones who put their dead up on scaffolds to let nature take its course. It must be peaceful, with the wind and sky all around, instead of being planted in the ground like a potato.

One thing about potatoes—if you've ever been unlucky enough to smell a pile of rotting potatoes, it's a smell you don't forget.

That's what I woke up to, a stench like rotting potatoes all around me in a darkness far too similar to the grave. The first thought that went through my mind was that I shouldn't have laughed during Philip Hollandale's memorial service, that I should have taken the preacher's warning more seriously. Obviously, I must be dead and buried in a grave that smelled of rotten potatoes.

Then, of course, I realized I must not be dead. For one thing, there weren't any flames or the stench of sulphur. And no deceased family members guarding the gates with pitchforks. Sad to say, the Truevine family has buried its share of rascals that St. Peter would never allow through heaven's gates.

My head hurt, my mouth was dry, and the silence too heavy. I put a hand to my head, felt something wet, and tried not to cry. Truth is, I was scared. The burst of light in front of my eyes had been eerily similar to the time I'd been accidentally hit in the head with a softball. I'd had the same reaction then, too. Only I had awakened with emergency employees sticking their fingers into my eyes and asking if I was all right.

The obvious conclusion was that someone had hit me in the head, stuffed me into a dark closet, and left me there. But I had no idea why.

"Bitty," I whispered in case whoever had done this still lurked in the dark, "are you here, too?"

There was no answer, so either Bitty was still unconscious, or—no. I just couldn't even contemplate that possibility. Maybe she'd escaped. Tears stung my eyes.

I don't know how long I sat there before I dared to move. It could have been just a few minutes, but it felt more like hours. Finally I began to explore a little bit. The wall behind me felt like old brick, that rough, uneven surface new bricks don't have. Damp old brick. Like in a basement. Sanders' basement? Or had I been moved elsewhere? I had no idea how long I'd been out. Maybe I'd been left for dead. The dent in my scalp oozed blood, but maybe the cool temperature kept it from being worse.

When I gathered some nerve, I rolled to my knees and felt around on the floor. Oval-shaped objects were piled everywhere. They rolled beneath me and felt vaguely familiar. I realized what they were about the same time as my right thumb slid inside one of them: rotten potatoes, of course. Coupled with the overpowering stench and squishy goo, my weak stomach rebelled. I promptly threw up. That certainly didn't help anything.

After a few minutes to recover, I wiped my hand on my jacket, stood up, and then headed in the opposite direction. Potatoes rolled under my feet when I stumbled along, half-crouched, the pitch black around me pressing down until I wanted to scream. Maybe I would have screamed if I hadn't worried my attacker might still be close.

Slowly I became aware of sound seeping in from somewhere. Other than my own rasping gulps of air through my mouth so I didn't choke on the heady aroma of rotting potatoes, and the thudding sound of my heart in my ears, this was the only other detectable noise in the darkness. I held my breath and listened.

Furtive scratching noises came from nearby. It was hard for me to judge distance when I had no internal compass point, so I just crouched in the pitch black darkness and tried to focus. It was a sound I'd heard before, but I just couldn't place it. Plumbing noises? Was this the root cellar under Sanders' house? Old boards creaking, maybe? If my head hadn't throbbed so badly, the answer might have come to me sooner.

Not until I heard a tiny squeak did I realize what I heard—rats. Now, while I'm not one to scream at the sight of a mouse, or usually even a snake, rats and spiders are entirely different. I have heard more than my share of rats eating people stories, and seen the results of brown recluse spider bites for myself, and as far as I'm concerned, all rats eat people and all spiders are brown recluses. Logic and a certain amount of education on these creatures assure me that this isn't true. I really don't care.

After realization came paralyzation. I was as rooted to that cellar floor as one of those potatoes. I'm not sure if I even took a breath for a while.

But when a squeak came from very close, and I felt something move past me in the dark, I became uprooted and unglued. I screamed. Very loudly. Over and over, while I did a panicked dance that totally destroyed half a bushel of rotten potatoes, my Nikes, and the eardrums of every rat in a quarter mile radius. I've been told I have a very piercing scream. No doubt, glass goblets shattered all over Marshall County.

The bad thing about all this was that my screams hurt my own ears; the good thing was that I was heard above ground. In a few moments, a door above me opened and light flooded in. I didn't care who opened it. If it'd been an armed terrorist with a machete between his teeth and an Uzi under his arm, I'd still have launched myself up and out of there like a rocket.

Apparently, the propulsion speed of a panicked woman who is twenty-pounds overweight is greater than the resistance of a man weighing a solid one hundred-ninety pounds. I flattened my liberator, first with the force of our collision, and second with the stench of rotting potatoes clinging to my hair, jeans, and Nikes.

In my zeal to leave behind rats and darkness, and with the thought at the back of my mind that my liberator could also be my assailant, I scrambled to my feet and kept going. Behind me, I heard this horrible gagging sound, and spared a glance over my shoulder as I sprinted toward the front of what I recognized as Sanders' yard. Recognition hit at the same time as a stitch in my ribs. I stopped, breathing heavily through my mouth and pressing a hand to my left side.

"Dr. Coltrane?"

I think he said something like "Gaghghh," which I took to mean, "Yes, nice to see you." I walked back to where he lay on his back looking up at the sky and holding a hand over his nose and mouth.

"Are you all right?" I asked, peering down at him.

Brown eyes blinked above the edge of his hand. "'Tand ober dere," he said, and gestured downwind. I nodded and continued to breathe through my mouth.

"Have you seen Bitty?" I asked as I moved to one side, and still holding his hand over his face, he nodded.

"Ad p'lith thtation."

"She's at the police station? Is she all right?"

"Fahn."

Relief made me want to sit down, so I did. Right there on the rutted clay by Dr. Coltrane. I saw that his eyes were watering. Or maybe he was crying. He sat up to look at me, and that's when I saw the blood coming from under his hand.

"You're hurt." My deductive powers were obviously returning. "Take your hand away so I can see."

He shook his head. "No 'fense, bud oo 'tink."

"Well, I've been in a root cellar with rotting potatoes. And rats." I shuddered at the last. "Do you think your nose is broken?"

"No," he said, making it sound more like *doe*. "Jut bleedink."

He pulled something out of his pocket, and I saw that he wore a white doctor's coat under a windbreaker. When he'd pressed a wad of gauze to his nose, he held his head back and pinched his nostrils, and after a moment, the bleeding stopped. He took a cautious breath, turning his head to keep from inhaling essence of potato.

Now that I was out of the cellar, knew Bitty was safe, and felt a little more secure, I said rather indignantly, "Someone locked me up down there."

Dr. Coltrane wiped away the last traces of blood and put the gauze into a bag he pulled from another pocket. *Always prepared* flashed through my mind. Maybe he'd been a Boy Scout.

"I had assumed you weren't in there by choice," he said, rather testily, I thought.

"What gave me away? My screams?"

"Certainly that, but the board stuck through the outside handles was a good clue."

I looked over at the cellar doors. It's one of those root cellars that looks like a storm cellar and may even have been originally used for that purpose. Double wooden doors can be pulled closed from the inside, and when shut from the outside, are kept shut by sticking a board through bolted-on iron handles. It's right behind Sanders' kitchen, back where pokeberries and bitterweed grow rampant, almost obscuring it from sight. Trampled weeds and piles of scuffed-up dirt were evidence of recent exploration, however.

When I looked back at Dr. Coltrane, he was gazing at me with what seemed to be a mix of awe and revulsion. Maybe he was just awed I could be so revolting, or at least smell that way.

"Your cousin thinks you've been abducted, you know," he said. "The police are putting together a search party. Horses and everything."

"So why aren't you with them?" I heard myself ask, and could cheerfully have bitten my tongue right in two at the implication he should be searching for me.

He smiled, eyes crinkling at the corners. "I've been helping Frank Dunlap with some of his cows in the pasture he leases from Sanders. Just thought I'd come over and check things out until the police could get here."

"How'd you hear about it?"

"I've got a CB in my work truck. Helps out when there's no cell phone signals. We need to call Sergeant Maxwell so he won't be out beating the bushes for you. Besides, it'll be safer if we get away from the house."

I went with him to his truck parked out on the road in front of Sanders' house, and leaned against it while he made the call. At least Bitty hadn't been hurt. How had she escaped? And just who had hit me in the head and why? The only rational explanation was Sanders. He knew Bitty had seen the senator in his foyer, and while that detail wasn't supposed to be released yet, odds were everyone in Marshall County already knew Bitty Hollandale had found her ex-husband with his head bashed in long before the police found his frozen corpse in her wine cellar.

Staring at the house, I wondered if Sanders was staring back at us. If he was angry that I wasn't dead, and that Bitty had somehow escaped.

"It was Sanders," I said when Dr. Coltrane got off the radio. "He locked me in the cellar."

"You saw him?"

I shook my head. "No, but who else would have done it? No one else has a good enough reason. My ex, maybe, but last I heard he's gotten a new job in Boise. Probably picking potatoes or selling insurance."

Mention of the potatoes made me think of something. I looked over at Dr. Coltrane, who had reached into a cooler in the back and taken out two Cokes.

"You know, I've smelled piles of rotten potatoes before, but this time, it's especially bad. Do you think they've fermented? Maybe there's a still down there. You know—to make vodka or something."

"Vodka?" He laughed. "I wouldn't be surprised at much of anything lately, but I can't see Sanders putting a still down there for vodka. Pure grain alcohol, maybe. Moonshine. Vodka is a far stretch."

"Hmmm. I just wondered how he's managed to support himself, you know, keep the house in good repair without any money. And of course, living with a cellar full of rotten potatoes can't be too pleasant. Why would he do that if he isn't using them for something?"

Dr. Coltrane nodded thoughtfully. "Sanders is a strange one. Cared about his dog, though."

"I heard his dog died of natural causes." When he hesitated, I wondered if I'd trespassed on client privilege—which made me wonder just how Bitty had really come up with all her information about Tuck—and said quickly, "Not that it's any of my business, but since I'm the one who found Tuck in the chicken house, I could tell he'd suffered some violence."

"Ah. Well, yes, he did, but it was post-mortem. He'd already died from complications of liver disease."

"So . . . someone hit him with something *after* he died?"

"Yes. Car tires."

That sounded gruesome, and I tried not to think about Sanders running over his own dog.

"Well, obviously it unhinged Sanders enough to hit me in the head and lock me up in his cellar," I said.

Coltrane straightened from where he'd leaned against the truck hood. "You've been hit in the head?"

"Yes, and contrary to some reports, it didn't happen when I was a baby." Talking about it made me reach up to touch the dent on the back of my head. The blood had dried, but my hair felt stiff.

Dr. Coltrane set down his Coke and despite my protest, examined the back of my head. Or more specifically, directly over my right ear. Then he made me sit down on his lowered tailgate while he got out gauze and some yellowish-red antiseptic that he probably uses on cattle, and he cleaned up the hole in my head and said it seemed superficial, long but not deep.

"You're fortunate. It could have been worse."

I looked at the squeeze bottle he still held in his hand. "That stuff isn't going to make me start mooing or anything, is it."

He grinned. "Maybe. Or you could start howling at the full moon."

"Oh, no problem. I already do that. I have very healthy lungs."

His grin widened. "So I've noticed."

I wasn't sure how he meant that, so I paused. No doubt, he meant that he'd heard me screeching loud enough to peel wallpaper. The other, more physical meaning referring to female attributes, couldn't be what he meant. Could it? Then his gaze flickered to my chest and back up.

My face got really hot, and I didn't know whether to be indignant at the obviously sexist, chauvinistic remark, or be glad he'd noticed something besides my wild hair, potato scraps, and *eau de decay* fragrance. It called for action, so I decided to go with deafness, and switch topics.

"I'm just glad Bitty's all right. Are the police on the way?"

To my shock, Dr. Coltrane reached a hand toward my chest. My reflexes were fairly quick and I grabbed his wrist just as he flicked away a bee hovering over potato remnants on my tee shirt. He looked a little startled, then chagrined.

"Oh, sorry. I saw that bee about to settle on your collarbone and didn't think."

All suspicions of potential ravishment evaporated, and I tried to think of something clever to say that'd smooth over the awkward moment. What came out was less than clever, but didn't stray too far into idiocy.

"I'm glad you weren't stung."

He smiled, and while I was thinking how really nice and warm his eyes are, a wonderful chocolate color, sirens blared down the road, getting closer. All I could do was smile back, and I let go of his wrist even while I admired the corded strength in his arm. Good thing we'd decided to just be friends, or this man might upset my complacent apple cart.

Sergeant Maxwell himself unfolded from a police car, and got out straightening his hat as he ambled toward us. Other officers fanned out, obviously knowing their roles, some with guns drawn, and others in black gear reminiscent of a TACT squad. A little overkill, I thought, for an old man in his late seventies. Then I remembered the dead senator and my own attempted murder, and I felt less sympathetic.

Bitty had already told the sergeant why we were there, though I'm not at all sure she told everything, and that she'd come back from chasing her dog to find me completely gone. When I hadn't answered her calls for me, she'd panicked and fled.

"Good thing," I said, "or she could have been down there with me." I shuddered at the memory of the cellar rats and that horrible rotten stench. "Wear boots when you go in there."

Folding his arms over his chest, Maxwell sent two deputies down into the cellar, sans boots, which none of them had with them. I empathized with their obvious reluctance. While we waited, the sergeant asked me questions about my reason for being there, and every detail I could remember. I left out nothing. Bitty would just have to cope.

"We already sent out a car earlier to check for Sanders," the sergeant said. "No sign of him here."

"Bitty's reasoning is that he'd hide from the police, but not from her."

Maxwell just looked at me, then up at the house. He wore one of those small shoulder radios that crackled incomprehensibly while he listened intently. Then he replied in a few of those numbers police like to use, and said, "Secure the area. I'll make the call."

He went around to the driver's side, got into his car and spoke into his radio, while Dr. Coltrane and I stood in the weeds and gravel and wondered what was going on. Or at least, I was wondering what was going on. Maybe Coltrane spoke police codes.

After a moment, the sergeant got out of the car and came around to talk to me again. He had that stone-faced look that police seem to wear when they're trying to be subtle. My stomach flipped.

"Is Bitty all right?" I asked anxiously.

"Mrs. Hollandale is safe. I'd like to ask you if you saw anything unusual in the cellar, Miz Truevine."

"As I told you, I couldn't see anything at all. It was pitch-black."

"Any unusual sounds, maybe?"

"Just rats."

"Before you were struck, did you see or hear anything unusual?"

Getting a little worried, I said, "No. What's going on?"

Instead of answering my question, he said, "How long were you separated from your cousin before you allege that someone struck you on the head?"

"I don't know, maybe ten minutes, and I wasn't *allegedly* anything. I have a hole in my scalp to prove it."

Dr. Coltrane put a hand on my arm, a solid, comforting pressure. "Sergeant, Miz Truevine sustained a head injury that I treated after my arrival. She'll need further medical care, however, so these questions should wait. Then she and her attorney will no doubt be glad to answer any questions you may have."

Maxwell didn't look happy, but that was probably in my favor. Something hard and cold sat in the pit of my stomach when I looked back at the house and saw increased activity. I just knew they'd cornered Sanders, or maybe found someone else. Did they think I was a part of it? And Bitty?

Apparently, Dr. Coltrane thought along the same lines. He looked at the sergeant and said, "If you prefer, I can have her call her attorney now and he'll come out and tell you the same thing I just suggested, or she can meet you later at the station after she's had medical care."

The upshot was that since I was a person with lifetime ties to the community and likely to hang around, the sergeant said my later presence at the police station would be sufficient. To me it sounded more like an arraignment, but then, maybe I watch too much *Law & Order*.

Dr. Coltrane escorted me to the passenger side of his truck even though I offered to ride in the back or wear a plastic bag. "I can't smell too pleasant," I added.

"That's all right. I've smelled worse." When I arched my brow, he smiled. "I hope you didn't expect me to say rotten potatoes smell just fine."

"No, that would be asking too much, wouldn't it," I agreed.

I don't know why, but somehow he made it all bearable, being locked up in a cellar filled with rotting potatoes and now being questioned—again—by the police. Like *I* was the one who had done something wrong, when I'd been hit in the head and left for dead. But I was alive. Bitty was safe. Could I ask for anything more? Oh yes. I'd almost forgotten.

"I hope they treat Sanders as least as badly as they just treated me," I said once I'd gotten into Dr. Coltrane's truck, sitting atop a big plastic garbage bag I'd insisted he place on the seat. "After all, he's the one guilty of bashing people in the head, not me."

Standing just outside the open truck door with his hand on it to close it, he looked at me. "I'd say Sanders is getting his just rewards if he's guilty."

It was the way he said it. I suddenly knew, even before he added, "They just found his body in the root cellar."

*

Jackson Lee accompanied me to the police station after I'd been to the emergency room where they used a different color antiseptic on my head and told me not to wash my hair. The last upset me more than the injury or the way I smelled. When I'd asked Jackson Lee if I shouldn't go home and bathe and get clean clothes first, he shook his head.

"No, they're less likely to keep you too long as you are."

That told me a lot about my current condition. No wonder Dr. Coltrane had taken off so fast when Jackson Lee showed up at the hospital. Of course, since the animal clinic is just across the road from the hospital, maybe he really did have work to do.

As Jackson Lee predicted, my presence in the police station was very brief. I preferred to think it was because of my innocence, but from the way the young officer taking my written statement kept gagging and coughing, my fragrance may have contributed to my swift release.

Jackson Lee took me to Bitty's, and she wouldn't even let me in the front door. She held her nose and said through wood and glass, "Oh God, Trinket—I'm sorry. I'll give you garbage bags to wear home, but if you come in here, I swear I'll throw up on you."

"That's all right. Just give me my purse so I can get my car keys. I'll talk to you later."

She stuck purse and garbage bag through the gap in the door and said, "I'm so glad you're all right. Go home and bathe," then shut the door on me.

It was that kind of day.

Fortunately, my parents had already heard all about everything by the time I got home, so I didn't have to go into lengthy explanations before I was allowed to leave my clothes in the laundry room for later burning and given a robe to make my way upstairs to the bathroom. Since I've been known to be rather defiant at times, I washed my hair anyway, although I did take care not to get too much water or shampoo into the cut. It was easy to find after emergency room staff had shaved around it despite my protests. Ah well. I'd been thinking of getting a new hairstyle anyway, I just hadn't considered the G.I. Jane look very attractive. I still don't.

Later, wrapped up against the evening chill in my thick terrycloth robe, I sat out on the sleeping porch with a cup of my mother's famous spiced tea. Even people who don't like to drink hot tea love this recipe. Mama brought me up a pot of it with an English cozy around the Royal Albert teapot to keep it warm. She sat down in the chair next to me, and for a while we just sat in companionable silence watching the shadows outside lengthen into night. It reminded me of my childhood, those precious times when it was just me and Mama together, all too brief in a rowdy household.

"I've missed this," Mama said after a little while. "Life just gets so busy at times."

"A bit busier than usual lately," I muttered, having not quite recovered from my day.

Soft light gleamed on the gold trim of the teacup rims, and Pachelbel's Canon in D Major played on my stereo system—one of those small cheap ones, since I'd given the best things to my daughter or sold them to strangers rather than let Perry have them. There's a lot of Bitty in me at times. I prefer to think of it as inherited Scotch-Irish thriftiness, but it's really more the Scotch-Irish long, vengeful memory, I fear. Throw in the Truevine Welsh ancestry, and what you've got are mean, stingy people, or happy, generous people. If there's a medium between the two extremes, I haven't yet seen it in our family. Somewhere in the attic is a detailed family tree with a rather interesting sketch of our ancestors who were either over-achievers or prison residents.

Mama reached over to pat me on the arm. "It's all right, sugar. Everything will work out just like it's supposed to do. This craziness will pass, and a new crisis will come along."

My eyes crossed. "Oh great. That really gives me something to look forward to. And to think I used to wonder if it was healthy to spend all my time alone. Now I realize how good I had it back then."

"You don't regret coming home, do you?"

I looked at Mama. "No, of course not." As I realized just how much I meant that, I added, "I'd thought about moving close to Michelle, but she has her own life and friends. Then I thought about how I always used to be so busy when you'd call, and how much of my adult life you and I have missed sharing. That's when I knew I wanted to come home. It was time to catch up."

"And of course," Mama added with a mischievous smile, "someone has to be here to take care of us old folks."

I laughed. "Right. I just hope I can keep up with the two of you."

Mama patted my arm again. "Take plenty of vitamins, sugar."

Early the next morning, before I'd had time to do more than get up and make my way blindly downstairs to the coffee pot, officers Stone and Farrell arrived. They'd come for the clothes I'd worn the day before, so Daddy, somewhat indignantly, put them into a plastic bag for them, along with my shoes. Truthfully, I wasn't sad to see them go. The thrifty side of me urged me to wash and keep them, but my inner coward said to burn them. So I really didn't mind giving the clothes to the police, though I had no idea what they thought they'd find.

Then Officer Farrell said, with a red face that should have warned me, "Um, ma'am, I've been told we have to, uh, get all your things."

"Those are all my things," I said. "I had on Lee jeans, an Ole Miss sweatshirt, and Nikes with sports socks. What more can—no. You can't possibly want *those*!"

Farrell turned purple. Horrified, I stared at him, while Daddy just looked perplexed. The thought of strangers—male strangers—pawing over my cotton Hanes and new underwire bra with lift was intolerable. It's not one of life's indignities that can be overlooked.

I drew myself up, standing at least two inches taller than scrawny Officer Farrell, and said in my iciest tone, "Young man, I will not have my unmentionables dragged into town. If Sergeant Maxwell wants them, he'll have to get a search warrant."

Farrell looked at me with pleading eyes that I ignored. Daddy made a low rumbling sound that took the officer three hasty steps backward. Not even Officer Stone, a more formidable man, could persuade me, and once I put in a call to Jackson Lee, he stopped trying. I have my limits.

Holly Springs police may not have all the new technical equipment of big cities, but they do have access to enough to conduct thorough investigations. What they need can be borrowed, and murder victims are sent nearly two hundred miles to Jackson for autopsies. Investigations may move at a slower pace, but that certainly doesn't mean they're not efficient. Trust me, they are quite efficient.

The upside to the police being so efficient is that while Holly Springs has its share of drug dealers and users, the police know them by first name, know their addresses, and who to look for and when. Burglaries are at a minimum, murders rare, and most crimes committed by one family member or friend against another. There are enough of the latter to keep the police busy, and give Holly Springs more than its share of lawyers. It's been said you can't throw a rock without hitting a lawyer, and that's probably true. Their offices run to one every four buildings around the court square. That may be a slight exaggeration, but Mississippi law is the state's premier industry.

While that has its advantages, the disadvantages are that the police also frequently know the family history of the citizens, and that includes when there's bad blood between husbands and wives, or ex-husbands and wives. They know why, and who got the best of whom, and if the feud is over or still on-going.

That's how they knew that Philip Hollandale had blocked Bitty's attempt to get the Inn on the historic register so far, and figured out that he'd tried to do the same to The Cedars. Since Sherman Sanders was no longer the prime suspect in the senator's death, having been killed at just about the same time, according to the local coroner, that left Bitty as the only logical suspect. When Sanders' autopsy report came back from Jackson along with his body for burial, it was expected that she'd be formally charged with his murder, too.

Bitty had already been charged with Philip Hollandale's murder. Jackson Lee argued there was only circumstantial evidence, but apparently traces of his blood on the parlor floor, her prints on the pot of chicken and dumplings, and the rancor she felt for the senator gave her motive and opportunity. Also, a search of her house had turned up shoes with traces of Philip's blood. The Sanders case wasn't quite as clear-cut, but police were still trying to connect it to Bitty.

And me? My choices were between being a prosecutorial witness, or accomplice. Neither of which I found especially appealing.

"Having been hit in the head and locked up in the cellar puts you in the position of being a victim as well," Jackson Lee explained to me when Bitty and I both sat on the edges of our chairs in his office and gripped each others' arms like life preservers. "That's good for you, but can be difficult for Bitty. Now, don't go looking at me like that, it's all going to be fine. There's a state full of people who wanted to hit Philip Hollandale in the head. He's done more than his share of questionable deals that made quite a few enemies. You're just the easiest suspect, Bitty. I wish you'd have listened to me and stayed away from Sanders'. You're the hard-headest female I've ever met in my life."

I bit my lip to keep from agreeing. Now wasn't the time. Bitty already felt lower than a snake's belly. She didn't need both of us reminding her that tenacity could be a liability.

"Now, you ladies try not to worry so much," Jackson Lee said as he walked us out of his office, "that's my job. I've got some people digging up facts, and as long as you told me every bit of the truth, we'll get through this. Just remember, when anyone asks you, *No comment* is what you should say. All right?"

Bitty sniffed a little, the traumatic experience of being fingerprinted, photographed, and held for arraignment having shaken her world quite a bit. "That doesn't include the Divas though, since they already know most of it and helped me hide Philip, right?"

Jackson Lee stopped, put his hands on Bitty's shoulders, and looked her straight in the eyes. "Bitty, I don't care if God shows up on your front porch. You and Trinket are the only ones who can talk about everything that happened. I know you and that girl's club you've got going are loyal, but this is serious stuff. Trust *no one*. Understand?"

Bitty nodded, but reluctantly. If she hadn't been holding Chen Ling, I'd have pinched her to make sure she paid attention. Since Chen Ling has a tendency to pee when squeezed, I didn't want to risk Bitty's reaction to a pinch.

"All right, Jackson Lee," she said, "but you know it's my nature to be trusting."

"I know, sugar," he said, slipping his arm around Bitty's shoulders and deftly avoiding Chen Ling's jealous snap at him, "that's part of your charm. But right now, there are only two people you can trust, and one of them is me."

Looking up at me, he added, "It might be good if you stayed pretty close to her, Trinket, since you're more cautious."

That was a nice, lawyerly way of saying that I'm a distrustful cynic, but since he went to all that trouble to phrase it so tactfully, I heard myself say, "I'll stay close."

"I know you can be counted on to move in with her for a while, just until the police find the real killer. I bet you two ladies will enjoy each other's company anyway."

My head buzzed. I'd been neatly trapped. I could refuse, of course, but then Bitty would think I'm a heartless relative, and if anything happened because she's a loose cannon, I'd always blame myself. Damn that Jackson Lee. No wonder he's got such an excellent reputation.

So that's how I found myself staying in Bitty's upstairs guest room where the expensive carpet that was once a debating point in divorce court, then used to hide a corpse, had left a very faint square outline on the bare wood floors. The transition from babysitting elderly parents to babysitting a cousin accused of murder really isn't that difficult. Both jobs hold a certain amount of surprise and an element of danger.

CHAPTER 15

Living in Bitty World has taught me the value of silence. When her phone isn't ringing or she isn't talking to Chitling or a neighbor, there's someone in her kitchen or tending to her yard, or the entire Historical Society is sitting in her living room drinking sweet tea and planning a ruthless coup to bring some run-down old house under their protective and loving wings. It's quite a change even from Mama and Daddy, who've taken to giggling a lot and making noises behind the closed door of their bedroom that I refuse to try and decipher.

Since Bitty decided on a self-imposed house arrest—which really only meant that she'd taken to dramatically reigning over a variety of visitors like some Queen of the Damned—I'd been kept busy monitoring her mouth. That's not an easy or enviable task, believe me.

I've figured out Bitty's secret to ignoring a crisis. As I'd suspected, she simply surrounds herself with so many distractions she has no time at all to think of what may, or will probably, happen. It's efficient but exhausting. Especially for those who prefer introspection and rehashing every action, past, present, and future. That would be me.

While Bitty hired Sharita's teenage cousin to pour sweet tea and serve angel food cake and peach ice cream to whoever stopped by, I gnashed my teeth and tried to focus on when and where I'd gone wrong. And of course, the teeny tiny little worm at the back of my brain that kept telling me I'd forgotten something important kept popping up at the most inconvenient times.

Again, it was the Nathan Bedford Forrest thing. I had no idea why I kept thinking about him, or about General Grant, but I did. Like Brownie fixated on squirrels, I fixated on Forrest. It was just the dumbest thing ever when there was so much else to worry about, like why Philip had been at The Cedars, and who had killed him if it wasn't Sanders, and why Sanders had been killed at just about the same time, and who had run over poor old Tuck. But did I focus on those concerns? No. Every time I'd start thinking about them, my stubborn brain would go right back to Forrest and Grant. There was only one thing to do, I decided after three days of nerve-racking hours spent in the queen's court. I'd reacquaint myself with both gentlemen and see why I just couldn't get them out of my mind.

Now, I know they're both dead. Grant is buried in Grant's Tomb, and General Forrest is buried in Forrest Park. But there had to be some reason I kept thinking about them in connection with the senator and Sanders. Until I'd satisfied myself they weren't at all important, I'd keep having internal arguments that made me gibber to myself in corners.

"But I'm not ready to go out and face everyone yet, Trinket," Bitty said when I told her we were going to the museum right down the street. "I mean, everyone knows I was arrested, and that Sergeant Maxwell is mean enough to say I killed Philip, and even Sherman Sanders, when I never would have lifted a hand to either one of them. Or Sanders, anyway, though I wouldn't have minded bashing Philip in the head."

"Now, see, Bitty, that's exactly why I can't leave you here by yourself. You say these things that some people might misinterpret."

Clutching Chen Ling to her chest, Bitty looked at me with resolution in her eyes. "Well, anyone I invite into my home is *not* going to be a traitor!"

"Bitty, you let in that reporter from the Memphis paper. Who knows what he could say in print?"

"It's unkind of you to even think that, Trinket. Why, Michael has been my friend for years and years, even before he bought that old house in Red Banks. He would never betray me. And I just don't allow anyone in my home that would, you should know that."

I sighed. "Just remember what Jackson Lee said, Bitty. Trust no one but him and me. And besides, you wouldn't want to put someone else in the position of having to testify against you or go to jail, would you?"

"Of course not."

"Good. Now, you can introduce me to people at the museum while I look up some things, can't you?"

Bitty smiled. "I'm just so glad you're developing an interest in our local history. I knew if you stayed around me long enough, I'd rub off on you."

As traumatized as I was at that thought, I managed a smile.

The Marshall County Historical Museum is located in an old buff brick school building at the corner of College Avenue and Randolph Street, just a short drive or decent walk from Bitty's house. It has a brick and iron picket fence around it that suffered some damage from a car mishap a few years back, but has since been repaired. Currently, however, it's under renovation, so one-fourth of the museum's items have been moved to The Square Museum on West Van Dorn until the renovations are completed.

Bitty introduced me to several people working there, and volunteers, like Cindy Nelson and Melody Doyle, two of the Divas. Cindy, you may recall, had been part of the team to bag the frozen senator, but didn't stay for the graveside relocation. Nor had she gone with us to retrieve him. Except for Georgie, only the older generation had been foolhardy enough to continue, and since Georgie is Gaynelle's niece, she'd probably felt an obligation to help. I'm glad to say all charges against participating Divas were dropped upon their complete cooperation with the police, by the way, which is really good since there's something called a Class D felony applied to the unauthorized toting of corpses around town.

Anyway, Cindy and Melody helped me research Generals Forrest and Grant, and both men's connection to Holly Springs and different houses here. Of course, I didn't share reasons for my sudden interest, just a desire to reacquaint myself with our history.

After Cindy showed me where to look, I thanked her and Melody, and said Bitty could help me with the rest of it. A tactful dismissal, I thought, since I had no wish to try to focus on a clue to my own distraction while keeping an ear out for Bitty's chatter.

Both of them seemed glad to leave us with the stacks of carefully logged newspaper clippings and journal ledgers and handwritten histories.

"I'm sure Mrs. Smythe wouldn't like anything on the clippings," Bitty said before I so much as touched one of the books, and handed me cotton gloves. "Wear these. It keeps oil from your fingers damaging the old books."

"I'd never have thought of that."

"Oh, poor precious! You shouldn't be here at all."

Chen Ling sneezed at the dust stirred up, but since I'd told Bitty not to bring her anyway, I didn't even listen to her fussing at me for dragging them out.

After nearly an hour of reading fascinating and often heart-wrenching accounts of Civil War exploits, I'd learned that Holly Springs had endured sixty-two raids during those years, and that afterward, Vicksburg, Jackson, and Holly Springs were the only nineteenth century towns to ever be federally occupied, and that Holly Springs was federally occupied for ten years during Reconstruction. While there were accounts of savagery on both sides, there were also accounts of men like Hiram Revels, who had been the very first black senator.

As for Grant and Forrest, I read about Grant's stay at Walter Place during his occupation of Holly Springs, and how the Govan women having been once burned out of their house by the Yankees, had already buried their family silver beneath the Walter Place's front walkway by the time the Union general got to town. An excellent example of foresight.

"Listen to this, Bitty," I said, even though she'd ignored my other gems of information, "'When Grant occupied Holly Springs, the Govan women who were staying at Walter Place by the owner's permission, shared the house with Grant's wife and son, as well as Mrs. Grant's slave, a gift from her father when she was born. The Govan ladies took much pleasure out of watching Yankee sentries walk over their family silver every day without so much as a hint of what lay buried beneath their feet.' Isn't that something?"

"Yes," Bitty said, nodding, "but I already knew that. Then Forrest chased Grant out of Holly Springs, and he left his wife Julie, their son Jesse, and their slave named Jule behind."

"Well, you've got part of that right. Van Dorn, along with a large troop of Confederate soldiers, chased Grant out of town. Then they took what they needed from Union supplies at the railroad depot, and burned the rest. One report says as much as four million dollars worth, but a more conservative estimate puts it at a million and a half. Whichever, it set General Grant back in his march to Vicksburg by several months."

"Did you get to the part yet where General Van Dorn sent a squad of Confederates to Walter Place to search for General Grant?"

"I did. And the Govan ladies barred the gates and wouldn't let them in, afraid they might try to take Mrs. Grant hostage."

Bitty smiled. "I love that story. And because Van Dorn was such a gentleman and did nothing to harm Mrs. Grant or the other ladies, General Grant returned the favor when he got to Port Gibson, Van Dorn's home town, and so spared it from being destroyed."

I read and reread the accounts, some by witnesses, some by more contemporary historians from stories handed down by family members who'd been there, but something eluded me. Some small fact that should be obvious. What on earth could it be?

"Well," I mused aloud, more to myself than Bitty, "Forrest was born in Bedford County, Tennessee, the name of which was later changed to Marshall County, not in Ashland, Mississippi like you and Rayna said."

"I said Salem. Or maybe it was New Salem. Not that it matters that much. He lived here as a little boy and grew up here, and that's what counts. Besides, Benton County was part of Tippah County first, I think. So, have you found out what you wanted to know yet?"

"No." I decided not to challenge her newest version of history. "I mean, I've found out a lot of new things, like Forrest wasn't at all the racist I always thought. After the war ended he spent all his pension money on soldiers who came home to nothing, both black and white soldiers."

Bitty stood up. "Now that we have the life history of Forrest memorized, may I leave?"

"I suppose."

Maybe I should have focused more on Grant than Forrest. Whatever it was I'd thought I'd find still eluded me. And yet I just knew I'd read the key somewhere in all that historical data and anecdote. It left me frustrated and unsettled, even after we got back to Six Chimneys.

I certainly wasn't in a mood to deal with legions of Bitty fans, or the people who came to try and dig out some nugget of information that could be passed along to others. The last gave me heartburn. I had to be especially attentive, and not get sidetracked by one person while another one waylaid Bitty.

So we compromised, Bitty agreeing to an evening of near isolation with only a few Divas as company. Gaynelle, Georgie, Rayna, and Melody played court to Bitty's tragic queen façade. Since it was the Divas, I didn't have to hover over Bitty like an avenging angel as most of them had taken part in our lunacy. Only Melody remained ignorant—or hopefully so—of the depths of our depredations.

"Let's get comfortable," Bitty said, and wearing a sour-faced Chen Ling against her chest like some kind of malignant growth, she led the way from the kitchen where we'd first gathered to stock up on food and drink.

Thankfully, she led us to the parlor, known less formally as the den, where the furniture is comfortable and we could kick off our shoes without feeling as if we'd committed sacrilege. Rayna stretched out on a plush chair and ottoman, her painted toenails a bright splash of color against the pale cream upholstery.

"This has all been such a mess," she said, and no one had to ask what she meant. "Who'd have thought Philip Hollandale would end up murdered?"

"I always did," Bitty said, and ignored my dirty look. "Someone was bound to do it. After all, look how many people lost their jobs when he voted against that tax bill that would have kept the bicycle plant in business. Over four hundred, wasn't it?"

"Hollandale wasn't the only one who voted against it," Gaynelle pointed out.

"No," Georgie said, "but his was the deciding vote. If he'd listened to the offers made by plant employees and CEO's, Roger would still be in Mississippi, not off in Arizona."

"Roger was Georgette's companion," Gaynelle said primly, and Georgie flushed.

"Just a friend," she said quickly, "a good friend. He went nearly a year without finding a job that'd pay near what he'd been making as a line supervisor at the bicycle plant."

"See?" Bitty said, waving a hand toward Georgie, "even her friend Roger has a motive for killing Philip. Not that he did, of course."

"Well," Melody said, "we all know no matter what you *felt* like doing, you'd never harm anyone, Bitty, even your ex-husband."

"Thank you, Melody, it's nice to know who my true friends are during this terrible time." Bitty smiled. Chen Ling sulked. Then Bitty looked over at me as she fed the pug a cracker spread with goose liver pâté and said, "Some people think I talk too much."

I sucked down an inch of white zinfandel and smiled. Agreement would be rude, but even a polite lie would sound too false.

After a moment, Rayna said, "Goose liver pâté is really bad for dogs, you know. Too rich. I had to stop, and poor Redd is just really upset about it. She loves pâté. Dr. Coltrane advised that I stick to dog food, so I started making it. Boiled chicken and long grain rice. It's very good for them and they love it."

"Oh my, poor Chen Ling," Bitty said, looking stricken. "Do you think I've poisoned her?"

"Lord no, Bitty. But it's not good for her. If you want, I'll give you the recipe for dog food that I got from Aunt Anna. I bet she loves it."

"So," I said, more a statement than a question," you've decided to keep Chitling."

Bitty made a face. "Trinket's being mean. She wants me to give Chen Ling back to Luann Carey, but I think she'll be much happier here. Unless . . . unless I go to prison, of course. Then I'll have to make sure she's cared for while I'm . . . while I'm gone."

The tears that suddenly welled up in Bitty's eyes were genuine, and I felt as mean as she said I was. "Oh honey, you know I want you to have what makes you happy," I said immediately. "I just don't want you to get attached to an older dog, that's all. It's devastating when they die."

Before I knew it, we were hugging each other, with Chen Ling squashed between us and growling. "I know, Trinket," Bitty said, sniffling a little, "but I'd rather have months of joy than years of just okay."

Since she'd made me cry, too, the horrible wretch, I said, "That's the worst paraphrase of Shelby I've ever heard," and we both laughed.

Gaynelle explained to a perplexed Melody, "*Steel Magnolias*. It's a movie, and Shelby is the character who dies. One of our favorites."

"Oh," Melody said as if she understood, but I could tell she didn't. Ah well. She was too young yet. Give her another decade or two, a marriage and-or child, and no one would have to explain it at all. "So, Bitty," Melody said next, "it's probably best y'all didn't get caught moving the senator's body around. That'd only make all this worse."

A brief silence fell, and we must have all looked a little surprised, since the only ones who knew about that were the Divas involved and the police. It was one of the many facts being withheld for the moment. Melody blinked when no one responded.

"Don't you think?" she asked a little tentatively.

"Where on earth did you hear that?" Gaynelle demanded, using her schoolteacher voice, and Melody seemed to jump a foot off the couch.

"Cindy said . . . well, I just heard . . . should I not have said anything?"

Leaning forward, Gaynelle put her hand on Melody's arm, "No, you should not. It's not something that needs to be said, and I'm quite surprised at Cynthia Nelson for being so foolish as to share such gossip. I'll have a word with her about this."

"Oh no! Please don't—I'll just die. I didn't know I wasn't supposed to say anything to you all, and Cindy and I are getting to be such good friends. I'd hate to ruin that with my big mouth."

Melody looked so upset, and kept apologizing, and finally Gaynelle agreed not to chastise Cindy for speaking out of turn. "But do not say a word to another living soul about anything like that," she added. "It could be very detrimental not only to Bitty, but to all of us."

I noted that Gaynelle neither denied nor confirmed Melody's information. She's good.

Since the festive air had dissipated, they left one by one, with Rayna being the last to leave. She took Bitty's hand in hers.

"Call me for that dog food recipe. And just be careful, okay?"

"Good heavens, Rayna," Bitty said with a little laugh, "I'm not at all sure there's anything bad left to happen."

Rayna didn't smile. "Well, there is. And I'd hate to see it happen to you. Stop poking your nose in places you shouldn't and stay home, please. Good night, Bitty, Trinket."

"Well, isn't that the strangest thing," Bitty said when she shut the door and locked it, "her sounding so . . . so much like a crossing guard. Warning me to be careful."

"She's right, Bitty. Think about it. Philip's dead. Sanders is dead. And someone tried to kill me."

Holding Chen Ling close, Bitty chewed on her bottom lip. "I'd hoped that maybe you just got lost, you know. Chen Ling ran so far so quickly—I mean, who'd have expected a little dog like her to be able to do that? And when I got back you were gone. At first I didn't worry about it since you're always so capable. And much bigger than Sanders, so I figured you'd just make him behave. Then when I realized you were really gone and Sanders wasn't there, and I heard this banging noise and I got scared . . . Trinket, I'm so sorry. I left you out there alone with whoever did that to you."

"You did exactly the right thing. Someone who's killed twice won't hesitate to kill a few more times, I think. You might have ended up in the cellar with me."

"Do you think they meant to kill you?"

I'd been wondering about that myself. The blow on my head had been nasty, but not fatal. Was that on purpose, or was I meant to be dead? From the angle of the cut in my scalp, doctors in the emergency room said it looked as if a much shorter person had struck me. Jackson Lee and I didn't want to alarm Bitty, but Sergeant Maxwell leaned toward the theory that Bitty had done it to me. Preposterous, of course.

But what really bothered Jackson Lee was how the prosecutors had shaped a damaging case against Bitty: wronged wife, an ex-husband determined to thwart her desire to get Sanders' house on the register, and Sanders himself being an obstacle to her goal. As the only eye-witness, I was a liability, they seemed to think, so she might have wanted to get rid of me.

As I said, preposterous.

"I don't know," I finally said to Bitty, "but if they did mean to kill me, they might be irritated they didn't succeed."

Bitty's eyes got wide. "You mean—they might try again?"

"Bitty, I can't help but wonder if *both* of us aren't dangerous to someone."

I really didn't want to frighten Bitty, but she needed to realize how vulnerable she was and how easily she could be hurt, physically as well as emotionally.

After sucking in a deep breath and apparently squeezing Chen

Ling a little too hard, Bitty got up to get a cloth to clean her pants. "It's a good thing my boys are coming home tomorrow," she said. "I'll make them stay here and keep us safe."

All the air left my lungs. Now, just so you'll know, I dearly love Clayton and Brandon. Two of the smartest, nicest, most wonderful hellions you'd ever meet. Alike as two peas in a pod, but just in appearance. Clayton is always ready for a party, gregarious and noisy. Brandon is more intellectual, but just as loud. Brandon would make an excellent attorney. Clayton would make an excellent prisoner. Brandon smokes Marlboros. Clayton smokes pot. Brandon has switched his major three times. Clayton doesn't have a major, other than professional student. Both are very attractive to the opposite sex, and wherever they are, there are always people and beer.

So it's understandable that the prospect of their arrival left me less than enthusiastic.

"Where on earth will they stay?" I finally squeaked as Bitty wiped pug piddle off the front of her pants.

"Heavens, Trinket, I have six bedrooms. There's enough room. I forgot to tell Sharita about it, though, so we'll have to run out tomorrow and get in enough food. Oh, and Jefferson is coming over for dinner tomorrow night. Did I mention that?"

"You didn't mention any of this. Bitty, I don't think this is a good idea at all."

She looked surprised. "Why not?"

There were so many reasons that I couldn't drag just one out as the most important, so I said at random, "Too many people, frat parties, beer, cigarettes, food—does Jefferson care that you've been charged with the murder of your ex-husband?"

Sometimes Bitty really does focus. "I told the boys not to bring anyone home with them, that I'm not up to parties, they can't get drunk or smoke in the house, we're going to Carlisle's and the Pig for food tomorrow anyway, and Jefferson is quite adamant that I'm not at all guilty so it doesn't matter to him in the least." She paused to take a breath, and then smiled. "See? Don't you feel better now?"

"Oh, much." My sarcasm went unnoticed. "Do you still have that prescription of Valium, by any chance?"

Bitty just laughed. I'm not known to take even an aspirin, so if I feel the need for any kind of medication, then the pain is unbearable or the doctor unmovable. I much prefer the medication that Mother Nature has given us: fermented grapes or barley and hops. And of course, chocolate.

I took half a bottle of wine and entire bar of dark chocolate up to my room and proceeded to self-medicate the hell out of myself. Don't scoff until you've tried it.

When I woke the next morning, it was to sweet, blessed peace. No awful sound marred the morning, one of those late March days that lets you know Spring has sprung. Birds chirped merrily in the tree tops outside my window, soft golden light streamed through window glass and sheers, and I could have sworn I heard angels singing. The heady aroma of brewing coffee teased me downstairs to find a singing angel in the kitchen.

"Sharita, aren't you here a day early?"

"Two," she replied with a laugh. "I had a cancellation, so I let Miss Bitty talk me into coming in an extra day."

"Has Bitty already been downstairs?"

"She drank three cups of coffee and left an hour ago."

In the act of reaching for a coffee mug, I stopped and turned to look at Sharita. "Tell me you're kidding. She left?"

"And took Yoda with her."

Normally, I'd have found that amusing, but the thought of Bitty being on her own with her mouth well-oiled and primed made me nervous.

"Did she say where she was headed?"

"To see Jackson Lee."

That made me feel a little better. I poured my coffee, and wondered if I should mention to Jackson Lee my persistent belief that General Forrest had something to do with Philip Hollandale's death. Probably not, though it would make an excellent insanity defense if needed.

"I shouldn't have slept so late," I said, and sat at the kitchen table to sample one of the freshly-baked cinnamon rolls Sharita put into the biscuit warmer. "I swear, Bitty and I are taking on each other's bad habits. She's getting up early now, and I've started sleeping late."

Sharita agreed. "Bitty certainly has changed lately. Guess I would, too, if I was the only suspect the police were looking at for two murders. I wouldn't sleep at all."

"That makes sense. What was that you were singing before I got down here?"

"*My Lord, What A Mornin'*. My grandmother used to sing it on days just like this one. It seemed appropriate."

I had to agree. "It's lovely. I thought I heard angels singing down here."

"You ought to come over to our church sometime. I think you'd like it. We do a lot of singing."

"I may do that. I love to sing."

"You'd be most welcome. We need a new alto in our choir."

With the new information I'd learned about Forrest, I decided to ask her a bold question. "What do you know about General Nathan Bedford Forrest?"

That surprised Sharita. She stopped stirring whatever it was she had in a big bowl that looked awful and smelled heavenly, and turned to look at me. Any fear that I'd insulted her by asking such a question disappeared when she said, "He wasn't always the terrible man a lot of people claim he was, not according to my granny, anyway. Granny's grandmother was born to slaves, and after the war, it was General Forrest who gave her granddaddy a mule and enough money to buy seed corn. Times were bad for everyone back then, black and white. Except for scalawags that came in like buzzards to buy land and property out from everyone."

"Like Sherman Sanders' family?"

Sharita nodded. "That's right. You know, my granny still says that her granny talked a lot about The Cedars, and how the family who owned it before and during the war lost it to Yankee carpetbaggers. One of them was a former soldier who came to Holly Springs with General Grant, a lieutenant, I think. He came back after the war ended and paid the taxes on The Cedars, and got it right out from under the family's nose. All their men had been killed, and only the women were left. Not that they could have paid the taxes anyway. There were a lot of bitter feelings back then, and for a long time afterward. The Richmonds claimed they'd had the money to pay the taxes but the Sanders got the tax men to stall just long enough so they could take illegal possession. Put the womenfolk and kids right out, with only the clothes on their backs. Didn't let them take a stick of furniture with them, either. Not even the kids' doll babies."

"Do you think the Richmonds really had the money for the taxes?"

Shrugging, Sharita said, "My granny says they did, but how could they? Confederate bills were worthless by that time, anyway. Worth more now than they were back then."

"A shame. There are hundreds of stories like that all over the South. Probably a few up North, as well, but of course, they didn't go through Reconstruction."

We dwelled on that for a moment, both from our own unique perspective, then Bitty came in and all conversation halted as she launched into one of her Bitty-tales. This one had to do with the indignities and shameful conduct of certain judicial members who'd denied Jackson Lee's petition to drop the charges against Bitty because of circumstantial evidence.

"Just what kind of evidence do they think they have?" she demanded from no one in particular. "A few specks of blood on my shoes, my fingerprints on an aluminum pot, of all things to worry about, and Philip thawing out in my wine cellar. It's police brutality, that's what it is, just police brutality!"

Sensitive to the fact that Sharita's brother is Marcus Stone, the officer who arrested Bitty, I looked at her, but she only smiled. She obviously knew Bitty meant nothing personal against Officer Stone.

Sharita and I made soothing, noncommittal sounds that Bitty viewed as agreement. She sat down at the table with Chen Ling tucked under her chin, and destroyed a cinnamon roll with her fingers, shredding more than she consumed. I eyed it wistfully. I really hate to see cinnamon rolls vandalized.

"Have the police found out where Philip was hidden?" I asked when it looked like she intended to massacre another cinnamon roll, and licking icing from her fingers, Bitty shrugged.

"Probably a warehouse freezer. They're still looking. Someone must have kept Sanders there too, though I don't know about that. And just think, Trinket, we had that same—"

"Bitty, when are the boys due to arrive?" I interrupted before she said more than she needed to say in front of a police officer's sister. It's not like Marcus Stone had to already know all the details anyway, but no point in putting Sharita on the spot.

"Any time now," she said, happily distracted. "I haven't seen them in ages. It's Spring Break and they'd planned on staying the whole time down in Florida, but I wish they'd stay here. They can go to Fort Lauderdale any old time."

I brightened. The likelihood of two college boys being persuaded to stay with their drama-prone mother instead of bikini-clad college girls wasn't great. I'd convince them they weren't needed here yet, and promise to summon them home when they were. It sounded so perfect.

And as in so many things that sound perfect in theory, reality proved to be quite different.

CHAPTER 16

Clayton and Brandon arrived in a whirlwind of noise and energy. It was both exhilarating and exhausting. Sometimes I wonder if that's my age or my intolerance showing, since after about ten minutes of high-level, frenetic activity, I'm ready for a quiet, solitary corner. But then, I've been that way since my twenties. While I prefer to think of it as achieving maturity, Bitty has referred to it as having a stick up my rear. Or words very close to that.

From the moment Brandon pulled his gleaming black sports car into Bitty's driveway, the walls rattled and roof shingles fluttered. Brandon is just naturally a loud speaker, which I think will be a great asset if he does go into law or becomes a carnival barker. Clayton, the younger by two minutes, is determined to be heard over his brother. The result is very similar to being caught in the middle of a volcanic eruption.

As I've said, Bitty's sons are identical twins, both tall, blond-haired, with brown eyes and the general physique of their father, who'd been a jock at Ole Miss when Bitty met him. Neither of the boys have their father's natural inclination to dishonesty, thank goodness, though I put that down to Bitty's high expectations rather than genetics. She's the kind of mother who expects the best from her offspring, and accepts nothing less. Her sons turn themselves inside out to please her, and while Bitty can be indulgent at times, when she says she's had enough, she's had enough and they toe the line.

So about the time my head began to vibrate at that high speed that shatters glass, Bitty said calmly to them, "That's enough, boys. Your Aunt Trinket's getting those unsightly lines between her eyebrows again."

Blessed silence fell, though my ears still hummed a little.

I sorted through the rapid-fire things they'd said since coming in the front door, and said, "So Brandon, you've changed your major to pre-law classes?"

"Yes, ma'am." Properly reared Southerners always use that courtesy with older family members and complete strangers. Most of the time, you just can't get them *not* to say it, it's that deeply ingrained. "Mama says I can argue the hide off a coon hound, so I figured that might come in handy." Brandon nudged his brother. "Besides, the way Clayton's going, he'll need a good lawyer in the family."

Clayton shoved back. "Better shut up, bro."

Bitty narrowed her eyes. "All right. What's going on?"

It was amazing, watching the transformation from often scattered drama queen to "I mean business" mother. Just as amazing, the two young men slouching in their chairs at the kitchen table sat up straight and looked nervous.

After a hesitation, Clayton said firmly, "We didn't want to worry you, not with all you've had happening lately, but I've gotten myself into a fix at school. I've been accused of cheating by one of my professors."

Bitty just looked at him with one brow lifted, and after a moment, Clayton added in a much less confident tone, "I didn't cheat, Mama. Not really."

"And what, pray tell, does 'not really' mean?"

"Well, I've been making a little extra cash, you know, so I don't have to keep asking for money."

"How have you been doing that, by stealing and selling tests?"

"*No ma'am!*" both young men said at the same time. Then Brandon said, "Clayton's just been helping out a few people with failing grades, that's all. He feels sorry for them, because most of them have to work all the time to pay for their tuition, while we've got trust funds and don't have to work, so have plenty of time for studying."

"So you *give* them the tests you've stolen? And I'm asking Clayton, not you, Brandon. Let him speak for himself." She trained her gaze on Clayton, who fidgeted like he was twelve.

"No ma'am, I haven't stolen anything, I swear. I write papers for them. Most of the time the professors don't know who we are anyway, so I write the paper and they sign their name."

"Out of the goodness of your heart."

Clayton's appeasing smile faded. "No ma'am, not quite. There's a small fee, you know, just for my time. But then they pass the class."

"Clayton Caldwell, that's *cheating*. It's turning in work they haven't done. Shame on you for being a part of something like that."

There were a few uncomfortable moments during which I decided this needed to be a private family discussion, and I eased away from the table and went out to the screened porch. It was once the old kitchen, separate from the house in case of fire, connected only by a breezeway. Over the years and renovations, it's become a nice-sized screened-in porch, accessible just off the new kitchen. It still has a fireplace on one wall, with one of the six chimneys sticking up and painted white. In cold weather, a nice fire gets the chill off the air. But I turned on the ceiling fan and sat down in a wicker lounge to reflect on the perils of motherhood. Then I had the sudden urge to call my daughter, so I did.

To my delight, she picked up her cell phone immediately. "Mama, I was just thinking about you!"

We both laughed. The miles disappeared, and it was like she was right beside me. Michelle has this laugh that makes everyone around her want to laugh with her, one of those full, joyful, from deep inside laughs. When she was little, she had a stuffed rabbit Mama gave her for Easter, with a voice box laugh almost identical to hers. She named it Thumper for the giggly rabbit in the movie *Bambi*. Whenever she laughs now, I think about Thumper, and I smile.

"How's Aunt Bitty?" Michelle asked after we'd gone down the usual conversational route of her health, husband, job, and new house-hunting. "Is she holding up all right?"

"Clayton and Brandon just got here. She's turned into Super-Mom. She'll be fine."

"That's probably just what she needs, a distraction to take her mind off everything."

"Any more distractions," I said, "and she won't be able to fit the murder charges into her busy schedule. She's adopted a dog, too."

"Aunt Bitty? A dog? Now, why didn't I ever think of that? It's just perfect for her. She needs something to mother. What kind of dog?"

"A pug. Looks like a small Yoda. Or one of those Muppets. The cranky one."

Michelle laughed. "Did she name it Oscar?"

"It's a female named Lady something. She calls it Chen Ling. I call it Chitling."

"I feel so much better now that you're back home. I hated it when you were off all alone, you were so unhappy, and I always worried so much about you."

That got my attention. "About me? I liked being alone."

"I know. That's what worried me. I think you're doing much better now that you've got Grandad and Grandma close by, and of course, Aunt Bitty."

Bitty isn't really her aunt, like I'm not Clayton and Brandon's aunt, but since it's always so confusing and troublesome to go through the kinship rituals, even distant relatives are called aunt or uncle. Unless they're disliked. Then they aren't called at all, but avoided if possible.

"Well," I said, "I'm glad *you* feel better. You may have to come visit me in Whitfield."

Even Michelle, who didn't grow up at all in Mississippi, knows that Whitfield is the state insane asylum. Of course they call it something else now, rehabilitation, or mental health facility, or some other name that really means the same thing. You're there because "you ain't right" in the head, whether through no fault of your own or self-inflicted substance abuse.

"Of all people in the world, you're not one I'll ever have to worry about checking into a mental facility of any kind," Michelle said firmly, and I sighed.

"That's too bad. I was looking forward to a little room service."

When we hung up, I felt able to face almost anything, and I hope she had reassurance that I'm never too far away from her. Sometimes I make the mistake of thinking of her as she was at three, or six, or fifteen, then I remember she's nearly thirty and on her own, and the love I had for her as a child has only grown, too. It's the nice thing about children. Mothers tend to forget most of the bad things sooner or later. The good things are forever.

Bitty joined me on the porch, and sat down in the wicker rocker next to me and handed me a Bloody Mary. "It's fresh," she said. "Brandon took a bartending class."

"Is that part of pre-law?"

"Must be mandatory. Every lawyer I've ever known can make any drink you name."

"So, all's well?"

"It will be. I'm going to have a talk with his professor to see if we can work out a way for Clayton to make up the classes he missed, but if we can't, then he'll fail the course. He's lucky they're not considering expelling him."

"This is very good," I said about the drink, "just spicy enough without being too spicy."

Bitty grinned. "Brandon said he learned how to make these for old ladies at Oxford garden club functions."

"I don't know whether to be insulted, or wish I belonged to the Oxford Garden Club."

We sat there for a little while, chatting aimlessly about our kids and the pretty weather, and everything except Philip Hollandale and Sherman Sanders. The ceiling fan stirred cool air, birds sang outside, and wonderful smells still came from the kitchen even though Sharita had left a few hours earlier.

For some reason, I thought about Melody Doyle saying what she had the night before. "How well do you know Melody?" I asked Bitty, who was stirring the last of her drink with the celery stalk.

"Um, not really well. She's so young, you know. But her family's always lived here. For a while she lived down in Georgia, went there after school, met a man and I guess that didn't work out so well. Marcy brought her to a Diva meeting, and since two of our members had moved, and since her mother was Maybelle Overton, we invited her to join us."

"Maybelle Overton . . . you know, I'd forgotten about her. Cancer, wasn't it?"

Bitty nodded. "Just terrible. She went so quick, and Melody just a little thing. Maybelle's mother raised her. Did as well as she could by her, but I always thought she was a scary old lady. Dressed in long black dresses and wore her hair pulled back into that tight bun."

"I remember her. She tapped me with the end of her cane once for talking in church."

We both laughed at that. Sunday morning church meetings had seemed to go on forever when we were kids, and Bitty and I used to try and sneak out if we got permission to sit in the back. My sister Emerald always sat up front with Mama and Daddy, dressed in her prim little dress and shiny shoes, with ribbons in her pretty blond hair and her hands folded in her lap. I rarely made it to church without getting dirt on my dress, and ribbons never stayed long in my unruly hair. Next to Emerald, I always looked like a cartoon character anyway. I can attest to the fact that there are three-hundred-sixty-eight bricks visible in the wall of the store next door to the church, in case you get stuck sitting in the first pew. There's a big window by that pew. I still think Emerald figured out how to sleep through the sermons with her eyes open.

"When are the boys due to leave for Florida?" I asked casually, not that I was anxious for them to go or anything, it's just that two more cars had pulled up outside and loud music rattled all six chimneys.

"Oh, they're not going this year. Clayton needs to learn consequences for his actions, and I told them they can both stay home. Besides, I like having them around. It's been too quiet lately without them, don't you think?"

By now my eyes had crossed and my head vibrated like a tuning fork to the beat of a song with lyrics something like *"don't you mess with me"* and a few other words I'd rather not repeat.

"Yes," I mumbled when I could speak without screaming, "much too quiet. How long is Spring Break?"

"Ten days. They're coming back for the pilgrimage, though. They can't miss that. It's the highlight of the year, and they're always so handsome in their uniforms, don't you think?"

Photos of Clayton and Brandon in gray Confederate uniforms sat atop the mantel in the living room. And hung on the wall in the living room. And on the wall above the landing at the top of the stairs. And in the hallway. And in Bitty's room, and—well, suffice it to say, there are photos of them in every stage of growing up, wearing Confederate uniforms with officers' hats and swords. There have been a few incidents with the swords over the years, but since most of them are too dull to slice bread, nothing more serious than bruises inflicted by the spontaneous—and unauthorized—battle reenactments.

"Handsome," I said truthfully, "very handsome."

An idea began to form in my brain. I knew if I stayed with Bitty much longer I'd be a candidate for Whitfield's caring embrace, so I decided to take my own spring break. With the permission of Jackson

Lee, of course. Just in case. So I went to see him in his office right after lunch and before a complete melt-down.

Jackson Lee, either convinced by the nervous tic under my right eye or the way my head occasionally jerked to one side, agreed that Clayton and Brandon were indeed quite capable of monitoring Bitty's unfettered conversation.

"Not quite as well as you can, of course," he said, smiling a little, "but I'll talk to them so they know how important it is that she doesn't say anything inappropriate."

"Every other word out of Bitty's mouth is inappropriate. I was thinking along the lines of incriminating," I said, then added, "Talk to Brandon. He's taking pre-law classes. Besides, he has the calmer nature of the two. Which isn't saying a whole lot."

Jackson Lee grinned. "I'm familiar with Clayton and Brandon. They're just three years behind my youngest son."

I'd forgotten Jackson Lee has three boys of his own. The oldest must be around thirty-five by now, the youngest, twenty-five. They still live up in Memphis, and all have jobs and two are married with kids, according to Bitty.

"That's just chronologically," I said. "Maturity-wise, Clayton and Brandon are still about sixteen much of the time."

"Well, so's their mama. It's not a bad trait to have occasionally; it just gets a little inconvenient when there are problems."

"An understatement if ever I heard one. So, do you think it'll be all right if I take a break from babysitting? Just while the boys are here, of course. If they don't work out, I'll buy ear plugs, a suit of armor and a stun gun, and go stay with her again."

Jackson Lee walked me to the door of his office. "Use that stun gun correctly, and you won't need any of the other stuff."

I really like Jackson Lee. He's practical.

So Jackson Lee had a talk with Clayton and Brandon, I told Bitty that I thought she and her boys needed some private time together, and I packed up my little carry-on case and went back to Cherryhill. It was like the difference between Oz and Kansas. The phrase "There's no place like home" kept going around and around in my head, and I truly appreciated what Dorothy must have felt waking up in her own bed again to black and white sanity instead of Technicolor insanity.

Cute little Munchkins aside, there hadn't been a single attraction in the Emerald City that justified one more moment in Oz.

Mama and Daddy were delighted to see me, and even Brownie greeted me at the door with a degree of enthusiasm only slightly more than that exhibited by France greeting the Nazi invasion. I felt truly welcome.

"I don't suppose he's passed my emerald earring yet?" I asked Mama, and as I expected, the answer was No. I sighed. A good earring, gone forever.

Apparently, the official arrival of Spring summons a new wardrobe in the Truevine household, as Mama wore cotton instead of wool, and Daddy and Brownie wore matching cotton tee shirts that said *N'awlins* in big letters. Souvenirs of their recent cruise, of course. My shirt is upstairs in my closet, a hot pink imprinted with *Bourbon Street* and a light pole that Daddy had chosen. He's never quite understood the color scheme-complexion connection. Mama had tried to tactfully dissuade him, but he'd insisted I'd be lovely in it. He'd picked one out for Emerald in a bright yellow that will turn her complexion sallow. We'll probably end up swapping if we can manage it without Daddy noticing.

Even though Cherryhill isn't full of antiques, just old furniture, and a lot of the decoration is more thirties and fifties style from the twentieth century instead of the nineteenth like Bitty's, it still felt so good to be home again. Floors creak under my feet in all the familiar places, the same windows stick, and I have to turn the hot water faucet on the tub in the opposite direction from where it's supposed to turn. Michelle was right. I need to be here.

That first day back home, I helped Daddy bring up some of the old furniture from the cellar where it was stored under covers and only used during the pilgrimage, fragile pieces that'd probably soon disintegrate if used daily. A lovely chest Great-Grandmother Truevine had used when she was a little girl still had scorch marks on it, souvenirs of the fire that'd destroyed their original house. It was one of the few pieces saved, along with a few framed photographs, and other odds and ends salvaged from the charred remains and nearby family members.

"My great-great-grandmother barely had time to stash the family silver before the Yankees got here," Daddy said, breathing a little heavily as we took a rest in the kitchen. "She buried it under the scarecrow in a just-planted cornfield. Not that it was worth that much then, just that it was all we had of any value. Rhondda Tryweryn, daughter of Griffith Jones, brought it with her when she married Dafyyd Tryweryn. That was back in the eighteenth century, before Morgan Tryweryn anglicized our surname to Truevine."

As I listened to Daddy tell the familiar story his father had told him, and his father before him, I felt a connection to all those who'd gone before me, all the Truevines and Tryweryns, the Joneses and others. There's something in the human soul that needs to make that connection, no matter if ancestors were common working people or royalty. It's a promise for the future, as well as a history of the past. Southerners in particular cling to that reassurance, maybe because there have been so many attempts to eradicate or deny it. While there are those who fictionalize their family roots, the real joy is in the truth. Endurance. Survival. Knowing that despite tremendous hardships and incredible dangers, your people survived to bring you into the world. I really think most Southerners recognize and respect the shared hardships and kinships with the people once enslaved. After all, many Southerners had come here as indentured servants or were enslaved by hunger and poverty, and most Southerners never owned a slave. Only the wealthy could afford to feed another mouth. And after the war, when devastation lay all around, black and white families struggled side-by-side to survive. It took another generation for prejudice to once more supplant basic survival. In my opinion, when some people have enough food to eat and enough time to waste, it's far too often spent unwisely.

Anyway, I helped Daddy prepare Cherryhill for the pilgrimage, brought up the heavy stands with velvet ropes to barricade certain areas, and unpacked the brochures the Historical Society had provided with the history of our house. Even though it was two weeks before the pilgrimage, I think Mama and Daddy just like to reacquaint themselves with our history. Mama has things she brought from the Crews side of the family, who had owned slaves up in Hardeman County. I'm not particularly proud of that part of our history, although I do understand it was a different era. Family legend says they were well-cared for, and hidden in the basement for the first part of the war, but after the Battle of Shiloh's catastrophic events very close by, they were set free. Many of them even wanted to stay, since it was all they knew, but there wasn't enough food for all. It must have been a terrible time for everyone.

Later, when I sat upstairs on the sleeping porch sipping sweet tea and watching clouds chase the sun away, I thought again about what Daddy had said. For some reason, I just knew his history lecture was connected to Philip Hollandale's death. How, I hadn't a clue. See how my mind works? It teases me with bits of information but never makes a connection, so all I have going around in my brain are all these unconnected pieces that make no sense at all. It's really maddening.

Right before I fell asleep, it occurred to me that maybe the Truevines were related to the Hollandales somehow, or even Sherman Sanders. As unlikely as it'd be that no relationship had ever been mentioned, there might be some dark tidbit of history that had been long-buried in our family ancestry legends. And how on earth that connected to Generals Grant and Forrest, I hadn't a single idea. But I intended to check it out.

Cindy Nelson seemed surprised to see me back at the museum. "Hey," she said, "you're getting to be a regular customer."

I smiled. "I insist upon paying my two dollars this time. If I'm going to take up space and use museum facilities, I might as well do my part to help support it."

Smiling back at me, Cindy took the two dollars. "Ever think about volunteering a day or two? Even once or twice a month would be wonderful. There's just so much to do, what with the restoration and all. If I didn't have to leave early every day to pick up my kids at school, or go to school functions, I'd probably spend a lot more time here. It's fascinating."

"You know," I said, "that's a thought. I'd hoped for a paying job, but no one seems to want a middle-aged woman whose skills range from typing to answering phones. I'm a little limited in my employability, I fear."

Cindy assured me I'd be more than qualified for a volunteer position, but there were some paying positions available in the county clerk's office if I was interested. I didn't want to admit I had already tried that and been turned down, so I said I'd consider it.

"Where's Melody today?" I asked to change the subject, and Cindy shrugged.

"She comes in just when she can. She's working for Dr. Johnston now, you know."

"I remember her saying that. It's very convenient for her, not having to drive to Memphis every day to work."

"Melody? When did she do that?"

"Before she took the job with Dr. Johnston. Didn't she? Maybe I misunderstood."

"Well, I haven't seen her since our last Diva day, so I could be wrong. Anyway, now she doesn't have as much time as she used to. I think business is picking up for Dr. Johnston since he always seems to be booked when I call to get an appointment. I've got this spur on my heel that's been bothering me."

Since she was wearing sandals, Cindy showed me the spur and I agreed that it needed to be seen, then someone called her to come help move another stack of files, and she left me alone in the room with old books and ledgers. These weren't yet copied to computers or microfiche files. The oldest ones were contained in special cases to retard deterioration, and the handwritten entries in old county ledgers are graceful, spidery loops and swirls peculiar to that century. I think that sometimes progress isn't all that pretty or progressive.

While I flipped through entries looking for deeds or sales, or any reference to the Sanders, Truevine, and Hollandale families having done business, it occurred to me Cindy Nelson hadn't been quite truthful. I had seen her in the museum just this past week, and Melody Doyle was here then, too. It probably meant nothing more than the forgetfulness of a busy mother and young wife, but still, it seemed a little odd that she'd say that.

My hours spent poring over local history and family roots as tangled as kudzu vines turned out to be futile. I found nothing linking the Truevine, Hollandale, or Sanders families except their burials in Hill Crest Cemetery. When I left, Cindy had already gone to pick up her kids at school, and I stopped to talk to Mrs. White, an elderly lady who belongs to the Historical Society, the museum register, and one of Holly Springs's oldest families. We chatted for a while about the weather, she asked tactfully if Bitty was holding up well, and then we discussed the upcoming pilgrimage.

"I just hope we have decent weather for it," Mrs. White said, "sometimes it's so cold and stormy hardly anyone comes out. We have charity functions and donors of course, but it's always nice to be able to put some money back into our Society funds with a lot of admission fees."

Since I'd already heard these same concerns expressed by Bitty, I knew to say that this year would be wonderful weather and draw tourists by the droves. "And there are more houses on the tour since renovations, even without The Cedars. Walter Place is opening the cottages behind the main house this year, and that should be a huge draw."

Mrs. White looked pleased, but added wistfully, "It would have been so nice to get The Cedars this year. I suppose now it will go to Mr. Sanders' heir, and heaven only knows what they'll do with it."

"He has heirs?"

"Why, I heard he did. It came as quite a surprise to me, too. I mean he was the last one of the Sanders left, which is one reason we've been trying so hard to get him to bequeath us his property, so it'd be protected. No one's supposed to know yet, but word gets around, you know."

"Does the heir live in Holly Springs?"

"My understanding is that the will goes to probate now, but the heir will be contacted very soon. We'll just have to wait to find out, I suppose. And cross our fingers."

Bitty would be crushed. She'd so counted on getting The Cedars on the tour. Of course, while she really does love old houses and antiques, I think a major part of her determination is to spite someone else on the committee. Madewell? Whoever it is, Bitty will just have to get over it.

Since Bitty might not have heard about this new wrinkle yet, I went by Six Chimneys just to prepare her for the disappointment. Even if I couldn't have found her house blindfolded, I'd have been able to find it by following the pulsing throb of loud music. Seven or eight cars were parked on the street and in her driveway, and I ended up parking down in front of Richard Simmons' house. He stood out in his front yard, and Mrs. Tyree stood on her front porch, and the neighbor across the street, Allison Kent, stood out on her sidewalk. They all looked irritated.

"Would you tell Miss Bitty that we're tired of listening to that racket?" Richard Simmons requested as I got out of my car, and I said I would.

As I passed Mrs. Tyree and Allison Kent, they both passed along the same message. By the time I got to Bitty's front porch, neighbors all along the street were standing in front of their houses with hands on hips. I sensed an imminent uprising.

No one answered my knock at Bitty's door, but that didn't surprise me. A lit stick of dynamite wouldn't be heard. I went on in, passing through the entrance hall and by the living and dining rooms, the breakfast room, and into the kitchen, where I saw evidence of food and drink. The parlor just behind the dining room was empty, as was the butler's pantry, a nice little nook Bitty also uses as a wet bar.

So I went down the steps onto the screened porch, and saw a lively group out on the lawn and in the gazebo off to one side. Music blared from a stereo system that looked very expensive. Most of the people were college-age, obviously friends of Clayton and Brandon, but it was a little startling to see Jefferson Johnston and Melody Doyle there as well.

Bitty and Jefferson were dancing on the paved drive in front of the three-car garage, and Bitty was laughing and bright-eyed. A little too bright-eyed. Fair, lanky Jefferson gave Bitty a spin, then whirled her back into his arms and bent her over his arm in a classic dance move that had nothing at all to do with the music blaring from stereo speakers the size of small cars.

It wouldn't do me any good to try and get her attention by shouting. I'd never be heard over the rat-a-tat-tat of lyrics blasting holes in my eardrums. Finally Bitty noticed me standing there, and dragged Jefferson along with her to greet me.

"Trinket! We're having a lawn party!" she said, or at least, I'm pretty sure that's what she said. I had to lip read, and only caught every other word, so it came out *Trinket– having– lawn*.

Instead of answering, I nodded with a smile that probably looked feral since Dr. Johnston took a startled step backward. Bitty just laughed, her amusement obviously well lubricated by whatever had been in her empty glass. My cousin is quite talented, able to dance, fall, carry on a decent conversation, and probably sleep, with a glass in her hand that remains unbroken and most of the time well-filled. Not that she drinks too much. Just on special occasions like moving a frozen corpse, or with company. Or getting arrested for murder.

"Brandon, fetch Trinket a mint julep," Bitty called over her shoulder, suddenly sounding much too loud in the quivering silence that fell when the noise disguised as a song ended.

"Bitty, the neighbors are complaining about the loud music," I said quickly before another song started and nothing less than breaking the sound barrier would get her attention. "I'm sure I heard someone mention tar and feathers."

"Oh, how inconvenient," she said, "we were having such fun. Jefferson is really a good dancer. Don't you think so, Melody?"

Melody had been talking to Brandon, smiling up at him like most members of the female persuasion do when faced with one of the Caldwell boys. As I've said, they're quite handsome young men, with thick blond hair streaked with shades of gold and brown no hairdresser could ever duplicate at any price. Like their mama, they have smooth California-beach skin that's only partially due to the sun, irresistible grins, and that smooth Southern charm that often borders on chauvinistic but doesn't quite cross the line. They're likely to call you darlin' or sugar or honey, open doors for you, and insist upon walking on the curb side of the sidewalk when escorting you anywhere, but they're just as likely to expect a young woman to stay home after marriage to keep house, husband, and babies happy. Southern men can't really help it. It's been imprinted in their genetic make-ups for just as long as the right to own guns and drink whiskey.

Curling his arm around Melody, Brandon grinned at his mama and said, "Melody was just telling me that Jefferson used to win dance contests all the time. You've been dancing with a professional, Mama."

Cutting her eyes up at Jefferson, Bitty gave him a little push with the flat of her hand and said, "Why, you mean thing, you should have told me!"

When Jefferson opened his mouth to reply, a piercing shriek came from one of the stereo speakers that made him jump six inches into the air. What followed sounded like a train wreck, but was, Brandon and Clayton assured us once they cut off the volume, an excellent band at the top of the music charts.

Bitty sagged into a lawn chair and fanned her flushed face with one hand. "What musical charts, the Top Ten in Hades? Mercy, I'm about done in. Where're our drinks, Brandon?"

Brandon and Melody went toward the house, and Jefferson excused himself for a few moments, either meaning he had to find a bathroom or keep an eye on Melody—the last just my own opinion and observation—and I grabbed Bitty's wrist to get her full attention.

"Sherman Sanders left an heir," I said without softening the blow, figuring that bourbon and crushed mint would be cushioning enough.

The smile on Bitty's face dimmed. I hated to see that, but I'd rather her hear it from me than for one of the legion of gossips tell her just to be mean.

"Well," she said after a moment, "is it someone we know?"

"No one knows who it is. Or if he or she or they even live here. Or anywhere near here."

Bitty's eyes got wide. "Oh my . . . what if it's someone who'll just tear it down to build a Mini-Mart?"

"Good Lord, Bitty, stop worrying about a Mini-Mart out there. It won't happen in our lifetimes, and probably not your grandchildren's."

Bitty looked startled. "I'm not a grandmother. I'm too young for that yet."

I sighed. "That's not the point. And anyway, I didn't hear this from a completely reliable source. I just know it's being said and I wanted you to be prepared."

She put her hand on my arm. "Oh Trinket, you're such a good friend. I just love the way you take care of me, and watch out for my feelings. I don't know what I'd do without you. If you ever move away again, I'll just die, I swear I will."

That was probably the Jim Beam talking. I smiled and nodded. My personal opinion was that Bitty didn't need any more bourbon, and I think Brandon agreed with me. He brought me a mint julep in the silver cups used especially for juleps, and told his mother that hers was specially made. She tasted it, frowned, and said, "I think you forgot the bourbon."

"No ma'am, I just grated a little nutmeg on top. Don't you like it?"

Bitty's eyes widened. "Good Lord, son, what have they been teaching you down there in Oxford? Nutmeg on my mint julep? That's sacrilege."

"I'll make you another one," he said, and gave me a wink. "I just thought the syrup might be old."

"Of course it's not. I make it up a quart at a time, and that lasts for months. Now, don't you be listening to people down there who tell you how to make mint juleps. My mother taught me, and her mother taught her, and since you've obviously forgotten, I'll show you again. Come on, and I'll give you the receipt my great-grandmother Mullen wrote out years ago."

I felt much better watching Brandon handle his mother. Obviously, he knows how to get her sidetracked.

It's funny that Bitty can't even make a sandwich properly, but makes the best mint juleps anyone ever tasted. I suppose it's a gift, rather like that of great French pastry chefs. Some people have their own special talents. My julep tasted excellent, with bruised mint leaves from the new mint that grows in huge flower pots by her garage—it'll take over the yard if not cut back—and crushed mint and sugar, and shaved ice packed into the cup so you have to suck the drink against your teeth to taste it. And of course, served in silver cups to hold the chill so when you get down to the very last, there's this exotic blend of sweet syrupy mint with a tang of bourbon. They taste nothing like the juleps purchased in bars and restaurants, or even from those little stands at the Kentucky Derby. The difference is similar to the difference between canned biscuits and scratch biscuits—they may look a lot alike, but one taste is all you need to realize that canned biscuits will never taste as good to you again.

Jefferson came to sit down in the chair Bitty vacated, and I saw Melody amble over to a cluster of young people she obviously knew.

"No patients this afternoon?" I asked politely, for lack of something else to say.

"Friday afternoons are always my free times," he replied with a smile. "I don't have a lot of patients yet anyway. You know. New in town."

"What brought you to Holly Springs? Do you have family here?"

"No, it's just such a lovely town, close to a larger city, but self-contained, far enough away from big city crime but with big city conveniences only forty-five minutes away. And if I don't want to, I never have to leave here as long as FedEx and UPS still deliver."

"Don't forget the new Super Wal-mart," I said, and we both laughed. Nothing about Easthaven had looked as if it'd come from a discount store. "I'm newly returned myself, and I've forgotten many of the people I used to know, and met quite a few new citizens. Holly Springs is no longer a well-kept secret, it seems."

Jefferson nodded. "It's my first time to live in a small town. I've been very pleased and gratified to be welcomed into the community."

"Have you tried one of Bitty's famous mint juleps yet?" I asked.

He shook his head. "I'm more a scotch and water man. Bitty tried though, took away my glass right before you got here, threatened to cut me off unless I at least tried her specialty."

"If Bitty wants you to do something," I said, "you might as well go ahead and do it. Save yourself a lot of time, because eventually, you'll end up doing it anyway."

Grinning, Jefferson said, "I'm beginning to realize that. She's a most persuasive woman."

"She always has been. If our military sent her into war zones, she'd have everything straightened out in no time."

"I don't doubt that."

I smiled at Jefferson, thinking he seemed such a pleasant man, even if quite a bit younger than Bitty. He looks to be in his late thirties or early forties, and that's a pretty big age spread in most opinions, though not so bad if it's the other way around. I've never completely understood that. Men in their forties can marry sweet young things in their twenties and no one bats an eye. But if a woman in her forties even looks at a man in his twenties, eyes roll, heads turn, cruel comments fly. Of course, while I can certainly see Ashton Kutcher's attraction to Demi Moore, I honestly wonder what on earth *she* can be thinking. Ashton either has to be very mature for his age, or Demi wears earplugs. But then, since I'm not really up on Hollywood gossip and star-mating, they may well be the perfect couple. Heaven knows, my generation of the Truevine family hasn't exactly been a good example of lasting relationships.

After some mundane conversation about the upcoming pilgrimage and undisputed queen of the antebellum homes, Montrose, hosting weddings and parties as well as being the most photographed house during the pilgrimage, Bitty returned to save me from making conversation. Brandon bore a silver tray holding more silver cups of mint juleps.

"Not me," I said when Brandon politely lowered the tray to me, "one is enough or I won't be able to drive home."

"Then you can stay the night here," Bitty said. "Besides, a proper julep is mostly ice anyway, so just one of them can't possibly intoxicate you."

Jefferson stood up and smiled at Bitty. "Why, you're the most intoxicating presence here, Miss Bitty."

It was an oddly jarring note. Even Bitty, obviously having had more bourbon than ice in her cup, looked a little startled. On the surface it was a bit of old-fashioned gallantry, but beneath the trite phrase it seemed false and overdone.

As Bitty recovered and said graciously, "Aren't you the sweetest thing," I caught the look on Brandon's face. It was an expression of dislike. It could have been because Jefferson Johnston seemed a little bit too attentive to his mother, but somehow I didn't think so.

When I got Brandon alone, I asked casually, "How did your dinner go the other night? I'm sorry I missed it, but I just felt like I needed to go home and check up on my parents."

"Oh, it was all right. You know Mama. She can put on the dog when she wants to, and we had all these different courses served in the dining room with candlelight and funeral music."

"Good Lord. On second thought, I'm not sorry I missed it."

Brandon laughed. "It probably would have been a lot more boring, but Mama insisted on having a real dog in her lap the entire time. Fed it right there at the table. I think Dr. Johnston nearly got sick when she used her fork." He grinned. "I told him not to worry, that we rarely feed our hunting dogs off the good silver."

"So where is Chitling?"

Brandon found that very funny. "Chitling is napping. I've missed you, Aunt Trinket."

I gave him a hug. "And I've missed you boys, too." I didn't say that because I should have said it, it's the truth. I just get over it quickly.

"So why don't you like Dr. Johnston?" I asked, and to his credit, Brandon didn't try to deny it.

"I don't know. There's just something about him. Why don't you like him?"

"I didn't realize I don't until just a few minutes ago. You know, I can't help but wonder why he's paying so much attention to Bitty when he obviously has a crush on Melody."

"You make it sound like he's in high school." Brandon paused, and then said thoughtfully, "I get the same feeling, though. Melody's a nice enough person, I guess, but she's got a sharp edge to her. Like she's mad at the world."

"Maybe she's upset because Dr. Johnston is paying so much attention to Bitty."

"Could be. But Mama's not serious. Anyone can see that. She might be flattered, and she's always been flirty, but that's just Mama. She's never outgrown the belle thing."

"Honey, it's something you're born with and you die with, not a childhood phase like thumb-sucking or bed-wetting. Bitty and my sister have it in spades, but in different ways. I've never had it." I didn't add *Thank God*, even though I was thinking it. It'd have been impolite.

"Now Aunt Trinket, you've always been a beautiful belle."

"And now you're my favorite nephew. I'd leave you something in my will, but I'm not really sure if it should be my one emerald earring or my four-slice toaster."

"The toaster sounds good."

"I'll make the arrangements. Do you think Jefferson is on the up and up?"

"He must be. He's got credentials and everything, and he bought Easthaven. Is that what you meant?"

"Yes, I think it is. Maybe he's just anxious to fit in, and maybe he's not comfortable with already having an affair with his receptionist. That could be all there is to it."

"Probably so," Brandon agreed, but he and I looked at each other and I'm sure both of us were thinking the same thing: That wasn't all there was to it.

Okay, now I had something else to worry about, and that was if Jefferson Johnston was some kind of fortune hunter. I mean, Bitty does have a lot of money, and she does like to have men buzzing around her, even if they are a lot younger. With all that'd been going on, Bitty probably didn't have any idea that there just had to be something between Melody and Jefferson, and I didn't really want to be the one to point that out. But who else was there?

Of course, Bitty surprised me, as she's prone to do.

Everyone was finally gone, even the boys off with their friends, and Bitty and I sat in her parlor-den with our shoes off, eating pimento cheese sandwiches and drinking sweet tea.

"Oh good heavens, Trinket, please give me as much credit as a sixth grade girl. If there's one thing I know, it's when a man is really interested in me, and Jefferson Johnston may say the right things and act like he is, but it's not me who keeps his pilot light burning."

"So whose furnace is he trying to light up?" I asked in an attempt to remain in the same ballpark with her metaphor.

"My best guess would be Melody Doyle, since she watches over him like a hawk." Bitty grinned wickedly. "I really enjoyed dancing with him and flirting with him, just to watch her squirm. That child should know better than to play games with me. I've got shoes older than she is."

"Why do you think they're keeping it a secret? And what on earth reason could Jefferson Johnston have for asking you out and hanging around with you?"

Bitty sat up indignantly. "Well really, Trinket, you don't have to be insulting."

"Oh, I didn't mean it that way and you know it. It just doesn't make sense, Bitty. I mean, he's been here for six months or so, he's establishing his business, bought an old house that's going to be on the tour, and obviously has money, and it's not like he'd be the first man to marry his secretary or at least sweet-talk her into bed."

A little mollified, Bitty took another bite of her sandwich and nodded. "That's true. I just thought at first maybe he wanted to make sure his house got on the pilgrimage, you know, since it all has to be done properly, but that didn't take long at all. Lately, he's taken to calling me a lot and dropping by . . . maybe he's trying to make Melody jealous?"

"At the risk of offending you, wouldn't it make her more jealous if he flirted with Cindy Nelson or Marcy Porter? Or Naomi Spencer?"

"Mention that last name in my house again, and I'll take back Mama's pimento cheese."

Since her mother's pimento cheese is unarguably the best in all of Mississippi, and maybe even the South, and Sharita is the only who can make Aunt Sarah's old recipe turn out at all like it should, I licked a glob of the delicious stuff off my fingers and nodded.

"Consider it unmentioned."

"Anyway, while Jefferson is certainly handsome enough, and it's been flattering in a way to have him hanging around, I'm not fool enough to lose my head. Although I have to admit, it's been amusing to see my boys concerned I'm going to run off with a con man and spend all their inheritance."

"Why do you call him a con man?"

Bitty frowned. "I don't know. That just popped out. I guess I meant younger man."

Sometimes Bitty says the right thing even when she doesn't mean to say it.

CHAPTER 17

When we were children, Bitty and I loved fairy tales. We acted out parts, with Bitty always being the princess or fairy queen, while I usually preferred being Robin Hood, a horse, or even the giant of Jack and the Beanstalk fame. There was something appealing about stomping around and saying in my deepest voice, "Fee fi fo fum, I smell the blood of an Englishman." I had no idea what that meant, but it sounded really menacing. Maybe because anything with the word blood in it had to be scary.

As an adult, I still like to frighten myself with dire possibilities. If I didn't, I wouldn't worry about things like Mama and Daddy snow-skiing in the Alps, white water river-rafting, or being shanghaied on clipper ships. Nor would I lie awake at night wondering if Bitty would run off with a foot doctor and spend all her children's inheritance on Dr. Scholl's shoe pads and Fed Ex shipping charges. Logic assures me that Bitty may have been unwise with men, but she's never been stupid with money. That annoying little voice in the back of my head whispers that there's always a first time.

Add to that the annoying little voice still muttering about Generals Grant and Forrest, and the persistent clamor that I'd overlooked the obvious, and I began to feel like a group meeting was going on inside my head without me in charge. Perhaps Whitfield takes reservations.

"Is this Sarah's pimento cheese?" Mama asked me when I went downstairs the next morning. She had her head inside the refrigerator, poring over plastic bowls of leftovers.

"It's all I could coax out of Bitty. If the US currency system collapses, she can use Aunt Sarah's pimento cheese as barter and still be a multi-millionaire."

"Do you think Bitty's a multi-millionaire?" Mama asked as she got out the pimento cheese and a loaf of light bread.

"Not yet. One more husband ought to do it. Is the coffee fresh?"

"It's the divorces that make her money, not the husbands," Mama said, and added, "It was fresh at five this morning."

I grimaced. It was nearly nine-thirty. "I really have to stop hanging around Bitty. Her bad habits are rubbing off on me."

"Nothing can rub off on you unless you let it," Mama said. I watched her slather spoons of creamy pimento cheese atop bread slices.

As penance for sleeping late, I poured stale coffee into a mug, and then added extra cream to cut the sharpness. And to punish my thighs for filling out my sweat pants a little too much, I only ate one pimento cheese sandwich along with my coffee. I can be a stern taskmaster if needed. A cold nose nudged my arm, and I looked down into Brownie's reproachful eyes. He's not allowed table scraps. He knows that, but it's done nothing to curb his mimicking of the big-eyed stray puppy left out in the cold and rain. Mama had her head in the refrigerator again, so I fed the dog the last crust of my bread that had only a slight smear of pimento cheese left on it.

In return for my kindness, he barked for more, and Mama straightened and turned to look at me. "Did you just feed him scraps?"

"Yes, ma'am. But it wasn't so much scraps as it was my last bite. And I shared. You've always encouraged me to share."

"Good heavens, Trinket, for a grown woman you've been doing some awfully silly things lately." Talk about the pot calling the kettle black . . . .

She came and picked up Brownie, cradling him in her arms like an infant as she scolded him for begging. He quivered, ears back and flat to his head, looking up at her with pleading eyes until she told him she knew it was all my fault. I propped my chin in my palm and my elbow on the table, and as Mama walked away, Brownie looked over her arm at me with a smirk. I don't know why people use phrases like "dog tired," and "dumb as a dog," when it's quite obvious most of them have mastered the art of getting exactly what they want. Brownie and Chen Ling are two excellent examples. I'm sure there are many more. There's a lesson to be learned here somewhere.

Mama was right about one thing, though, and that's that I'd been doing some awfully silly things lately. I needed to be smarter. I needed to have a plan. And first, I needed to figure out my priorities.

Since I'd been drifting along, letting odd questions temporarily inhabit my brain until some other distraction came along so I could worry about that for a while, I decided to be ruthless and focus on one thing at a time. Number one priority: Generals Grant and Forrest. There had to be a logical reason I kept thinking about them both in connection with Philip Hollandale's murder. Grant was easy. Philip had been killed with a statue of him. But why fixate on Forrest? What on earth could he have to do with the murder? I just had to try and remember when it'd first begun to bother me.

My process of elimination required meditation. It'd been a long time since I even tried to meditate. I knew I was supposed to have a mantra, but it'd vanished about the same time as my confidence in myself. First, I must clear my mind of all thoughts other than one that'd bring me peace. I chose an image and sound of a waterfall. Then I remembered that usually made me have to go to the bathroom, so I thought about focusing on a mountain scene, but that reminded me of the time our U-Haul broke down on the steep road going up the Continental Divide and Perry left me and Michelle with it while he went into the next town to call a tow truck. It'd been a long time ago, and if not for a friendly trucker who called U-Haul and got us a tow truck, Michelle and I might still be there by the side of the road waiting for the U-Haul to just start sliding backward while Perry drank beer and played pool.

Okay, a mantra wasn't going to be as easy as it'd been when I was thirty. I got out a pad of paper and started going backward, jotting down key points, some in remnants of shorthand that's been outdated by technology. Finally I got stuck at the point of going back with Bitty to wipe her fingerprints off the statue of General Grant.

The statue . . . there was something about that statue of General Grant that bothered me. I had no idea what it could be, but it felt like it was key to the murder. Of course, the statue had been sent to Jackson, the state capitol, for DNA analysis, along with Philip's body and all the evidence collected. Only Philip had been returned. But Jackson Lee, the attorney, may well have photographs of the crime scene I could see. Since the photographs would only be of an empty space in the foyer, not pools of blood, my stomach would be just fine. All blood trace had been sent along with the murder weapon, and Sanders' and Bitty's antique carpets as well.

So that's where I found myself by eleven, sitting in Jackson Lee Brunetti's office waiting on his secretary to get permission from him to show me the crime scene photos. Jackson Lee was out in a pasture somewhere with a cow and a vet. I wondered if the vet was Dr. Thompson or Dr. Coltrane. My stomach did that annoying little flip again. Maybe I was just coming down with a stomach virus. That'd certainly be preferable.

As Bitty's defense lawyer, Jackson Lee gets copies of the crime scene photos, as does the prosecutor. The secretary showed me into a small room with a big conference table—antique, of course—thick carpet, soft chairs, and the kind of strong lighting usually only seen in hospital emergency rooms.

"May I get you some coffee?" she asked when I was seated at the table with the folder of photos, and I nodded.

"If it's strong, please."

She grinned. "We've got three strengths, one-hundred yard dash, five-hundred yard sprint, and marathon."

"Five-hundred yard sprint, please. I'm not sure it's marathon time yet."

Laughing, she went off to get the coffee and I flipped open the folder. Scenes from Sherman Sanders' foyer slid out in eight by ten glossies. I spread them out on the gleaming pecan table. Tags gave date, time, and place of photographs. After a few minutes, during which Diane Wright, Jackson Lee's secretary, brought me coffee strong enough to have hiked in there on its own, I picked out the photos I thought might give me my answer.

I lined them up the way I recalled seeing things when walking in the door that first time with Bitty. Foyer, parlor to the left, dining room to the right, staircase rising up on the right-hand side just outside the double doors leading into the dining room. The little table holding the statue sat there at the bottom of the staircase. A closet door had been built under the staircase, obviously added after the home had originally been built. I didn't remember seeing that. I did remember the walnut mantle carved with hunting scenes, and the array of photos sitting atop it, along with the crystal candlesticks. I studied that more closely. Something looked different about it. I wasn't sure what. I set it aside after a few minutes, in a pile I designated as Questionable.

There were photos of the carpet in the foyer, with little markers like the kind steak places use to put on your plate so the servers will know if you'd ordered the well-done, medium, or rare. I assume the numbered markers point out evidence to the crime team.

Anyway, when I got to the photo of the table and the statue, I pulled the pair of what my father calls "cheaters" out of my purse, those drug store reading glasses that magnify things. It's not that I'm too vain to wear glasses; it's just that I have a habit of putting even my sunglasses in odd places and forgetting where they are. As long as I can pay just a few dollars for cheaters and they work when I need them, I'm going to go that route.

I studied the photo closely, admired the graceful curve of wood and intricate top of the table, and then focused on the statue. The bronze statue is nearly a foot high, with the general wearing his uniform and hat. I thought about Bitty picking it up and Sherman Sanders' reaction that first day we went out there. Was there something special about the statue, something that might hold a hint to what was driving me crazy?

The general had struck a militant pose, head lifted as if in defiance of the enemy, his body straight with military discipline even mounted on his horse. Then I looked a little closer. Where was the sword he'd held up? Wait—I didn't remember a horse. While details weren't that easily seen in this photo, it looked to me as if the insignia on the hat said CSA instead of US. I held the photo up right to my nose. General Grant would hardly wear the enemy's hat, not even in the fevered imagination of some crazed sculptor. Why, this wasn't General Grant at all, this was General Forrest!

I sat up straight. So that's what had been bothering me all this time. Sherman Sanders had said it was Grant, but it was Forrest. But then, Bitty had said it was General Grant, too, and while she may very well be as scattered as chickens in a tornado, she definitely knows General Grant from General Forrest.

Diane gave permission for me to use the telephone, and I called Bitty immediately.

"Bitty," I said, cutting into her surprise at hearing me call from the Brunetti offices, "I'd like for you to answer a quick question for me, then I'll tell you why I'm here. That first day we went out to Sanders, you know, when the mule ate the chicken and dumplings, do you remember looking at the statue on the small table at the foot of the staircase?"

"Well for heaven's sake, Trinket, of course I do. It was a heavy bronze statue of General Grant. Don't you remember Sanders getting all huffy when I just politely mentioned it?"

"Yes, I certainly do. You're sure it was Grant."

"I think I can tell the difference between Grant and Forrest by now. You're not saying my eyes have gone bad, are you?"

"No, no, nothing like that. I'm just trying to remember everything, that's all. You know, for the court case." No point in saying anything to Bitty until I talked to Jackson Lee. There may be a good explanation for General Grant having turned into General Forrest.

When I hung up after giving Bitty a promise to come right over after I left the law offices, I went back to the table and studied some of the other photographs again. I pulled a few from the Questionable stack, and focused on the one of the parlor and the mantel. A fire had been burning the day we were there. It looked cold and dead in the photo. I studied the hearth, then the mantel. Photos, candlesticks . . . and an oddly empty space. Something else had been there the day I visited, though that didn't necessarily mean it had anything to do with the murder. Still, sometimes the smallest details make the biggest differences.

Jackson Lee came in before I'd finished studying the photographs, and while he had a bit of mud on his boots, fortunately, there was no hint of cow manure.

"So," he said genially, sitting down in a chair at the head of the table by me, "did you find anything?"

"Yes. Or at least, I found an answer as well as some questions without answers."

"That works." He leaned forward as I pushed two photographs toward him. "Let's look at it."

"I haven't mentioned this, because I thought maybe I was just unhinged by everything, but I've been really bothered since the beginning about Generals Grant and Forrest." Jackson Lee kept his expression of polite attentiveness, and encouraged, I went on. "The first day Bitty and I were out there, we admired the statue of General

Grant on this table." I tapped the photo.

"That's General Forrest," Jackson Lee corrected me, and I nodded.

"I know. But it was General Grant when we were there. We did say that in our statements, I'm sure." Jackson Lee nodded, still without a change of expression. "And now there's an empty space on the mantel. I remember looking at the mantel that first day, there was a fire on the hearth . . . anyway, there was a bronze statue on the mantel. I recall seeing it, though I can't say for *certain* that it was General Forrest. I didn't look that closely. I just remember there being a bronze statue of a man on a horse. I know this may seem completely unrelated, but I don't think it is.

"And when I went back with Bitty to wipe off her fingerprints it wasn't Grant then, either. I was too rattled to notice, at least consciously, but the statue I wiped clean was this one, not the one Bitty says was on the floor next to Philip, or the first one we saw. The one that goes on this table. I think that the murder weapon is missing, that the statue here on the table in this crime scene photo is *not* the one used to kill Philip Hollandale." I ended with a Perry Mason flourish, and Jackson Lee sat back with a little smile.

"This morning we got the preliminary test results back from down in Jackson. There was no blood or fingerprints on the statue taken from the crime scene. It's not the weapon that killed Senator Hollandale."

"Then that's good for Bitty, right?"

"I wish I could say that, but the prosecutor is probably going to claim she killed him with something else. Since you and she both say it was a statue of General Grant, and Forrest is the only statue in evidence, it's going to be difficult to prove she didn't dispose of it. We need to find the murder weapon. The senator's fatal injury is consistent with a blow to the head from a heavy object like that statue, so since Grant is missing . . . . "

He left the sentence unfinished. I filled in the blanks. "And since Bitty had motive and the opportunity, my brilliant deduction doesn't help at all."

"Not much," he agreed.

I felt deflated. All this time worrying myself to death about a tiny detail like the difference between Grant and Forrest, and it didn't help at all when I finally figured it out. Apparently I'm more Pink Panther than Perry Mason.

"So," I said, "Inspector Clouseau strikes again."

Jackson laughed. "But it does help a theory that's been forming in the back of my mind. I researched that Nissan plant you told me about, and the senator's possible involvement, and if Sanders had been contacted by Nissan. It's fact that Nissan has been looking in this area, and it's fact that Sanders' land backs up to Highway 7 and is in a good spot for a plant. Nissan denies talking to Sanders. Hollandale is known for making deals that benefit him more than landowners, unless they're corporate donors."

"So Sanders and Philip might have gotten into an argument, and Philip ended up dead," I said. "Then who killed Sanders?"

"The trick is finding out who benefits most from Sanders' death."

I remembered what Mrs. White had told me and said, "I've heard he has an heir."

"That's interesting. I haven't been able to find any record of one. No will was filed in the Marshall County probate court. As far as is known, he died intestate."

"That's not in Bitty's favor. I mean, she doesn't benefit from Sanders being killed at all, so doesn't that mean she has no motive to see him dead? She'd convinced him to put his house on the tour, after all, and anyway, just who kills someone for a house that won't be theirs?"

Jackson Lee nodded. "I think we've got a pretty strong defense on Sanders. It's Philip Hollandale that worries me. And don't share that last with Bitty. By the time this comes to court, we'll have all the DNA results back and a lot more evidence than we do now. The labs might be backed up and slow, but they're thorough."

I sighed. "They get it done so quickly on CSI. Instant DNA results."

"Just on TV. Not available in reality yet, but I'm betting it will be. After all, used to, it took a lot more blood evidence to get DNA, and now all they need is a speck."

Because talking about blood made me a little queasy, I thanked Jackson Lee for allowing me to access the crime scene photos, and he walked me out to my car. I turned to look up at him.

"Jackson Lee, do the police already know about the statues being different?"

He nodded. "As well as the prosecutor. I just haven't said anything since I hoped Bitty wouldn't remember it yet. If this case does get to court, Bitty can be a lot more convincing when she's telling the truth than when she's trying to make folks believe she is. She's hard to shake when she thinks she's right."

"And any shade of doubt that she did it—"

"Can put reasonable doubt in play. The police have blood evidence, motive, opportunity, and Bitty saying she'd like to see the senator dead. Not to mention him turning up in her cellar after you ladies hauled him around town a while first. That can be pretty damning. Believable doubt might help with a jury."

"That's depressing. Too many people already know about us trying to hide Philip in the cemetery anyway." When Jackson Lee looked at me, I added, "Melody Doyle says Cindy Nelson told her about it, so I imagine most of Marshall County knows about it by now. Or will soon."

"Unless I can get that thrown out, it's going to look bad for her in court." Jackson Lee blew out a heavy sigh and rocked back on his heels. "What the hell made you ladies do that in the first place?"

"I don't know. Some kind of hysteria, I think. It just seemed like a good idea at the time."

He put a hand on my shoulder. "Next time anything like this happens, call me before you do anything."

"My God. I can't imagine anything like this ever happening again. Not to us. Even Bitty hasn't ever found one of her husbands dead and in her coat closet before."

"Let's hope it's not a new phase she's going through."

I thought about that when I pulled up in front of Bitty's house. Despite her exemption of loud parties and visitors, the house was once more a parking lot and way-station for college kids. Thank heavens, the music was much more subdued, however, so I went inside to find Bitty in the thick of things, as usual.

A crowd was gathered in the basement "playroom" that looks like it was decorated by Tony Soprano. Some sat at the card tables engrossed in poker, but the liveliest of the group were throwing sharp objects. Naturally, Bitty was among them. The electric dart board lit up, while I looked around for a suit of armor.

"Trip twenty!" Bitty shouted, giving one of the hops from her former cheerleading days at Ole Miss. True to form, none of the coffee in her cup sloshed out but stayed firmly in place as if held with a clear seal or magnets.

Since I wasn't sure what a trip twenty was but thought it must be good, I said, "Excellent, Bitty" in hopes that she'd quit before hitting someone with a dart. Like me.

Turning, she came to me with a pleased smile and an offer of a drink. "We have whatever you might want, sugar. Bailey's and coffee?"

"Thanks, but I'm considering a twelve-step program. I'm sure it'll last as long as my diet plan, so don't throw away any booze just yet. Any Coke?"

We ended up in the kitchen where it was quiet, or quieter than the basement. Instead of Coke, I had sweet tea, and my ice clinked against the glass as I sucked down three inches of it.

"So why were you at Jackson Lee's office?" Bitty asked as she shoved a plate of cream cheese and pineapple mix spread atop crackers at me.

Since Jackson Lee and I had decided that Bitty would benefit most by not mentioning the statue switch, I stuffed one of the Ritz crackers into my mouth and swallowed before replying. "I just had some silly idea I'd missed something, that's all."

"And did you miss something?"

"Just my breakfast. And lunch. These are delicious. I've always loved this stuff."

"So have I. You're keeping something from me, Trinket. I can always tell. What is it?"

"You always say that, but I've kept plenty of things from you and you've never even suspected."

Bitty sat up straighter. "Like what?"

"Like the time I didn't tell you that Stewart Carmichael and Cady Lee Forsythe were stirring up more than dust in his hayloft. You didn't know for a month after I did. And even then you didn't hear it from me."

"I mean secrets about *me*. You haven't ever been able to keep secrets about me without me knowing."

"Yes, I have. Remember your surprise birthday party? You didn't know about that."

"We were sixteen, and I knew about it a month before. You're really awful at that kind of thing. You kept smiling like the Cheshire cat."

"I did not. Wait—something's missing from your chest. Where's Chitling?"

"Chen Ling is having her day at the spa. Bath, nails trimmed, even a massage."

"When I die, I hope I come back as your dog. Does Luann Carey know she's not ever getting Chitling back?"

"Luann and I have come to an agreement. She realizes that Chen Ling is much better off here with me than with all those other dogs she has running around. I can give her more attention and see to her needs. In return, Luann's rescue group gets a nice donation. So why were you at Jackson Lee's office?"

Occasionally Bitty isn't so easily distracted.

"Oh for heaven's sake, Bitty," I said, "don't you think if it's something you truly need to know, I'll tell you?"

She thought about that for a moment. Then she nodded. "Yes, I know you would. And it's not like I haven't kept some things from you lately."

When she got up as if to leave the kitchen, I said, "Wait. What have you kept from me?"

"Oh no, Trinket. Trust is a two-way street. If you won't confide in me, then I should spare you details that I think may upset you. It's probably best, anyway."

Sometimes I just want to smack Bitty. Not hard, of course, just one of those "you drive me crazy" smacks to get her attention. But then, I have no doubt she feels the same way about me at times, too.

So I looked at her standing there in pretty pink cotton slacks and blouse, hair all done and make-up on, while I wore my favorite Lee jeans and a pull-over jersey, no make-up, my hair only slightly less scary than my bank balance, and I knew we'd have to come to some sort of a compromise. I wouldn't get a moment's peace until I knew what she was keeping from me. And it better not be gossip about someone's face lift or cheating husband, either.

I patted the other side of the kitchen table in invitation. "You come and upset me, and I'll upset you, honey. It's the least we can do for each other."

To her credit, Bitty voiced no triumphant murmurings, but came and sat down across from me. "I'll tell you first," she said, "I've just been dying to anyway. Cindy Nelson called me, really upset with Melody Doyle. It seems that Melody has let slip quite a few things Cindy told her in strictest confidence, and Cindy doesn't know what to do. She wants to confront her, but then, she doesn't want to get anything started with the Divas, either. You know, it could really get uncomfortable if one won't come if the other one's going to be there, and if one holds it at their house, then the other won't come—although Melody Doyle has never held it at her house, not that I can blame her, it being kind of rundown and all. Still, we all understand, and it's not like all of us have enough money for that kind of thing. That's not what the Divas are about. We just like to get together for some fun.

"Anyway, Cindy said that she and Melody had this little disagreement because Melody's cousin Serena had everyone out looking for Sherman Sanders on Highway 4 when we now know he was deader than bacon that whole time. Then Melody confessed Serena had only made it up so the police wouldn't stop looking for him. But most of all, Cindy's mad because Melody said she'd told her about us taking Philip to the cemetery when she didn't even know it herself."

My head swam a little. I came up for air before Bitty could catch her breath and asked, "How did Cindy find out Melody told us?" I asked. "Gaynelle said she wouldn't tell Cindy that Melody had told us."

I began to feel like I was in the middle of that skit about Who's on First. Bitty seems to handle this kind of thing better.

"She didn't. After Melody mentioned it to us, she told Cady Lee Forsythe, too. I mean Kincade."

I drew in a deep breath. "She *didn't*. Everyone knows Cady Lee couldn't keep her mouth shut in a sandstorm. She's sweet, but she tells everything. Bless her heart."

"Just goes to show you. Beauty and brains don't always sit side by side."

We nodded at the wisdom of that old saw. I wondered why Melody seemed to be going out of her way to incriminate Bitty. Naturally, the first thought that sprang to mind was Jefferson Johnston.

"Well, I told you Melody is sweet on Dr. Johnston," I said, and Bitty shrugged.

"That's no reason to go telling things you've no right to tell. I'm of a mind myself to just go tell Melody exactly what I think. After all, I'm the one who invited her to join the Divas, even though Marcy is the one who brought her. I let my better nature get the best of me, thinking about Maybelle and how poor Melody had to live with her grandmother all those years after her mama died and her daddy took off. You know how spiteful Mrs. Overton was to everyone. She only got worse after Maybelle died. Poor Melody got the brunt of it, I guess. And look how she repays me for inviting her to join us, by telling wicked lies about me."

"It's not a lie, Bitty," I pointed out. "We did cart Philip's body down to the cemetery."

"But I didn't kill him, and she shouldn't have said things to make it seem like I did."

"Which brings me to wonder—just why would she do that?"

Silence fell. We looked at each other.

"It's not really because of Jefferson Johnston," I said after a moment. "I've changed my mind. I don't think Melody worried about that for even a minute. At the St. Patrick's Day party, she encouraged both of you to get better acquainted. So how did the dinner in Oxford turn out? And has he been attentive in other ways?"

"Dinner was fine, but I told you that already. By attentive, if you're asking if he tried to get in my drawers, no. We just talked antiques and old houses. Though come to think of it, *I* talked antiques and old houses. He just asked a few questions." Bitty frowned. "I suppose I do tend to monopolize conversations at times, especially when it's something that interests me."

It hurt, but I managed to swallow the words that kept burning the tip of my tongue. I might have heartburn for a week, but Bitty's feelings were spared.

"There's something funny going on with those two," I said, and

Bitty agreed. "And after all, you don't really know much about Melody since she came back from Atlanta, do you? What do you know about Jefferson Johnston?"

Bitty thought for a moment. "Not much. But I know someone who probably does. Do you remember Ted Alston?"

"The banker?"

"That's the one. Bankers know more about a person than their mothers do. That's who I need to talk to about Jefferson."

"But Bitty, he's a *banker*. He won't tell you anything about a client."

She smiled. "Not unless I ask him just right. Then he won't even know he's answered my questions. It's lunchtime, so I'll let him take me to Budgie's."

It seemed like a plan.

CHAPTER 18

There are times when I think I have too much trust in human nature. Despite my cynicism and low expectations, occasionally I'm still surprised by the things people do. It takes a lot, but it's possible. That's not usually a good thing.

Oddly enough, I still have that hope buried deep inside me that there'll be a Happily Ever After down the road, not just for me, but everyone I care about. It'd be nice if the world would cooperate so everyone could have a Happily Ever After, but it doesn't seem to be going in that direction. I'm not surprised, of course.

You can see how these two opposite ends of the pole can be conflicting: My hope for the happy ending against my certainty it won't happen. I'm sure I'd be a therapist's nightmare.

So I carted my contradictory viewpoints right over to Rayna Blue at the Inn. She may not be a therapist, but she seems wise beyond her years. Besides, I've known her since we were both in grade school. She taught me how to finger paint. Yes, there's an art to it.

"How well do you know Melody Doyle?" I asked when we were sitting out in her garden with her three dogs, five cats, and baskets full of flowering crocus, tulips, and daffodils. It was a nice day again, so I expected one of our seasonal storms to rip through anytime. Just to remind us Mother Nature has the upper hand.

"Well, she's so much younger," Rayna said, frowning a little. "I was more friends with her mother, Maybelle. Melody had a hard time growing up with her grandmother. Mrs. Overton was always filled with bitterness anyway, and after Maybelle died, she didn't get better."

"Why was Mrs. Overton so bitter? A man?"

"Surprisingly, no." Rayna laughed. "I think she and her husband got along well enough. He died when Maybelle was fairly young, but I never heard of any trouble between them. My mama always told me that the Richmonds never got over losing everything after The War."

Of course, I didn't have to ask which war she meant. Most

Southerners only refer to one war as *The War*.

"Richmond? Mrs. Overton was a Richmond?" I asked. Rayna nodded, and I said, "I don't recall ever hearing that before. But of course, Mama never used to gossip. Until lately."

We both turned when we heard a voice at the garden gate, and Rayna waved to Georgie Marshall, then got up to go unlock the gate for her and invite her to sit with us.

Rather shyly, Georgie said, "Are you sure I'm not interrupting anything?"

"Lord no," Rayna said, "we're talking ancient history. You know, about the Richmonds, the Sanders, and the war."

"Oh yes," Georgie said, "I just read about that recently. The Richmonds and Sanders, I mean. I found some old records. I've always wondered what started that feud."

"Once, the Richmonds owned a sawmill, lumberyard, that sort of thing, but they lost it all when Grant came through," Rayna said. "Yankees burned everything except their house."

It suddenly hit me about the time Rayna said, "You know, The Cedars," that I'd found my connection. My heart beat a little faster.

"Melody Doyle's family once owned The Cedars? Why don't I remember hearing that?" I asked.

"Well, it is ancient history, but a matter of record if you look in the ledgers. No one still talks about it too much, since there's so much bitterness about it. The Richmonds never forgave the Sanders for stealing their home out from under them like they did. Besides, Melody is the last Richmond left, and I don't imagine she cares about that old feud. Young people today don't get as upset over things like that, so it'll die out on its own, I suppose. Especially now that Sanders is dead."

Georgie said, "Not all young people feel that way. I certainly don't."

"Well honey, you're an exception, and I'm glad of it," Rayna said. "A lot more historic houses would be saved if there were more people like you."

Thinking of what Sharita had told me, I said, "I've heard the Richmonds were rumored to have the money to pay the taxes, but the Sanders somehow got the tax man to foreclose anyway so they could buy it."

Rayna nodded. "That could be true."

"But how could the Richmonds have the money if they'd lost everything? Their business was destroyed three years before the war ended, wasn't it?"

"Like a lot of people, they had a Plan B. The Govans buried their family silver under the front sidewalk of the Walter Place, and rumor has it that the Richmonds buried their valuables at The Cedars somewhere."

"Confederate money would be worthless after the war ended," Georgie said.

"But gold wouldn't be. Elijah Richmond was supposed to have buried a fortune in gold somewhere out there, but if he did, no one's ever found it. That's probably just rumor, too. If he had buried it, it'd have either been found by now, or the Richmonds wouldn't have been as poor as sharecroppers the past hundred and forty years."

My brain started spinning and spewing out random thoughts like some gumball machine gone mad. Maybe the Richmonds had been poor for a hundred and forty years, but the Sanders seemed to have done well enough. Sherman Sanders had no visible means of support, yet he managed to keep up the house, buy food, and get along quite well. But how would he get rid of the gold? It's not like he could just tote a gold bar or coin into town to pay for a loaf of bread. If he did, everyone would know it. And wasn't there some kind of law prohibiting average citizens from owning gold bars? If he started trading in bullion, the Feds would be down on him like a ton of bricks.

Startled back to our conversation by Rayna snapping her fingers and saying "Helllooo," I shrugged and laughed.

"Sorry. Sometimes I have these trances. Usually harmless."

"I know what you mean," Georgie said, and stood up. "Here I am, when I only meant to stay a minute or two. I'm supposed to meet Aunt Gaynelle over at Phillips. I'll see you two soon, maybe on the next Diva day." She waved good-bye and left out the garden gate again, but I lingered.

Rayna and I chatted a little while longer, but I'm afraid my mind wasn't really on our conversation. I had too many questions battering my beleaguered brain. And I just knew Melody Doyle was in this up to her pretty little neck.

For once, I decided to do the sane thing and tell Jackson Lee instead of Bitty what I'd found out. It may be just a wild idea anyway. After all, despite everything, Melody really didn't seem like the type of person who'd kill two people. But I'm sure Ted Bundy never seemed like a serial killer to all his victims until it was too late, either. That thought gave me the shivers. Then I thought about Bitty "belle-ing" information about Jefferson Johnston out of Ted Alston, and I got a cold chill. Surely, she wouldn't act on anything she found out?

From the Inn, I went straight over to Bitty's house, only a block and a half away. Her car wasn't there, but Brandon and Clayton were entertaining friends.

"Where's your mama?" I asked Brandon, and he looked a little surprised.

"I thought she was with you."

"No." I turned to his brother. "Clayton, did she tell you where she was going?"

"Yes, ma'am. She had to go to the bank. She'll be right back."

I nodded, and went right to the phone to call Bitty's cell phone. As much as I dislike the thought of distracting her while she's driving, I felt it important.

Bitty answered on the second ring, and I gave a sigh of relief. "Where are you, Bitty?"

"On Highway 4. I'm on the way to pick up Chen Ling from her spa treatment. Brandon took her out there early, so she's already done for the day. Pugs dry quickly."

"Did you already go to the bank?"

"I sure did," Bitty said, "and wait until you hear what all I found out. Ted is just the sweetest thing, but he's getting a little careless now that he's seventy. Or is it seventy-one? I can't ever remember. He's right around the age my mama would be, I think."

"Listen, Bitty, I've got to go back to see Jackson Lee, and I want you to meet me there. Don't go anywhere else first, okay? It's important."

I didn't want to scare her or get her all stirred up, because an indignant Bitty can be a dangerous Bitty. More to herself than anyone else most of the time, but there was no point in taking that chance.

"Well, I have to get Chen Ling first, you know."

"Yes, of course, but then go straight to Jackson Lee's office, okay?"

"Ooh, this sounds good. I can't wait. I think Jackson Lee is going to be quite happy with what I have to tell him."

"That sounds promising. You have proof Jefferson's a fraud?"

"Oh no, this is too good to tell over the phone. I'll see you in about thirty minutes."

Bitty can be very annoying.

Jackson Lee was out when I got to his office, but his secretary said he was due back shortly. "I can get you a Coke or coffee while you wait," Diane said, and I shook my head.

"Any more caffeine and I'm liable to start vibrating at high speed. It's not a pretty sight."

Diane laughed and showed me into Jackson Lee's office to wait for him. It's definitely a masculine office, but without the prerequisite deer head or big mouth bass hanging on the wall. It seems to me that most men consider proper wall decoration to include at least one dead animal. A rite of passage, or declaration of manhood, or just a "Look what I killed" statement. Instead, Jackson Lee has photos of his sons, his late wife, and an older couple I presume to be his parents. Diplomas hang on the hunter-green colored upper walls, a dark stained chair rail defines the line from the lower burgundy-colored walls, and big comfortable chairs make a half-circle in front of his big mahogany desk. His chair is burgundy leather, built-in shelves with cabinets line the wall behind him, and smoky glass deflects dust from a few keepsakes that look like the stuff kids do in elementary school. Misshapen bowls, a ceramic cup with *World's Best Dad* obviously painted by a child and fired in a kiln, and a collection of wood objects that defy description were lit up by one of those hidden lights found in many cabinets. Any man who proudly displays such ugly things in his office has to be an excellent father. My original estimation of Jackson Lee's fine character was only confirmed.

Jackson Lee showed up about fifteen minutes later. He'd obviously changed boots but not his clothes. Mud and something I had no intention of examining too closely stained his Levi's. It overpowered the air freshener, but recently I've learned to breathe through my mouth fairly well.

"You look like you're about to bust, Trinket," he said, grinning at me. "Just what have you found out?"

I promptly told him what I'd heard, all unsubstantiated rumor, of course, but surely could be verified. Jackson nodded, his expression noncommittal. Then he sat back in his chair with a creak of leather and locked his hands behind his head.

"I've been investigating Johnston myself. I hadn't really considered a link with Melody Doyle until now."

"You have? Why have you suspected Johnston of being involved?"

"Something he said at that St. Patrick's Day party. It just didn't sound right. Not for a foot doctor. Of course, I don't know much about podiatry, so I didn't think much of it at the time. It just hit me later."

We looked at each other, both tangled in our own thought processes, his much more legal and thorough than mine, I'm sure. Still, if Jefferson Johnston warranted investigation, and Melody Doyle was involved with him, the two of them were likely to be up to something that had to do with The Cedars. That might explain Sanders being killed, but why the senator?

After a few moments of thinking, Jackson Lee leaned forward and clasped his hands atop his desk. "You should know that Philip Hollandale got a measure tacked on to the supplemental appropriation bill to pay for the war in Iraq. It involves the increase of a previous twenty million dollar cap for the Regional Utility Authority. New trunk lines, an interceptor, and a centralized wastewater treatment system that involve Sanders' land."

I just looked at him for a minute. "Uh, does this involve the Nissan plant, too?"

Jackson Lee shook his head. "No. Apparently, that was just a rumor. Although Nissan is looking at possible sites in our area for their new plant, Sanders' land isn't one of the sites listed. I checked it out. Sanders' land is earmarked for sewage trunk lines that stop any Nissan deal."

"So Philip wasn't really trying to make a deal to buy Sanders' land for Nissan? What does he get out of it?"

"Maybe the senator was paying back favors to some big donors in the Utility Authority."

"So maybe Sanders did kill him. Then that still leaves the question of who killed Sanders and why. And how is Johnston involved in this, and Melody?"

My brain started to throb. I seemed to be going in circles. Then I remembered Bitty.

"Bitty should be here any minute. She has some information on Jefferson Johnston she's going to share. It may be something you already know, but she sounds quite excited about it."

Jackson Lee glanced at his watch, an inexpensive sports watch when he could probably afford a top of the line Rolex. "Where is she?"

"She went to pick up her dog. It's being groomed."

"Willow Bend?"

I shook my head. "No, the dog grooming place farther down the road, halfway between here and Snow Lake. Bitty says they give specialized care."

He grinned. "Bitty sure is particular about that dog."

"Bitty can be fiercely protective of someone or something she loves. I sure wouldn't want to get in her way."

We both smiled, thinking of Bitty wearing that dog like a new ornament all the time, as obsessed with it as she'd been her boys when they were younger. That's just Bitty's nature. She's always been like that. One thing about Bitty, she loves deeply. That may sound like a funny thing to say about a woman who's had four divorces, but while she may make light of it at times, each decision had been heart-wringing for her. And once the decision was made, there was no going back. She had to reach the point of No Return, and after that, while she could be civil to them, and may even love them as a friend, nothing any of her husbands could say would coax her back.

After another half hour passed, Jackson Lee called Bitty on her cell phone to see what was keeping her. She didn't answer, so he called the grooming place to see if she'd left yet. The expression on his face made me uneasy, and when he hung up, he took a deep breath.

"Bitty left an hour ago with her dog. Rachel said she saw her talking to someone in the parking lot, but she couldn't see who. Bitty's car is still there."

I gripped the edge of his desk hard enough to break a nail. "Was it Melody Doyle, do you think? Or . . . or Jefferson Johnston?"

"I think we need to bring in the police. Whether or not she's in danger, we can't take any chances."

I didn't argue. Bitty isn't stupid. Bitty wouldn't get in a car with either, especially if she'd just found out things about Jefferson Johnston, since she and I had already decided that Melody is somehow connected to him. So if Bitty did get in a car with one of them, even Melody, it had to be because she was forced.

Jackson Lee was on the phone with the Holly Springs Police Department when I stood up. He waved me to sit back down, but I shook my head. I couldn't just sit. I had to do something. I had to go to Bitty's house to tell Clayton and Brandon before they heard it from someone else.

"Tell Jackson Lee that I'm going to Bitty's house," I said to Diane on my way out, and she nodded. He'd know why.

Clayton was gone with some friends, but Brandon was there. Most of the boyishness in his face vanished, and his mouth thinned into a taut line when I told him my fears. He nodded.

"Mama isn't a fool. Scattered, yes, but she's not known to be stupid. If she thinks it's not right, she wouldn't get in a car with one of them unless she was forced."

"I know the police are efficient, but the more people out looking, the quicker we can find her, I hope. But Brandon," I added when he reached for his cell phone, "tell everyone not to get close if they find them, just call the police immediately. If Melody has been desperate enough to kidnap Bitty, she might be desperate enough to kill her if anyone goes blundering in."

"If that bitch touches one hair on my mama's head, she'll wish she hadn't," Brandon said in a growling tone that reminded me a little bit of his grandfather. John Truevine hadn't been any man to mess with when it came to his family. Just like my daddy.

Knowing a force of determined college kids was about to be mobilized, I felt a little better about Bitty being found. Give young adults an important mission, and my experience has always been that they are more than capable of succeeding.

"Oh," I said as Brandon headed for the door, "you might go by and pick up Georgie Marshall, too. Gaynelle Bishop's niece. She's probably at the museum or the cemetery."

Brandon stopped in the foyer. "Why her?"

"She's more than familiar with the history of Holly Springs and is likely to know the best hiding places."

Making an "okay" sign with his thumb and forefinger, Brandon left. I headed over to the Inn. Rayna could mobilize the Divas, and would know who to trust.

I caught her in the midst of her new painting, a rendition of the Audubon gardens out at Strawberry Plains. She was working from a photograph taped up to a small easel nearby.

As soon as I told her about Bitty, she stripped off her work clothes and grabbed a dog leash off a hook. That startled me.

"What are you doing?"

"Jinx is a tracker. We'll take him with us if we find a location where Bitty might have been taken. I'll call the Divas. You go back to Bitty's and get an article of her clothing that she's recently worn."

I looked doubtfully at Jinx, a rather pudgy golden retriever mix who'd sat up alertly the minute Rayna picked up his leash. He doesn't look like a tracker, unless it involves ham hocks or roast beef, but then, as I'd recently been reminded, appearances can be deceiving.

I left for Bitty's.

Maybe Bitty's much neater than I am, or better at hiding her sloppiness. It took me several minutes to find an article of her clothing that I knew she'd recently worn. Her nightgown lay in a white wicker clothes hamper hidden under a shelf in her bathroom closet. How tidy. My discarded clothes go into a rattan hamper in plain sight in the bathroom. I like organization, but don't feel a need to hide it.

By the time I got back to the Inn, Rayna had changed into sensible shoes with socks, khaki pants with pockets on the legs, a long-sleeved windbreaker, and wore an *Atlanta Braves* baseball cap. Jinx looked very business-like in a spiffy little orange vest and his brown leather leash. I felt inappropriately dressed, as usual.

"You're fine," Rayna said when I mentioned my clothes, and tossed me a windbreaker. "Just take that along. We've got a storm brewing."

A glance outside showed me bright sunshine, soft breezes, puffy clouds, and gently swaying grass. But like Rayna, I know how quickly a storm can blow across the Mississippi river and the delta, coming from the west with colder air that clashes with the warm, humid air coming up from the Gulf Coast. It usually creates thunderstorms at best, tornados at worst. Part of the price for living in an area rich with history, cotton, and eccentric relatives.

"Is anyone coming here to meet us?" I asked, and Rayna shook her head.

"Gaynelle's calling Sandra and Georgie. We've all got cell phones to keep in touch."

"Oh good. Then Brandon doesn't have to find Georgie. What about Cindy?"

Rayna hesitated. "After all the confusion, maybe it's best to leave her out right now."

I understood. "Five of us should be enough, anyway. Clayton and Brandon and their friends are out looking, too. And of course, the police. I imagine Jackson Lee has his own posse rounded up by now."

"We'll find her." Rayna put her hand on my arm. "She'll be all right, Trinket. Nothing bad ever happens to Bitty. Or bad enough to really hurt her, anyway."

Nodding, I said, "I know. Mama says it's because she's crazy as a Betsy bug, and we should be as smart as the Indians. They knew to leave crazy people alone."

Rayna smiled. "See? Bitty comes with her own built-in protection."

I just hoped we were right.

*

Jackson Lee showed up at the Inn with Kit Coltrane. I was too worried about Bitty to do more than nod at Dr. Coltrane.

"I've joined the search party this time," he said, and it took me a moment, but then I remembered my comment to him the day he'd found me in the root cellar.

"Civic duty is always appreciated," I said, and Dr. Coltrane smiled.

"Jackson Lee shared the basics with me, but what do you ladies think? You'd have more of an idea where they might have gone than we would."

While I was a little surprised that the male ego was so ready to relinquish any kind of control, even just asking our opinions, Rayna immediately said, "It'd have to be somewhere she feels safe. Melody, I mean. I'm sure the police are checking Mrs. Overton's house and probably The Cedars, as well as Easthaven and Dr. Johnston's office. Those are the most obvious places. I think she might go to her cabin."

"What cabin is that?" Jackson Lee asked.

"Snow Lake. That's how she met Cindy, you know. At one of the Snow Lake community dinners. And that's how we met her."

"So Cindy joined the Divas at Melody's invitation?" I asked. When Rayna nodded, I wondered if I had overlooked a connection there. Truth is, my brain darted from one possibility to the next, and I didn't rule out anyone as a suspect. I told you I'm a cynic.

Gaynelle arrived at the Inn then, parking in the rear like the rest of us. Sandra was with her.

"Where's Georgie?" Rayna asked Gaynelle, and I slapped my forehead.

"Oh, I didn't call Brandon. He probably picked her up. I figured she'd know the best places to look since she knows this area so well."

Gaynelle nodded. "So that's why she didn't answer her cell phone. I thought she might be here already, so Sandra and I came on over. I'm glad she's with Bitty's boys. She'll help them."

"Okay," Jackson Lee said, "now that we know where everyone is, we need to decide where everyone searches. As Rayna said, the police are covering the obvious places first, but they won't stop there. We don't need to be covering territory already covered, or backtrack."

The tone of his voice was grim and urgent. My stomach flipped. When I looked over at Dr. Coltrane, I recognized urgency in his expression, too. While I'd already realized the danger, it hadn't seemed truly real until that moment. Maybe somehow I'd still held out hope that it was just another one of Bitty's melodramas.

Maybe I swayed or something, because Kit Coltrane grabbed my arm and held it. "We all need to split up into pairs and search different areas first," he said. "The Marshall County police are checking here, so someone needs to check Snow Lake since it's in Benton County."

Jackson Lee got out a legal pad and wrote down specific areas to search. Then he gave them out. "Sandra, you come with me. We'll take horses out to the old Richmond place where they lived after they lost The Cedars. Kit, you and Trinket check the Snow Lake cabin. Gaynelle, you and Rayna see if the dog can find a trail at the groomer's. We'll keep in touch by cell phones. My number's on here, everyone swap cell numbers. Call as soon as you find something or rule it out."

I rode with Dr. Coltrane in his red four-wheel drive truck. It still smelled faintly of rotten potatoes and pine cleaner. Three car deodorizers had been hung in the front of the dual cab. The bed has one of those covers over it to protect his supplies.

"It seems much later than two o'clock," I said after a few moments of silence. Kit had taken the back way behind the railroad depot, the truck rocking a little bit in white gravel ruts as it climbed up the hill to Salem Street. Salem turned into Highway 4 a half mile or so down the road.

"That's because you've been so busy this morning." He glanced over at me. "We'll find her, Trinket. Do you mind if I call you that?"

I shook my head. "No, of course not. You always seem to show up in dire emergencies, so you can call me anything you like. Within reason, of course."

"I'll keep that in mind. Call me Kit."

"Now that we have that out of the way, do you think we should stop and talk to Rachel at the dog grooming place? She might have remembered something else by now."

"Sure. That's on the way. It won't take long, and we can leave when Gaynelle and Rayna get there."

We turned right to head east for Snow Lake, my stomach muscles thumping in time with my heartbeat. Poor Bitty. Was she scared? I remembered being locked in that root cellar, waking up to solitude and black dread. I'd heard that fear makes a person's senses more alert, but it had only sent me into overdrive. Bitty might fare even worse.

I looked out the window at the rolling pastures and stands of trees we passed, the kudzu along the road still in hibernation. Leathery brown vines clung to trees, telephone poles, clambered up banks and down into ditches, and smothered deserted shacks that had once housed families. Here and there, a blackened chimney stands testament to a fire having consumed a structure. House trailers squat atop hills, magnificent brick homes built like French villas sit behind trees at the ends of long driveways.

Rachel's dog grooming shop sits close to the road, concrete blocks painted beige with big brown dog and cat prints decorating it. Bitty's car sat out front, and a police officer was already there searching it. That made it even more real. My fingers tightened on the door handle.

"Easy now," Kit said, and I wondered if I'd made a noise, "they might find something useful."

Gravel crunched under truck tires as we pulled in and stopped. The officer straightened. I recognized Marcus Stone. We got out of the truck and went over to the Miata. He nodded at Kit, then me. I noticed he wore plastic gloves.

"Miz Truevine, can you identify this purse?" He held up a Dooney & Bourke shoulder bag, black leather with brown trim.

I nodded. "That's Bitty's shopping purse. It holds her checkbook, keys, cell phone, things like that." My last couple of words came out in a choked whisper. Just seeing Bitty's purse left in her car, when I knew she'd rather leave behind her underwear than her purse with credit cards, was the final proof she'd been abducted.

Kit put a hand on my back, lightly, but enough to let me know he was there. I had no idea why, but it was very comforting.

"Was Rachel Tompkins able to provide any more description?" he asked Officer Stone, and for a moment, I thought Stone didn't intend to reply. Then he shook his head.

"No. From her viewpoint through the small window, she only saw Mrs. Hollandale go to the driver's side window of the other car. A dark blue sedan, maybe a Pontiac. There didn't seem to be any problem, so she didn't think anything of it. When she looked up again, the sedan was gone but Mrs. Hollandale's car was still here."

"Chitling?" I asked suddenly. "The dog? Has she picked up her dog yet?"

Stone nodded. "Had it with her when she walked out of the shop."

There's not much around the grooming shop, just a house a few hundred yards behind that has nothing to do with the grooming and boarding, and a few white Charolais grazing in a pasture that butts up to the kennel's fenced back yard. A road goes beside the kennel leading to the house, but it's private. A wide stretch of pasture lies on each side, thick trees across the road, and a couple of houses scattered within the next half mile.

"It's possible Chen Ling ran off again and Bitty's gone after her," I said, but it didn't really seem likely.

"We're checking out all possibilities, Miz Truevine," Officer Stone said. "We've got a few men from the crime scene unit coming, and horsemen alerted if we don't find her pretty quick. Don't you worry, we intend to find her and make sure she's in good shape for her trial."

"I assume that's meant to be comforting, so thank you," I said, and as if just realizing how it'd sounded, Officer Stone looked embarrassed.

"I didn't really mean it like that," Stone said, and I nodded.

"I figured you didn't. This is just all so upsetting."

Gaynelle and Rayna arrived then with the dog, saving us all from the awkward moment, and Officer Stone nodded grudging permission for them to let Jinx try and find Bitty. Rachel Tompkins came outside, visibly upset, and said she had the towel she'd used on Chen Ling if it'd help.

"Just keep away from this area," Stone said, gesturing to markers cordoning off a wide section around Bitty's car. "We don't want any evidence compromised."

Rayna took out the nightgown I'd brought from Bitty's hamper, and knelt down beside Jinx to show it to him. He sniffed it for a few moments, tail wagging, then put his nose to the ground. Apparently he caught the scent immediately. He went from Bitty's car to the shop door, then kept circling and coming back to one spot, where he'd sit down and look up at Rayna. He didn't go near the road, just stopped at the spot where Rachel had seen the dark blue sedan.

Rayna looked up at me, and I saw the answer in her eyes. "Sorry," she said. "I hoped it'd turn out differently."

"I know. So did I. It just means we have to look a little harder, that's all."

"We should take Jinx over to Melody's house," Gaynelle said, "or Dr. Johnston's. It's worth a try. Call if you think they've been to the cabin, and we'll come out there."

Kit and I returned to his truck, and we sat there for a moment. Shadows skidded over the road and fields, sunshine flirting with storm clouds. Pine tree branches danced and whistled their soft song that promises rain.

"Do you want to look for her along the road?" Kit asked finally.

"No. She didn't leave here on foot."

He started the truck. "You still have the directions to the cabin?"

I nodded. Just down Highway 4, Kit pulled in to the paved parking lot of a white-painted concrete block store and gas station. It has big beer signs out front, the last chance to buy beer before crossing into Benton County, which is still dry. Not to say residents don't drink there, they just can't buy it in Benton County. All those tax revenues are enjoyed by the surrounding counties.

He went in, and came back out with a big bag of ice and a case of soft drinks that he put into a cooler in the back seat of the cab. I hadn't realized how thirsty I was, and accepted the can of Coke very gratefully.

Snow Lake itself isn't that big, but houses are flung out around the shores and up on hills in a haphazard pattern. Home-owners have a few sailboats, but the lake is mostly for fisherman. After passing over the dam that spills under the bridge and into Little Snow Creek, we took the next left onto Snow Lake Drive. Recently repaved roads wind up and down the hills and around, houses anywhere from one-bedroom cabins to five and six bedroom houses that sprawl over three lots. Ashland is the county seat and home to the only stop light in all of Benton County.

Behind Snow Lake the Holly Springs National Forest curves around in a horseshoe. It has an abundance of deer, squirrels, doves, wild dogs, and a few panthers. Hawks hover over lake and forest, riding wind currents.

Melody's cabin backs right up to the forest, almost hidden in the trees. The road dead-ends right next to it. Another road probably formed by four-wheelers dips down into high grass and weeds, then into a gully before rising sharply to a rim thickly crowned with pines, oaks, ash trees, and a hundred other species of bush and tree and weed. If she was out there, we'd never find her.

"It looks so desolate," I said. "Why would Melody want a place out here?"

"Maybe to get away from her own demons." Kit had gotten out

of the truck and come to stand beside me as I looked out over the gully. "From what I've heard, she has a few."

"Don't we all."

He nodded understanding, if not agreement.

The cabin door was locked, and it looked as if no one had been there in a while. Cobwebs hung like tattered lace in window corners and above the door of the small porch. Dust had settled on wood planks. Kit took something out of his pocket, and in just a few seconds, twisted the door knob and swung open the door.

"I see your career hasn't always been honest," I observed, stepping a little closer to him as he held the door wide. "You go first."

"A trick learned when I used to lock myself out of my own house. One of my clients used to be a burglar. It's very simple to learn. I'll teach you. After you, my lady."

"A useful trade when you get out of Parchman. No. Seriously. After you."

Kit went in first, and when no one hit him on the head or shot him, I stepped inside. It's not that I'm completely selfish, but I just figured that anyone who knows how to pick locks is much better than I am at deflecting blows to the head and bullets. My past experience with blows to the head has taught me that avoiding them is always less painful.

The cabin interior wasn't especially neat, but it wasn't a disaster, either. A rather ratty old couch had a blanket thrown over it, a wood stove sat in one corner below soot-covered walls and ceilings, and the kitchen sink held clean dishes that looked like they'd been there a few days. That sign of life kept it from being completely dreary.

I stood just a few feet inside the open door, poised to run, heart slamming against my ribs like a jackhammer, while Kit poked around in a bedroom behind the living room. Then he swung open the door to another room, and I heard him say something under his breath. The hair stood up on my entire scalp. I'm sure I looked like the Bride of Frankenstein when he turned back to me and tossed me his cell phone.

"Call 911," he said, and as I caught the phone, I heard myself babbling, "Bitty? Bitty?"

"No," he said, squatting down where I couldn't see him, "it's Cindy Nelson."

CHAPTER 19

Cindy Nelson was still alive, but not by much. The Snow Lake volunteer fire department has a great EMT group, an ambulance, and some up-to-date equipment even big city hospitals are proud to own. Someone called Cindy's husband, and another neighbor went to pick up her kids from school.

It didn't help much that the storm broke over our heads, rain slashing down and wind so fierce I thought a few of the trees around Melody's cabin were going to come crashing down on us. The police had cordoned off the cabin, and since no one could go inside, I waited on the front porch. My clothes were soaked through. I couldn't stop shivering.

"Nothing like this should happen," I said when Kit held a cup of coffee out to me, "it's not right."

"No. It's not. And just because it happened to Cindy doesn't mean it's happened to Bitty. We don't know anything like that."

"I know what you're trying to do, but this has to be connected. Melody tried to kill Cindy, and now she plans to kill Bitty. If she hasn't already."

Another shiver made my hand shake so badly I spilled coffee on my shoes. Kit took it from me, and guided me to his truck. He'd turned up the heat so that the smell of rotten potatoes, pine fresheners, and manure was really strong.

"Look, I don't know all the details," he said when he lifted me into the truck cab, a feat that even in my distress I thought remarkable, "but I trust Jackson Lee. He'll find her. He must have an idea where she could be. I bet we hear from him before long that he's handed Melody over to the police, and has Bitty safe with him."

Kit was half right. Not an hour later, just as we reached Bitty's house, Jackson Lee pulled up and got out of his truck. Thunder rumbled in the distance, and a flash of lightning briefly lit up his face as he reached the front porch where I waited, as jittery from the hovering storm as I was with dread.

"Did you find Melody?" I asked, ignoring the courtesies, and he nodded.

Relief swamped me, and Kit opened the door for us all to go inside. Clayton and Brandon met us in the foyer, strain showing on their faces and in their eyes. I'd forgotten what a strain this must be on them, too. Sometimes I can be very selfish.

"So where's Bitty?" I asked Jackson Lee. "Is she at the police station?"

"No. We didn't find her. She wasn't with Melody."

Stunned, I gaped at him. "But . . . why not?"

Jackson Lee shook his head wearily. "I don't know. We found Melody out at the old Richmond place, or what's left of it. She was hiding in the attic. The police are talking to her, but she claims she hasn't seen Bitty."

A chill went through me. "If Melody doesn't have her, then Jefferson must. Right?"

Jackson Lee looked at Clayton and Brandon, then Kit before looking back at me. "He's in custody. They caught him a half-hour ago at The Cedars."

The unspoken fear had to be in all our eyes. Bitty was hidden somewhere and left to die. Or already dead. It didn't seem possible. Not Bitty.

Brandon said it first, his tone calm. "Mama's alive. She's strong, and she'll get through this. We just have to find her. How long can they hold Melody and Jefferson before they have to charge them or let them go?"

"Wait," I said since I needed time to cushion my disappointment, "we all need to get something to drink and to sit down. Jackson Lee looks like he's about to fall down."

Because it was so obviously true, deep lines of weariness and resolute despair in his face, we went into the kitchen and Kit and I got out platters of leftovers and two pitchers of sweet tea. I made coffee, after Kit showed me how to work the state of the art monster Bitty has, and gave some to Jackson Lee.

"Now," I said, "tell us everything, good and bad. We'll handle it."

A faint smile briefly lit his face. "I know. You Truevine women are something else. Here is what I know for sure, and then I'll share some speculation. Jefferson Johnston's real name is Jerry Ray Dean. He's from Conyers, right outside Atlanta. He's got a record a mile long, but his daddy was a doctor. A podiatrist, which is where Jerry probably got what little he knows about it from. Jerry's been in trouble with the law since he was fourteen, mostly minor stuff until he got a little older and decided it's a lot easier to get someone else's money than it is to earn his own. He has a history of running scams that I won't go into right now. Suffice it to say, he's pretty good at running a con, then skipping town before people realize they've been had."

I thought of when Bitty had called Jefferson a con man. She'd been right.

"Anyway," Jackson Lee went on, "apparently he met up with Melody in Atlanta. They came back here once they had everything set up, phony certificates, credentials, all that, and he ran a scam on Ted Alston down at the bank, made some big deposits, some legit, others cashier checks he'd stolen, bought Easthaven mostly on credit and a good yarn, and hasn't made a single payment on it yet. He and Melody headed up the charity auction with proceeds to go to the Holly Springs Historical Society, but of course, they didn't. It was all about to fall in on him anyway. That's fact. Here's the speculation. I think he and Melody targeted old man Sanders. Growing up with Mrs. Overton, all her life all Melody heard was how The Cedars belongs to the Richmonds. They went out there, things got heated, there was a struggle, Sanders gets killed, and the senator just happens to show up at the wrong time, so they killed him, too."

"But that wouldn't have gotten Melody the house," Brandon broke in. "If he died intestate she'd have to wait until probate settled everything, then buy it like anyone else. If he had a will, she still got cut out."

"Unless they faked a will that left The Cedars to Melody," I mused. "Or made Sanders sign one. I heard he left an heir. So what does this have to do with Bitty? Why take *her*?"

"Because Mama talked to the banker and found out about Jefferson and the stolen charity funds and was going to tell," Clayton said, but Jackson Lee slowly shook his head.

"Johnston, I mean Dean, had to know it was all about to fall in on him. Maybe he got desperate. Just because he hasn't ever killed anyone before doesn't mean he's not capable of it. What bothers me is, why take Bitty? It doesn't fit."

He was right. Why take Bitty? Unless maybe she knew something no one else knew. But what could it be? And why hurt Cindy Nelson?

"Do you think the police will let me talk to Melody?" I asked Jackson Lee, and he shook his head.

"Doubtful."

"Ask them. Please. Maybe she'll tell me something that might help. We have to find Bitty soon, Jackson Lee."

He had a tortured look on his face that said he felt the same. I imagine what he saw in our faces mirrored his own distress.

"I'll try," he said finally, "but it might take some time. Give me an hour."

Kit drove me home for dry clothes, and Mama and Daddy met us at the door. They had worried looks, and Daddy kept muttering things about high crime in Holly Springs. Mama kept clasping and unclasping her hands, saying over and over that Bitty just had to be all right. For the first time since I'd come back home, she almost looked her age.

"It's going to be okay, Mama," I said, and hugged her. "Bitty is going to be just fine."

Mama clung to me a bit, then stepped back and shook her head. "Bitty never has been one to give an inch or give up. I almost feel sorry for whoever took her."

"Well, Melody Doyle is responsible for it, and right now she's in police custody," I said.

"Yes, I'd heard that." Mama frowned. "You know, that child always had it rough when she was young, growing up with hate and bitterness, but I never thought Melody capable of hurting anyone. She's always had such a sweet nature."

"Hate and bitterness change people," Daddy said. "Not usually for the better."

While I went upstairs to get dry clothes, Kit stayed downstairs talking to my parents. By the time I got back downstairs, he held an adoring Brownie in his lap, and had managed to make my mother laugh. If for no other reason, I'd have to like him for that.

Jackson Lee met us at the police station. "You've got ten minutes," he said. "And that's only because I called in an old favor. See what you can do."

Melody sat in a straight-back chair with wrists cuffed and a chain running to ankle cuffs. Her pretty brown hair looked dull and matted, her eyes wary. I sat across from her.

"Hi, Melody."

"Hi yourself. I know you're not here as a friend, so say what you want to say then leave me alone."

"I just want to find out what happened."

"Why ask questions? You won't believe me anyway. No one does. I don't care." She gave me a defiant look, chin lifted, some of her spark coming back.

"My mama says you're not capable of hurting anyone. She says you're too sweet."

Melody stared at me. Her chin quivered slightly and she looked away. "Mrs. Truevine's always been nice to me. She taught me in Sunday School. That was a long time ago. I've changed a lot since then."

"Yes, people change, but not their basic character. Not that much. Melody, we're just so worried about Bitty. Do you know where she is?"

"No. I've told the police that but they just keep on saying it'll be better for me to tell them where she is instead of face three murder charges."

For some reason, I believed her. Incredible, I know, but sometimes it's the way a person says something that lets you know they're telling the truth. Not that I'm the best judge of character since I usually figure everyone's capable of almost anything, but my mama isn't a fool.

"How did you get mixed up in all this? The police think you killed Philip Hollandale and Sanders, and kidnapped Bitty. They have to have some reason for it."

"I haven't claimed I'm completely innocent. But I didn't kill anyone. I'd never do that. I might feel like hitting someone at times, but doesn't everyone?"

"Yes. For me, it's a daily occurrence. But I'm known to be bitchy, so it's expected."

Melody smiled. Then she leaned forward. "Trinket, if I tell you what really happened, do you think you can help me? You know, find a real lawyer?"

"I'll do my best. Jackson Lee knows every lawyer in Marshall County, and that's a lot better than Legal Aid."

Chains clinked softly as Melody put her clasped hands atop the table and looked at me. "I admit that Jerry Ray and I came back here for The Cedars. We never meant to hurt anyone, not to kill them or anything. I swear to you, Trinket, neither one of us hurt the senator or Sanders. I may not know who killed Sanders, but I do know what happened to the senator."

By now, every nerve in my body was thrumming. I nodded, and hoped I didn't look as on edge as I felt. "I believe you."

"Jerry Ray and I had a plan. My grandma always told me about how the Sanders stole our house and all our money. I knew I'd never get Sanders out of the house legally, but I knew he had something he didn't want anyone knowing about, too. I figured I'd make a trade with him, you know, if he gave me back The Cedars, I wouldn't tell about the hidden gold."

"Gold? That story is *true*?"

Melody nodded. "I don't know how much is left of it, or even if any is left, but Elijah Richmond had been hiding gold for a long time once he saw the inevitable coming. Enough to keep the house, get the family back on their feet when the war was over. But he didn't tell anyone where it was hidden, and then died before he could. He'd left behind papers, but the Yankees came through and burned the businesses, so that destroyed everything. All that was found was what he wanted engraved on his tombstone when he died. 'Money is the root of all evil.' If you go out to Hill Crest, it's still readable, right below his name and dates. After the war ended, no one could find where the gold was hidden, and then it was too late. But the Sanders had plenty of time to look."

Even though I nodded, my mind was shrieking *Get to the point! What does this have to do with Bitty?*

"Anyway," Melody said as if sensing my impatience, "all this does connect to the senator and Bitty. I just want you to understand first. Jerry Ray and I figured Sanders wouldn't want to go to jail for hiding gold bullion, so if he signed over The Cedars, then we'd let him take his gold and go. It'd be mine, just like my grandma always said it should be. Elijah Richmond built that house, and it should be *ours*." She said that last a little fiercely, and I imagined how often she must have heard it.

"But Sanders refused," I said, and Melody nodded.

"Crazy old goat. Said he already had both, and no one would believe me anyway. Said it was just a rumor, and everyone knew the Richmonds would do anything to get back that house. Then he said he'd make sure I never got it, even after he died. Jerry Ray got mad, and said we should go back out and talk to him again, tell him that he'd be risking prison if we told about the gold bars he'd kept hidden."

"So you went back out there," I prodded when she fell silent, and she nodded.

"There was a car in the driveway up by the house. We parked out on the road, then went up, just to see who it was since it had official license plates. That's when we heard Sanders and the senator arguing, really loud. Sanders kept yelling that he'd killed his dog, and the senator kept saying it was an accident, and the dog shouldn't have been sleeping in the driveway. I wanted to go, but Jerry Ray said we should hang around, see what was going on." She shivered, and her voice faltered a bit. "The yelling stopped suddenly. It got really quiet. Too quiet. I looked in one of those long windows, and when we saw the senator lying in a lot of blood on the floor, Jerry Ray and I just took off.

"Then we got to thinking—now we really had something to make old man Sanders sign over the house. We'd go back and tell him what we saw. All I wanted was the house, but Jerry Ray said we should make him give us the gold, too, said he had connections that'd buy it off of us a little at a time so no one would know, said we'd be rich and I'd have my house, too. We had a fight about that, since the house means a lot more to me than the gold, you know? But when we got back out there, Sanders was deader than dirt, lying almost where the senator had been. I didn't see the senator, so I thought at first maybe he'd just been knocked out. His car was gone, so it seemed likely. We just figured the senator had come to, and killed Sanders."

"So you hid Sanders," I said when she paused, and she nodded.

"Yes. We figured the senator wouldn't say anything about the body being missing, since then the police would know he'd killed him.

Politicians don't usually like to get involved in things like that since it's bad for their image. Dirt gets swept under their rugs."

She said the last mockingly. Out of the mouths of babes.

"But why hide Sanders' body? And why put the senator's body in Bitty's house?"

Melody bit her lip. "We were out there when you and Bitty showed up. We barely had time to stick Sanders in the closet before y'all came barging in. We'd cleaned up most of it, just so no one would know Sanders was dead. That'd give us time to find the gold, then be ready to buy the house once it came clear. We knew y'all would go straight to the police, so as soon as you left, we got Sanders out of the closet and took off with him. I thought of the old ice house. It isn't used now, but since it's for sale, it still has a back-up generator that works. I thought I was being so smart, thinking of that.

"Imagine my surprise when we got out there to find the generator running and Senator Hollandale frozen stiff as a board in the cooler. We didn't know what to do. Everything went so wrong so fast . . . and we got scared. Really scared. If the senator was dead, and now Sanders was dead, we'd probably end up charged with both murders. No one would believe us, especially since it's no secret how badly I want The Cedars. We panicked. Then Jerry Ray said he'd find a place to hide the senator so no one would suspect us, and we'd just put Sanders back in his root cellar for someone to find, hopefully after a long time. Rotten potatoes smell so bad, it didn't seem like he'd be noticed for a while."

"It was very bad of you to put Philip Hollandale in Bitty's coat closet, then in her wine cellar," I said, a little angrily.

"I didn't know that was where Jerry Ray put him, really I didn't. Not until Georgie told me about y'all hiding him in the cemetery. And I don't know who took the senator from the cemetery and put him in Bitty's wine cellar. I swear I don't. It wasn't me, and Jerry Ray says it wasn't him."

"Do you trust Jerry Ray?"

"When it comes to getting money." Her smile was mirthless. "I know he's a con man, but we were both going to get what we wanted out of this. I'd get The Cedars, he'd get to scam a few folks before he took off again."

"But why involve Bitty with Jeff—Jerry Ray? For money?"

"No, nothing like that. I knew none of the Divas would say anything about what happened or was going on, so Jerry Ray thought he might be able to sweet-talk a little information out of Bitty. That was all. We just wanted to know what was going on and when, you know." She drew in a deep breath. "When I found out, I told Cady Lee about y'all taking the body to the cemetery. We just had to keep folks from thinking we had anything to do with it. I'd never have hurt Cindy, either. I really hate it that things got all messed up."

I heard someone just outside the door and knew my time was almost up. I leaned closer. "Do you have any idea who else might be involved? Who might have taken Bitty and why?"

Melody shook her head. "It'd have to be someone who wants The Cedars as much as I do, and I don't know anyone like that. Except maybe Bitty."

That was true.

After I repeated what Melody had told me to Jackson Lee and the police, who'd already heard everything anyway, I'm sure, we went back to Jackson Lee's office. He made a phone call to a friend to get Melody an attorney, just as I'd promised her.

"So what now?" he said, frowning. "If Melody and Jerry Ray don't have Bitty, then who does?"

"Someone as fanatical about The Cedars as Bitty is, and the only person I can think of is Trina Madewell. She's Bitty's arch-rival in acquiring houses." I paused. "But that bothers me. I mean, yes, Bitty loves saving old houses, loves antiques, and loves even more beating someone to the punch, but that's not enough reason for anyone to kill Sanders. Even Melody, who feels the house rightfully belongs to her, stopped short of murder."

Jackson Lee shook his head. "The police are ahead of us there. They've already checked out Trina Madewell—and most of the rest of the historical society—and Trina has an iron-clad alibi. She's been in the Baptist-Desoto hospital for knee surgery, and is at home with her leg in a brace. I doubt she could haul around bodies, much less drag an unwilling Bitty anywhere. Or hit Cindy Nelson so hard it nearly killed her."

"Has Cindy said anything?" Kit asked, and Jackson Lee shook

his head.

"Not yet. It'll probably be tomorrow before we can talk to her, if then. She nearly bled out before y'all got there. Good thing you went on in, Kit."

"I don't suppose Rayna's dog found any scent at the cabin?" Kit asked, and once more Jackson Lee shook his head.

"The rain came down too hard before they got there. Washed away a lot of evidence."

"That's not what I want to hear." I rubbed at the crease between my eyebrows.

"Could it be one of the Divas?"

That question came from Kit, and I gave him a thoughtful look. "Well, they have had a security breach lately," I said, then explained, "Cindy Nelson was accused of telling Melody that we'd hidden the senator's body. Only the Divas directly involved knew about it, and all swore to keep it a secret."

Jackson Lee reached for the yellow legal pad on his desk, flipped through some pages, then stopped. "Rayna Blue, Bitty Hollandale, Gaynelle Bishop, Cindy Nelson, Sandra Dobson, Georgette Marshall, Trinket Truevine. Cindy Nelson didn't make the graveyard detail. Am I right?"

I nodded. "But word got out. Cindy says she didn't tell anyone, but Melody told Cady Lee Forsythe, who has the biggest mouth around, and it spread from there."

"So how did Melody find out about it if she wasn't there?"

That stopped me. He was right. Who'd told her about the cemetery detail? If all were to be believed, no one had breathed a word of it except to the police. That meant all of us could be suspects. I knew I hadn't said anything, and I was fairly sure Bitty hadn't said anything, even to Jerry Ray, though that's always a bit iffy. Bitty's known to let her mouth get ahead of her at times. Rayna, I felt sure, could be trusted. Cindy had sworn she hadn't said anything, but had admitted to repeating other things, so I felt inclined to believe her. Besides, she'd had her head bashed in so that pretty much ruled her out. Gaynelle certainly wasn't the type to repeat things that needed to be kept private, and by default, Georgie wasn't either. That left Sandra Dobson.

I said, "It's either Sandra Dobson or Bitty. Since Bitty's been abducted, I tend to lean toward Sandra, though I never would have thought it of her. She's a nurse. They know how to keep secrets. Really, I just can't believe it'd be her, either."

Jackson Lee said, "Sandra might have spoken out of turn, but not intentionally. She's just not the kind. I don't think she's the one."

I stood up. "Tell you what. You convince the police to let me talk to her again, and I'll go ask Melody who told her. Then see what the police find out about Sandra. We can go from there."

"I'll make the call," he said, but still looked troubled. I didn't blame him.

"I'll take you to the police station," Kit said, and I nodded.

"Great. Just drop me off out front. Would you mind running by Bitty's house to see if the boys are all right? Then pick me back up at the police station. I should be finished by then and we'll know a little more than we do now. I hope."

Kit nodded. "I'll check on the boys. But stay at the police station until I get back, okay?"

"Good heavens, it's daylight. I'm a big woman. No one's going to drag me kicking and screaming anywhere I don't want to go."

"I'd rather not take any chances. Bitty wasn't dragged off kicking and screaming either."

He had a good point.

Kit watched me walk into the police station, then he left, his red truck making the curve back onto Market Street. The lady who'd been so nice to me when I'd been there in my caftan and no underwear said she'd have to check with the officers. I'd have to wait. She pointed to a bench beside the door.

"If you wouldn't mind sitting over there. It may take a little while."

I sat for a few minutes, fidgeting as different scenarios kept battering my brain. It'd be dark soon. While there was a lull in the storm, it didn't look like it was going anywhere fast. Rain threatened, in the distance thunder growled, and the air had a faint yellowish tinge that always makes me nervous. If you've ever seen it, you know what I'm talking about. I got up to go to the door and look out, watching for a suspicious cloud or funnel.

Bitty might be caught in this. Out somewhere, maybe tied up. Left to die of exposure or thirst or starvation, or God only knows what kind of injuries . . . .

That line of thought can make me crazy very quickly, so I tried to summon a mantra. I'd have taken any distraction at that point, so when I saw Gaynelle's pale blue 1985 Cadillac Seville cruise slowly by, I seized at it gratefully.

"Hey," I called, stepping out to flag her down, "did Jinx find anything?" The car stopped and the passenger side door opened. It was Georgie, not Gaynelle. She beckoned for me to get in as rain began to patter down again.

"Any sign of Bitty yet?" she asked when I got in.

"Unfortunately, no. That's why I'm here. I talked to Melody—I guess you've heard she was found and picked up on suspicion of murder—but I'm waiting to talk to her again. There's something else I need to ask her. There's been a delay, though."

Georgie nodded. Her clothes were damp, hair pulled back into a knot on the nape of her neck, and she looked distressed. "That must be why Jackson Lee sent me after you."

"Has something else happened?" A sense of dread marched with spiked shoes along my spine, but Georgie shook her head.

"Not yet. We have to hurry." She pulled out of the parking lot and onto Spring Street.

"Oh Lord." Tension contracted my muscles so hard I got actual spasms. "The boys? They aren't hurt, are they?"

"No, no. Of course not. No one could hurt them." She laughed a little. "They're ten feet tall and bulletproof, like all young men. None of them ever think anything bad can happen to them. Not until it does. Then it's too late. I'm rattling, aren't I . . . it's just been so stressful lately, with everything happening. I can't believe . . . it's just gotten out of hand."

"Yes," I said, "it certainly has."

We both fell silent, each lost in our private thoughts. I wondered what Jackson Lee had found out that'd be important enough to drag me away from the police station, but then, he may not know I hadn't talked to Melody yet. A growing sense of urgency bit at me sharply, but I kept it under control by reminding myself that we'd find Bitty, that she'd be all right. With all of us out looking for her, loving her, how could she not be?

"Where is Jackson Lee?" I asked when we passed his office without stopping. "He's left his office?"

"We're supposed to meet him—he got a call so should already be there waiting on us. At least, I hope he is."

"Meet us where?"

"In the industrial complex. I have the address written down there on that scrap of paper."

I looked at it, *11052 Industrial Park Drive* scrawled on a torn sheet of paper. "I haven't been over there in ages," I said, remembering it as a rather barren part of town, railroad tracks, propane gas businesses, truck depots, and lumberyards.

It hasn't changed much. Tall brown weeds choke empty lots; lines of warehouses, some new with pretty green grass in front of office buildings, some old and tumbling down, like the compress building by the railroad depot. Old creosote railroad ties are piled here and there, and some of the corrugated metal walls of abandoned warehouses are rusted out and look as if a giant can opener has peeled away entire portions. Not much different than the vacated industrial area of any decent size town, I guess.

Georgie pulled up in the front parking lot of gray gravel and stunted weeds. The building looked deserted. Long deserted. Empty windows stared out like vacant eye-sockets, a padlock on the front door and a For Sale sign in fading red paint against a peeling white background. Rain pelted the ground, spattered on the windshield, and pinged against corrugated metal roofing. The only sign of life was a dark car parked at the far end by a stack of rusted iron rebar.

I checked the address. "This is it?"

Georgie peered through the windshield of Gaynelle's car. "I think so. What does it say above the door?"

"It's the right address," I said after a moment, rather skeptically since it certainly didn't look like any place Jackson Lee might ask me to meet him. "What is this place?"

"I think it's the old ice house and feed and supply warehouse."

"Ah." That made sense. The senator and Sanders had spent some time here, so maybe a clue had been left. Then my heart started beating really hard. Or maybe Bitty was here?

I opened the car door and Georgie said, "Don't you want to wait on Jackson Lee?"

"If he's on his way, he should be here any minute. Come on."

Georgie followed me, keeping one hand on my arm as if for comfort. While there may be a huge chain and padlock on the front door, an entire section of clapboard wall left bare a support post. Since there was a hole big enough to drive a small car through, I was able to get in.

It smelled musty inside, no big mystery since it was raining outside and this had been an ice house and feed supply. Straw bale remnants were scattered around, dark brown with age and humidity. A set of iron tongs big enough to lift a Volkswagen lay rusting on the floor. Long trolleys with high handles and wooden wheels slumped against a few walls. Those looked really old. Bitty would love them.

Electrical cords with crackling, broken wire hung from the high ceilings, but none of them held light bulbs, not that I'd want to test them anyway. This place was a fire waiting for the right match, humidity or not. Sawdust and straw lay inches thick on the floor.

"Let's wait here," Georgie said when I started toward a door at the far end, and I paused.

"If Jackson Lee told us to meet him here, it can't be too dangerous. Maybe Bitty's here. Or maybe there's evidence he needs me to see before he shows it to the police. Maybe we should wait on him. I don't know."

Georgie's eyes looked huge behind her glasses. The glasses slid down her nose a little, her face still damp from the rain, and she nodded as she pushed them back up. "You might be right. Jackson Lee wouldn't tell us to meet him if he didn't know it was safe. What kind of evidence do you think could be here?"

I shook my head. "I have no idea. The police would have already checked it out pretty thoroughly, I imagine."

"Unless whoever took Bitty has been back here."

Georgie and I looked at each other. Her eyes were white-rimmed and dark in the dim light of the warehouse, as mine must have been. Another chill shivered down my back all the way to my toes. Rain beat harder against the metal roof, sounding like bullets. Or hail. For a minute, I felt rooted to the spot, unable to move, fear riveting me to the floor. Then I thought of Bitty, and I sucked in a deep breath that smelled of moldy straw, sawdust, dirt, and rain.

"You don't have to go with me," I said. "Stay here. It's safer. But I have to see if Bitty's here somewhere, maybe needing me . . . I know. It's crazy. I just have to know. Okay?"

Nodding, Georgie glanced toward the parking lot. "I'll keep an eye out for them and come and get you. Just holler if you find anything."

"I will."

Resolute, terrified, and soon in need of dry jeans, I set my shoulders so I'd be taller and walked toward the door at the far end. It was one of those heavy doors with a huge handle on the outside. It reminded me of that old *I Love Lucy* show when she'd been locked inside a freezer, and had icicles on her brows and nose and hair when they found her. While I didn't really expect it to be in operation, or find anyone in there, I wouldn't rest until I knew for certain.

Before I reached the door, I glanced back at Georgie. She stood almost where I'd left her, watching me. Another chill went through me. This was crazy. Maybe I should wait on Jackson Lee to arrive. Something wasn't right. Georgie and I never should have come here.

It was the weirdest thing, but I felt somehow as if I was caught in a time warp. Or in some kind of contest between good and evil. Metal roofing and loose boards rattled furiously in the rising wind. A banging sound came from somewhere deeper inside, a dull, steady thud as of a loose board. Shadows almost hid the door, yet seemed safer than the light where Georgie stood. I didn't know why. Like I said, it was one of the strangest things I've ever experienced. I started to call and tell her to come with me, but hesitated. Then it didn't matter anyway, because she came toward me, her steps a little quick as if she was frightened to be alone. I turned back to the door.

It had one of those thick metal pull handles, the spring kind like on old refrigerators that Mama always called Frigidaires regardless of brand name. Sometimes she still does. Daddy still calls the side-by-side refrigerator with ice-maker that he bought at Sears an ice box. Old habits are hard to break.

Anyway, I tugged on the door, but it didn't give easily. I decided to put all my weight into it. If that doesn't work, it's usually not workable. Even without the extra twenty pounds, I'm no lightweight.

Grabbing it with both hands, I gave a tremendous heave and the door came open so quick and easy it threw me off-balance. I staggered sideways a little. If not for holding on to the handle, I'd have probably fallen on my nicely cushioned rear. An old barrel stave lay up against the wall, and I used it to prop open the door. Cold dank air drifted out, but at least it wasn't freezing.

"Are you all right, Trinket?" I heard Georgie ask, and as I regained my balance, I nodded.

Then realizing she probably couldn't see me well in the thick shadows, I said, "Fine. I'm still on my feet, anyway."

"That's too bad."

I laughed, a little shakily, but with an effort at humor. "Gee, thanks."

"Go into the freezer. See if she's in there."

Something in her tone had changed, a subtle alteration that put me immediately on the defensive. For one thing, I've never really liked being bossed around that much, but especially not by someone twenty years younger. It could be a problem in the workplace, but at least there, I understand the chain of authority.

"You first," I said, probably more sharply than she expected.

"I don't think so. Get in there."

I turned to look at her. She was silhouetted against the gray light coming through the big hole in the front of the building. Tension radiated from her, made her seem larger than her slight size, lent her an air of menace.

"What on earth's the matter with you?" I demanded.

"Nothing if you'll just do what you're told."

That really made me mad. "Look, you little twit, I don't blame you if you're scared, but I have no intention of just walking into some dark hole without a few precautions."

It occurred to me that Georgie had her own agenda. And I didn't think it was going to be one I liked. While I never joined the Girl Scouts, I am familiar with the *Be Prepared* motto of the Boy Scouts. It never hurts.

Georgie's voice rose a little, a sure sign of uncertainty. "I'm not scared, you idiot, but you should be. Now walk into the freezer."

Crossing my arms over my chest, I gave her a belligerent stare. "Make me."

"Dammit, Trinket, why won't you just cooperate?" Georgie actually sounded aggrieved, and I started to be really rude, then I saw the small pistol in her hand. That complicated things.

Going with the *Be Prepared* advice, I'd already considered the barrel stave as a possible weapon just in case Dr. No waited in the wings. I hadn't expected treachery on my own team, however, an oversight that can be fatal. Since James Bond wasn't likely to come to my rescue—Sean Connery is and always will be 007 to me, even if he's bald as an egg now—I knew I was on my own.

Georgie stepped forward, pistol clutched in both hands aimed right at me. I reached for the only weapon within range, grabbing the barrel stave, but she shot me before I could swing. I spun around just like I've seen them do on TV, not from the force of the bullet, but the surprise.

It burned like I'd just laid a curling iron against my arm, but before my life started passing in front of my eyes, Georgie let out a shriek that drowned out the storm overhead. As she started violently shaking one leg, I took immediate advantage of her convulsion by clutching that barrel stave in both hands. In a move that would make Jackie Chan proud, I swung the stave up and out, caught Georgie right on the side of her head and laid her out like a slab of beef. The pistol went spinning across dirt and sawdust, and that's when I saw the cause of her St. Vitus dance.

Chitling let go of Georgie's ankle and took off after the pistol. Since I wasn't sure which of her three teeth might actually catch on the trigger and cause damage, I dove after it like an NFL star, sliding face-first in a whirlpool of sawdust that tasted like . . . well, sawdust. Good thing I'm a lot taller than Chitling is fast, or the outcome could have been very different.

Since an ill-tempered Chitling had to mean an imminent Bitty sighting, I took hold of the pistol like I knew what I was doing just in case Georgie woke up, and backed toward the open freezer door. My arm throbbed, but apparently wasn't fatal.

"Bitty? Bitty? Are you in there?"

The only reply was something that sounded like a cross between the Tasmanian Devil and Bugs Bunny. I told you I watch too much TV. Anyway, since Bitty hadn't come barreling out to check on her darling Chitling, I immediately deduced that she must be incapacitated.

Actually, it was such a relief to hear her making any noise at all, that I'm afraid I was much too cheerful for her liking. Almost to the point of giddiness.

"Ah, my *precioussss*," I said as I stepped inside and saw a pink blur sitting up against a wall and glaring at me, mouth, hands and ankles bound with duct tape, "I found my *preciousss* . . . "

Really, Bitty shouldn't have kicked me so hard. Especially when she totes around a dog with a face just like Gollum's. Or am I thinking of Yoda? Sometimes I get *Lord of the Rings* and *Star Wars* characters confused.

Anyway, by the time I worked the duct tape off her mouth, wrists, and ankles, then kept her from stomping Georgie to a bloody pulp like she insisted she wanted to do, the storm had finally stopped and more light came in from the hole in the wall. For a woman whose mouth had been taped up for nearly seven hours, Bitty's healing time was remarkably swift.

"That simpering, sheep-faced little bitch," she snarled, hovering over me like an avenging angel of death while I was still wrapping the tape I'd prudently saved around Georgie's wrists—a precaution I felt necessary. "She had the audacity to tell me that this was all my fault! That I should have acted my age and not like some idiotic high school girl! Can you imagine her saying that to me?"

"No," I said honestly. "She always seemed so quiet."

"Well, Daddy always said it's the quiet ones you've got to watch."

"Then you and I should be the most unobserved people since the dawn of time. Now go out to Gaynelle's car and get Georgie's cell phone, and call Jackson Lee. Please?"

Bitty got a crafty look on her face. "You go. I'll keep an eye on Georgie."

"Looks like we'll be here a while, then. I'm not leaving you alone with her."

"Really, Trinket, sometimes you can be so annoying. Look at my clothes. My hair! And I broke a heel on these shoes. Besides that, she scared poor little Chen Ling to death. She didn't leave my side the entire time we sat there in that cold, filthy hole. If for no other reason than that, Georgie should be shot at dawn."

"The sooner you call Jackson Lee, the sooner she might be shot at dawn," I suggested.

Georgie should have appreciated my efforts. I'm sure she didn't, but watching Bitty scoop up her precious dog, the three-toothed Hydra—to whom I'm very grateful, by the way—I knew I'd made the right decision not to turn Bitty loose on her.

Still lying out on the floor, breathing a little shallowly but steadily, her broken glasses lost somewhere, Georgie had a lot of explaining to do. And since I was dying to hear what on earth had gotten into her, I wasn't about to let Bitty spoil that.

When Jackson Lee arrived with five police cars, a TACT squad, a crime scene unit, two ambulances, and the coroner, I looked at Bitty. "Just what in the name of God did you tell him?"

Bitty, busily inspecting one of the old trolleys I'd known she'd appreciate, waved a hand. "Just that we're at the old ice house, you've been shot, and we're being held by a madwoman. He said he'd come right away."

"You did tell him the madwoman is unconscious and tied up, didn't you?"

Bitty looked up. "Why, I'm just certain I did. I think."

For a few minutes it was a little dicey, what with bullhorn orders being bayed at us and sharpshooters and miniature Darth Vaders running all around the parking lot, but finally I was able to convey the facts that we were all right, that our assailant was unarmed, and in fact, taking a nap, and if they just wouldn't shoot us, we'd like to come outside.

There was a tense moment when Bitty refused to put her arms over her head, but as she was only armed with a pug, no one shot her. Maybe they should have. I was pretty irritated by that point. It'd been a long, stressful day. And it promised to be even more stressful.

So imagine my surprise when Kit Coltrane ran interference for me, insisting that Bitty and I be seen at the hospital before the police could barrage us with questions.

"You're welcome to go along," he said firmly to Officer Stone, "but Trinket's been shot and needs to be seen by a doctor."

Marcus Stone didn't blink. It didn't matter that my bullet wound was just a scratch that had already stopped bleeding. "There's an ambulance right over here. I know where to find her when we need her," he said, obviously trying to make up for false accusations. He probably knew we understood about the arrest, but I thought it a nice gesture anyway.

Jackson Lee did the same for Bitty, of course. I walked to the ambulance, protesting that I felt silly about it, but Bitty, who'd been held hostage all day, rose to the occasion like a true belle. I fully expected her to swoon just like Aunt Pitty-Pat—another *Gone with the Wind* reference for the only person on the planet who hasn't read the book or seen the movie—and to call for Uncle Peter and her smelling salts.

Medics swarmed around her and Jackson Lee hovered anxiously, insisting upon holding her hand. He kept patting it as if he expected her to expire at any moment, and of course, Bitty ate that up with a spoon. She loves focused attention, even when it's undeserved.

With Bitty safely loaded onto a gurney for the three yard trip to the waiting ambulance, she stretched out her free arm dramatically, calling, "Chen Ling! Where is my darling? I must have her with me. She's the only thing that kept me alive during that terrible time . . . . "

"Oh yes," I muttered rather irritably as I climbed into the back of the other ambulance on my own, "that terrible seven hour ordeal sitting on your butt in a warm freezer far outweighs a bullet wound." I told you I can be bitchy.

Kit, who had checked over the dog and pronounced her as fit as a bow-legged, knock-kneed dog with an underbite and three front teeth can be, valiantly carried the grumpy pug to Bitty's waiting arms. Then, with Chitling sitting on her stomach and looking like something out of *Star Wars,* Bitty was borne to the ambulance with all the pomp of Cleopatra on her barge.

I had to move my feet quickly before the attendant shut the ambulance door on them.

Then Kit showed up, demanding to be allowed to ride with me and demanding to know why my wound hadn't already been tended. "Damn, son," he snapped at the young man in the white coat, "don't you know that she could go into shock?"

"But . . . but it's just a scratch," the young attendant protested, and the look in Kit's eyes made him fumble for the door latch. "It's stopped bleeding," he added as he got the door open.

Kit was undeterred. "Are you telling me you aren't familiar with infection? If I'd known she hadn't already been prepped, I'd have been in here doing it myself."

He sounded furious. The attendant looked terrified. I was fascinated. I've never had a man treat me like I need protection. Most men take one look at me and figure a big strapping woman like I am can take care of herself. It's quite a novel feeling to be treated as fragile.

Anyway, I had my first ride in an ambulance, which made me suspect that I must look pretty awful, but Kit rode with me, and while that was a little awkward, he did make me feel better. In a way, it was almost romantic, even if the rose and purple sunset was only viewable by peering through those little rectangular ambulance windows, but I didn't mind. I felt safe.

Kit held my hand. "You're just fine," he said.

"I've always known that, thank you," I replied, and we both grinned at each other like two tenth graders. Then he kissed me. I liked it a lot.

It's almost embarrassing to remember. Our new EMT made funny noises in the back of his throat, but springtime always brings out people's allergies.

CHAPTER 20

I've always known that Happily Ever Afters aren't really possible. Not like in fairy tales or Disney movies. But sometimes, the next best thing is better than you ever thought it might be. As a card-carrying cynic, of course I expect it to blow up in my face at any moment, but I've decided that the fun of the ride is worth the price of the ticket. Whatever happens, happens. One way or the other.

Not all has been well in Fairy Land, however, at least, not for the villains. Melody Doyle, whose lawyer got her a really good deal, still has to do a year in a minimum security prison for her part in the charity funds fraud and the Class D felony of the traveling corpses. All the Divas were able to get off in exchange for their testimony—and are the newest town celebrities—and poor Gaynelle Bishop, who didn't know anything at all about her niece's activities, has still stood by her. We all understand that. It's what family does. In fact, we'd be shocked if she didn't.

Thankfully, Cindy Nelson has a concussion but no long-lasting effects from Georgie hitting her in the head after Cindy realized that Georgie had been the one to tell Melody about hiding the senator in the cemetery. And Cindy doesn't hold any grudges against Gaynelle, either. Georgie's another matter.

Working so often in the cemetery provided Georgie with perfect access to the senator's frozen body, and no one thought anything about her moving things around with a furniture dolly, since she occasionally did that, too. Now Georgie's on industrial strength anti-psychotics. I hope her reservations at Whitfield are for a lifetime residency.

Jerry Ray Dean, the former Jefferson Johnston, is on the list of Favorite To Be Extradited, so when he gets out of Parchman, no doubt Jerry Ray will become best friends with a cellmate named Bubba in Georgia. Easthaven is up for sale again, and Bitty is thinking of buying it. Bless her heart.

We discussed that very thing out on the screened porch of Six Chimneys while the ceiling fan recycled cool air over our heads and we drank tall frosted glasses of fresh lemonade.

"I swear, Sharita makes the best lemonade ever," Bitty said, using her straw to swirl the festive sprig of mint around in the glass.

"I gave her Mama's recipe," I replied after a moment, feeling very lazy and relaxed for the first time in a long while. Warm days do that to me, especially when everything's blooming and birds are singing and I have a glass of high-calorie lemonade in my hand.

"Really? I didn't know that. What is it that Aunt Anna does different?"

"Mashes the sliced lemons up in all the sugar first to make that thick syrup, then adds ice a little at a time, stirring it until it melts. It takes a lot of ice. And a big metal bowl or pan. A couple dozen lemons. I think she used a stockpot when we were kids, we drank so much of it."

We thought on that, probably both of us recalling long summer days, lightning bugs, and cups of lemonade. The smell of freshly cut grass, sleeping out in tents until the mosquitoes got so bad we had to come inside, then the smell of pink calamine lotion on all our bites. Nice memories.

"So, do you think I should buy Easthaven?" Bitty asked, and I said *Good Lord, no.* She craned her neck to look at me. "Why not?"

"What do you need another house for, Bitty? You've got this one, and it's a wonderful house. Even with Clayton and Brandon and half of Ole Miss and Mississippi State here during their spring break, it wasn't so bad. You don't need anything bigger."

"Oh, you're right. I guess I was just thinking of the fun it'd be to work on another house. You know, fix it all up."

"If you're looking for another distraction, buy Chitling a set of false teeth."

"Leave Chen Ling alone. She's beautiful just as she is. Besides, she saved our lives."

"I remember that a little differently," I said rather crossly. "She was a distraction. I saved our lives by smacking Georgie in the head with that barrel stave."

"A shame about all that. And I never even suspected. Why, that girl is just deranged. I mean, I wanted to get The Cedars on the tour and definitely on the Historical Register, but I'd never have gone to the lengths she did."

"Certainly not. I'd have had you a room at Whitfield long before that," I said. "Maybe I should make reservations for you, anyway. Getting into the car with Georgie just because she said Jackson Lee had been kicked in the head by a cow and was at the hospital. You knew he was at his office with me, waiting for you to get there."

"Well, I just didn't think, Trinket. I mean, when she said that, all I could think about was Jackson Lee laid out like a big old tree on some hospital bed."

"Once she passed up the hospital, you should have jumped out of the car."

"And risk hurting Chen Ling? I couldn't do that. You know I couldn't."

I looked at the pug cuddled up next to Bitty and wearing a pretty lace bib that said, "My Mommy Loves Me," and recognized the truth in that.

Bitty turned over on the lounge to look at me, uprooting Chitling, who gave her a sour look and disgruntled growl, then got down to waddle over to her empty food bowl. Diets are hell.

"Besides, *you* got in the car with her," Bitty pointed out.

I'd been hoping she wouldn't remember that. I sighed. "Yeah, I know. Good thing for you I did or you'd have frozen to death."

"No, I wouldn't. The generator ran out of gas. Thank God."

We both said our silent prayers of gratitude again.

"What do you think set Georgie off?" Bitty asked.

"Well, according to her deposition, it was right after Sanders killed Philip. She got there in time to see Melody take off, and then saw what Sanders had done. She helped him drag Philip into the closet, clean things up a little bit. It's not that she cared so much that he killed Philip, but then Sanders said he intended to sell The Cedars to Nissan anyway. That's what set her off."

"That was stupid," Bitty observed. "Nissan never even seriously considered his land."

"We know that *now*. It was part of Philip's pork barrel promise. A pay-back to one of his big donors. He teased Sanders with promises he never intended to keep, just to get him to sign an agreement or waiver for that land. One thing about Philip, he always had a much higher opinion of his intelligence than he did of anyone else's. But Sherman Sanders knew enough to recognize a smooth-talking politician with a promise in his eyes and a lie in his mouth."

"I hope you're not trying to rub in the fact that I married Philip," Bitty said. "Anyway, she should never have believed Sanders. He used to say all kinds of mean things to me. But I think he might have liked me a little, too. You know, since I used to take him all those goodies. And he knew I admired The Cedars and his work on it. Such a lovely old house."

She said that last a little wistfully. The fate of The Cedars was in the air. Hollandale had designated the land facing Highway 7 for the sewage project, so it'd probably be appropriated by imminent domain, but no one knew what Sanders' heirs might do with the house and the remaining two acres it sat on.

"Maybe it'll be on the pilgrimage next year," I said to be nice, though it didn't seem likely to happen. People get greedy, and if money could be made by selling the house, then that's what would happen. "It wasn't even missed this year, you had so many wonderful houses."

"This year's pilgrimage went very nicely, don't you think?" Bitty said, and I was glad she didn't look sad anymore.

"The best one yet. The weather was perfect, and attendance was up, and all the houses were beautiful. Clayton and Brandon looked so handsome in their uniforms, too. And of course, you were gorgeous as always."

Bitty smiled. She does love to hear that.

"You should have worn a costume," she said. "I could have had one altered to fit you."

"In what parallel universe? I'd have looked like a drag queen, or that Britney Spears guy we had at the Mardi Gras Diva day."

"You should know, Trinket, that I submitted your name to the Divas for membership. It was unanimous. You're now a Dixie Diva."

My head got a little light and I considered switching my lemonade for Jack Daniel's. But then I reconsidered. After all, it's my civic duty as a Holly Springs resident to belong to local groups formed for the betterment of society, and certainly, the Divas make things better. Entire wine and chocolate industries enjoy record sales since the forming of the group.

"I'm so proud," I said, and Bitty smiled as we lifted our glasses of lemonade in a toast.

"Good. We're having it at your house this month. Rayna's got to get the Inn in shape for the inspectors' visit. It's almost certain it's going to be on the Historical Register, so it'll qualify for state funding. Isn't that nice?"

"The third Saturday, right?" I managed to get out, wondering just how this had suddenly gone so wrong. "That's my birthday."

"I know! Won't that be fun? Don't worry about the entertainment. I've already lined up a huge birthday cake with just the right kind of filling. Six-two, hard abs, and wearing a thong."

"Urk," I said. "My parents," I said. "My mother," I said, then, with horror, "my *father*!"

"I thought they're going to be gone on their next trip."

"God." I closed my eyes and sighed. "They have pamphlets on backpacking across the Yucatan. I suggested the cruise to Cancún."

"Did it ever occur to you that they suggest those outrageous things just so you'll happily agree to the trip they really want to take?"

I opened my eyes. "My God. I've been so blind. And it's working—I'm so glad to get them to do something sensible, I commit myself to caring for their deranged dog and crazy cats."

"Well, you didn't think they got to their age without learning something from their kids, did you," Bitty said, and I looked at her thoughtfully. Sometimes, she's a lot sharper than she pretends to be.

While I mulled over my lack of suspicion of two sweet, elderly parents who'd seemed so guileless and been so treacherous, Bitty leaped to a former topic of discussion.

"Speaking of deranged, Georgie Marshall needs to be in jail instead of Whitfield. Why, she killed Sanders and almost killed Cindy, and would have killed you and me."

"Yes, but she *is* unbalanced."

"Not so unbalanced she couldn't figure out exactly where that gold was hidden, when no one else was able to do it for a hundred and forty years."

"Apparently," I pointed out, "the Sanders family was able to find it. They spent enough of it over the years."

"Still, I think it was pretty smart of her, figuring out that the clue to where the gold was hidden was carved on Elijah Richmond's tombstone. 'Money is the root of all evil.' And so he buried all that Richmond gold in the root cellar."

"And Sherman Sanders kept rotten potatoes on top of it just to discourage anyone who might come looking. That's probably why she buried Grant's statue next to the gold." I shuddered. "It'd certainly discourage me. I don't care how much he has down there, I wouldn't go digging for it. No wonder Melody and Jefferson never found it."

"Well," Bitty said practically, "now the state of Mississippi is taking care of it. Along with the estate. Such a shame. The Cedars would be really wonderful on our tour. All those beautiful old things, and the attic—I do hope they get those clothes out of plastic bags before they go to ruin."

Bitty really can be single-minded.

"I'm sure they will, Bitty. You know, if Georgie hadn't gone off the deep end like she did and kept hitting people in the head with General Grant, you might have ended up convicted of murder. Do you ever think about that?"

"Not much. I mean, it didn't happen, so why should I worry about it? It's a shame about General Grant, though. Even if it's Grant, it's a really nice statue. I hope the police return it. And I definitely want my carpet back. Jackson Lee said he'd make sure it's cleaned and returned. Aren't happy endings nice?"

After a moment, I said, "I'd love to live in Bitty World. It must be so nice there. Blue skies, rainbows, golden streets—"

Bitty said something rude and threw a pillow at me. I managed to deflect it before it made me spill my lemonade.

"Well, that was childish, Bitty. And you almost fifty-two years old."

"No, you're almost fifty-two years old. I'm nearly fifty."

"I know, I know, fifty-one is just as close to fifty as forty-nine. God, you're vain. And in just a few months, you'll be fifty-two."

"You're calling *me* vain? Just who put a henna rinse on their hair last week to cover the gray?"

"I just did that so Mama's dog will stop barking at me every time he sees my hair," I said in my defense. "Brownie thinks it's a squirrel on my head."

"Then stop wearing it with that little squirrel tail hanging down your neck. Wear it loose. It makes you look years younger."

I didn't say anything to that. I'm happy being fifty-one, fifty-two this month. I earned the right to get here. It's been a journey with a lot of interesting sights along the way. Some not so good, but just when I think things can't get any worse, they do. That's how I know I'm alive. If I lived in Bitty World, I'd feel like every day was a walk with Willy Wonka. No thanks. Bitty's good at handling her world, I'm satisfied with handling mine. The occasional overlap creates havoc, but we're working on that.

Bitty said thoughtfully, "You know, I've been thinking of buying a house in Florida."

"Hurricanes, senior drivers, alligators, Donald Trump, OJ Simpson . . . ."

"Or California."

"Earthquakes, mudslides, brush fires, Michael Jackson, Arnold Schwarzenegger . . . "

"Canada?"

"Canadians."

I meant that in jest, since I think Canadians are a lot smarter than most Americans. They have socialized health care, cheaper medications than in America, and a monarchy they mostly ignore. Politicians there aren't much different than here, however. It's a universal virus that turns sweet infants into crafty, double-dealing, double-talking criminals thinly disguised as honest, upright citizens who have only their countries' best interests at heart. If scientists can find a cure for that virus, they've found the key to world peace.

"What's the matter with Canadians?" Bitty asked in surprise.

"Nothing. But they'd probably put you in a strait-jacket an hour after you got there. Stay here, Bitty. You're much safer. And so are they. Let's keep international relations peaceful."

Whatever Bitty might have said to that went unsaid, thankfully, since Chitling started barking at the arrival of visitors. She makes an excellent doorbell, if you don't mind the puddles.

"Hope you don't mind, sugar," Jackson Lee said as he came down the steps, "but I just let myself in since I figured you couldn't hear the doorbell out here."

Bitty sat up, going into instant belle-mode. "Why Jackson Lee, you sweet thing, I don't mind at all."

With Bitty, The Scarlett sounds perfectly natural. If I said something like that, I'd get another ride in an ambulance. Or to Whitfield.

But then I found myself on the verge of breaking into a belle myself as I saw Kit Coltrane right behind Jackson Lee, looking straight at me and smiling. Sometimes it's hard to remember I'm not sixteen anymore.

"Just thought you ladies might like to hear some good news," Jackson Lee said, grinning at Bitty like she'd just given him a new pair of boots. She patted the lounge in an invitation, and he settled himself on the end of it, looking a little awkward and much too big, but determined to perch there if it killed him. It might. Bitty's been known to be devastating.

"We sure would, honey," Bitty cooed, "good news is always welcome."

"Oh, you'll like this, sugar," he said to her, and I rolled my eyes.

"With all this sugar and honey being slopped around, I might go into insulin shock before you get around to telling us anything, Jackson Lee," I said, and heard Kit laugh.

Jackson Lee's face got a little red, but he got over it pretty quickly. "All right, here it is. I just heard that Sherman Sanders left The Cedars to the Holly Springs Historical Society, and—"

Bitty gasped and clasped her hands together when he paused, then he finished:

"He stipulated that Mrs. Elisabeth Truevine Hollandale be designated caretaker—in his own words, 'Because she worried the life out of me about that house and I know she'll take good care of it.'"

"I can't believe it," Bitty breathed. "The Cedars is saved! Oh, Sanders must have wanted to atone for all those years of hate and bitterness brought about by his ancestor's actions."

"More than likely," I pointed out, "he was just hoping for a ticket into heaven."

"Oh, Trinket, you can be such a cynic." Bitty turned back to look at Jackson Lee. "This is really true? The Cedars will be on the Historic

Register?"

Jackson Lee nodded. "Not only that, sug—Bitty, but Sanders gave instructions on where to find the gold buried in the cellar. Said it was too big a temptation to some folks, and it should be used for the upkeep of the house. He did leave a couple other bequests, one to some Japanese woman he knew years ago, and even some things to the Richmond heirs. Photos of their kin, that statue of Forrest—and a solid gold bar with Elijah Richmond's name stamped on it."

"Well, that's a little late," I said wryly, "Melody could have used it twenty years ago."

Bitty turned to look at me. "It wouldn't have helped, Trinket. The money didn't mean to her what the house does. And, unless there's a stipulation in his will that says differently, I'd like to put the entire history of the house on our brochures. I'll do it tactfully, of course. No point in stirring up old fires, but the Richmonds deserve their history, too."

She looked back at Jackson Lee with one of those smiles that have been known to blind men for days. When their sight returns, it's never quite the same.

"You've been wonderful, Jackson Lee. I just don't know what I'd do without you."

"Well," he said, grinning at her, "I don't intend for you to find out. Not for a while yet, anyway."

"Jackson Lee Brunetti, you sweet bit of sugar, are you flirting with me?"

"Good Lord, Bitty," I said, and stood up. "Kit, I don't know about you, but I'm going up to the kitchen to check my glucose levels. Care to join me?"

"Well, I am feeling a little lightheaded." Grinning, Kit followed me into the kitchen. Then he got really close, trapping me against the counter with an arm on each side of me. "But not just because of all that sweet talk."

"Hm," I said, looking at him, "this might be serious enough to require a doctor."

He put his arms around me and whispered in my ear, "I love to play doctor."

In response, I unclasped the hair at the back of my neck and shook it free. It just seemed like the thing to do. You know, I think my parents have the right idea after all. A healthy libido just makes life so much more fun.

Sometimes Bitty isn't the only one who has things turn out all right.

About Virginia Brown

As a long-time resident of Mississippi, award-winning author Virginia Brown has lived in several different areas of the state, and finds the history, romance, and intrigue of the Deep South irresistible. Although having spent her childhood as a "military brat" living all over the US, and overseas, this author of nearly fifty novels is now happily settled in and drawing her favorite fictional characters from the wonderful, whimsical Southerners she has known and loved.

Reader's Guide

Trinket Truevine Wants To Know:

1.   Does caring for aging parents relate to experiences in your own life? Do you wish there was a *Guide For the Proper Care and Feeding of Senior Parents* to help you maneuver the minefield of playing the role of their child/parent? Does it help to know you are not alone?

2.   Ex-husbands: An interesting species that rarely end up like Bitty's ex, thank heavens. So why is it so much fun to read about unpleasant exes expiring in unusual ways? Not that I'm asking for ideas, of course.

3.   Do you know someone else who rescues stray animals? Are they the responsible kind of animal rescuer who spays and neuters the pets they save? Do they find them good homes eventually, or do they create space in their own homes for too many so that you end up having to take care—oh, never mind.

4.   Do you own a pet? If so, do you treat your dog or cat as a child like Bitty does Chen Ling? Do you think it is healthy for Bitty to lavish so much attention on her dog? For that matter, do you think it is too much for Anna Truevine to dress Brownie in coordinating sweaters? (Please be specific so I can pass on this information to the parties involved).

5.   Have you recently returned to your hometown? If so, have you found it greatly changed? Do you think you would fit right back in with all those who remained, or would you find it awkward to reacquaint yourself with extended family and friends? Especially the ones you think are crazy?

6.   Has a failed relationship left you overly cautious about embarking upon another romantic foray? What would you do if you met a handsome, intelligent, charming man who makes your toes tingle? Would you take a chance, maybe dye your hair auburn and buy a new bra?

7.   What do you think about Bitty's divorces? Do you think she is still in love with any of her ex-husbands—not counting the dead one? Do you think she and Jackson Brunetti have a chance for a lasting relationship? Or will Bitty find a way to run him off? Would you reunite with an ex-husband?

8.   Do you have grown children who live far away from you? Are you able to see them often? How do you deal with them being out of your daily life? Do you ever feel as if you have switched roles with your own parents in some way, that now you feel as if you are intruding on your children's busy life by wanting more frequent contact? Really, don't you think they should call more often than they do? Not that I am whining.

9.   Do you have a passion for old homes, antique furniture, and local history? Are you involved in maintaining the integrity of these cherished memories of times long past? Do you think people feel a connection to those who lived before them when they collect antiques? Do you think Bitty feels that way, or do you think it is more about the acquisition than the memory?

10.   Are you a member of a group of friends who get together regularly like the Divas? If so, does your group play card games, go out to eat, or just celebrate one another's company with wine and chocolate? Do you keep one another's confidences? If asked, would you help hide the frozen body of a friend's ex-husband? Forget the last question. Your answer could be incriminating.

LaVergne, TN USA
26 October 2009

162077LV00007B/66/P